ACTS OF HONOR

by
Richard H. Dickinson

RH Dickinson

Praise for *Acts of Honor*

"*Acts of Honor* has become mandatory reading at the Pentagon. The first serious fiction to arise from the American experience at Abu Ghraib, Dickinson spins a believable military thriller with epic violence, an evocative sense of place, and characters who spring off the page."

> **Susan Mathews**, author of *Prisoner of Conscience,*
> *Hour of Judgement, An Exchange of Hostages*

"*Acts of Honor* is unsettling at many levels, forcing us to reexamine everything we think we know about love, war, torture, West Point, and human beings. It is a sophisticated thriller that reminds us that good men can do bad things."

> **Pepper Schwartz**, author of *The Great Sex Weekend,*
> *Prime:Adventures and Advice on Sex, Love, and the*
> *Sensual Years*

Acclaim for *The Silent Men*
by Richard H. Dickinson

"Dickinson has written a war novel chock full of suspense, sweat, blood and corpses. I felt as if I was lying in the jungle grass waiting for the sniper's bullet. *The Silent Men* is the real deal."

> **Stephen Coonts,** author of *Flight of the Intruder, Point of Impact*, and *Under Siege*

"Air Force veteran Dickinson debuts with one of the most authentic Vietnam War novels since Tim O'Brien. Dickinson captures the grit and intensity of the war by getting inside the soldiers heads, without politicizing or moralizing."

> **Publishers Weekly**

"*The Silent Men* is an extraordinary thriller, filled with a dynamic cast of believable, dedicated and realistic army grunts and officers serving in Vietnam. With a gift for riveting combat action, a keen sense for time and place, and a depth of military knowledge, Richard H. Dickinson has produced one of the year's outstanding debuts."

> **W.E.B. Griffin**, author of *The Brotherhood of War, The Corps, Honor Bound, Badge of Honor,* and *Final Justice*

"Dickinson writes convincingly in a debut that both stimulates and informs."

<u>Kirkus Reviews</u>

"Page-turning exciting! A very grisly and graphic novel, a down and dirty war story with attention to the smallest detail."

<u>Booklist</u>

"Dickinson's story is so compelling you will be hooked from the first page."

<u>Rocky Mountain News</u>

DEDICATION

Dedicated to the Cadets of Company F-2, United States
Military Academy, West Point, New York

And to Mark Harrison
Semper Fi

CHAPTER 1

August 15, 2003 (Friday)
Fallujah, Iraq

The bomb that destroyed Major General Robert Tannerbeck exploded in Fallujah while he sat at his desk at the Combined Joint Task Force Headquarters, sixty miles away in the bleeding heart of Baghdad. Iraq was rattled by a dozen blasts that day, and any one of them could have been the one that caused the American gloves to come off in the increasingly nasty war, but this IED killed too many of the two things that the United States Department of Defense held most precious: soldiers and children. When the decision was made to deal with the terrorists in a manner worthy of their crimes, it was Tannerbeck who would harvest the consequences.

The bomb was similar to other Improvised Explosive Devices used by Sunni Muslims in their guerilla campaign to kill foreigners: three 82mm mortar rounds looted from an Iraqi armory, stashed in the trunk of a Toyota and wired together with a manual trigger. The finger on the trigger belonged to Ahmad Nidal, a twenty-two-year-old martyr with a scraggly beard and the gentle hands of a musician, who had come to Iraq from Cairo. The youngest son from a family of cigarette peddlers, Nidal was determined to show the world that it had underestimated him. After a week of high living in Damascus, he had been smuggled across the Iraqi border with the help of Syrian soldiers, who turned him over to his Sunni handlers. These men scoffed at Nidal's idealism, but they buffed his ego while locking him in a safe house with a Koran until it was time to die. After posing for a photo for his family, the young man consecrated himself to Allah. Bracing himself with faith, he chanted in a whisper, "*Al Allah Il Allah. Muhammad rasull Allah,*" as he steered his vehicle over the curb, aiming for the American combat vehicles in the school courtyard. "There is no God but Allah and Muhammad is his prophet."

Sergeant First Class Ricardo Baltizar hopped down from his HMMV and signaled for the other two vehicles in the patrol to park in combat lager, weapons facing out, engines running. A driver stayed with each vehicle, along with a gunner who kept his finger on the trigger of the MK19 grenade launcher and his eyes on any potential threat. The others disembarked and followed Baltizar to the shade of a eucalyptus tree within the schoolyard where they had parked.

The men did not like stopping their vehicles, or leaving them, for mobility was a key element of survival on the urban battlefield. But Baltizar understood, even if his men did not, that the battlefield they had trained for was out in the desert somewhere, not here in Fallujah. He did not like the new tactics any better than his soldiers, but he was an NCO, a lifer, ready to make sacrifices to accomplish the mission. So he grabbed the last of the humrats (humanitarian rations) from the HMMV and displayed them to the kids, who had gathered with their teachers in the doorway of the school when the Americans' vehicles had barged into the schoolyard. The teachers had ignored the GIs during previous visits, keeping the children inside and pretending that heavily armed men in body armor were not on the school grounds, staring in the broken windows or walking the halls. Later, after American contractors had repaired the windows and the school's sewage system, the teachers would nod shyly to the troops who visited once a week, though any discourse could not be permitted between a female Muslim teacher and an American soldier. The children were a different matter, however, and today the principal allowed the male students to approach Sgt. Baltizar and his men. The kids approached warily, like squirrels seeking peanuts, and Baltizar handed out the precious yellow humrat packs to the boldest of the bunch.

Baltizar spotted the Toyota as it hopped the curb and instantly raised his M4 carbine to firing position. "Run!" he yelled at the children, who understood no English and who were focused on the humrats that now lay on the ground where Baltizar had dropped them. But the children grasped their peril and turned away as their teachers screamed and tried to gather them up in the folds of their black *abayas*.

Baltizar saw Nidal's calm face clearly and fired three rounds through the windshield as all three gunners in the squad opened up behind him. The Toyota shuddered as if it had run into a wall of lead, but Nidal lived long enough to trigger the bomb. The car leaped into the air and came apart, adding itself to the wave of metal fragments that ripped through the courtyard. Only when the fragments actually embedded themselves in human beings did they technically become "shrapnel."

The blast lifted Baltizar off his feet and peppered his flak jacket with bits of metal and glass. He lay for a moment, stunned, struggling to sit up and catch his breath, the air crushed out of him. His hearing returned gradually, but for many seconds there was nothing to hear, since the explosion had quieted all living things within the blast radius. Baltizar felt blood on his face, but did not realize that the concussion had crushed his internal organs, or that he was dying.

As he struggled to sit up, something moved in Baltizar's lap. He saw the face of a child, the brave kid who had approached him first while the other boys hung back. The explosion had decapitated him, and Baltizar jerked with horror as the boy's head rolled into the dirt between the sergeant's legs. The boy's body hung like bloody fruit from the limbs of the scalded eucalyptus tree. Baltizar's eyes rolled slowly back into their sockets as he lost consciousness, thinking, *What kind of religion issues virgins to men for killing a school full of children?*

CHAPTER 2

September 1, 2003 (Monday)
CJTF-7 Headquarters, Baghdad, Iraq

Baghdad was an energized city of traffic and noise despite the omnipresent threat of gunfire that hovered in the air with the drifting dust. People drove with their windows up and their car doors locked, pitiful measures against the brute violence of an AK47. Speed was the best defensive measure, and the streets were lawless and fast, except at intersections, where accidents and murders took place. The city bustled with new freedoms and fresh capitalism, yet it had the anxious air of the apocalypse about it. Baghdad had become a city under siege, not from any gathered army outside the city limits, but from Sunni terrorists who lived in the neighborhoods of al-Baya'a, al-Shaab, and al Khadra. The enemy was not a cancer that could be excised with a bold stroke of a scalpel, but an infection that required flooding the body with antibiotics. The U.S. Army had been set to that task of relentless, holistic attack throughout every neighborhood and alley, but Baghdad seemed as drug-resistant as the incurable cases of TB that had begun to surface.

The U.S. forces had taken over the administrative offices of the Baathist regime, Saddam's old headquarters nestled into a bend in the Euphrates River. This complex of four square miles had become the American "green zone," a fortified bastion of civilization surrounded by a sea of anarchy. Here, in offices with marble floors and crystal chandeliers, the Coalition Joint Task Force 7 established their headquarters.

The commander in chief was an old-school warrior recently promoted to a position that demanded a modern appreciation for the role of politics in all aspects of any military exercise. A darling of the White House, he had risen from squalid beginnings through a calculated combination of battlefield prowess, personal charm, and an unrelenting focus on administrative reports and deadlines. As he assumed command of the most complex and politically explosive assignment in the world, the CINC must have realized how unqualified he was, but his civilian benefactors were already paving the way for his next star, as if CJTF-7 was a done deal, a stepping stone to greatness.

Second in command was the Deputy CINC, Major General Robert Tannerbeck. Tannerbeck sat now in his office, tending to the minutia of leadership—performance reviews and budgets—irksome chores that should have been required only in peacetime. For the first time in his life, Tannerbeck was a "Fobbit," army slang for soldiers who hunkered down in their FOB, or Forward Operating Base, and who rarely faced the enemy. In Vietnam, where Tannerbeck began his career, the term of endearment was REMF, Rear Echelon Motherfucker, and that was how Tannerbeck thought of himself now: pure bureaucratic overhead. In every combat operation since Panama, Tannerbeck had commanded the point of the spear; first as a company commander, then battalion, then

ten years of experience in Military Intelligence, a career field he detested. He longed for the battlefield, where chaos could be conquered with violence, where performance reports were written in blood, and where prisoners of war were a nuisance to be handed off to rear echelon troops and forgotten about. Now, he found himself in command of forty-six POW camps throughout Iraq. His feelings toward the men in his custody were ambivalent. Even on the battlefield, he had never mustered hatred for the hungry and shoeless Iraqi soldiers who begged to surrender. He saw no value in incarcerating them now, except for a few Baathist terrorists and those on the famous "deck of cards." Volpe advocated releasing 95 percent of the men detained under his authority and shooting the rest.

Volpe sat in Tannerbeck's conference room, thumbing through e-mail on his Blackberry while scratching the scar that ran from his forehead to his chin. After twelve years, the damn thing still itched, a constant reminder of the piece of shrapnel that had knocked him from the turret of his tank during Desert Storm, nearly splitting his head in two and taking out most of his teeth, along with one eyeball. Rather than accept a disability pension, Volpe had fought to remain in uniform, accepting reassignment to MI, where a savvy combat leader with one eye was not a liability. He still spoke with a lisp because the oral surgeons never quite got his false teeth right, but he was generally pleased by the way the army had put him back together. He even found his face to be a career enhancer; if the fruit salad on his uniform didn't impress the men above and below him, the scar never failed to get their attention. He rubbed his face again and sat quietly at work, forcing himself to remain uncurious about the upcoming meeting. Volpe knew who he was about to meet, but not why.

The conference room door opened abruptly. Volpe pushed his chair back and stood to attention as General Tannerbeck entered, followed by another two-star general and a third man that Volpe did not recognize.

"At ease, Colonel Volpe."

Tannerbeck motioned toward an empty chair at the head of the table for General Piersal, and claimed the seat at the opposite end for himself. Volpe found himself staring across the table at a Lt. Colonel Makin, according to the tag on his crisp new desert BDUs. He saw that Makin, too, was from Military Intelligence, the petal-like collar insignia as undecipherable as the branch itself. He should have felt a sense of camaraderie among fellow members of the shadowy career field, but Volpe still thought of himself as a tanker, whatever the insignia on his collar.

"Everyone," said Tannerbeck, "please be seated."

Volpe watched Makin with some amusement as the man took care to avoid staring at Volpe's face.

Tannerbeck wasted no time in bringing Volpe up to speed. "Rick, this is General Piersal, commander of JTF-GTMO in Guantanamo Bay, Cuba. And Lieutenant Colonel Makin, also from Gitmo, where he has been in charge of POW interrogations. Colonel Makin and I served together during Desert Storm. We were younger then, right, Elliott?"

Makin nodded politely, and Tannerbeck did not mention that he had reassigned Makin back to Kuwait as soon as he had realized that Makin spent more time theorizing about breaking the enemy's spirit than he did finding ways to kill him. Tannerbeck resumed, "General Piersal is here at the direction of the Joint Chiefs to assist us in the way we generate battlefield intel. I've asked you to join us because your troops will be directly impacted by some of the changes that will be coming down."

Volpe sensed a hint of disdain in Tannerbeck's introductions, as if the Deputy CINC was not pleased to receive advice from another general from a civilized place like Guantanamo Bay. He glanced at Piersal and nodded slightly at Makin.

"General," said Tannerbeck, "would you clarify your orders and explain your intentions?"

"Thank you, Bob." Piersal cleared his throat, and Volpe was surprised by the high pitch of his voice. He did not have the presence of a combat commander, but this did not surprise Volpe. MI was an intellectual command, filled with philosophers and political science majors who spent wars breaking codes and grading battle damage from satellite photos. These were important jobs that saved American lives, but the officers who rose to the top in MI were not the kind of combat leaders who inspired others to levels of atavistic violence. MI officers knew where they ranked in the army pecking order, but Piersal refused to be intimidated by the condescension he encountered every day. Though he sensed Volpe's disdain, he began his presentation bluntly, not about to be stared down by a colonel with a glass eye.

"Colonel Volpe," began Piersal, "I've already briefed General Tannerbeck on my orders, but he would like to review our plans for your benefit. Therefore, let me begin with a comment on what we already know.

"We defeated the Iraqi army due to the skill and aggressiveness that men like General Tannerbeck displayed on the battlefield. We are faced now with a more ticklish task, of rooting out the remaining resistance forces that have resorted to a murderous, illegal, and immoral guerilla war. Not only are these people taking an unacceptable toll on our own troops, many of whom are on humanitarian missions, but they are killing thousands of Iraqi women, children, and civilians. They kidnap foreign nationals and behead them on television in a successful attempt to terrorize other countries that might be inclined to send assistance to stabilize the country and help nurture a democratic society."

Volpe wondered who Piersal was preaching to.

"Suffice it to say, Colonel, these people are animals and we need to get rid of them."

Volpe nodded in agreement, but maintained an expressionless face behind his scar. Piersal had said nothing so far that required comment.

"The president is concerned about the level of American casualties, not to mention the threat these forces pose to the success of our mission here."

The president is concerned about his reelection, thought Volpe, cynical despite the fact that he planned to vote for the man again. Casualties were a political liability and the war was supposed to be over by now.

Piersal seemed to read the smug disdain in Volpe's good eye, for he sat up and stared directly at the colonel and continued. "The fact of the matter, Colonel Volpe, is that you have not been taking advantage of the assets available to you. Specifically, I am referring to the Iraqi prisoners currently detained in your facilities."

Piersal now had Volpe's attention. The general stared harder at Volpe's scar. The combat arms were full of savages like Volpe, who wore their scars like badges of honor instead of evidence of their foolhardiness for getting themselves shot in the first place.

"I'm not sure I follow you, General."

Piersal stared him down for a moment. "Well, Colonel, you were a tank commander, trained to destroy everything in front of you. More often than you might like to admit, your targets were identified for you by us gnomes at MI who spend night and day poring through reams of data. Unfortunately, urban guerilla warfare is not so simple. High-tech data-gathering tools have limited value in urban guerilla warfare, where satellite photos and telecom intercepts are no longer effective in pinpointing enemy locations or intentions. What we need now is HUMINT, human intelligence: spies, confessions, tips, and POWs willing to spill their guts." Piersal paused for a moment. "I don't mean to be condescending. The point I am trying to make is that battlefield intelligence is important to success in traditional combat, but it is absolutely critical to success in urban guerilla warfare. And combat intel is what I do."

"Yes, sir," said Volpe. "I fully appreciate the need for HUMINT. We interrogate our POWs as best we can, but we don't have the staff to do much more than keep them locked up. We would welcome any additional manpower that MI might be able to provide."

"Colonel, I'm not here to bring additional manpower to the problem. I'm here to change the way you gather intelligence. We don't advertise it, but we have been very successful in Guantanamo in developing interrogation techniques against Muslim prisoners. The SecDef has directed the Pentagon to take the lessons we learned in Gitmo and employ them here in Iraq."

Volpe glanced at Tannerbeck, who said, "Rick, this is no reflection on your performance. On the contrary, your responsibilities and authorities will be expanded. The decision to 'Gitmo-ize' our POW operations is strictly a matter of applying lessons learned elsewhere to our situation here.

The purpose of this meeting is to discuss the implementation of that decision."

Piersal sensed that Tannerbeck's words were not as heartfelt as they should have been and that Volpe, too, was suspicious. But the Guantanamo commander cared nothing about Volpe's attitude, or even Tannerbeck's. He was there at the behest of the Joint Chiefs of Staff, and CJTF-7 was about to learn the lessons of Guantanamo Bay whether they wanted to or not. He said, "I have concluded that there are a number of areas of operation that require improvement if we are going to increase the velocity and effectiveness of interrogations. Of most immediate concern, however, is the fact that there is no unified strategy to detain and interrogate internees. Part of the problem is a lack of resources; you just don't have the manpower. But the other problem is that you don't use the resources you have."

Tannerbeck kept his eye on Volpe and wondered if General Piersal noticed the hardening of Volpe's horrible face. Volpe sat attentively and kept his mouth shut.

Piersal continued. "Currently, Colonel, the responsibilities of the MP units under your command are to escort prisoners and to maintain the physical security of the facility. At Gitmo, we expanded those responsibilities to include the preparation of prisoners for interrogation, to soften them up so that they are less able to resist interrogation by MI. This will facilitate the rapid exploitation of detainees, resulting in more actionable intelligence."

"What do you mean by 'soften them up'?" asked Volpe, suspicious.

"To shake them up a little; to disorient and intimidate them so that they will be more willing to talk," replied Piersal with a hint of irritation. He was convinced that Volpe knew perfectly well what the hell he meant.

But Volpe had little tolerance for intentional ambiguity. He was plainspoken man and demanded the same clarity from others, including his superiors. "Are we talking about torture?" he asked bluntly.

Piersal glared at Volpe, but responded calmly. "The specific measures used to prepare the prisoners for questioning are currently under review by JAG and civilian lawyers, but they include stress positions, sleep deprivation, isolation, hoods, nudity, twenty-four-hour interrogations, and mild physical contact.

"I have proposed," continued Piersal, "to create a Joint Debriefing and Interrogation Center at Abu Ghraib prison. The JDIC will consist of interrogators, translators, and analysts under a single commander. In addition, the JDIC will be supported by a dedicated MP unit that will be trained to implement the enhanced interrogation techniques. Lieutenant Colonel Makin will remain here for a few weeks to oversee the creation of the JDIC and commence the training of the dedicated guards. Lieutenant Colonel Makin supervised interrogations at Guantanamo and he is an expert in Muslim culture and psychology."

Makin felt Volpe's eye upon him, and he forced himself to look up and nod slightly.

Volpe asked, "Who will Lieutenant Colonel Makin report to?"

Piersal smiled at last. "To you, Colonel."

General Tannerbeck spoke up. "Rick, we are preparing a frag order that will appoint you as the new FOB commander at Abu Ghraib, responsible for all forces there. You should prepare to move your office ASAP."

Tannerbeck's announcement was a surprise, but Volpe's face betrayed nothing. He simply nodded and said, "I'll transfer my command immediately, sir. But so there is no misunderstanding, I assume that I am responsible to assure that all of my soldiers, including the JDIC, observe the rules of war as defined by the Geneva Conventions."

"Colonel," said Piersal testily, "The SecDef has determined that these prisoners are terrorists, unlawful combatants, not entitled to the protections of the Geneva Conventions."

"So you're saying that these techniques do violate the Conventions, but that they simply don't apply to our POWs?"

Tannerbeck almost smiled.

"These men are civilian criminals, not soldiers, and are thus subject to civilian rules regarding their treatment," said Piersal. "We're talking about sleep deprivation, minor humiliation, nudity, and solitary confinement. We don't pull out any goddamn fingernails."

Volpe didn't buy it. With a hint of insubordination, he said, "My men don't subject our POWs to this sort of thing; we protect them from it."

"Colonel, these men are unprivileged belligerents, not prisoners of war. In fact, many of the interrogations will be conducted by Other Government Agencies and civilian contractors." Piersal leaned forward to reinforce his point, "Civilians interrogating civilians."

OGAs, thought Volpe, increasingly alarmed. Other Government Agencies usually referred to the cowboys from the CIA who reported to invisible nobodies and operated outside any local authorities. Volpe had dealt with them before and he wanted nothing to do with them now. He leveled a stare at Makin, and his scowl turned grim.

Piersal stood up, prompting Makin and Volpe to pop to their feet as well. Speaking to Tannerbeck, who remained seated, Piersal said, "If there are no further objections to the SecDef's orders, Colonel Makin and I have work to do. Good luck, General."

Piersal exited the conference room, Makin in tow.

The room was silent for a moment until Volpe sensed Tannerbeck looking at him. "Civilian contractors are trouble," he growled.

Tannerbeck nodded. "Men without fingerprints."

"I can't obey these orders, sir."

"I admire your professionalism, but I don't give a damn about those POWs. I'll shove a cattle prod up every ass in Iraq if that's what it takes to send my men home in one piece. And if the SecDef says it's OK to do it, so much the better." Tannerbeck spoke with sincerity, despite troubling thoughts. There could be no resistance to Piersal's recommendations, since the authority of the Joint Chiefs and the secretary of defense were behind them. The CINC had the political instincts to see this one coming and had dumped it on Tannerbeck, a man he could count on to do his duty and to protect them all.

CHAPTER 3

October 8, 2003 (Wednesday)
Abu Ghraib Prison, Iraq

The prison at Abu Ghraib was built in 1961 by British contractors for the Iraqi government. The new regime, threatened by internal enemies following the Baathist ascension to power, needed a prison of extraordinary proportions to house their political opponents, along with a smattering of common criminals. The prison eventually became the depository for many Baathists themselves, as Saddam Hussein purged the ranks of his own party and sent any potential rivals to their final resting places inside Abu Ghraib's walls.

Stretching across 280 acres in a wilderness of sand, the prison was surrounded by three miles of masonry walls, twenty feet high, punctuated by guard towers every 200 meters, twenty-four in all. The central facility consisted of administrative offices and two wings of cell blocks. The cells themselves were twelve feet square, enough room to pack a hundred men like cigarettes. Here they lived for months, released only long enough for the prison staff to attach electrodes to their genitals or to dip them in vats of hydrochloric acid. Abu Ghraib was where Saddam's son Uday peeled the skin from the soles of the feet of Iraqi soccer players whenever they lost a match.

The carnival of sadism finally ended with the American invasion of Iraq. Sometime during the fight for Baghdad, Abu Ghraib's staff of torturers slipped away, the prisoners escaped, looters stripped it bare, and the prison became a ghost town, a foreboding ruin in the windy desert occupied by crows and the miserable spirits of its dead.

American combat units swept through Abu Ghraib during the initial assault toward Baghdad, but finding no enemy resistance, no arms, nothing but drifts of sand and shattered toilets and a dead man hanging from a meat hook in one cell, the army left the ruin to the ghosts and headed on to Baghdad. When combat operations ended a week later, Abu Ghraib was forgotten—until the prisoners began to pile up. So it was that on May 1, 2003, the 72nd Military Police Company arrived with orders to clean the place up and prepare it for occupancy.

Their tour of duty ended in August, when the 229th MP Company from the Virginia National Guard arrived. The 229th was one of a dozen odd-lot units consolidated in Iraq under the command of the 800th MP Brigade HQ in Baghdad and assigned to guard prisoners at Abu Ghraib. While some units pulled internal duties, handling high-value detainees in the cell blocks, the 229th focused on force protection, patrolling the perimeter walls, manning the guard towers, and riding herd over the tent city of Camp Vigilant, where two thousand miserable and mostly innocent Iraqi detainees lived in one of five internal compounds within the walls of Abu Ghraib, each compound surrounded by its own security wall and rolls of razor wire. Each detainee was issued a blanket and a hospital-style name tag was secured to his wrist. There were no prison uniforms, so the prisoners wore whatever they had on at the time of their arrest, which for those picked up during nighttime raids was nothing more than a bathrobe. They were fed in chow lines run by corrupt Iraqi contractors, and they relieved themselves in unsanitary portable toilets that overflowed when the maintenance convoys failed to arrive due to insurgent attacks on the only road to Baghdad.

Like army units everywhere, the 229th fought the stress and tedium with irreverent humor. The company had a clown, a self-appointed NCOIC of Comedy, whose brand of humor gravitated toward the lewd, crude, and socially unacceptable, which made him immensely popular with his fellow soldiers. But like most jokers, Vic Tetra was not the fool he pretended to be. He was a man of unusual maturity for his age, a bodybuilder with the neck of a bison who believed in personal responsibility and clean living, but not God. He was tattooed like a snake and tittered like a bird when he laughed, which wasn't often despite the fact that he kept everyone else in stitches. Raised like the rest of the soldiers of the 229th on rap music and video games, his wit was hip, urban, and blasphemous.

As a buck sergeant E4, Tetra had the authority to pick his own partners on perimeter patrol and for duty in the guard towers. He chose his partners in ways that baffled the others, for Tetra's friends were soldiers unlike himself. They were solitary men who accepted Tetra with a shrug, who shared Tetra's amoral vision of a perverse universe, but who accepted it without the need to ridicule it. He paired himself frequently with Morgan Buckner.

Buckner was a mystery to the soldiers of the 229th MPs, including Tetra, whose every nickname for Buckner seemed to slough off after a day or two because so few people knew Buckner or liked him well enough to call him anything at all. When rumor spread that Buckner had submitted an application for reassignment to the U.S. Military Academy at West Point, people shook their heads with amused incredulity, baffled by such ambition unfounded by any evidence that he had what it took to graduate. The two men were an odd couple; Tetra, the hulking white kid from some hick town in Maryland, shambling along with the taciturn black man from Baltimore, who seemed almost unaware of Tetra's wisecracking presence.

Dusk was like dawn at Abu Ghraib, the sun rising or setting behind a veil of dust that rose a thousand feet into the atmosphere and hung there like the desert version of the aurora borealis. Even at midday, visibility across the desert was limited by the powdered dirt in the air, and the guards in the towers kept a wary eye out for any movement in the hazy area where the landscape crumbled into the sky. Nights were especially dangerous, when the prison floodlights cast a glow into the air. The lights were aimed low to keep their beams inside the prison walls, but the dust reflected enough photons upward that they radiated over the walls like effervescent lava, advertising their position like a neon bull's-eye to any insurgent mortar team members who might dare to travel off road in the desert with their headlights off, hidden in the dust of their own pickup trucks.

An hour before sunset, the floodlights flared on with a bang. In tower 09, Buckner checked his wristwatch, glad that the relief crew would be arriving soon. He was hungry.

"Anything out there?" asked Tetra.

Buckner shrugged. "Can't see shit."

Tetra settled onto a row of sandbags that had been arranged as a sort of chair and withdrew a pair of envelopes from his pocket. Nobody received much mail, so two letters in a single day was an event to celebrate. Most men ripped open their mail immediately, like children attacking Christmas presents under the tree, but Tetra had carried his letters in his pocket all day, waiting for the best moment to savor them. Privacy was unheard of at Abu Ghraib, and time alone with a single friend was as good as it got. Besides, Tetra wanted to share one of his letters with Buckner. "Smell it," he said, holding the fragrant envelope. "The girl wants me, Dude."

"She's thirteen years old."

"Not according to her perfume."

"She's my sister," said Buckner, "I know how old she is."

"She wants to meet me."

"You pervert."

"Yeah, but you don't mind if I bang her, do you?"

"She's too mature for you."

Tetra laughed his effeminate twitter. "She says you gotta bring me home with you 'cause you're the man of the house now. What's with that?"

"I bashed my old man over the head with his bottle and threw him out."

Tetra nodded, as if no explanation was required as to why such action might have been necessary. "What about your mother?" he asked, suddenly serious. "She work?"

"She gets welfare. That's why I joined the army, because I needed to take care of them, and MPs was the only MOS available for me, guarding ignorant dirtbags who are just one step lower than me."

"According to the Koran," said Tetra, "the natural state of man is *jahilyya*, a condition of ignorance and animism. *Animism* is like dirtbags, right?"

"You read the Koran?"

"I read The Koran for Idiots."

Buckner was impressed. Few soldiers took any interest at all in Muslim culture, including himself. Waving his
hand toward the prisoners in the yard below, he said, "They
should call it The Koran for Jahilyyas."

Tetra laughed and added, "The army'll make it into
Field Manual 01-205: The Koran for Shit-Eating Jihalyyas."

Buckner began laughing, too. "You're crazy, Tetra. Crazy fucking white man."

Tetra broke into song: "People are crazy and things are
strange."

"I'm locked in tight, I'm outta range," sang Buckner. In
unison, they finished the verse: "I used to care, but things
have changed," two men quoting Bob Dylan thirty years after their fathers sang his verses in a different war. The songs
were different, but the relationship between soldiers would
never change; they were locked in tight.

Tetra spotted the relief team hiking toward them along
a trail bordered on one side by the original high walls of
Abu Ghraib and on the other by coils of concertina wire that
encircled the tent city where the prisoners were held. The
wired compounds were huge, with open space for prayer,
thousands of men with their asses in the air as they knelt
in the dirt and faced toward Mecca whenever the muezzins
called the faithful to prayer. The tents were hot and filthy,
filled with the fluffy moon dust that permeated everything
because the canvas walls were raised up to catch whatever
breeze there was. There were too few showers and too few
latrines, and usually too little food. A few of the soldiers of
the 229th wished they could do more to alleviate the suffering of their prisoners, but most were like Buckner and Tetra;
not mean-spirited or evil, merely consumed with their own
problems and as indifferent to the Muslim prisoners as they
would have been to a prison full of California beach boys.

The relief team climbed the steps into the guard tower and exchanged passwords. "Keep an eye on that group over there," said Tetra, pointing, as he grabbed his ruck and slung it over his shoulder. "They've been hanging there since the last prayers, trying hard to look casual, you know?"

The relief team looked over a sea of prisoners toward a dozen Sunnis who smoked cigarettes and shuffled furtively in the dirt near the portable toilets, shooing flies that hovered over them. The fiberglass shitters stunk with overflow because the service trucks were delayed again by threats of ambush on the main drag to Baghdad. Most prisoners stayed as far from the foul area as possible, so a congregation of any kind that close to the latrines was a suspicious event.

"OK," acknowledged the relief. "Anything else?"

"Not that I can see," said Buckner. Same desert, same dust, same vacant scrubland of weeds and rocks with clumps of desert vegetation along the road to Baghdad. There might be someone out there, or there might not. Buckner grabbed his gear and climbed down the ladder with Tetra right behind.

Guards were relieved at staggered intervals to assure continuity of surveillance, so Buckner and Tetra had the barracks nearly to themselves as they lumbered in and tossed their gear on their bunks. Two hundred additional cots filled the cavernous bay where the enlisted members of the battalion slept, a room that could have been a gymnasium at one time, but nobody really knew. Buckner thought of chow and was checking his watch when suddenly the door flew open behind them.

"Tetra! Buckner!" called Lt. Brewer, leader of Camp Vigilant's Quick Reaction Force. "Get to the gate NOW!"

Every uprising was serious enough to command the attention of the FOB commander, who now peered from his second-story office window at the gathering tempest in the confinement yards below. Colonel Volpe watched nervously, shifting his eyes from the reaction team to the guards in the towers and praying that none of them overreacted.

Volpe was not alone. He was joined in his office by Lt. Colonel Makin, who watched the action over his commander's shoulder. The relationship between the two men had never warmed up after their initial meeting in General Tannerbeck's conference room, in which Volpe learned that Makin would assume command of the Joint Debriefing and Interrogation Center (JDIC) to facilitate prisoner interrogations. Volpe was objective enough to acknowledge that Makin was no fool; he had done a superb job of cobbling together the elements of his command to create the JDIC. But Makin's carefully drawn line between legal and illegal interrogations seemed like quibbling to Volpe, who had little tolerance for anything that was not black or white. On more than one occasion, Volpe had upbraided Makin for the performance of his troops in the JDIC, whose treatment of prisoners seemed to Volpe to be not only criminal, but ridiculous.

"Makin," said Volpe, eager to wrap up the meeting and get down to the action below, "I called you here to advise you that your replacement has arrived in country and will be reporting for duty to take command of the JDIC in forty-eight hours. You are free to return to Gitmo at your earliest opportunity."

Makin sucked in his breath. He was eager to get back to his unit in Guantanamo, an almost academic environment where they were learning fascinating things about breaking the human will, but the JDIC was his baby, too, and would be hard to leave. He was confident, however, that he had found the right men to carry on the operations of the JDIC; men with the dispassionate ability to break a man the way a biochemist might dismantle a string of DNA. "If it's OK with you, Colonel, I'll stay on long enough to get the new commander up to speed."

Volpe turned away from the window and retrieved his sidearm from the bottom drawer of his desk. With no further comment, he strapped the pistol belt around his waist and headed downstairs to join his troops.

The QRF formed up outside the wire, Tetra shifting chameleon-like from jester to NCO as other soldiers joined the team. The team was composed of men of superior strength and military prowess, who received specialized training with clubs and shields and in martial arts. Their mission was to operate inside the wire, among the detainees, to subdue troublemakers or break up fights. Tetra moved efficiently down his rank of soldiers, checking their gear and hurrying them up. "Secure your chin strap," he admonished Buckner, any trace of their previous camaraderie lost in professionalism. "Batons in your right hands, gentlemen." Every man was right-handed, to avoid the dangers of entangling arms with a southpaw if everyone started swinging his billy club. "Heads up," ordered Tetra. "Here we go!"

Inside the compound, a group of Iraqis screamed across the razor wire at the assembling Americans. Buckner recognized them immediately as the cluster from the latrine. The other detainees gave the men a wide berth, not because of any respect for the Americans, but solely to avoid any more trouble than they already had. Every few seconds, a different man would emerge from the scrum to shout insults at his captors, and throw stones at the floodlights that illuminated the area, one of which was already out. The prisoners moved closer to the gate, and from the rear of the mob a wad of human excrement flew into the air, shredding into pieces overhead before splattering short of the wary reaction team.

The gate was opened and the reaction team stepped forward like a Roman skirmish line. They outnumbered their foes and were better armed, but Buckner felt the tightness in his chest common to soldiers everywhere as they go into combat. Anything could happen in a melee, which was why the prisoners wanted to mix it up in close quarters.

The prisoners stood their ground and puffed out their chests and taunted their enemies with English obscenities and international hand gestures. A few of the men wore Arab robes and *kaffiyeh*, but most were dressed in western clothes typical of city dandies: pleated slacks, sleek loafers, and bright cotton shirts open at the neck, now filthy with dust. "Fuck you, America! Fuck you, George Bush!" The Quick Reaction Force approached to within fifteen feet.

The last few feet would be closed in a headlong rush, an old-fashioned charge worthy of a medieval clash of knights, so as to maximize shock and confusion among the prisoners. As Lieutenant Brewer prepared to issue the command, however, a hand thrust forward between two prisoners in their front rank. The hand bucked as a 9 mm automatic handgun barked once, then again, and five more times in rapid order.

"Gun!" yelled Tetra, bolting forward without waiting for the command to charge, for only immediate aggressive action could thwart an ambush. Retreat was suicide, as was any response slower than instantaneous.

Buckner felt a tap on the corner of his headgear, a bullet passing his ear like a supersonic hornet. Terrified, he dropped to ground, knowing he'd been hit but not how severely. Buckner opened his mouth to summon a medic, but another member of the QRF jumped over him, following Tetra into harm's way. From his prone position, Buckner saw the shooter drop his weapon into the dirt, as other members of the QRF crashed into the gang of troublemakers.

The prisoners scattered like a flock of birds, fleet boys daring the Americans to come after them deeper into the tent city, one-on-one, where each soldier could be engulfed by a dozen prisoners. From the guard towers, the crack of M-16s echoed across the compound, three shots in rapid order. One boy pitched face-first into the dirt, killed by a bullet that entered his back and blew his heart out through his mouth. The other prisoners immediately surrendered, somehow surprised that the Americans would actually shoot back.

Mortified by his initial reaction, Buckner sprang to his feet to pursue the others into the melee. But Lieutenant Brewer ordered, "No pursuit! Regroup!" as chaos erupted around him.

"Medic!"

"I'm hit!"

"Where's the medic?"

"Tetra, you OK?"

"Open the gate! Get a medic in here!"

"Oh shit! Oh SHIT!"

"MEDIC! Where's the fucking *MEDIC?*"

"Tetra?"

Iraqi translators now broadcast over the compound in broken Arabic: *"Koll al masajeen, enbateeho a'laa alarrdh! Dhaa' aydeekom khalf ra'sekom! Ayy wahed yoqawem sawfa naqtoluh!"*

Brewer grabbed Buckner by the collar and ordered him into a defensive perimeter. Those members of the QRF who had charged into the crowd stumbled into position as Brewer rounded them up. One man returned with a prisoner in tow, his wrists secured with plastic zip cuffs. Buckner pointed at the prisoner and yelled, "Lieutenant! That's the one who had the gun!"

The QRF guard jerked the man upright, so as to present him to Brewer. The lieutenant gave the man a quick once-over as other guards swarmed into the compound, armed this time with 12-gauge Benelli shotguns to protect the reaction team that had now wrangled themselves into a perimeter around the wounded, where a medic tended to them. "Take him to the hard site," ordered Brewer. "Buckner, you go with him. I want to know where he got that weapon."

Buckner grabbed prisoner's arm. As the two guards shoved the man forward, Buckner spotted Tetra, motionless on the ground, ignored by the medics. Even at a distance, Buckner could see the clumps of dust coagulated by a spoor of blood. Tetra seemed diminished, like an inflatable doll with some air leaked out, and he knew by the medic's lack of attention that his friend was dead.

Stunned, Buckner relied upon professionalism and training to guide his actions as he held numbly to the prisoner's wrists, keeping the man's hands high in the air while forcing his head down. The man staggered in discomfort, but Buckner made no effort to ameliorate the pain, kicking the man's feet to keep him moving toward the guarded steel door that was the entrance of the old prison, staffed by members of another company, the 372nd MPs, a reserve unit from the state of Maryland. This was the "hard site," a real prison, with cells and doors and bars and locks, used to hold the most dangerous prisoners.

The prisoner entrance was as innocuous as a back alley service door to any restaurant, except for the chain-link cage topped by razor wire that extended fifteen feet from the door. The enclosure was guarded by two members of the Iraqi Police, and Buckner wondered which one of them had provided his prisoner with the handgun that had killed Tetra. Nervous and agitated by the brawl at the other end of the prison, the IPs quickly opened the chain-link gate as Buckner approached and without a word rapped on the steel door to the building.

When the door opened, Buckner pushed the prisoner ahead of him while maintaining a positive grasp on the man's handcuffed wrists. Another MP closed the door behind them, and Buckner found himself in a passageway six feet wide with a concrete floor and walls of painted cinder block. The reception hall opened into a larger space, a vestibule thirty feet across and one hundred feet long, with other corridors every forty feet leading away into the cell blocks. Faint human voices emanated from the block labeled "1A" in black paint above the entrance. The guard led them to a metal desk, the surface bare except for a radio, a telephone, and a torn copy of *Sports Illustrated* magazine. Prisoner records filled a row of filing cabinets that lined the wall behind the desk. In a metal chair sat a female soldier, her feet resting on the desktop.

"Got a prisoner," stated Buckner.

"Trouble in the yard?" she asked.

"This one got a gun and started shooting."

The girl from MI sat up. Like the other members of the JDIC, she rarely went outdoors, the routine of the exterior guards as mysterious to her as were her responsibilities to the soldiers of the 229th. "Any casualties?"

"One KIA. Some wounded, I think." Somehow, Buckner kept an emotional lid on the fact that the KIA was Tetra. Buckner pushed the man's head down, keeping him doubled over at the waist. With his free hand, Buckner removed his headgear and placed it on the guard's desk. The headliner was smeared with blood and Buckner realized he was bleeding.

No one spoke as their hatred for Buckner's prisoner, and for all Iraqis, grew palpable. After a moment, the guard sighed deeply and commanded the prisoner, "Stand up!"

Buckner released his grip on the man's wrists and straightened him up with a tug on his hair. "I only need one of you here," said the guard, glancing back and forth between Buckner and the other member of the QRF who had captured the prisoner.

"You stay," said Buckner's QRF teammate, eager to rejoin his buddies in their hour of peril. "They need me out there." He gave Buckner a frank stare as he headed for the door, and Buckner realized that this was the man who had leapt over him to follow Tetra when Buckner had hit the dirt.

But Buckner thought only of Tetra, who didn't need anybody anymore.

"You speak English?" asked the female guard. She noted that the prisoner had removed his wrist ID.

"Better than you," said the man, his eyes pouring out hatred as if it were tactile. With a sneer of dismissal, he pursed his lips and calmly spit on the floor. Buckner next heard the sound of trickling water and realized that the prisoner was urinating in his pants, an act of contempt especially satisfying to perform in the presence of a woman. The man almost laughed when the girl spotted the puddle of urine spreading at his feet.

With an ominous sigh, the girl withdrew a ring of keys from the top drawer of one filing cabinet. While she crossed the room to a heavy door that was locked with a pair of deadbolts, the male guard kicked the man's feet out from under him and pushed his face into the pool of his own urine. The guard said, "You ain't the first dog I've had to house train."

The girl threw the latch and held the door while Buckner jerked the prisoner to his feet and pushed him ahead of them. They entered a short hallway without doors or windows illuminated only by a pair of fluorescent bulbs. Buckner saw brighter lights and heard a wave of human sounds—yelling, crying, and laughing—that carried down the corridor to greet them.

"What's going on?" asked Buckner, the noise reminding him of a few drinking establishments in East Baltimore where his father had blown too many paychecks.

The cell block consisted of ten rooms along each side of a wide center aisle. The doors to each cell were open. Naked men quailed outside each door, some with women's underwear on their heads, while American guards in olive drab T-shirts roamed among them, yelling and slapping at them. A well-muscled man in a civilian polo shirt stood at the head of the aisle, observing the scene with his arms folded across his chest. As Buckner pushed the prisoner into the cell block, the civilian's attention turned to the new arrival. "Who are you?" he asked, with a faint accent that Buckner could not place. The timbre of his voice was raspy, as if his vocal chords had been damaged. Buckner held the prisoner in position as the girl related to the civilian in charge what Buckner had already told her, raising her voice to overcome the bedlam in the cell block. The civilian nodded and asked Buckner, "Where'd he get the gun?"

"IPs, probably."

"We'll see." The man grabbed the prisoner by the hair and smiled at him. The prisoner smiled back. "What's his name?"

"He ain't talking," said Buckner.

The man shook his head slowly, as if amused by prisoners who thought they could resist interrogation. "Come with me." He led the way to an open cell and closed the door behind them. Only then did Buckner release his grip on the man's wrists. The prisoner straightened up carefully and stared at them with insolence.

"Careful," said Buckner. "He spits."

"Just like their fuckin' camels." The man withdrew a cloth from his pocket and quickly lowered it over the man's head. When he stepped away, Buckner saw that the prisoner now sported a pair of women's panties that covered his face, the elastic cinched around his neck. "The humiliation really does a number on these guys, but I like the panties because they prevent them from spitting on you."

Buckner said nothing, but glanced through a small window in the door into the cell block where the yelling and braying continued.

"I'm an interrogator," explained the man. "The prisoners are being prepared for questioning."

Buckner snorted. "You're shittin' me, right?"

"Not at all," the man replied, enthusiastic and proud of his work. "We smack 'em around a little, take their clothes, Psy-ops the shit out of them. After a night naked in their cell, freezing their ass off, they usually tell us anything we want to know. Personally, I just like fucking with their heads."

Buckner peeked again into the hallway, where the girl who had escorted him into the cell block now strutted among the naked prisoners. Like the other guards, she wore no fatigue shirt, maintaining anonymity by wearing an OD T-shirt with no name tag. She appeared to be enjoying herself, yelling obscenities at the prisoners and mocking their genitalia.

"Women drive these idiots crazy," said the man, reading Buckner's mind. Turning to the prisoner, he added, "The woman that wore these was menstruating, my friend. She was unclean, just like you."

The prisoner mocked him with a grunt.

Ignorant of Muslim sensitivities toward menstrual blood, Buckner was perplexed. He nodded toward the chaos outside the cell, where only a single prisoner seemed discomposed. "These ragheads don't give a shit about blood. They shit on the ground right in front of us, like dogs." The prisoner snapped his head toward Buckner with a blatant gaze of contempt. Buckner continued, "These people chop off heads and smear the blood all over themselves. You think a pair of panties freaks 'em out?"

The interrogator shrugged and suddenly yanked down the man's pants. "All it takes is one." He pointed out a prisoner outside the cell whose demeanor was less stoic than the others. "See that guy? He'll give it up in a minute."

Turning to the prisoner, the interrogator said, "You want to go join your naked friends? Let everyone see you? Rub your bodies together? We take your photo, you know. We'll show it to your family. You want that?"

The man said nothing, but extended each middle finger of his shackled hands.

The interpreter grabbed one finger and pulled it backward, eliciting a grunt of pain from the prisoner. On the back of the prisoner's hand was a tattoo. "You know that this says?" the civilian asked Buckner. "Without waiting for an answer, he translated the Arabic words: "Only Allah rules."

"Fuck Allah," said Buckner. "Who gave him the gun?"

The man refused to speak, though the pain had finally wiped the smile off his lips.

"Tell us where you got the gun, and I'll return your pants. Your family will never need to see naked photographs of you," said the civilian.

The man almost laughed. "My family was already murdered by an American bomb. If you are so fascinated by my penis, go ahead and photograph it."

"This is bullshit," said Buckner, embarrassed by the silliness. He closed his fist and buried it in the prisoner's solar plexus. The man collapsed to the floor with a pneumatic wheeze as the civilian jumped back.

Kneeling beside the breathless prisoner, Buckner growled with laconic intensity that belied the violence of his attack, "You shot my friend. I don't care about any stupid photographs. I'm just gonna kill you unless you tell me who gave you the fucking gun."

The man coughed and said, "I killed an infidel and I am proud of it."

Buckner yanked the panties from the gasping man's head and stuffed them into his mouth. The prisoner's eyes bulged and he began to gag. Buckner grasped the man by the hair and jammed the wad of cotton further down the man's throat. "That infidel was my friend," growled Buckner, as he pushed the man to the floor and knelt on his chest. A burst of vomit shot from the man's nostrils and his body convulsed. Buckner stared into the prisoner's wide eyes and said calmly, "Tell me where you got the gun, or you're going to choke to death on these bloody panties, you camel-fuckin' asshole. You understand what I'm saying?" Increasingly furious, Buckner grabbed the man by his shirt and slapped him viciously across the face. "You understand?" Buckner hit him again and yelled, "You understand what I'm saying?"

The man nodded vigorously and gagged again. Buckner pulled the underwear from the man's throat and the prisoner inhaled desperately, like air rushing into a vacuum. Grabbing the prisoner by the hair, Buckner tilted the man's head backward and said, "Who gave you the gun?"

"The guards," gasped the prisoner.

The civilian knelt down next to Buckner. Nonchalant, he said to the prisoner, "What guard? I need his name, please."

The prisoner muttered the name of a member of the Iraqi security force. Buckner dropped the prisoner's head to the floor, where the man continued to breathe raggedly. He had been ready to die, but he had expected bullets, not suffocation. He gulped the air greedily, even though each breath reminded him that he was a coward before Allah.

The civilian tugged Buckner by the sleeve. "What'd you say your name was?"

"Buckner."

The civilian looked him over and nodded. "Go on back to your unit. Keep everything you saw here to yourself, understand?" Without waiting for an answer, he turned back to the prisoner. "I'll take care of this guy. I suspect he has more to tell us. Once they give it up, they blabber all night."

Buckner stared down at the prostrate prisoner, still struggling to catch ragged breaths. He had suppressed thoughts of Tetra for nearly an hour, and as the adrenalin depleted itself in his body, emotion flooded back into him. A wave of hatred overcame him; hatred for the man who had killed Tetra and hatred for all Iraqis, miserable cowards who refused to fight their own war and who allowed animals like the one on the floor to dominate them. In a parting act, Buckner shifted onto his left foot and threw his weight into a vicious kick with his right, the toe of his boot burying itself deep into the prisoner's lower rib cage and paralyzing his diaphragm. The man curled into a fetal position, helpless to breathe, and his eyes rolled back in his head.

Buckner glared at the civilian, challenging him to step in. Buckner thought to kick the prisoner again, but the man vomited and Buckner knew that no payback would ever be sufficient. He left the prisoner on the floor and exited the cell. A trickle of blood dribbled down his cheek from a tiny cut in his skin that oozed another drop of blood.

The female guard came up behind him to escort him from the cell block. Noting the blood on Buckner's face, she said, "You'll get a Heart for that."

Buckner's adrenalin had dissipated, and he remembered the sight of Tetra lying in the dirt outside. Tetra would be buried with a Purple Heart of his own, an award as insufficient as it was unfair. Buckner strode past the quaking prisoners with his eyes on the floor, wishing he could kill them all.

CHAPTER 4

October 20, 2003 (Monday)
Fallujah, Iraq

Fallujah was another Baathist shithole of two hundred thousand Sunnis southwest of Baghdad. The city was notorious for the murder of four unarmed American civilians in June 2003, gunned down in broad daylight, after which hundreds of Fallujah's citizens danced like animists as they chopped the corpses apart with shovels before stringing them up like sides of beef from the superstructure of a railroad bridge over the Euphrates River. So grotesque was the brutality and so proud were the perpetrators, that Fallujah earned a nickname that mocked the avowed piety of the Muslims who lived there: The City of Atheists. American commanders would later remind their soldiers of this act of barbarity during the destruction of Fallujah in November 2004, but the U.S. military had higher priorities in October 2003.

In an act of forbearance intended to defuse the situation in Fallujah, and hoping to facilitate civilian control and political stabilization, Central Command agreed to keep American troops out of the city. Instead, Iraqi troops were deployed to keep the peace under the command of General

Mohammed Lahifa, a Baathist general with flexible loyalties. But intimidated by the insurgents, Lahifa's battalion withered away within a week. Iraqi troops guarded checkpoints at various entry points into the city, but only the politicians in Baghdad succumbed to the fantasy that the guards served any purpose other than to alert the insurgents of any American presence in their vicinity. The City of Atheists thus became a haven for the enemy, a place where sacred mosques became arsenals, where kidnapped civilians were tortured and beheaded, and a place from which to stage terrorist attacks without fear of reprisals.

Like the other entrances into Fallujah, the notorious railroad bridge was guarded by Iraqi soldiers, who lay a few meters from the tracks on a large slab of cardboard, snoring gently. Looking down at them stood a man in desert BDUs and Night Vision Goggles, wearing scuffed boots as silent as moccasins. The man picked the guards' pockets of their cell phones and tossed away their AK47s, and then signaled into the darkness. Four additional marines materialized and headed across the bridge. Only when the Marine Recon snipers were mid-span on the trestle, invisible in the darkness, did the marine kick the sleeping men roughly in the ass.

The stupefied sentries snapped awake when their eyes focused enough to recognize the goggled figure standing before them like a gargoyle. After fumbling quickly for their missing rifles, then their cellular telephones, they gradually realized that they were alive only because the gargoyle had elected not to cut their throats. Terrified, they meekly obeyed the marine's pantomime to sit quietly on their cardboard pad. Nobody spoke and nobody moved, even when the shooting started.

The night turned calm, the dust sifting to the ground gradually, allowing a sliver of a moon to penetrate the haze; perfect hunting conditions for skilled men with high-powered rifles and vision-enhancing eyewear. Led by Sergeant "Chippie" Halloran, the Recon marines scuttled silently across the bridge, converted now from a railroad trestle to a span for motor vehicles eighty feet above the filthy stream that was the Euphrates River, the aorta of Iraq. Among "the brave, the proud, and the few," Recon marines were elite: human destroyers as mystical as ninjas. Tough and smart, they were dangerous veterans who killed efficiently with knives or with their bare hands, but their mission tonight would call upon their other deadly specialty, sniping. Halloran's team carried an assortment of weapons selected specifically for the mission. In the lead, Corporals Pitkin and Rivas carried Squad Automatic Weapons. SAWs could lay 750 rounds per minute downrange, a curtain of fire that would intimidate a battalion or cover a retreat. Stripped of all nonessential combat gear to eliminate "battle rattle" typical of marines on the move, the team carried little more than ammunition, night vision equipment, and sophisticated radio gear that included a hands-free bone mic and earpiece. The two corporals glided across the bridge to the far shore, where they scanned the empty road that ran into the city toward the Abdul-Aziz al-Samarrai Mosque. Through their goggles, the blue dome shone bright green. Closer to their position, the city was a squalid zigzag of alleys surrounded by low buildings with flat roofs covered with household trash, rusted mufflers, and busted appliances—individual garbage dumps on top of each residence. Televisions flickered in the windows of several apartments, satellite dishes mounted amid the refuse on the roofs. A couple of dogs caught the

Americans' scent and skulked away. Otherwise, the terrain was unoccupied and quiet, the moon high, the river black.

"Bridgehead clear," muttered Pitkin, as he and Rivas hunkered into defensive positions on either side of the road. With their bodies under the bridge and only their heads and weapons exposed, the dual sentries could decimate any large force that might approach from the rear.

"Roger," acknowledged Halloran. At the bridge center, Halloran set up his position alongside his spotter, Broussard, a man who would have outranked him if he had not been busted to corporal on three separate occasions for various peacetime offenses related to violations of uniform standards and personal appearance, including a tattoo of a swastika on his ass. The loss of rank seemed to not discourage Broussard from a military career, however, and no marine officer had yet been foolish enough to rid the service of a man with Broussard's deadly skills. For this mission, he carried a powerful spotter's scope and a CAR-15 with iron sights. Unlike Pitkin and Rivas, the sniper team eschewed NVGs in favor of the light enhancing technology built into their scopes. Strapped to Broussard's back was a SwiftLink satellite dish in a hardened suitcase, which he proceeded to open.

Wordlessly, Halloran set up his own weapon, the M70 Marine Sniper Rifle, a 30.06 instrument of death designed and built to marine combat specs. A beast of a weapon, the gun was capable of felling a rhinoceros at one thousand meters. Equipped with a Leothold 3x9 sight and firing a match grade round, it had a fabled history in the Marine Corps where sharpshooters had taken out enemy targets in Beirut, Mogadishu, and Panama. Snipers often named their rifles after women, and Halloran caressed "Xena" as he laid it gently on the pedestrian railing of the bridge and sighted across open space to the intended kill zone, another bridge that crossed the river downstream. Broussard checked the distance to the target with the laser range finder. "Four hundred yards," he muttered. Halloran adjusted Xena's elevation knob and set windage at zero while Broussard turned to the SwiftLink pack, powering up the battery and aligning the tiny BGAN antenna with the predetermined azimuth where somewhere in the night sky waited the correct Inmarsat satellite.

The kill zone was a two-lane span of concrete still known as the Saddam Bridge to the loyal Baathists of Fallujah. Because the river curved, the bridge was perpendicular to the railroad trestle where Halloran and Broussard waited, allowing a clear line of sight down the length of the bridge. Any targets crossing the bridge would be traveling toward the snipers or away from them, rather than across the view in the shooters' scopes. The bridges were at equal elevation, so there was no extra drop to consider. The wind died. If the target showed up, it would be like shooting fish in a barrel.

On the opposite side of the Saddam Bridge, a second team of marines set up their hide. Alpha Team's sniper carried a different weapon, the .50 caliber Barrett. A weapon of devastating power, the "Dirty Harry" of sniper rifles fired a copper-jacketed cartridge the size of a Havana cigar. The gun was massive, but so was the man who wielded it, a linebacker from UCLA who had quit the Pac Ten for something more exciting than football. It took a big man to carry the Barrett, as well as to absorb the recoil. The gun was a portable cannon designed to take out aircraft engines, generators, and power stations at a distance of nearly a mile. It was well suited for its mission tonight. In his headset, Halloran heard, "Alpha Team ready."

"Bravo Team ready," said Halloran. The men got comfortable. They would wait until 0500 if necessary, but the target was due at midnight, sixty minutes away. They killed the time by watching the Iraqi guards at the Saddam Bridge, who, unlike their counterparts at the railroad trestle, were awake tonight. They wandered across the bridge from time to time and tossed stones into the water, listening for the splash since it was too dark to see. Alpha Team had not bothered to take out the guards, for it was imperative that the bridge seem normal to anyone approaching it. Besides, Alpha Team had no intention of actually crossing the bridge, as Bravo Team had done on the railroad trestle.

Twelve thousand miles away, Captain Rachel Varnell slipped a headset over her ears and took a seat at a work station in the basement of the Pentagon. Her laptop flared to life, demanding a password. She logged in, and then opened the application she had helped design with the assistance of some geniuses from a little company in Maryland called TeleCommunication Systems. The company name was as generic as they came, an anonymous group of retired Naval Academy graduates who built black boxes full of electronics for anonymous agencies.

She clicked on a button labeled "Falluja" and a map appeared, covered with crosshairs, each representing the exact location of a cell phone, whether in operation or not. Friendlies were green; bogies were red, and she had to look hard to pick out Halloran's green crosshair from the sea of red ones. Checking her notes from the Intel briefing, she punched a phone number into her laptop. She knew only that the number had been acquired from a prisoner during an interrogation somewhere in Iraq and that MI had been monitoring the cellular phone for a week. One of the red crosshairs began to flash. With a click of her mouse she zoomed in on the target while filtering out extraneous bogies. She thought, *OK, asshole, let's play.*

She keyed her radio and muttered, "Spider, this is Miss Muffet. Commo check, over." Somewhere over the Atlantic Ocean, a satellite operated by the same little company that built her cell-phone tracking software relayed the words to a SwiftLink receiver on the bridge in Falluja.

"Miss Muffet, this is Spider. You're five by five, over." Halloran had no idea who Miss Muffet was or where she was, but she had watched his back on a dozen missions, keeping her cool in the diciest situations. Miss Muffet was the only woman he could think of who rivaled the Warrior Princess after whom he had named his rifle, and he was determined to meet her someday.

"Spider, this is Muffet. You're loud and clear." Amazing, she thought, dazzled by the technology at her fingertips. A West Point graduate, she found it hard to believe that Tele-Communication Systems was run by a bunch of crabs from the Naval Academy, but she nevertheless resolved to apply for a job there when her hitch was up.

The crosshair moved.

"Spider, this is Miss Muffet. Target is seven hundred yards from your position, heading one twenty, speed twenty." She forced herself to sound bored. With a keystroke, she removed the filter that suppressed the flashing crosshairs of other cellular bogies. Five additional crosshairs appeared, all moving together. She recorded the numbers for future reference. MI would pull their records to see who they had called in the last few days. One of the crosshairs, she suspected, was the trigger device. "Spider, the target consists of at least five individuals."

"Roger."

The crescent moon arced slowly across the sky, low on the horizon, providing the Fertile Crescent with enough light to feed the marines' night vision gear. To the un-enhanced eye, however, the world was as dark as the Fayadeen leaders had hoped it would be as the convoy of three vehicles made its way through the streets of Fallujah toward the Saddam Bridge.

"Vehicles approaching," muttered Halloran, who spotted the movement first. The convoy drove slowly without headlights, for the drivers had only the eyes that Allah had given them. The marines, however, had what Raytheon had given them, and the vehicles registered clearly in Halloran's scope. "Pickup truck in the lead," he whispered in his mic. "Pickup truck in trail. Sedan in the middle."

"Roger," acknowledged Miss Muffet.

Both sniper teams watched as the convoy approached the bridge, surprised that MI seemed to have finally called one right. If the intel was correct, a 155 mm artillery round lay in the trunk of the sedan, wired to a cell phone and set to explode when the bomber dialed the phone's number.

"I count four hajjis in the bed of each truck," reported Halloran. "Two in each cab. One driver in the sedan. Thirteen tangos."

Miss Muffet announced, "I show the target stopped, three hundred fifty degrees from your position, range four hundred meters."

The vehicles approached the bridge and halted. One of the Iraqi guards jogged the length of the bridge, sixty yards, and spoke to the lead driver.

"Must be giving him the all clear," grumbled Broussard. "I love our allies."

"We'll take out the guards, too," said Halloran.

"Roger," affirmed Alpha, dialing in the Iraqi guard who remained on the opposite end of the bridge.

"Miss Muffet, this is Spider. Target confirmed. Stand by."

Captain Varnell knew what was about to happen, and she wished the boys at TCS could put some video into her tracking system. The crosshair started to move again.

The convoy surged ahead, quickly now. As all three vehicles crossed the center of the bridge, Alpha Team fired. A .50 caliber round roared through the grill of the lead truck, shattering the engine block and blowing the hood backward against the windshield. The report from the Barrett was lost in the sounds of the disintegration of the Toyota, which stopped dead in its tracks, tossing the men in the bed against the rear window in a clatter of AK47s and yells of surprise. In the darkness, the sedan plowed into the rear of the Toyota, further terrifying the men in the truck, who scrambled out in panic, lest the sedan's cargo detonate. But the shell was stable, well packaged to protect the driver from potholes or accidents. The driver of the trailing pickup managed to stop before ramming the sedan, but unaware of the situation in that first second of chaos, he made no effort yet to reverse course. The lead Toyota's engine flickered into flame with a quiet whoosh, for the ruined engine block had scattered metal fragments that cut the fuel line. The remaining men in the bed of the truck leapt over the fender and raced to the edge of the bridge, where a concrete railing offered some protection from incoming fire.

Only two made it, however, as Halloran now opened fire with Xena, hitting one Fayadeen squarely in the back, blowing his heart onto the pavement, fifteen yards from where the body fell.

"Hit," announced Broussard, confirming that Halloran's windage and elevation were correct. With little else to do, and not content to merely watch the action through his spotter's scope, Broussard now reached for his weapon and added well-aimed shots into the men scurrying across the bridge. Halloran jacked in another round and directed his next shot through the rear of the trailing pickup truck and into the driver's back. He fell dead against the steering wheel, causing his foot to fall from the clutch. The vehicle hopped forward and stalled, trapping the sedan between the two disabled trucks.

Both doors of the rear pickup truck flew open and two men bailed out of the cab, pushing the dead driver onto the pavement. One passenger raced to join his comrades behind the railing, but the other, more combat-savvy than the others, motioned urgently for everyone to get off the bridge. As he ran back toward the narrow streets and protective buildings of Fallujah, Halloran could see his face clearly, green in the night vision scope, his eyes wide. Before Halloran could pull the trigger, however, Rivas opened up with his SAW, pulverizing the bridge deck and hitting the man twice in the head. If any of the other men on the bridge had ideas of following their leader back into town, those thoughts vanished as the man's brains sailed away into the night.

By stopping the lead vehicle, Alpha Team had accomplished its mission. The Barrett was not designed for human targets and was not as accurate as Halloran's gun, which could fire a shot group the size of a quarter at one thousand yards. But these targets were only four hundred yards away; a shot that any sniper could make with his eyes closed. So the Alpha Team sniper shouldered his massive gun and drew a bead on the Iraqi guard who had spoken to the lead driver. The man was the only person in the kill zone to determine the origin of Alpha Team's initial round, and he turned to stare toward the marine's hide, reacting to the sound faster than he could discern the need to run. He spotted the muzzle flash of Alpha Team's gun a split second before the gigantic bullet hit him in the sternum, plowing through his torso and shattering against his spinal column. The guard's head, left arm, and shoulder landed in the mud on the banks of the Euphrates, while the rest of his corpse skittered down the bridge surface.

The carnage was duplicated at the opposite end of the column, where Bravo Team took out the other Iraqi guard and two men with AK47s who leaped from the bed of the trailing truck. From both pickup trucks, some men had jumped left and some right, and now nine targets huddled against the railings on either side of the bridge. The driver of the sedan, perhaps dazed by the collision, staggered from his vehicle and was immediately shot by Alpha Team, the bullet driving him to the pavement as if a giant flyswatter had come out of the heavens and flattened him.

"I'll take the north side," said Halloran calmly into his bone mic. "Alpha, you take the south."

"Roger."

"Miss Muffet," continued Halloran, now switching to the satellite frequency, "the target is stationary and isolated."

"Spider, confirm no civilians in the vicinity."

"Affirmative," said Halloran. "Start dialing for dollars, Miss Muffet."

Captain Varnell programmed the first of the bogie phone numbers into her keypad and pressed "send." Via satellite, the call connected with the cellular network in Iraq, and within seconds the men cowering on the bridge were startled to hear the distinctive ring tone of Beethoven's "Für Elise" emanate from the cellular phone in the pocket of the driver of the rear pickup truck, who now lay dead on the pavement. Without waiting for an answer, Varnell dialed the next number on the list. Eventually, she would dial the phone that was the trigger device, blowing everything on the bridge to smithereens.

On the bridge, the men huddled together and pointed their weapons toward the sky, imagining at first that they were under attack from the air. In the melee, they had not seen a muzzle flash or heard the sounds of any rifle. Some of them considered that they might have run across one of their own mines. They had less than fifteen seconds to consider their situation, however, before Halloran's next bullet struck. His target suddenly sat up straight as the bullet slammed him against the concrete railing. The man slumped against the terrified teenager next to him before anyone heard the gunshot, belatedly catching up to the supersonic speed of the bullet.

Halloran drew back the bolt and jacked another round into the smoking chamber. As heads turned to the sound of his first shot, the second round struck the teenage boy in the teeth, clipping his head neatly from his neck as the bullet shattered upon impact with the boy's the vertebrae just below the skull. Aware now that the shots were coming from behind them, one man leapt to his feet and ran toward the opposite end of the bridge.

Halloran let him run. "Coming your way, Alpha."

"Roger."

The man went down. Halloran lined up the final target in his crosshair. Suddenly, the man jumped to his feet and thrust his hands into the air, standing motionless in the classic position of surrender. Strangely, the cell phone in his pocket started to ring. He thought to answer it, but dared not lower his arms.

"Shoot him," said Broussard.

"Cease fire," said Halloran. "Cease fire. Cease fire."

"Miss Muffet," said Halloran, "We have one clown trying to surrender. What do you want us to do with him?"

"Can you go get him without risk?" Varnell was unsure what to do. There had never before been enemy survivors.

Risk? Halloran and Broussard turned to each other and grinned. *The entire fucking city was now awake, every swinging dick reaching for his AK47, and Miss Muffet herself trying to set off a bomb six feet away from the poor bastard.* "Miss Muffet, as long as you keep your fingers off that dial pad, we'll bring him in." To Alpha Team, Halloran ordered, "Go get him." He warned Pitkin and Rivas to stay alert on rear guard.

Halloran swung his scope toward the opposite end of the the river and saw one man glide out of the darkness and onto the bridge. The Alpha Team sniper had stayed behind to provide additional cover, while the spotter retrieved the prisoner. Halloran watched as the spotter skirted the flames of the lead pickup truck and leveled his weapon at the man who still stood with his hands in the air. Alpha moved up carefully until the man saw him, barely ten feet away. Motioning for the man to lie on the ground, Alpha quickly cinched his wrists with plastic flexicuffs before hauling him roughly to his feet. "Got him."

"Roger," acknowledged Halloran. "Bug out now." He watched the Alpha Team spotter trot the prisoner off the bridge and into the darkness. "Miss Muffett, we're clear of the area."

"Roger." Captain Varnell dialed the last phone number.

In the trunk of the Toyota sedan, a cellular phone received a signal from a local tower advising it of an incoming call. The device responded with an electrical pulse to the ringer, which had been replaced with an electronic trigger attached to the fuse of the artillery shell in the trunk. The car disappeared in a blinding concussion that beat the breath out of even Halloran, still covering Alpha's withdrawal. When the smoke cleared, only shards of all three vehicles remained on the bridge, and a four-foot hole existed in the bridge deck where the sedan had been.

"Rear guard, pull out now," ordered Halloran. "I'll cover."

"Roger," said Pitkin. "Moving now."

Halloran turned his weapon down the road into town, scanning for any approaching enemy. The city lights and the blue flickering TVs had gone out the instant the shooting had started, and he saw only Pitkin and Rivas as they emerged from the darkness. The rear guard moved past Halloran, taking up defensive positions at the end of the bridge, where the two terrified Iraqi guards still sat on their sheet of cardboard under the watchful eye of the silent gargoyle. Broussard packed up the SwiftLink and Halloran gave him the signal to move out.

Captain Varnell monitored their retreat, watching for any unknown crosshairs that might approach them in the dark. All over town, the crosshairs had sprung to life as their owners responded to the gunshots by calling families, friends, or fellow terrorists. Their conversations were already being recorded.

Back at the cardboard, the Iraqi sentries prayed, placing their heads to the ground as they beseeched Allah. As if in answer to their prayers, the marine was gone when they looked up, having drifted silently into the dusty night like the ghosts of the American civilians who had been murdered and strung up from the Fallujah bridge.

CHAPTER 5

October 21, 2003 (Tuesday)
Abu Ghraib Prison, Iraq

Prisoners arrived almost daily at Abu Ghraib by truck, HMMV, or helicopter, depending upon the transport available to the units that captured them. Upon their arrival, members of the internal reaction team were on hand to receive them and to escort them through in-processing. The procedures had become routine, though dangerous, since many prisoners, unhooded for the first time in hours or days, often suicidal, and in close proximity to American troops, would attack the guards with their fists or teeth. For this reason, firearms were never allowed into the reception area; prisoners remained cuffed until the last minute and some remained hooded; and guards wore only T-shirts to maintain their anonymity, lest fanatical clerics issue *Fatwahs* against their wives or children, placing a religious obligation upon all Muslims to kill them.

Buckner was roused from his cot by the duty NCO, who watched over the sleeping soldiers and their gear and who responded to officers' calls for manpower when demands arose.

"What time is it?" asked Buckner, as the soldier shook him gently awake so as to not bother the other men in their cots. The sound of breathing and snoring created a sort of white noise that droned in the background.

"Midnight. They want you at the hard site."

"I'm not on duty."

"They said to send you."

"What for?"

"How should I know? Put on your boots and go ask 'em."

Buckner reported grumpily to in-processing, the big chamber empty except for the sentry. "What's up?" asked Buckner, his voice echoing. The cell blocks were quiet.

"Marines are bringing in a prisoner," responded the guard, who sat at his desk checking the daily change sheets that tracked prisoner rolls and transfers.

"Just one? They can't wait until morning?"

The guard shrugged.

"What am I supposed to do with him? He's your fucking prisoner, not mine."

A voice behind him said quietly, "I'll in-process him." Buckner recognized the raspy whisper and cocked his head around. The civilian lit a cigarette and nodded cordially. "I asked for you."

Buckner looked him over, a short man with ropy arms and a powerful chest barely concealed by his polo shirt.

"What do you want with me?"

"You seem to be a man who can handle himself with prisoners."

"So?"

The man shrugged. "Not everyone is cut out for interrogating people."

Slowly, Buckner got the man's drift. The two men exchanged frank stares until Buckner said, "You never told me your name."

"Levi. I'm a civilian interpreter with MI."

"I thought civilian terps were all OGAs."

Levi smiled, impressed. "Actually, I'm not sure who funds my paycheck. Main thing is that I'm a civilian, and civilians scare these *arabushes* to death. They trust the uniformed soldiers to respect the rules of war, but they piss in their pants when they see me coming."

"These people piss anywhere."

Levi grinned wider. "Muslim men are highly religious, sexually inhibited, morally rigid, poorly educated, group-oriented, and devoted to their family and clan. These character traits serve them well in combat; their poor performance on the battlefield reflects a lack of training and incompetent leadership, not any failure in individual motivation. As prisoners, however, these character traits can be exploited.

"We focus on two things: isolation and humiliation. On one hand, we isolate the detainees from each other, destroying their support group. On the other hand, we humiliate them in front of their peers, further breaking their group bonds. Emotionally broken, many of these men are inclined toward martyrdom and suicide, but many others grasp for a lifeline. We offer a way back from the brink, and they spill their guts."

Buckner had heard parts of Levi's lecture before. "Isn't it easier to just beat the shit out of 'em?"

"Sometimes. I was impressed by the way you handled yourself last week. I wanted someone I could rely on for processing this prisoner."

"You got a whole company of goons in there. What do you need me for?"

"I always have an eye out for good men. You think you'd like to come work for me?"

Buckner shook his head.

"You did a great job on the last one," said Levi. "He gave us great information."

"With him," said Buckner, staring at his boots, "it was personal."

Levi took another drag of his cigarette and shrugged. "Men like us, we know what it means to lose someone close. I know about revenge, Buckner, and it can be sweet."

Suddenly, the radio at the sentry station rattled and the guard put the handset to his ear. "Roger. Out." Turning to Levi, the guard said, "Marines just cleared the gate, sir."

Levi peeped through a small window in the door, then pushed it open and stepped into the chain-link enclosure that surrounded the entrance. The IPs stumbled to their feet on the other side of the gate as Levi ordered them to unlock it. An HMMV approached in the dark and parked next to the open gate, shedding dust in a billow that washed up against the side of the building and burst gently through the door. The diesel ground away with the sound of an engine that had absorbed too much dust and violence, and the driver did not turn it off for fear that it might not start again. The vehicle had no doors; Sgt. Halloran stepped out of the shotgun seat as though the HMMV was a dune buggy. In back, Corporal Pitkin dragged the hooded prisoner roughly from the cargo compartment, jerking him to his feet by slipping one hand under the man's armpit. The prisoner's wrists remained secured behind him with flexicuffs.

Buckner followed Levi toward Halloran, who removed his goggles and glanced at Pitkin to confirm that the prisoner was under control. Ignoring the IPs, he said, "I have a prisoner to be turned over to MI."

"I'll accept him," said Levi."

"Can I see some ID, sir?"

Levi handed over his military identity card, which Halloran held in front of one dusty headlight to view. Halloran nodded and withdrew a set of orders from his breast pocket. He glanced at Buckner, then Halloran, and said, "You got the preliminaries on this guy, sir?"

"Yes," said Levi.

"OK, then." Halloran handed over an envelope. "Here's his passport, cell phone, and press credentials." With a final nod toward the prisoner, Halloran said, "You want the hood on or off?"

"Leave it on for now." Levi pointed with his finger to indicate for Buckner to take the man in tow. No words were exchanged as Pitkin released his grip on the prisoner's shirt collar and Buckner grabbed his wrists. As Buckner pushed the stumbling man ahead of him toward the door, Halloran saluted smartly and hopped back into the HMMV.

"Hit it, Rivas. Let's get the fuck outta here." The driver hit the gas, and the HMMV disappeared into the same silent cloud of dust it rode in on.

Levi followed Buckner into the building and closed the door. Buckner pushed the prisoner up against the cinder block wall and patted him down. His clothing was unusual. The filthy khaki trousers and denim shirt were well suited for rugged wear, an uncommon thing for most of the hajjis, who wore clothes more suited to a night of disco dancing than combat. Thin-soled loafers and cheap suits with pleated slacks were typical of the Fayadeen, while the Iraqis more often wore *dishdashas*, the flowing robes that were equally dysfunctional in the wear and tear of battle. But this prisoner also wore combat boots, and a fisherman's vest with a dozen pockets. Whoever he was, this guy had known what he was getting into.

"No personal effects," announced Buckner. Every pocket was empty.

Suddenly, the man spoke though his hood. "The fucking marines stole everything I had! They owe me five hundred dollars and a Nikon!" Buckner pushed him harder against the wall, surprised by his English. The man grunted in pain. "Where are we?" he gasped. "Take off this hood, will ya'?"

Levi reached over and yanked the burlap sack from the prisoner's head. The man's face and hair were as filthy as his clothes, the dust irritating his sinus membranes so that a stream of mucus had dribbled from his nose and mixed with the dust and three days of stubble. His hair was long enough to cover his ears, and powdered with beige dust that had filtered down to his scalp. The only clean parts of him were his blue eyes that blinked in the sudden light.

He drank in a gasp of air and exhaled. "Fuck. I was suffocating with that thing on." With Buckner still pushing his face into the wall, the man continued, "Now the handcuffs. They're killing me."

Levi put his own face against the wall and looked the prisoner in the eye. Very quietly, he said, "One more word out of you, the hood goes back on. Understand?"

"I'm an American."

Levi immediately shoved the sack over the prisoner's head.

"OK, OK!" the man pleaded, but Levi only grabbed the bottom hem of the burlap and yanked the man's head around to face him.

"Too late, asshole. I said the hood would go back on if you said another word. This time, we will inflict pain if you say another word. If you understand, nod your head."

The man nodded.

Buckner asked, "Do you want me to fingerprint him?"

"No processing for this one. Just follow me." Levi led the way down a short corridor that terminated at a steel door, which Levi opened with a key. Buckner pushed the man ahead of him and found himself in the cell block he had seen before, three tiers of cells around an open center aisle. Tonight, however, the block was quiet. The prisoners were asleep, except for one man who squatted naked and shivering in his cell, with his fingers interlaced behind his head. His blue eyes and red hair pegged him as a Syrian. A pair of American guards in OD T-shirts stood behind him with canteens, pouring water over his head and shoulders.

"How long has he been awake?" asked Levi.

A guard checked his watch. "Sixty hours."

"He'll crack in the morning."

The guards nodded and went back to work, while Levi led the way to the far end of the cell block, past the latrine and the common shower room. As they passed across the open door to the shower, a bundle on the floor caught Buckner's attention. Only after a second of disbelief did he recognize the corpse of a human being swathed tightly in plastic wrap, like a huge ham and cheese sandwich in a New York deli. "Keep moving," ordered Levi, apparently irritated that the body had not been removed. He motioned for Buckner to bring their prisoner inside an open cell. Buckner pushed the man ahead of him and released his wrists.

Levi stood behind the prisoner and ripped the hood from the man's head. "Don't speak. You will answer my questions when I ask them. If you say anything else, anything at all, I'll put the hood back on and leave you here for twenty-four hours. Nod your head if you understand."

The man's eyes darted back and forth, but he found himself staring at a cinder block wall six inches from his nose. Meekly, he nodded.

"Good," said Levi. "State your name."

"McGowan. I'm a reporter for *The Citizen Times.*"

Levi edged closer to him, placing his nose almost in Mc-Gowan's ear. "You speak English, but you don't understand it. Did I ask you for your occupation?"

McGowan trembled slightly and shook his head. "No."

"If I put this hood back on your head, you will receive no food, no water for twenty-four hours. You will be required to stand the entire time. And then we'll start all over. DO YOU UNDERSTAND THAT, ASSHOLE?"

"Yes."

"What's your occupation?"

The man's eyeballs bounced around, left then right, as he tried to orient himself, but he could see only the painted wall in front of him and the hint of a man in his peripheral vision. Panic welled up within him as if he had entered some sort of Twilight Zone. "I'm a reporter for *The Citizen Times,*" he murmured. "In New York."

"What were you doing in Fallujah?"

"I wanted to report the war from the insurgent point of view."

Levi held up the passport and the press badge he had received from Halloran. "According to these, you're a French reporter for *Le Monde.* And your name is LeBlanc."

"The passport is fake. There was no way any American could embed himself with the insurgent forces. So I got the French to hook me up with the Syrians."

The man was chatty again, but he was being forthcoming, so Levi cut him some slack. "Well, the French will embed themselves with anyone, won't they?"

McGowan kept his mouth shut.

"The marines tell me you are lucky they didn't shoot you. What was your mission last night?"

"They were going to set up a roadside bomb in Baghdad, and then ambush the police when they came."

"And you were going along for the show?"

"You could say that."

"You like watching Americans die?"

"I don't like watching anyone die."

"But somebody's gotta do it, eh?"

McGowan said nothing, but finally surrendered to curiosity and fear and turned his head to the left. He found himself staring directly into Buckner's eyes, barely a yard away.

"Keep your eyes straight ahead," warned Levi. McGowan complied. "We recovered a few Nikon flash drives in you pockets," Levi resumed, "with your digital photos. Looks like you were there when they beheaded poor Michael Pastor. You remember him, right?"

"Yes. They insisted I photograph it."

"Of course. They probably saved him just for you."

"I urged them not to do it. I told them it was counter-productive to their cause."

"Sounds like you were more than simply an observer."

"I am a reporter. What do I have to do to convince you?"

"I want a list of all your contacts." Levi plucked from his hip pocket a small green notebook, the sort issued to all military officers to record daily schedules, rosters, etc. "Start with Fallujah. Who organized the convoy? How do we find him?"

"I don't know," said McGowan, a hint of nervousness creeping into his voice, for he sensed that this was not the required answer.

Levi acted as if he had not heard him. "I need the names and cell phone numbers of every person you met between New York and Paris and Damascus and Fallujah."

"I don't know," repeated McGowan. "My contacts were arranged by my editor. He'll confirm everything if you'll just make a damn phone call."

"I already did," said Levi, a slight look of amusement on his face. "I spoke to the editor in chief personally. He refused to comment on any contacts that the *Times* might use to place its reporters with insurgent groups around the world. 'Priviledged information,' he called it, protected by the U.S. Constitution."

"But at least you confirmed that I'm legit!" said McGowan indignantly. "Now let me out of here."

Levi sighed and signaled for Buckner to replace the hood over McGowan's head.

"No!" complained the prisoner. He shook his head violently as Buckner slipped the burlap over it and cinched the drawstring around his neck. Levi stepped forward and grabbed McGowan by his still-cuffed wrists. With a sudden and powerful yank, he spun McGowan around and propelled him into the opposite wall of his cell. The reporter's face hit the concrete hard, and he bounced backward into the center of the small cell where he collapsed to the floor. "Stop! I'm an American citizen!"

"If you're an American," said Levi quietly, "then you are a traitor. Either way, you're in very deep trouble right now. I could have you shot." Levi turned to Buckner and pointed at McGowan's feet. "Take off his boots and socks." Levi unbuckled McGowan's belt. "Take his pants, too."

"What's the matter with you? This treatment is prohibited by the Geneva Conventions," cried McGowan through his hood. "This is illegal."

"The Geneva Conventions exist to protect soldiers. You are a civilian terrorist, a common criminal. The Conventions do not apply to you, any more than they apply to some car thief in Kansas."

"Goddamn it, you know I'm no terrorist! You spoke to my employer! You know who I am!"

"I don't know how to break this to you, Mr. Whoever-You-Are, but I never asked about you when I called the editor in chief at the *Times*. We are about to do some very unpleasant things to you, and it might be politically awkward to do these things to a citizen of a friendly country. So, frankly, we really don't want to know who you are."

"My God!" cried McGowan. "You know I'm telling the truth!"

Motioning to Buckner, Levi ordered, "Get him up." Buckner grabbed the reporter by the collar of his shirt, hauled him to his feet, and lifted McGowan's wrists into the air. Doubled over at the waist as his arms were raised behind him, McGowan gasped and struggled, conscious of the pain in his shoulders, and his nudity from the waist down.

"But we digress," said Levi. "Back to business, Mr. LeBlanc."

"McGowan. My name is McGowan!"

"I want names and phone numbers. You will remain in this position until you talk, or until you die. You have no friends, no allies, no rights, no lawyers, and not a soul knows you are here. You are a confidante of men who kidnap innocent civilians and chop off their heads. We really will kill you. If you give us good, actionable intel, we'll check out your identity. Are you starting to understand your predicament?"

"You're crazy. You can't do this."

Turning to Buckner, Levi instructed, "Call me if he starts talking."

"How long do I keep him like this?" asked Buckner, his own arms starting to tire.

"Until he talks." Levi walked out of the cell.

Ten minutes passed; the only sound McGowan's labored breathing and an occasional groan. Buckner's arms felt like lead. "You really an American?" he asked, almost to pass the time.

"Yes," grunted the prisoner.

Buckner lifted McGowan's hands higher, eliciting a wavering scream. Buckner's own arms were in pain now, from holding the reporter in position. He was angry, too; angry because he didn't know what he was supposed to do; angry at Levi for leaving him; and angry at McGowan for getting him out of bed in the first place.

"You're wasting your time," grunted McGowan, his emotions settling down. "I don't know who those people were. I only traveled with them, documenting their cause."

Buckner distrusted all men with causes and saw no value in documenting them. Tetra was dead because of some fanatic with a cause. "One of your Fayadeen pals killed my friend last week."

"That has nothing to do with me."

McGowan's statement, uttered with a lawyer's self-righteousness, filled Buckner with such a rage that he yanked McGowan's hands over his head, forcing him to his knees with a scream. "Get up!" yelled Buckner, as he dragged the prisoner toward the open cell door.

McGowan stumbled to his feet, lest his arms be pulled completely from their sockets. "Stop! God, stop it!" he begged between sobs. But Buckner stormed from the cell toward the cell block showers, the hooded and half-naked McGowan stumbling and hopping behind him while the guards in the other cell looked up with amused curiosity before pouring another glass of water over their own prisoner's head.

In the shower, Buckner finally lowered McGowan's arms as he flung him, still hooded, onto the slippery floor. The newsman collapsed, landing on something soft, another person. The relief in McGowan's shoulders was like a breath after too long under water, but the respite was short-lived. Buckner leaned down to rip off the burlap hood, and with his hand on the back of McGowan's neck, he pushed the prisoner's nose to within an inch of the shrink-wrapped face. When McGowan recognized the mackerel eyes of a corpse and the battered face of a man beaten to a pulp, he recoiled in horror, but Buckner kept his face nose to nose with the dead man.

"We kill people here!" Only when Buckner recognized the tattoo on the corpse's hand did he realize that the bloody face of the corpse was that of the prisoner who had killed Tetra. Grabbing McGowan by the hair, he twisted the reporter's head backward with one hand and grabbed his nose with the other. That, too, he twisted until he felt it break. He refused to let go, despite McGowan's frantic and useless spasms.

"Please!" cried McGowan, a spray of blood now coming from his mouth.

"I want the names!" yelled Buckner, pushing the man down and rendering a pair of violent slaps across his face.

"Ahmad Jibouri!" gasped McGowan. "He's my contact in Paris." He stopped resisting and the pain seemed to melt away. Consumed with self-contempt, he muttered, "I'll give you the others. I'll give you whatever you want." What was Jibouri to him?

Levi appeared from nowhere. "I'll take it from here." He patted Buckner on the back and escorted him from the shower room, leaving McGowan groveling and bloody on the floor. "There's just one more thing," he added.

Buckner looked at him.

"When you were here the other day, didn't I tell you to keep your mouth shut about what you had seen?"

Buckner said nothing. He owed no explanation to Levi; not that he could explain even to himself why he had reported to the first sergeant the fact that he had stuffed a pair of panties down a prisoner's throat. He felt no remorse about what he had done, but in the adrenalin crash that followed he had needed an excuse to talk to someone about Tetra. "The First Shirt said it was 'exigent circumstances' and told me not to worry about it," said Buckner. He did not mention that the first sergeant had also left him alone in his office for a few minutes, because it was the only place at Abu Ghraib where a man could cry without a dozen people watching.

"That's not the point. Your sergeant does not want to know what goes on in here, 'exigent circumstances' or not. You got that?"

"I got it."

"Good, because there was nothing 'exigent' about what you just did to that American citizen in there. You see what I'm saying, Buckner?"

Dazed, Buckner wandered back into the central cell block area. The other two guards stared at him and smiled.

One man gave him a thumbs-up while the other kicked at the shins of the shivering prisoner, whimpering now, frightened by the sound of another man's surrender. Buckner was not sure who he hated more: Levi, or himself.

CHAPTER 6

October 24, 2003 (Friday)
CJTF-7 HQ, Baghdad, Iraq

The photographs on General Tannerbeck's desk were a surprise only because the interrogators at Abu Ghraib had been stupid enough to allow them to be taken. The grinning faces of the American guards betrayed a childish innocence, like toddlers joyfully beating a Christmas puppy. As he flipped through the photos, he felt no pity for the hooded man, his supplicant hands wired to some unseen power source, or for the naked prisoner on his hands and knees, the leash around his neck held in the hand of an amused female guard. These men, reckoned Tannerbeck, had blood on their hands. But he was mortified by the silliness of the abuses and mystified by how any professional soldier could derive such apparent glee from it. Tannerbeck pondered what he would say to Colonel Volpe, who stepped into his office at that moment.

The general motioned without speaking toward a chair across from his desk. Volpe took it quietly. A new tenseness characterized their relationship.

"What do you expect me to do with these?" asked Tannerbeck, shoving the photographs across the desk at his subordinate. "The guards look like idiots in these photos. Their behavior is clearly in violation of the Geneva Conventions."

"Sir," began Volpe, "this is the nightmare I have been worried about since the day we established the JDIC. I have already disciplined several of the soldiers guilty of abuses, but I'm being undermined by my own chain of command. MI is being pressured to get results and I'm being squeezed to look the other way."

"I know, but this has to stop. There will be hell to pay if these photos get out."

Volpe exhaled a huge sigh of relief. "Thank you, sir. I'll put a stop to it, but I'll need your support all the way up the chain of command. The fact of the matter is that the abuses documented in these photographs have been very successful in getting these prisoners to talk. If we stop the extreme methods, the flow of actionable intel will stop with them. We should anticipate higher casualties."

"That's not acceptable, Rick. There's an election coming."

Volpe put his head in his hands, like a Muslim rug merchant who really wants to make a deal for such a deserving customer, but nevertheless has mouths of his own to feed. "General, do you want me to stop it or not?"

Tannerbeck stared at Volpe for a long moment and said nothing.

At last, Volpe nodded his head. "Very well, sir. I'll follow up with a confidential memo acknowledging that you want the interrogations to continue."

"I don't want any more memos."

"Duty requires me to document this, sir, just as it requires you to conceal it." Volpe felt insubordinate, lecturing a superior officer. Black and white were the only colors in Volpe's world, a trait that comforted subordinates and superiors alike, for it made him predictable. But it was with surprise that Tannerbeck now realized that while Volpe could tolerate no gray, he at least had the capacity to realize that black for some men was white for others.

"Sometimes," acknowledged Tannerbeck, "duty and honor are too flexible."

"Sir, if you order me to stop the documentation, I will be forced to resign my commission." Resignation was the ultimate choice for any officer faced with an unconscionable order.

Tannerbeck knew that Volpe was incapable of bluffing. With a frustrated sigh, he said, "Document what you have to. Just don't take any more of these goddamn photographs."

Tannerbeck waited for Volpe to rise and excuse himself, so he would not have to dismiss the man he regarded as his protégé. But Volpe remained because he had more information to convey.

"Sir, we've experienced one death so far."

"What are you talking about?"

"One of the prisoners has died of injuries sustained in a beating administered by one of the guards."

"Christ, it sounds like an insane asylum."

"The prisoner was escorted from the general population into the MI wing by an MP named Buckner."

"I already received your report on Buckner. It doesn't mention anything about killing the prisoner," said Tannerbeck.

"Buckner filed his own report with his company commander a couple of weeks ago, immediately after the incident. The prisoner was alive at the time of the report. I checked the prisoner myself. He died later."

"The man is as much a fool as you, Rick, reporting his own malfeasance." But Tannerbeck spoke with an undertone of admiration.

"I am forever impressed by the professionalism of our enlisted men," said Volpe. Returning to the subject, he added, "The prisoner probably died of internal bleeding related to Buckner's kicking the hell out of him. Fortunately, the prisoner gave up a couple of extremely useful cell phone numbers before he died, simply because the interrogators threatened to bring Buckner back in to work him over some more. The cell phones were monitored, leading to a subsequent ambush by U.S. Marines that led to the deaths of at least ten terrorists who were planning a roadside bomb and ambush. We also captured an additional prisoner who in turn provided even more valuable intel, leading to the destruction of French financial networks and infiltration routes from Syria."

"So, what are you suggesting? That we give the boy a medal?"

"No, sir, but Buckner is a problem. We cannot prosecute him without exposing the activities at Abu Ghraib, but the longer he's there, the greater the opportunity for his buddies or superiors to become aware of what he's done. His report is bound to start rumors within his company."

"You want him transferred?"

"I'll leave that decision up to you, sir. I've lost faith in my immediate chain of command to do anything about it. General Piersal urged me to keep you informed."

"Piersal?" Tannerbeck growled with unchecked scorn. It was one thing for a general to advise another, as Piersal had done during his visit to Iraq, but no commander could tolerate back-door meddling by another, no matter how dysfunctional the chain of command. Volpe reported through

MI channels, who reported to both CJTF-7 as well as the DC-SINT in the Pentagon. Tannerbeck was an unofficial authority, since the CINC wanted no part of Abu Ghraib. It made sense that Volpe might go to Tannerbeck in the absence of guidance from his own commander, but it was a mystery to Tannerbeck why Piersal would encourage him to do so.

Volpe watched Tannerbeck's hackles rise. "I don't trust the man any more than you do, sir, but he has been surprisingly supportive. He calls me regularly about the JDIC."

"Let me deal with it," said Tannerbeck, "before Piersal manages to get his fingers into this any deeper than they already are."

Volpe stood and saluted. "Thank you, sir."

Tannerbeck returned the salute with a nod. "God help us, Rick."

Tannerbeck was awake when his phone rang at 0200. He barely slept at all anymore, and he grabbed the receiver before the phone could ring again. *Another bombing*, he surmised. "This is Tannerbeck."

"Hello, General. This is John Piersal, returning your call. I'm glad you called, actually, because I need to talk to you, too."

Tannerbeck swung his feet onto the floor of his quarters. "General, what are you doing meddling in our business at Abu Ghraib? We have your recommendations. We'll implement or adapt them as appropriate for the local situation."

"I'm sure you will, General, and I think Volpe is doing an excellent job. I understand that the intel is flowing better already."

"Then I would appreciate it if you would leave Abu Ghraib to us."

"Absolutely," said Piersal. "But we have a problem: a Private First Class Morgan Buckner."

"I know all about Buckner. We'll deal with him."

"He needs to be transferred out of Abu Ghraib. The longer he's there, the greater the opportunity for him to discuss his report with other soldiers, and eventually they will pass the story on. We'll have to prosecute him sooner or later, at which time the whole mess will get out."

"I understand the problem, Piersal. I spoke with Volpe earlier today. He informed me of your continuing interest in the interrogations at Abu Ghraib, and I want you to stay out of this, understand?"

Piersal ignored the warning. "I've arranged for his transfer."

"What are you doing in personnel decisions? I can work this through the chain of command."

"Certain assignment come from above," said Piersal, "such as appointments to the Military Academy Prep School."

"What are you talking about?" grumbled Tannerbeck.

"It seems that Buckner already applied for an appointment to West Point and was rejected due to a lack of qualifications. But he's a good soldier, if you ignore the murder of a prisoner. I've already greased the skids for his appointment."

Tannerbeck jumped to his feet. Designed for enlisted soldiers with poor academic credentials but promising leadership skills, the USMA Prep School was a prestigious assignment. No ivy-covered high school, USMAPS was an academic boot camp located at Fort Monmouth, New Jersey, whereupon successful completion of the curriculum of English and math, graduates received an appointment as freshmen to the U.S. Military Academy at West Point. "You want to send a murderer to West Point?"

"We don't know how that prisoner died."

"Bullshit." Tannerbeck squeezed the handset of his telephone as if it were Piersal's throat. "You've abrogated the Geneva Conventions, and now you want to cover your ass by compromising West Point. What's the matter with you?"

"Get off your high horse, General. My recommendations at Abu Ghraib were well within the Geneva Conventions, which don't apply to unlawful combatants anyway. You're the one who has chosen to ignore the abuses that have occurred as a result of poor supervision and enforcement, despite complaints from the commander on site. Now, you can prosecute this boy, or you can hide him. If you prosecute, your own failure to report the abuses will come to light and the whole JDIC will likely be shut down amid the howling protests of the civil liberties crowd. If you hide him, we can continue to deliver actionable information while fixing whatever supervisory problems might exist. Who knows how many lives we might save?"

"I don't need a lecture from you about saving lives."

"Listen to me," said Piersal, exasperation in his voice. "The SecDef is determined to win this war by any means necessary. We are in the end game now, where skullduggery is more effective than brute force and your warrior mentality. This is my bailiwick and I know what the hell to do. You can cooperate and help me win this war, or you can beat your chest and scream about duty and honor while a few hundred more American boys get themselves blown to pieces."

"Don't patronize me."

Adding insult to injury, Piersal said, "I've arranged for Buckner to pass through Baghdad on his way to the Prep School. So, you can personally welcome him to The Long Gray Line, and then remind him that the army will be forced to prosecute him for war crimes if word gets out about his actions."

You bastard, thought Tannerbeck.

"If it's any consolation to you," continued Piersal, "Buckner will never make it to West Point. He hasn't got a chance of making it through the Prep School. A year from now, he'll be back where he came from, guarding civilian inmates in the county jail in Baltimore. And you'll be the superintendent of the U.S. Military Academy."

Tannerbeck hung up the phone and checked the clock: 0215. There would be no more sleep tonight, so he headed for the shower, feeling the need to wash away the greasiness that seemed to have seeped into his quarters through the telephone.

Master Sergeant Baker Voltaire had ten years of active duty under his belt, plus another six in the reserves. He had run convoys across battlefields all over the world, usually without incident, but not always. The trip to Abu Ghraib from Baghdad had been uneventful, but that was typical of outbound legs on the main supply routes. There was only one way back to Baghdad, and the hajjis would be ready when the convoy returned. The drivers were edgy and eager to get going before too many insurgents could round themselves up for an ambush. Inbound supplies were unloaded in minutes, but it would take hours to pump out the portable toilets into the tanker trailers. Not even an NCO as professional as Voltaire could explain to his drivers the military necessity of hauling shit back to Baghdad.

The trucks also had some human cargo for the return trip, and Voltaire hustled a lieutenant with a satchel of passports and other confiscated documents into the back of an M1114 HMMV gun truck, one of three that accompanied the convoy. The gun trucks were protected with level-one Armox Armor, the highest level of armament available, and the lieutenant gratefully made space for himself among the crates of ammo for the M2 .50 caliber gun mounted on the roof while Voltaire paced in the dust, waiting for his final passenger. Unlike many non-coms, Voltaire was no blusterer. He saw himself as an ordinary grunt, a soldier whose responsibilities had been elevated by the stripes on his sleeve. He had no love for the army—it scared the hell out of him—but he was too close to retirement to chuck it all now for a soft job with some civilian trucking firm in Pittsburgh. So, when Buckner showed up with his duffel bag slung over his shoulder, Voltaire simply put his clipboard under his arm and said, "You Buckner?"

"Yeah."

"Get in."

Buckner rolled into the back of the HMMV along with the ammo and gear and the lieutenant, and made himself comfortable against his duffel bag. The bag contained all of his belongings and an envelope with orders directing him to report to the USMA Prep School. Only one person would have appreciated the absurdity of a man like Buckner being accepted to a place like West Point, and he wished Tetra could be there to see him off. *People are crazy and things are strange…*

An hour later, the convoy finally rolled eastward on the empty blacktop at forty-five miles per hour, the diesels growling comfortably. A daylight moon rose, white in the afternoon sky. In the passenger seat of the lead HMMV,

Voltaire kept a steady eye out for what lay ahead, while the gunner standing behind him aimed the MK19 grenade launcher mounted on the roof of the vehicle from threat to threat as they passed farmhouses and abandoned cars along the road. The drivers communicated on secure CB radios, keeping everyone aware of suspicious objects—animal carcasses, trash bags, boxes—anything in which an IED could be concealed. Voltaire kept the I-COM transmitter in one hand and the UHF radio in the other, tuned to the AWACs overhead. The air force broadcast warnings of IEDs or insurgent attacks, and in the event of ambush, the AWACs Eye in the Sky summoned medical dustoffs and the local Quick Reaction Force. In the trailing vehicles, the drivers kept their eyes on the road, while the assistant drivers in the right seat kept their M-16s pointed out the windows, ready for anything.

For several miles they drove in silence, with no conversation or radio chatter. They saw few people, only children playing near the houses or working in the date groves. As the convoy approached an unpaved crossroads, however, Voltaire felt the hair rise on the back of his neck. The intersection was populated by a tiny village that had existed for centuries. The place still retained a biblical air despite the power lines that hung over it, a crappy little settlement of cinder block buildings crumbling into the debris of antiquity. Since the days of the Hittites, a thousand battles had been fought at similar crossroads throughout Mesopotamia, and now began one more.

The assault was well planned, but like most insurgent ambushes, ineptly executed. The IED designed to halt the lead vehicle exploded prematurely when the trigger man miscalculated the call setup time for the cellular phone that acted as the detonator. Fifty yards from Voltaire's HMMV, the mortar shell was still close enough to kill a man, but Voltaire's gunner merely heard the shell fragments hum past him as he instantly swung his MK19 toward the explosion and opened fire at a wall of concrete block that surrounded a nearby home, where a dozen men now added the weight of AK45 rounds to their attack on the American convoy.

"Keep moving!" ordered Voltaire. He grabbed the I-Com and notified his drivers, "IED, right side! Hajjis behind the concrete wall! Light 'em up!" The commo was superfluous, as everyone put his accelerator to the floor, and the soldier riding shotgun in every passenger seat returned fire with an M-16, while the trailing HMMVs added .50 caliber rounds to the convoy's volume of fire. The heavy weapons blew away the satellite dish mounted on the flat roof of the farmhouse and chewed away at the wall surrounding the ambushers, blowing holes through it and creating a cloud of pulverized concrete and human remains stitched through with the incandescent trail of tracer rounds. Across the road, ragamuffin children indifferent to the violence of the firefight threw rocks at a wild dog trapped in a drainage ditch along the side of the highway, pausing only for a moment to watch the Great Satans roar through.

In the HMMV in the middle of the column, Buckner reacted to the sudden gunfire by diving to the floor of the vehicle to take maximum advantage of the armor plating. Glancing out the back of the truck, he glimpsed with horror the loopy vapor trail of an RPG fired from the opposite side of the road as it sailed between Buckner's gun truck and the M915 loaded with shit behind them.

The shooting stopped as suddenly as it began, as the convoy barreled through the kill zone without casualties. Two drivers reported punctured windshields, but further damage to the vehicles would be assessed when they reached their destination. As Buckner dusted himself off in the back of the HMMV, giddy bravado crackled across the I-Com net. "Hey, Sarge, you think those hajjis know they just died for a trailer full of shit?" They laughed all the way to Baghdad.

The suburbs of Baghdad sprawled for miles, a third world version of Los Angeles built of concrete blocks and sheet metal, with intermittent electrical power that ran forests of satellite dishes while raw sewage and rats ran in the streets. Peering from the back of the HMMV, Buckner saw nothing exotic about the single-story homes, gas stations, and filthy roadside vendors who hawked everything from kebabs to televisions in an Old West atmosphere of shifty-eyed men and scurrying women in black *abayas,* working like mules. *Good thing the women aren't in the army,* thought Buckner, *or these people would have kicked our ass.*

The approach to the city had the merciless charm of Bakersfield, California, except that it stretched forever, eight hundred square miles teeming with six million frightened and angry people. The convoy entered the city along a boulevard lined with concrete barriers, a manmade canyon topped with razor wire and guarded by sandbagged checkpoints. Behind a neighborhood of houses with blown-out windows stood an abandoned Ferris wheel, an odd memory in a city full of violence. As traffic increased, the convoy traveled in tighter formation, scaring away tailgaters by pointing the .50 caliber machine gun in the trailing HMMV into the faces of oncoming drivers, who responded with contemptuous aplomb by backing off only slightly, as if daring the gunner to blow their heads off. They rolled through streets that smelled of sewage and diesel. If dread had an odor, they would have smelled it, too, for it permeated everything.

But the city was indifferent to them today, and at last the convoy rolled to a halt, a billow of dust catching up to the vehicles and then mushrooming into the air. Voltaire beat on the side of the HMMV.

"Buckner, you still with us?"

"Yo!"

"This is your stop. Get your ass outta there!"

The lieutenant disembarked as well. He seemed to know where he was and he motioned for Buckner to follow him. Voltaire moved on, checking with his drivers on engine temperatures, fuel status, tire pressure, and battle damage. Stinking streams of effluent dribbled onto the street from several holes in the tanker.

The convoy had come to a halt on the side of Al Kindi Street under the guns of American sentries at Checkpoint 12, the entrance to the Green Zone, headquarters of CJTF-7 and a dozen embassies, and an odd lot of various division headquarters and other agencies of the occupation government. The Iraqi Police presence in the area was intense, armed men in body armor directing traffic around concrete barriers on the far side of the street. Buckner followed the lieutenant across the street toward a sandbagged checkpoint manned by heavily armed MPs.

He threaded his way through a maze of concrete barriers designed to thwart any vehicles from approaching too closely and then down a sidewalk bordered with razor wire. An MP in sunglasses motioned for him to approach.

"State your business."

"I have to report to General Tannerbeck." Buckner handed over a copy of his orders and his military ID.

The guard noted that the crossed flintlock pistols on the collar of Buckner's BDUs matched his own. "Military Police?"

"Yeah. Abu Ghraib prison."

The guard directed Buckner to assume the proper position for a pat-down, feet apart, arms outstretched. After a quick search, the man returned Buckner's paperwork. "Welcome to the Green Zone. You know what to do?"

"No."

The guard pointed down the continuing channel of wire. "Next stop, they'll do this all over again."

There were, in fact, two more checkpoints and two more searches before he finally received an ID badge and was directed to a bus stop inside the blast-proof T-walls that surrounded the Green Zone. He waited with the lieutenant and a few others, disappointed by the grimy similarity of the view that greeted them. The Green Zone was no Emerald City; just more brown and dusty buildings with trash blowing in the streets. An olive drab school bus arrived, piloted by an affable old civilian from Texas. Someone had written "wash me" on one dirty side panel. The doors opened and the driver drawled, "Welcome to Baghdad, y'all!"

They drove past a guard detail of Nepalese Ghurkas in front of the ten-story HQ of the Iraqi Interim Government before the bus pulled up at the Baath Party Convention Center, now the headquarters of the Combined Joint Task Force 7. Few privates first class wandered the marble halls of CJTF-7, and fewer still in uniforms soaked with perspiration and trailing a river of dust. Buckner followed an officious captain through the atrium that bustled with "fobbits" and a few resolute civilians who gave him a surprised once-over. They descended into the basement, where a nondescript corridor led to an ante-office staffed by two colonels and another captain.

"Private Buckner says he has an appointment to see General Tannerbeck?"

The other captain nodded, while the colonels interrupted their respective telephone conversations to study the enlisted man with an appointment to see the Deputy CINC, a man with whom they themselves had difficulty getting face time, despite the proximity of their offices. The escort knocked on Tannerbeck's door, then opened it. With a jerk of his head, he said, "Go ahead, Private. You know how to report?"

Buckner nodded and stepped into the room. The door closed behind him, leaving him in a windowless office with concrete walls, unpainted and unadorned. A row of filing cabinets stood against one wall, along with a combination safe the size of a small refrigerator. Bookshelves lined the opposite wall, stacked with army field manuals and the UCMJ. In the center of the room, General Tannerbeck looked up sternly from his paperwork and lowered his reading glasses onto his gray metal desk. A comfortable red leather easy chair flanked the desk, out of place in the Spartan environment. An American flag stood in the corner behind him.

Buckner snapped to attention. "Sir! Private First Class Buckner reports as ordered!"

"At ease." Tannerbeck stared at him briefly as Buckner assumed a position of parade rest. He motioned toward the leather chair. "Have a seat."

Buckner sat awkwardly, not sure if he was required to sit at attention, for Tannerbeck was the first officer above the rank of captain to whom he had ever spoken.

Tannerbeck flipped open a folder on his desk and began reading. "I've been reviewing your personnel file, Private. On paper, you do not appear to be qualified for an appointment to West Point." The general lifted his eyes over the top of his reading glasses and fixed them on Buckner, who stared straight ahead. "You do have the skills of a soldier, but I am concerned about your academic credentials. I am even more concerned about comments in here indicating that you are a loner, without much concern for your fellow soldiers. At West Point, that's a one-way ticket home."

"Yes, sir."

Tannerbeck was impressed that Buckner had the sense to minimize his responses, to avoid familiarity, excuses, or tap dancing. The boy had poise, but Tannerbeck wondered if it stemmed from unusual maturity, or if he was a player, working the system. "Tell me something, Private. Why did you report the illegal treatment of prisoners? Were you concerned about the prisoners, or were you concerned about the army? Or were you just looking for a way to cause trouble and somehow get yourself out of Iraq?"

"Sir, I don't give a damn about those Iraqi prisoners. But I thought that somebody needed to know what was going on."

Tannerbeck looked at Buckner for a prolonged moment, causing Buckner to drop his eyes to the floor. "Your own behavior was worst of all, yet you turned yourself in. I'm not sure if that shows commitment to duty, or lack of concern for your fellow soldiers, all of whom could end up being court-martialed."

"I never thought of it that way, sir." Buckner was embarrassed to hear the nervousness in his voice.

"From what I hear, Private Buckner, your squad leader took a bullet for his men. That's the kind of commitment I expect from every NCO and officer in the army. Are you ready to make that commitment?"

This was another thing that Buckner had never considered, whether he could make the kind of sacrifice that Tetra had made. He said, "I don't know, sir."

Not all high-ranking officers were comfortable with enlisted troops, but Tannerbeck savored his rare conversations with the young warriors he commanded. He understood nothing of hip-hop music or computer games, but he understood his soldiers the way fathers understand their sons, and he knew that Buckner, like most adolescent males, had probably never given a thought during his short life to anything as spiritual as Duty or Honor. So he broke it down as personally as he could. "I'd jump on a grenade to save any man under my command, including you. And I'd expect you to do the same for me."

Buckner imagined himself fighting with Tannerbeck over a grenade for the privilege of blowing themselves up. He had heard of Tannerbeck since the day he had arrived in Iraq, stories of gallantry and devotion told by admiring non-coms and passed along through scuttlebutt. Like most enlisted men, Buckner had no love of officers, especially generals, and he was perplexed by the way even the lowest-ranking privates ate up the stories, as if they were true. In Tannerbeck's presence, however, Buckner felt his cynicism slipping away under the weight of the man's sincerity.

Tannerbeck continued. "Men don't die for the flag, Buckner. They die for each other. That's what our profession is all about—sacrifice. We revel in it. You will be called upon to sacrifice. At West Point, we will imbue you with honor and steel you with professionalism. Then someday, you may be called upon to sacrifice it all in order to save your men."

The intensity and emotion in Tannerbeck's speech deepened, increasing Buckner's sense of awe as well as discomfort. He had no idea what the man was talking about.

"You sacrificed your honor and professionalism when you beat the daylights out of the prisoner who shot your friend Tetra. Most soldiers only get one chance to throw away their careers. You'll reclaim your honor and professionalism at West Point, but the next time you throw them away, it had better be done in order to save the men you love, not to satisfy a selfish craving for revenge."

"Yes, sir." Buckner's voice was a whisper.

"Very well then." Tannerbeck imagined that he saw things in Buckner that leaders were made of: cockiness, maturity, self-righteousness, emotionalism. The references in his fitness reports regarding his aloofness were of little concern to him. Tannerbeck himself was no back-slapping extrovert, but he could motivate soldiers to do things that they never thought they could do. "You've got your work cut out for you at the Prep School. You're starting the semester late, and from what I can see of your high school transcripts, you are going to need all the extra trigonometry, calculus, and English you can get. The odds are against you, Son, but if you can cut the mustard for the next eight months at the Prep School, I'll look forward to swearing you in on July first next year. You ready for the challenge?"

"Yes, sir." Buckner felt his composure return and his excitement grow, like a running back listening to his coach's pre-game pep talk. He felt silly responding to Tannerbeck's cheerleading, but allowed himself to be swept away by it. Suddenly, he wanted to please this man.

Tannerbeck pushed his chair back and stood up, announcing the end of their meeting. Buckner popped to attention. "Have a safe trip home, Private Buckner. I'll give you one final word of advice."

"Yes, sir."

"Keep your activities at Abu Ghraib to yourself. The army is prepared to overlook some of your actions there, but if word gets out that you beat up a prisoner, you could face a court-martial. Not many people understand the necessity for what you did, and we won't be able to help you once legal proceedings commence. So keep your mouth shut. You understand what I'm saying?"

"Yes, sir."

"Good. You're dismissed, Private."

Buckner saluted. After a smart about-face, he could still feel the general's eyes upon him as he opened the door and left the office.

CHAPTER 7

May 17, 2004 (Monday)
New York

According to some people, Roger Simmons was the most powerful man in New York. As editor in chief of *The Citizen Times*, Simmons reported to the CEO, who reported to the board of directors, but he was the only real newspaperman in the corporate circle. The others ran the business; Simmons ran the newsrooms.

Upon his appointment, Simmons inherited a newspaper that was already at the pinnacle of influence and financial success. The *Times* raked in Pulitzers, along with dozens of lesser awards for journalistic excellence. The newspaper had become a virtual branch of government, the embodiment of the fourth estate.

But after a decade of imperious domination of the nation's media, Roger Simmons was on the hot seat. The Internet had begun to undermine all print media, and the *Times*' own reporting scandals had shaken the newspaper's self-confidence. The administration in Washington had suckered the paper with selected leaks, leading the *Times* to beat the drums of war with unsubstantiated articles about weapons of mass destruction. Readership was declining as steadily as the stock price, but most worrisome to Simmons was the specter of irrelevance that haunted the *Times'* newsrooms.

Part of the problem was Doug McGowan, whose brilliant reporting and natural distrust of authority had filled his office with Pulitzers. His reporting was old school: factual, terse, devoid of personal ideology, unlike the articles written by the younger hotshots that had begun to fill the ranks. The new generation lacked McGowan's seasoning and maturity, making them vulnerable to the elixir of power that oozed from the politicians they interviewed. "They aren't reporters," complained Simmons. "They're stenographers." In their efforts to emulate McGowan, they sensationalized rumors and printed every leak, but failed to verify, verify, verify. By his dogged brilliance, McGowan had helped create the problem, and Simmons had determined that McGowan was going to solve it.

Simmons expected the knock on his office door and rose to greet his star reporter as McGowan entered. He waited behind his desk while McGowan made his way across the executive office, moving so slowly that Simmons wondered if the reports on McGowan's condition were understated. Six months in prison could do a number on anyone, but until now Simmons had only heard that McGowan was suffering from bacterial infections and exhaustion. They shook hands. "Welcome home, Doug."

McGowan settled into a comfortable leather chair. "Looks like you've put on some weight, Roger."

Simmons was a bulky man with thinning hair and the mug of an aging prizefighter. He was shocked by McGowan's emaciated face. "You look like hell."

They had been friends for years, but the jocular edge that should have characterized their conversation was missing.

"I should have come to see you when you got back from Iraq," said Simmons, "but you never returned my calls."

"I haven't felt much like socializing."

"I've heard."

McGowan snorted. "What have you heard? That I'm even more of an asshole now than I was before?"

"Something like that."

"Yeah, well, I'm borderline homicidal. Or suicidal. It varies from day to day."

Simmons realized he was still standing, and sat down. He sensed that any further small talk would be useless. "Doug, I want you to take over the editorship of the International Desk."

McGowan raised his eyebrows and stared across the desk at his boss. "Why? I don't need some charity assignment."

"Doug, I want somebody to go in and clean that place up. The whole department has become a liability, full or antiwar zealots or government sycophants who don't question anything the DOD feeds them. Nobody's checking anything, and it's only a matter of time before something else blows up in our face, like this WMD crap. I don't give a damn about the war, Doug. I want to start printing big stories again, and winning some more Pulitzers."

"I already wrote a Pulitzer story for you, Roger, a first-person account of the abuses at Abu Ghraib. You rejected it." McGowan stared at his boss directly, challenging him to justify holding back the story of the year.

Simmons was ready. "I've seen your drafts. I want you to print the stories about your experiences while embedded with the insurgents. This is the kind of writing we need—raw, firsthand stuff. These stories alone should get us a Pulitzer."

"But Abu Ghraib—"

"We'll publish it, Doug. You better believe it. But when we do, I want to blow the lid off that scandal. If we print what you've got so far, all we have is a firsthand confirmation of the abuses. Ordinarily, this would be a big scoop, but this is all secondhand news now. Hell, those photographs tell the whole story. But if we print it, every source we have is going to shut down—no more embedded reporters, no more visits to the Pentagon. If we're going to absorb that sort of retaliation, I need something to justify it, something more than a "me-too" account of old news. I want names. Get me the names of the men who tortured you, and we'll have the story of the year. We'll reveal not just the abuses, but we'll expose the cover-up as well. Someone is protecting the men who abused you, and I want you to find out who it is."

McGowan said nothing, stewing in old memories. The abuses had ended after the first week, when any information he had was no longer current. He had survived the solitude and sleep deprivation, had told them everything he could remember, and had pleaded for mercy like all the rest of the pathetic prisoners in Cell Block 1A. They had locked him away then like a crazy aunt, afraid to discover that he actually was an American, not knowing what to do with him. What could be written about five months in solitary confinement? "I almost died for that story."

"You've almost died for less."

"Roger, I'm no desk man. I belong in the field."

"Not anymore." With convincing vehemence, Simmons said, "I need you here. You've got two Pulitzers, and more talent than the lot of them. Those morons should be writing for television. I want you to make reporters out of those people, reporters like you."

"The first thing I'll do," threatened McGowan, "is publish Abu Ghraib."

Simmons leaned back in his chair. McGowan had too much blood invested in his story of Abu Ghraib to simply let it go. If the *Times* didn't publish it, McGowan could sell it to any number of other papers: the *Post* or the *Daily News*, or some provincial rag like the *Seattle Post-Intelligencer*. "Doug, if you want to publish it, OK. But you know as well as I do what that story needs."

McGowan blinked slowly and locked eyes with Simmons. "I know."

"You claim there were others, like the man who beat you that first night, that have not been identified, who are still out there getting on with their lives, like the anonymous Nazis who moved to Argentina after World War Two. All you have to do is—"

"Find 'em."

Silence descended between them as both men looked away. Finally, Simmons asked, "How much time do you need to recuperate?"

McGowan shrugged. "Whenever you're ready, I suppose."

Simmons watched as McGowan struggled to his feet, an old man at fifty. He paused before opening the door. "We're family, Doug, and I'm counting on you. We can turn this paper around."

McGowan nodded. "I'll find them, Roger."

"I'm counting on it." The two friends shook hands.

CHAPTER 8

June 16, 2004 (Wednesday)
New York

As far as Doug McGowan was concerned, one of the few advantages to being an editor was the opportunity to work in a private office where he could escape from the noise of the newsroom. Five months of solitary confinement had taught him the value of silence. Forbidden to speak, he had learned to listen to the changing of the shifts, to the coming of meals, to other men breathing, until he had become comfortable with solitude. Now, the mere buzzing of his telephone raised the hair on the back of his neck. From his glass office, he could observe the comings and goings of his staff, but the phones and the clicking of the computer keyboards chattered in blessed silence.

There were, besides the silence, two aspects of the job which made it tolerable. First, for reasons which McGowan did not understand, his staff was devoted to him. He insisted upon reading every word they wrote and he frequently gutted their stories, often with stinging verbal criticism. To McGowan's astonishment, his young reporters responded by working harder, and later into the night. Rarely did McGowan come to work in the morning without finding at least one staffer draped over his keyboard, surrounded by empty coffee cups from an all-night rewrite.

They responded to him because McGowan brought something to the newsroom that they had never experienced before: incorruptibility. For once, the young reporters in McGowan's newsroom were guided by journalistic principles they had learned in school, but had promptly forgotten in the commercial frenzy that consumed their peers. McGowan's code of ethics transcended morality, particularly the morality of the war in Iraq. Righteousness was replaced by truth. "It's easier to be honest than it is to be right," lectured McGowan, "because most of us are too stupid to remember what is right or wrong from one day to the next." With a wink, he added, "And the truth does a hell of a lot more damage."

There were those who disagreed, who believed it was their duty to use the press to end injustice by shining light on shameful things, real or imagined. McGowan had no use for ideology, and so he fired them. Thus, he embarked upon the other obligation of his office which he found surprisingly interesting: hiring new reporters.

McGowan did not have the budget to hire experienced news hands. Most of them were prima donnas, anyway, with egos as large as McGowan's own. McGowan preferred younger reporters, and there was no shortage of supply. A dozen journalism majors knocked on his door every week, naive college graduates with pathetic resumes that listed their favorite sports and pastimes and included a clipping or two from their school newspaper. McGowan didn't mind, although he eventually determined that it was a waste of time to interview journalism majors, since too many of them were political activists. English majors had a better command of the language, but they had a boring habit of trying to impress, rather than inform. McGowan would have preferred physics majors above all, were they not illiterate, for at least they were analytical thinkers who could spot the false premises that always accompanied intentional deception. Ultimately, he hired anyone who could recognize bullshit from shinola, and if he or she could string two sentences together, so much the better.

But McGowan nevertheless enjoyed the fire in the adolescent bellies of journalism students. They were students of the industry who knew all about Doug McGowan and who revered his credentials, his Pulitzers, and his reputation. McGowan was not above toying with the overtly sexual ploys of attractive young women who would do anything for a job with *The Citizen Times*, but there was a limit to how many cub reporters the paper could use, even if they *were* willing to work for nothing and fuck the boss on the side.

He stared now through the window at the carefully revealed cleavage of a young woman who, according to his appointment calendar, must be Angie Darrow. Her cheerleader smile would have stopped work in the newsroom even if she hadn't been wearing a skirt far too short for proper interview attire. By the time she reached McGowan's door, every eye in the office was fixed upon her.

McGowan rose as she entered. "Don't pay any attention to the animals," he said, jerking his thumb at the still-gawking staff.

She laughed comfortably, her breasts bouncing like pom-poms, as McGowan offered her a chair.

"I must apologize," began McGowan, "but I have apparently misplaced your resume. I'd misplace my head if it wasn't attached. Do you have another copy with you?"

"Well, I do have one, actually." She rummaged in her briefcase and then handed him the one-page document.

"But I don't think I ever sent you one. I'm not here for a job interview."

"Oh?" McGowan stared at her for a moment, flustered and enchanted.

"I have an article from *The Bard Observer* that I'd like you to consider publishing. I'm majoring in journalism."

"Of course." Every journalism student had at least one freelance article, like poets and novelists, sending their crap out to anyone with a printing press. The writing was always florid and belligerent, full of idealistic indignation about some minor campus brouhaha. The articles came across McGowan's desk every day and went immediately into his trash can. "Most people mail their stuff to me."

"We did that two weeks ago," she said. "Look, I know you don't appreciate my making this appointment just to show you this article, but I think it has a great angle. Read it."

He glanced at the article, and then at Darrow's breasts. With a sigh, McGowan reached for his reading glasses, then leaned back in his chair and heaved his foot onto the desk. He began to read.

> Yesterday, 200 female members of the Bard student body forcibly occupied the office of Bard President, Ms. Elaine Casswell, in a demonstration against the war in Iraq. The women remained in the hallways and administrative offices of the president for three hours. The demonstrators remained peaceful at all times, their sole demand being that Ms. Casswell issue a public statement condemning the presence of U.S. troops in Iraq. Ms. Casswell complied with the student demands without hesitation.

The text of her statement was submitted to the demonstrators, and was approved by voice vote. The text of Ms. Casswell's statement follows:

The administration and student body of Bard College declare our opposition to the immoral war currently being waged against the innocent people of Iraq by the government of the United States. We call upon our government to immediately withdraw all U.S. personnel from that country.

Immediately after release of Ms. Casswell's statement, the demonstrators were escorted from the administration building by campus police. No arrests were made. The women returned to their dormitory rooms, chanting, "Hell no, we wouldn't go, even if we had to!" Susie Chaffee, leader of the demonstrators, stated, "The participation of women in the antiwar movement is especially significant. First, we have shown here that we can take aggressive action without dangerous and angry confrontation. Second, and most important, the voice of women should be heard because we are a relatively disinterested party. We women are far less likely to face combat then men. We protest for one pure and simple reason: the war is wrong."

"Standard bullshit," said McGowan. "Kids are doing this everywhere. What's so different about Bard? Nobody poured gas on themselves and lit a match, did they?" He remembered watching on TV as Buddhist monks in Vietnam did exactly that, piquing his interest in world events and war and journalism. *Ancient history to this girl.*

"You don't get it," said Darrow. "Two hundred women took part in this demonstration; women of privilege who can ignore the military, who don't need the military as a path to success, who won't ever be going to Iraq, women with nothing to gain. It was a demonstration based on the pure ideological antiwar sentiment across the campus, rather than any fear of having to serve in the armed forces. Women are an unbiased measure of public opinion."

With growing disappointment, McGowan removed his glasses and tossed them onto his desk. This girl was like the rest, he concluded, grinding her ax in the press. Slowly, he crumpled the paper into a ball and tossed it into his trash, indifferent to the feelings of the woman in front of him.

"You think you know enough about Iraq to write stories like this?"

"I wrote what I saw," she replied, her eyes following the arc of her article as it sailed into the trash can.

"How many people do you know in Iraq?"

Her silence confirmed that she did not know anyone in uniform.

"And you also think women have some sort of special vision into righteousness just because you have the privilege of turning up your noses at men who serve?"

"That's not it at all," she said. "It's about the war, not the soldiers. The soldiers are the victims of war, just like everyone else. They should come home."

"Look," said McGowan, "we print news here, not opinions. If you want to make a point, contact the editorial pages."

Tears had begun to cloud Darrow's vision, but she refused to show them. "Everybody reads your byline; people think you're a hero. They think you actually write things that make a difference. How can you support what's happening there?"

"Don't assume anything about me. I do hate the war in Iraq. But people listen to me because they know that I don't take sides and I know what I'm talking about. I don't report things in order to whip up public indignation; I report them because they're true."

Darrow turned away for a moment, but did not blink, forcing her eyes to dry. She felt suddenly out of her league, which she was. She was silent for a long period of time, and McGowan said nothing more. But this was not the first time in her life that Darrow had found herself in over her head, and she had learned that a little pluck could go a long way in regaining the initiative, so long as a girl was pretty enough. She focused her penetrating eyes on him, radiating like microwaves until he squirmed. At last, she said, "So, I guess the Paris beat is out of the question, huh?"

"I thought you weren't looking for a job."

She stood to take her leave. "I don't seem to be accomplishing much at Bard."

"Sit down." He liked her effrontery; there was a toughness about her that made him believe she was trainable and far more intelligent than she pretended to be. And her breasts were remarkable. "You ready to quit school and work for six months at minimum wage doing research?"

"What kind of research?"

McGowan reached in his desk drawer and tossed a sheaf of photographs into her lap. She immediately recognized the famous images of the abused prisoners at Abu Ghraib, but their garish perversity had a riveting quality that forced her to view them again. McGowan waited while she struggled to collect her thoughts. He stared at her pretty face, so devoid of pain or memories or character, and imagined what she might be like in bed. "There were other people guilty of abusing prisoners besides the guards in these photos."

"How do you know?"

"I was there."

She stared first at him, then at the photographs, as if to spot him among the prisoners. Suddenly, her story about the protest at Bard seemed infantile.

"I was stripped naked and beaten. Deprived of sleep and threatened with death. The guards in those photos were the only ones stupid enough to show their faces. I'm looking for a research assistant to help me find the others."

Darrow could not take her eyes off the photographs as she digested what he told her. "And you think I'm qualified?"

"Why not? I'm not interested in your college credentials. You can write as well as anyone on my staff. More importantly, you just picked yourself up after absorbing an ego-crushing critique of your work. I need people who can go toe-to-toe with me, and lose, and come back for more."

"Masochists?"

"Maybe." He pointed toward the newsroom, where the staff had resumed work. "Those are the best reporters in the world out there. Every one of them has been in this office at one time or another, crying, ready to resign. But then they drag themselves back to their cubicles and pull an all-nighter and turn in a Pulitzer. I'd die for them."

McGowan's voice had grown husky, and Darrow detected a trace of embarrassment as he cleared his throat. She did not know what caused the shiver to run up her spine, but no man had ever vowed to die for her, not even her father. Glancing again at the photos, she said, "When do you want me to start?"

CHAPTER 9

June 21, 2004 (Monday)
New York

Angie Darrow reported for duty at *The Citizen Times* one week after her interview with Doug McGowan. After two days of filling out forms and attending benefits meetings, she was issued a laptop computer and a cubicle as nondescript as the dozens of others others that surrounded hers. The other reporters introduced themselves, some of the men stopping by her desk more frequently than necessary to see if she needed help with anything. Even the women invited her to lunch each day, until Darrow's shallow resume, smoldering sexuality, and ill-defined responsibilities became the subject of water cooler gossip. By the end of the week, she was alone, baffled by the sudden indifference of her coworkers, who thought they had figured out she was there for the boss's entertainment, not to perform any real work. She sat at her desk contemplating resignation when a thin file folder landed in front of her.

"You know what that is?" asked McGowan. He said nothing more, but scanned her tiny cubicle, pleased that she had not immediately adorned it with cute photographs of puppies and other people's children that cluttered the work spaces of every other woman in the office. He watched her for a silent moment, as Darrow opened the folder and saw only a photo of a soldier and a snippet of newsprint announcing his name, rank, date of birth, hometown, and the date of his death.

She read the name and asked, "Who is Tetra?"

"I don't know."

Increasingly perplexed, she asked, "Am I supposed to do something with this?"

"Find his mother."

"Why?"

"This newspaper has an archive of all soldiers who have died in Iraq, along with their photograph and hometown. This guy Tetra died at Abu Ghraib about a week before I got there, the only death recorded any time close to my arrival. The man who beat me referred to his friend; said I had helped kill him. If we can find Tetra's family, they might be able to identify the man's friends."

She nodded, and McGowan was pleased to see that she was considering how to begin.

In his other hand, McGowan held a thin phone book, which he tossed onto her desk with a thud. "The army listed his home of record as Frederick, Maryland. Call every Tetra in the book. Then call every Tetra in the surrounding area. Maybe you'll get lucky."

Darrow did not get lucky, but she did keep busy, leaving messages, chatting with perplexed people named Tetra, tracking her calls and the results of each one. She forgot about her unhappiness and the office innuendo, excited as she was by every call, each a new adventure that might or might not lead her to Victor Tetra's family, but fascinating either way. She ignored McGowan's antiquated phone book, relying instead upon the internet to find every Tetra in the entire state of Maryland. At the end of the week, however, she reported to McGowan defeated. If anyone in Maryland was related to Vic Tetra, they were not in any telephone directory.

McGowan listened to her report as he reviewed the records of each call, which she had tabulated on an extensive spreadsheet. Her notes were thorough; she seemed to have chatted up half the people in the state. Satisfied, McGowan tossed the papers aside and turned the computer screen on his desk toward her so she could see it. "This is the mock-up of tomorrow's edition," he said. "Page thirteen."

She saw the headline immediately: War Protest at Bard. She read it quickly. Not a word had been changed.

"It wasn't complete horseshit," he said.

Willing herself to remain calm, she mumbled, "Thank you."

Immediately back to business, McGowan said, "Wear a dress tomorrow, something professional. And comfortable shoes. We're taking the train to Washington."

Angie Darrow was awed by the gigantic parking lot of the Pentagon as Buster Lambeau escorted her and McGowan across the expanse of asphalt. From the looks of him, nobody would have believed that Lambeau had paid his dues as a reporter alongside McGowan, reporting from Panama, Sarajevo, Beirut, and Moscow. He was the bureau chief in Washington DC, now, working a desk and glad of it, for his body had eroded with age and was no longer fit enough to be running with military units or chasing the Taliban through the caves of Afghanistan. Lambeau and McGowan had been a swashbuckling pair at one time, but Darrow found it hard to imagine that the bald and pudgy man who gasped now as he escorted her up the Pentagon steps had once beaten McGowan to a pulp in a bar fight over a hooker in Subic Bay. The two men laughed like brothers over the incident while Darrow followed along, wondering how they could be so relaxed as they approached the most powerful building in the world. Like most civilians, she understood that the Pentagon was the nerve center of the U.S. military, but she had only a vague idea of what went on within its walls. The building itself was intimidating, its stern façade evoking the foreboding character of a prison. To the eyes of the silent American majority, the squat and functional Pentagon was a properly austere edifice for a military headquarters. Even the rebuilt section destroyed by the terrorists of September 11 evoked a sense of warrior spirit. But to those like Angie Darrow, who held the military responsible for the debacle of Iraq, the Pentagon was menacing and closed, a bunker where the generals isolated themselves from the American people. With a sense of dread, she climbed the stairs to the visitors' entrance.

Access to the Pentagon had been dramatically curtailed since the terrorist attacks of September 11, 2001. Visitors were still admitted, and even the press was tolerated, but authority to wander the halls unescorted was limited to Pentagon employees and properly credentialed others. Although the brass would have liked to toss the entire press corps into the parking lot, the military succumbed to political pressure and did offer credentials and access badges to members of the press who could pass security vettings. Many reporters were found to have dubious histories and associates, but most eventually passed muster and were awarded the coveted press badge. Fully credentialed, Lambeau passed through the metal detector first, and then stood by while Darrow and McGowan underwent full screening of their briefcases and garments. McGowan explained their business while another guard entered their names in the visitor's database, where they were crosschecked against the FBI's terrorist watch list and other lists maintained by the Immigration and Naturalization Service and by the DEA of international criminals of all kinds. As they were about to be released into Lambeau's custody, the guard spoke up forcefully. "Sir!" he said to McGowan. "Step aside, please." While Darrow and Lambeau stood by, perplexed, the guards escorted McGowan into a small room adjacent to the screening area. McGowan glanced over his shoulder and offered a puzzled and disgusted shrug as the door closed behind him. The other guard directed Darrow and Lambeau to remain where they were while he worked the phone.

"What's going on?" asked Lambeau. The guard spoke quietly on the phone and pointed with his finger to a bench, indicating for Lambeau and Darrow to sit. As they obeyed the command, Lambeau muttered to Darrow, "What the hell has McGowan done now?" Frightened, Darrow said nothing.

They waited for an hour, until the door to the interrogation chamber opened and McGowan walked out, his disgust replaced now by anger communicated to Lambeau in a single glance. As Lambeau jumped to his feet, a guard escorted McGowan out of the building and released him at the top of the granite stairs. With the permission of the other sentry, Lambeau and Darrow followed.

"What have you done this time?" asked Lambeau.

"Nothing. My name is on the terrorist watch list. Some goddamn government bureaucrat decided to put my name on this list and suddenly I'm a terrorist. No trial, no explanation, no discussion."

"We can fight this. It's got to be unconstitutional."

"Yeah, well, we have don't have ten years to push it through the courts," said McGowan. "The only way I'm getting into the Pentagon today is to fly another airplane into it."

"Don't talk like that; they'll put you back in prison. I'll get the information you want," volunteered Lambeau. "Why don't you two take the car, and I'll meet you back here in two hours."

"I'll wait here," said McGowan. "Take Darrow with you. She needs the education."

"I can work faster alone," said Lambeau. His voice carried no impression of disapproval, but Darrow sensed that he did not like her. She guessed that Lambeau, like everyone else at the newspaper, assumed she was sleeping with McGowan.

"We've got all day," replied McGowan. "Take her with you."

Lambeau nodded and offered his arm to Darrow, a gentleman despite himself. She allowed herself to be escorted back into the building and through the screening devices, where she repeated the purpose for her visit to the guards, who reentered her name into the database. After again coming up clean, she was released finally into the custody of Buster Lambeau. Forbidden to leave her alone at any time, Lambeau would be her escort everywhere, even waiting outside the ladies' room door if Darrow felt compelled to go there. In the event that Lambeau needed to use the men's room, he would return Darrow to the guard at the entrance for supervision until he could retrieve her.

Lambeau took her to the press room, a cramped and windowless space with a dozen cubicles reserved for credentialed reporters. The *Times* had a cubicle, alongside the cubicles of the *Washington Post* and the *Los Angeles Times*, a prestigious row occupied by old cronies like Lambeau and McGowan. The *Citizen's* cube was empty, however, recently vacated by another old member of the *Times'* family who had been unable to resist an offer of higher pay and regular hours at CNN. The empty space seemed a lonely oasis of calm in comparison to the hubbub of the newsroom.

"I'm waiting for Doug to fill this position." explained Lambeau. "I'm too old to waste my time sitting through Pentagon briefings every day." He checked the phone for messages and sorted through the mail while Darrow gazed around the room. A dozen men, all over forty, huddled in their cubicles to file stories or tend to e-mail, but most of the cubes were empty while the reporters assigned to them chased the news somewhere in the Pentagon. "There aren't many of us left who know their way around this place anymore."

"Why not?" asked Darrow. "The army seems to find enough brass to fill this building; are reporters any harder to find than generals?"

Lambeau looked at her like she was an idiot, but there was something naively insightful in her question, so he answered it seriously. "There are qualified reporters out there, but they opt to work for television. Better pay, more glamour, easier hours, and shallow reporting that requires little effort. A waste of talent, if you ask me." Thoughtlessly, he added, "You should look into television, too."

"What do you mean?" she asked. If McGowan had said such a thing, she would have teased him about the interchangeability of breasts and talent, but Lambeau's comment left her crestfallen, reminding her again that few people took her seriously.

Lambeau realized from the look on her face that he had insulted her. "I didn't mean to imply anything about your talent, Angie. You may have all the talent in the world, but a woman who looks like you can do very well without it. But Doug seems to think you have what it takes in this business, so who am I to send you to the competition?"

"Doug said that?"

"Why else would you be here?"

"You know why."

Lambeau snorted. "I've known Doug McGowan for a long time, Angie. I've never known him to lie about anything to anyone. He's dysfunctional that way; hurts a lot of people's feelings along the way. He may like the way you look in a miniskirt, but unless he's told you specifically that all he wants from you is sex, then you can believe he sees a potential reporter in you."

"We're not sleeping together, you know."

He raised an eyebrow. "Come on. I'll take you to the Media Relations office."

As she followed Lambeau through the maze of corridors, Darrow was thunderstruck by the artwork on the walls. It had never occurred to her that artists went to war, or that they could render moments of such human anguish and glory. She had always considered war a political event. While not indifferent to the human tragedy, Darrow was aware of it only in the abstract, despite the graphic images from Iraq shown every night on television. The paintings here moved her, and she wondered how military men could engage in war while surrounded by such evocative reminders of their handiwork.

Lambeau stopped abruptly at a metal door labeled only with the room number 2D245: second floor, D ring, the

245th room out of 850 that occupied the outermost ring of the Pentagon. This portion of the building was new and still smelled of paint, but Darrow was too dazzled to put the clues together to realize that 150 people had died here when Hani Hanjour had hijacked American Airlines Flight #77 and flown it into the building.

A plastic plaque on the wall identified the office: Media Relations Division. The room was protected by a digital scanner against which Lambeau pressed his security badge. The electronic deadbolt released with a crisp thud. Lambeau held the door for Darrow and followed her inside.

Martha Rose looked up from her computer and greeted Darrow with a professional but sincere smile. It was Rose's responsibility to manage the press, to facilitate their research when possible and to thwart them when necessary. A quick-eyed woman with an unflappable air who had run her three-man office for twelve years, there was hardly a reporter she didn't know. Darrow was a mystery to her, but her smile turned personal when Lambeau entered the room.

"Buster!" she exclaimed, slipping her reading glasses from her nose as she stood to greet him. "How long has it been?"

"Way too long, Martha. I've missed making your life a living hell."

She laughed. "Don't flatter yourself. Not many like you left anymore." She turned her attention to Darrow, as if to make her point. "And you are…?" she asked, extending her hand.

"Angie Darrow, *Citizen Times.*" The women shook hands and Darrow absorbed a measure of Rose's warmth. She was smooth but earthy, with the deep voice of a smoker, the kind of gal who might have been a reporter herself at one time, tough enough to compete with the men in a combat zone without letting them forget she was a lady.

"Angie works for Doug McGowan out of our New York office," explained Lambeau. "We need your help for a story we're working on."

"McGowan!" Rose shot a horrified glance at Lambeau. "Good Lord, are you two back together again?" She turned to Darrow and grumbled coyly, "You tell Douglas McGowan that he still owes me dinner. He'll know why."

Darrow smiled awkwardly, more intimidated by this woman than anyone she could remember. There was a hint of beauty remaining in Rose's face, but Darrow knew that this woman had never traded on it. Whatever debt Mc-Gowan owed her had nothing to do with sex, and Darrow wished someday that men might owe her favors the way they owed Rose.

Lambeau said, "I'll buy you dinner myself, Martha. I need for you to bend a rule for me."

She narrowed her eyes and said, "That's all you ever needed me for, Buster. What is it this time?"

"I need the next of kin for a kid killed in Iraq."

"You know we don't release that information," she said. She turned to Darrow and asked, "You understand why, of course?"

Darrow shook her head.

"The army learned its lesson in Vietnam," explained Lambeau. "The press started printing the names of the next of kin of men killed or wounded, thinking people would want to express condolences or do something to help them. But the antiwar crowd started harassing them, calling parents at midnight to tell them that their son was a murderer who deserved to have his legs blown off."

"Have you checked his hometown phone book?" asked Rose, trying to be helpful.

Darrow nodded. "I called every Tetra in Maryland."

"Why do you want his NOK?"

"Martha," said Lambeau, "you know we aren't going to harass the poor boy's parents. We're looking for someone else, and are hoping that they can help us find him. We won't publish their names, phone number, address, anything. You have my word on that. Anything you tell us is off the record."

Rose sighed. "Your word has always been good, Buster." To Darrow, she added, "This business is all about trust. Right now, for example, Buster is trusting that I will cut off his balls if I lose my job for releasing this information to you."

"Hey," protested Lambeau, grinning. "I'm just here doing a favor for McGowan!"

"Ha! I castrated that bitch a long time ago!" Rose and Lambeau burst into laughter, leaving Darrow with a horrified smile on her face. With a sigh of resignation, Rose turned to her computer. "What did you say the name was?"

Darrow told her, and then listened to the keystrokes as Rose's fingers opened up one database after another. Finally, Rose snatched a Post-it from her desk and scribbled down a name, address, and phone number of Mr. and Mrs. Jacob Tetra in Morgantown, West Virginia.

"The obituary said he was from Maryland," said Darrow.

"People move," replied Rose, "when their lives fall apart."

CHAPTER 10

June 22, 2004 (Tuesday)
Washington, DC

The summer of 2004 was brutally hot, the heat along the banks of the Potomac heavy enough to remind Major General Piersal of his tour in Guantanamo, recently completed. He was glad to be away from Cuba, where the interrogations had become increasingly futile because the prisoners had finally coughed up everything they knew. Despite the efficacy of the interrogation techniques that he had pioneered in Gitmo and in Iraq, the war had taken an ominous turn. The press ranted about torture and demanded the heads of American generals to atone for it, while trumpeting the photos of Abu Ghraib and proclaiming the war lost. As a lieutenant in Vietnam, Piersal had seen the Americal Division come apart at My Lai, and he had learned a thing or two about lost wars. The best place to protect himself from the coming crisis, he knew, would be at the center of power, in the Pentagon, far from the scene of the crime. So, while the West Pointers with Purple Hearts fought for glory assignments in Iraq, Piersal came home to save his career.

Piersal engineered his promotion to the Pentagon with perfect timing. As Chief of Staff for Military Intelligence, he assumed command over all aspects of MI, reporting directly to the Joint Chiefs of Staff. The Chiefs were warriors like Tannerbeck—fools, thought Piersal—except for a level of political savvy that served them well among their patrons in the halls of Congress. It had been difficult to cultivate the politicians while he was isolated in Cuba, but once in Washington, Piersal moved quickly to ingratiate himself with those high-powered civilians who could do him some good. As the war spiraled into a quagmire, Piersal believed that the leaders of the loyal opposition would become the power brokers of the future, and he met with them whenever he could, off the record, in private homes or isolated bars in Georgetown. They were fools, but Piersal smiled and listened and nodded as they talked.

Piersal still spent his days immersed in the challenges of winning the battle for Iraq, but a lot of his work was merely a matter of going through the motions. He managed budgets and personnel now, allowing subordinates to deal with the technologies and challenges of operations. He kept his finger on things that interested him, things that could harm or help his career, like Abu Ghraib, which could do both. Piersal had ensured from the beginning that his part in the drama was obscured, documenting objections he never voiced and always operating through others, like Elliott Makin. And while CJTF-7 in Baghdad struggled with damage control, Piersal pondered how each new disaster could contribute to his next star.

Piersal's scheming was interrupted by a crisp rap on the door of his office, followed by the arrival of his aide. Elliott Makin, now promoted to colonel, entered with information that he believed would be of keen interest to his boss. Without protocol, Makin said, "General, do you recall a combat reporter in Iraq by the name of McGowan? Doug McGowan, of *The Citizen Times*?"

"Vaguely," replied Piersal. Then he sat forward at his desk, suddenly intent as memories kicked in. "Yes, of course. He was of some concern to you at Abu Ghraib."

"Yes, sir, a very big problem. We finally confirmed that he was an American journalist, but there was no way we could release him without blowing the whole operation. So we kept him in solitary until the scandal broke, and then we had no choice but to send him home. I put his name on the terrorist watch list just to keep tabs on him."

"What has he stuck his nose into now?" asked Piersal, more curious than alarmed.

"His name popped up this morning right here in the Pentagon. I think he's looking into Abu Ghraib."

Piersal motioned Makin to a chair in front of his desk. Makin leaned forward, his elbows on his knees, an unmilitary posture acceptable only in MI or with a military mentor. He was a gloomy man with mysterious aura that he cultivated by hoarding information and scuttlebutt, which he shared only with his boss. Piersal had recently brought Makin back from Cuba with him, a reward for loyal service. They were both intelligent and arrogant men, but their difference in rank precluded any rivalry. Makin relished his role as Piersal's bulldog, imagining himself as the muscle behind the brains.

"The security team detained him and then escorted him from the building when he refused to state his business. But he was accompanied by a credentialed colleague, the *Times'* Washington bureau chief named Lambeau, who proceeded on his own to the Media Relations Division while McGowan cooled his heels outside."

"He suddenly shows up out of nowhere for a visit to Media Relations?"

Makin replied, "The reason McGowan dropped out of sight was because he was in various hospitals between Baghdad and New York. We were a little too rough on him, I suppose. As soon as he got home, *The Citizen Times* promoted him to the editorship of the International Desk."

"Fascinating," said Piersal. "So McGowan has lain dormant all this time with this nice little bombshell just eating his guts out, I'll bet. So why hasn't he published?"

"My guess? I suspect he's seeking names. He knows he's already been scooped with respect to the actual events at Abu Ghraib. His first-person account might sell to *Reader's Digest*, but the only way to really earn the Pulitzer will be to name the men at the top, and to prove what they knew and when they knew it."

"Does he have information that the rest of the press doesn't?"

"He must know something. We tracked Lambeau's travel through the building by auditing the scanner trail of his access badge. I spoke with the woman in Media Relations and asked her what he wanted. She advised me that he was searching for the NOK of a soldier named Tetra."

"Who?"

"Tetra was a guard at Abu Ghraib, killed in a prison riot a few days prior to McGowan's arrival."

"What does McGowan want with his next of kin?"

Makin shrugged and shook his head. "I have no idea. But I suspect that McGowan must have found some sort of connection between Tetra and the men who abused him— Private Buckner and a contractor named Levi."

Piersal sighed, recalling clearly now the name of Morgan Buckner. "Levi has disappeared back into whatever kibbutz he came out of, but Buckner can be found." Slowly, a thin smile formed upon Piersal's lips, as if a plan was falling into place. "Makin," he said, "do you see an opportunity here?"

"There is opportunity in every development, sir, but we've tried manipulating the press before. It has always been a debacle. They cannot be trusted."

"That's because we've always fed them lies. What if we simply lead them to the truth?"

"Now there's a novel concept."

Piersal laughed heartily, and then turned serious. "Elliott, you worked closely with Colonel Volpe at Abu Ghraib when you set up the JDIC."

"Yes, sir," replied Makin carefully. "He was a problem, actually, very by-the-book. Levi kept Volpe in the dark about McGowan because we feared that Volpe might insist that he be able to speak to the Red Cross or an American consulate rep. McGowan was a ghost detainee, not on the books anywhere."

"Volpe objected to our techniques from the beginning," agreed Piersal. "I directed him to document his objections and to copy me on everything. It was Tannerbeck who insisted on continuing the interrogations and then covering them up."

Makin was puzzled. "Sir, encouraging Colonel Volpe to document our own abuses can only implicate us in the event of an investigation."

"Elliott, in this business, it is a good policy to document your objections to illegal policies, even as you push to implement them. Our success at Gitmo is the reason we are here in this office today. Volpe's classified objections, passed up-channel to Tannerbeck—who had no choice but to ignore them—are what will get us to the next office."

"We may have some explaining to do."

Piersal could see the alarm in the eyes of his protégé, and relished the opportunity to impart more lessons in the dark art of political knife fighting. "CJTF-7 came to us for help. The White House tied themselves into knots trying to parse the law in such a way as to justify our methods and to explain away my concerns for the Geneva Conventions. Despite our documented misgivings, Tannerbeck gave the green light and Buckner was the result."

Makin nodded, admiring his boss's rationale. "So you want to pin this on Tannerbeck?"

"Damn right. He's not your favorite general, is he?"

Makin spoke freely to his mentor. "I reported to him during the drive to Baghdad. There were times that I felt he was too eager to charge into a battle that could be won with fewer casualties if he was willing to exercise a little patience and brain power."

"But his units did more fighting with fewer casualties than any other in the army," replied Piersal.

"I meant enemy casualties," said Makin. "You don't win hearts and minds by killing fathers and sons. But he didn't want my advice."

"I agree, Colonel. The man is a West Point barbarian, contemptuous of all of our initiatives in Iraq. He despised MI and anyone who didn't go right for the jugular in combat."

"He'd rather wade through a lot of blood than a little shit."

Piersal smiled. "Tannerbeck authorized MI to proceed with the techniques at Abu Ghraib, and then treated us with contempt, as if we forced him to authorize the abuses. He outranked me, for Christ's sake. We were the architects of the interrogations, but Tannerbeck was the executor. He could have stopped it at any time, but it was working, saving American lives. I required Volpe to document all communications with him, but I knew there was no stopping the train. So, MI was a hero either way: we got credit for the improvement of intel as long as nothing went wrong, but if things went south, MI was the only one to have raised any flags of warning."

Makin could only smile with admiration, so Piersal continued. "The battlefield is no place for Renaissance men like us, Elliott. That is where inspirational commanders like Tannerbeck are in their element, wreaking havoc and leading ignorant soldiers to hell. We have always operated in the shadows and we must continue to do so. His values are black and white—duty, honor, country. Simple enough for fools to comprehend, while our values are complex, colored in shades of gray."

"I didn't realize you knew him so well."

"I was an infantryman before I was a spook," said Piersal. "I was Tannerbeck's commander in Desert Storm, the first Iraq war. We were sent north to secure several enemy airfields while Schwarzkopf conducted his left hook into the Iraqi armored divisions. Most of the war was fought by armor, but we were isolated without support and we fought some of the only true infantry battles of the war. I had been ordered to secure a ridgeline just south of Baghdad. I planned a double envelopment, with Tannerbeck's battalion in the center. His orders were to feint—to attack, then turn back, thus holding the enemy in place while we outflanked them on both sides. Tannerbeck argued that such an attack was too complicated and would expose his men to enemy fire as they attacked, and more enemy fire as they retreated. We argued until I told him to act like a soldier and move out."

"What happened?" asked Makin, as entranced as a boy listening to his father's tales of war. He could not imagine anyone challenging Tannerbeck's professionalism to his face.

"He attacked. But when he reached the point where he was to turn back, he marched to the front of his battalion and drew his sidearm. He ordered 'fix bayonets' and personally led an infantry charge up that ridge worthy of Pickett at Gettysburg."

"Suicide."

"To my knowledge, it was the only bayonet charge in modern history. His men maintained a perfect line abreast as they humped up that ridge, until every man in the company crested the enemy lines simultaneously."

"Casualties must have been devastating."

"Casualties amounted to two wounded, including him," spat Piersal, anger building as he told his story. "His men kept up a well-disciplined rate of fire as they advanced, keeping the Iraqis' heads down. Once Tannerbeck broke through their lines, it was utter carnage. His men killed over four hundred and thirty Iraqis and had one hundred prisoners waiting for us when we arrived from the flanks. He reported back to me soaked in blood, head to toe."

"I can't believe that any Iraqi unit would stand and fight like that. They would have surrendered long before they took that kind of slaughter."

"I doubt that he gave any of them much of an opportunity to surrender."

"He should have been court-martialed."

"On the contrary, I was required to award him a Silver Star and a Purple Heart. Three months later, he was in command of my regiment and I was with MI."

"Sir," began Makin, flattered nearly speechless that Piersal would confide such a story to him. Professional humiliations were unbearable to most soldiers, even ones as enlightened as General Piersal. "Tannerbeck has the power to make men do superhuman things."

"So does the Devil."

"What do you propose to do about him, sir?"

"Tannerbeck has enemies, Colonel. He inspires sacrifice; he preaches duty and honor to his cadets at West Point, but our civilian leadership is becoming demoralized by this war. Iraq is the best thing that could have happened to us. If we can winnow the Tannerbecks from the army, the new administration will be inclined to listen to our advice instead of the old guard. There is an election campaign underway, Elliott. The challenger is an enlightened man, like us, more inclined to fight wars with brains rather than blood."

"He needs to win the election first, sir."

Piersal almost smiled. "Then we'd better help him."

Makin nodded. "But what about us?" he asked. "How do we avoid being caught up in the investigation?"

"Let me worry about that." Piersal knew his fingerprints were nearly as transparent as those of the CIA, and he had friends who, if not yet in high places, soon would be. "McGowan is looking for this Private Buckner, who tortured him at Abu Ghraib. Even if he finds him, Buckner doesn't know anything about us. But he knows Tannerbeck. The administration could be seriously embarrassed if McGowan discovers that Tannerbeck was promoted to Supe at West Point in exchange for covering up the events at Abu Ghraib. Tannerbeck can fall on his sword and accept responsibility, or he can blame it on higher authorities. Hopefully, the finger-pointing will go all the way to the Oval Office."

"Shall I discreetly guide Mr. McGowan to Tannerbeck's involvement at Abu Ghraib?"

"Yes," answered Piersal. "See what you can concoct that will connect this fellow Tetra with Tannerbeck. Then have Media Relations leak the NOK information to McGowan."

"They already did, sir."

Piersal glanced at the ceiling, amused by the breach of regulations.

CHAPTER 11

June 28, 2004 (Monday)
Baltimore

She was drunk again.

Buckner gazed at her, formless and fat, and willed himself to stony indifference. He had expected this, even though she had talked for weeks of little else than the fact that her son had somehow survived months of schooling at the Army Prep School to earn an appointment to West Point itself. His mother had but a vague notion of what that meant, but when Buckner had explained to her that it was a four-year academic institution, she seemed to think it was the most natural thing in the world that the army would send her son there, all expenses paid.

The bottle lay on the floor, a puddle of booze still in it. Buckner scooped it up and swallowed the last belt. He shuddered and sucked in his breath, and wondered how she could consume so much, and why.

No, he knew why. The reasons were all around him, within the apartment and outside. Despair drifted on the air in the McEldery Park neighborhood as distinctly as the odor from garbage in the alleys. He surveyed the room, their third apartment in as many years, each one worse than the last. Buckner sent money every month, but most of it went for booze, the rest for rent. There was no phone, other than the pay phone in the hall that was usually out of order. The couch was covered by a blanket, a patch to contain the stuffing which threatened to explode from every seam. Flies hovered over the remains of last night's pizza that lay on the floor in front of the TV. Threadbare curtains wavered in a draft of stifling air, which drew in the sounds of sirens and a woman yelling, and gallons of humidity. Of course he knew why she was drunk. Why not?

"I'm leaving now," he announced.

"You go on, baby." She took a ragged breath, followed by a salvo of coughs. "I'll be along." Her head lolled toward the sound of his voice, and her eyes opened but did not focus. By the way she gripped the back of the couch, Buckner knew that her room was rolling. And he recognized the smile. It was the honeyed smile she had offered Buckner's father when she knew he was going to hit her, back when he was still around. It said, "Please don't be angry with me." It meant nothing.

"Good-bye, Mama." He closed the door behind him.

He found his sister in the hall, playing with the girl next door. They were both pubescent, but their eyes could pass for forty. They knew about drugs and booze and cops and death and sex, yet they played on the floor with a pair of stolen Barbie dolls as if they were a couple of suburban white girls.

"Anna, lookit my brother! He's prettier'n this fuckin' doll!"

Anna put aside her lanky blonde toy and admired Buckner's uniform. She sat on the floor and allowed her eyes to drift upward from his spit-shined shoes to the brass buttons on his jacket. A row of campaign ribbons and a Purple Heart adorned his left breast.

"You be careful, Morgan Buckner. All them New York girls gonna be chasin' you. Too bad I'm only twelve." Anna studied him as frankly as a streetwalker, but sweetly enough to imply that she still had dreams.

"Where's Mama?" asked Lydia. "Ain't she going to the bus station with you?"

"No."

"Oh," she said, understanding. "Morgan, when you comin' home again?"

"Soon," he said. "Christmas, maybe."

"I'll be thirteen," said Anna.

"We'll see, Jailbait." He stood at the stair landing.

"Morgan," said Lydia, "is Sergeant Tetra going to West Point with you?"

"No, Lydia. He went home."

Lydia turned back to her doll with a sigh. "Good-bye, Morgan."

CHAPTER 12

June 28, 2004 (Monday)
Morgantown, West Virginia

Victor Tetra's parents lived in a mobile home park that occupied a few acres of land just west of Morgantown, where the Appalachian Mountains become rugged enough to make winter truckers consider chaining up before heading north on Interstate 79. Monique Tetra served coffee at the truck stop where I-79 crossed I-68. Tetra's father, Jacob, had not returned to work as a diesel mechanic since the day the telegram arrived announcing that his son was dead.

Darrow could not imagine a place more isolated or forlorn, for the Tetras' trailer park was not a neat settlement of modest retirement homes with pink flamingos like those Darrow had seen from the Florida interstates while en route to her parents' annual winter pilgrimage in Boca Raton. The Coal Dust Mobile Home Park was a huddle of worn-out trailers, many with blue tarps on the roof to keep out the drizzle, which gave the settlement a sense of melancholy that seemed appropriate for the lives that were lived there.

The Tetras' doublewide seemed bigger than the others, though no less disheartened. An empty propane tank sat next to the front door, but otherwise the place was typical: shabby but not destitute. McGowan noted the new TV antenna bolted to the metal siding and a Taurus in the driveway with a magnetic yellow ribbon stuck to the trunk lid. The road through the small complex was gravel and there were no sidewalks. As McGowan killed the engine, Darrow opened her passenger side door and stepped into two inches of mud.

"My God," she said, "how do people live here?"

"You should see how they live in Iraq."

She was sick of McGowan's stories about Iraq, where everything was filthier, more decrepit, less civilized. "I've seen better-looking chicken coops than this."

McGowan glanced sideways, doubtful that Darrow had ever seen—or smelled—a chicken coop. Chickens came from Arkansas, not Westchester. Although she was learning quickly, Darrow was at heart a mall rat, uncomfortable in situations where her good looks and fashion sense were not valued. He had brought her along because she had performed well at the Pentagon and because he found her increasingly infatuating, but he wondered now if it would be a mistake to expose her to people so unlike herself. *Too late now*, he thought.

Monique Tetra stood inside her home, watching through the storm door as McGowan and the pretty woman made their way to the front porch. She was expecting McGowan, but not Darrow, and she didn't like the idea of a girl from New York entering her house and passing judgment. Monique would not have recognized the Franco Sarto label on Darrow's pumps, but she could tell they were expensive and she derived a bit of satisfaction in watching Darrow struggle to clean the mud off of them before stepping into the Tetra home.

Mrs. Tetra was overweight, but not obese, never having lost the weight gained during her pregnancy with her son, her only child. Her hair was in a net, as if she was leaving soon for work. Light-skinned, her cheeks were sprinkled with freckles. A basset hound began to howl as the two journalists approached. From inside, a male voice yelled, "Shut up!"

She held the storm door open for them. Introductions were not necessary; she knew McGowan was the man from New York, and she didn't care about Darrow. Nevertheless, McGowan took pains to present himself more gallantly than Darrow would have expected, even shaking hands with the dog, who took an immediate liking to him. Jacob Tetra climbed out of an ancient easy chair and shook McGowan's hand curtly, giving the city man a careful once-over. A different side of McGowan emerged from the brusque manager who regularly drove grown men to tears with a few strokes of his editing pencil. Darrow saw that McGowan had a way with people that allowed him to be honest and polite at the same time, without a hint of pretense. He spoke to Monique and Jacob Tetra the way he would speak to Palestinian refugees on the West Bank, or to Saudi princes outside Mecca. Monique Tetra offered coffee as they took seats on the worn living room sofa.

"Don't trouble yourself," said McGowan. "We don't want to impose any more than necessary."

"I don't get many visitors, not since the man came with the telegram." Mrs. Tetra spoke very quietly.

"Has anyone come to take care of you since your boy died?" McGowan asked. "Survivor's benefits?"

She stared at him blankly. "The officer from the army base came by in his green car and said 'sorry' and then gave me the telegram and left as fast as he could. I don't blame him."

"Sit down, Mrs. Tetra." Gently, McGowan took charge of the meeting. "Forget about the coffee. I'll see to it that the army knows you need somebody to come out here and help you take care of things."

She sat. "Call me Monique." She waited expectantly.

"I'm looking for some of your son's friends."

She nodded, for McGowan had already explained his purpose on the phone. Mr. Tetra, almost forgotten in his chair, spoke up angrily. "Those boys didn't have anything to do with that crap at the prison."

"I have no reason to believe they did," acknowledged McGowan. "Vic just happened to be in the wrong place at the wrong time. But there were others there who did evil things. Until I track them down and expose them, their abuses will taint the memory of a lot of good men like your son."

Monique dabbed her eyes. McGowan waited calmly, while Darrow squirmed in her chair. "I miss him so much," said Monique. "Lord, I miss him."

"They gave him a medal," said Jacob Tetra. "We don't need you to prove anything. They gave him a medal, for Chrissake."

"Jacob, be quiet," said Monique. To McGowan, she explained, "He hasn't been himself since the telegram came. We moved here after Vic died to be closer to my mother, but there isn't much work my husband in these parts."

Mr. Tetra grunted and pushed himself out of his chair. "Come here," he grumbled. "I'll show you."

McGowan glanced quizzically at Monique, who nodded, as if to give permission to follow her husband. Jacob Tetra led them down a narrow hallway to a spare bedroom, where his wife's sewing machine sat in one corner. In the other corner, McGowan saw a chest of drawers, on top of which lay a triangularly folded American flag, two framed photographs, and a small hinged box with a velvet cover: Vic Tetra's shrine.

"That's him," said Mr. Tetra, pointing at the five-by-seven photo that grinned back at them, the same official photo from his personnel file. McGowan wondered if it was the only photo ever taken of him. He glanced at Darrow and noticed that she was blinking back tears, for even modest shrines are packed with emotion. Jacob Tetra handed the little jewelry box to McGowan. It could have been a string of pearls, but McGowan knew a medal was inside, probably a Bronze Star. The award had been cheapened by the war, although those with the "V" device for valor still meant something. He opened the box politely, and nearly gasped when he recognized the Silver Star. Under the medal was a written citation, which McGowan carefully unfolded:

> On October 8, 2003, while serving as a reaction team leader assigned to the 229th Military Police Company during a disturbance at Camp Vigilance at Abu Ghraib prison in Iraq, Sergeant Victor Tetra came under surprise small arms attack from a prisoner armed with a handgun. At extreme risk to himself, Sgt. Tetra immediately charged the attacker. Despite mortal wounds, Sgt. Tetra's attack disrupted the assailant's plan, thus protecting his men and limiting additional casualties. Sgt. Tetra's courageous actions were directly responsible for saving the lives of his men. His actions reflect great credit upon himself and the U.S. Army.

"Do you know what this means?" asked McGowan.

"My boy was a good soldier." Monique's understatement almost brought tears to McGowan's eyes.

"Mrs. Tetra," he said hoarsely, "there are a lot of medals being passed out in Iraq just for showing up. But not this one. These only go to real heroes."

Darrow noticed a shiver of movement in Mr. Tetra. His lips began to tremble and he closed his eyes tightly in an unsuccessful effort to staunch tears. "I knew it," he whispered. "I knew it. I knew it." He lost control then and fled from the room, gently pushing Darrow aside.

After a moment of awkward silence, Monique said quietly, "Vic was a handful. Jacob told him to join the army, to straighten him out. It did, too. But he blames himself." She dabbed her own eyes again with a tissue from the sewing table, and handed one to Darrow, whose tears had also begun to flow.

McGowan waited politely for the emotions to settle down, and then reached for the photographs. The company commander had added a group photo of the 229th to Tetra's personal effects, along with his own note of condolence. McGowan snatched his reading glasses from his pocket and perused the 120 tiny faces of smiling men taken just prior to their embarkation to Iraq. The images were small, but he recognized immediately the African American face of the soldier who had threatened to kill him before breaking his nose. Fighting his excitement, he held the photo so Monique could see it and pointed at Buckner. "Do you know this man?"

Mrs. Tetra squinted and shook her head. "That's my Vic," she said, pointing at a different member of the company, "standing next to him."

"Can you identify any of the men in the photo?" he asked. Darrow leaned over and raised an eyebrow: *Is that the man we're looking for?* McGowan nodded.

She shook her head. "Vic had a lot of friends."

"Did he write letters?"

"Not much." She opened the top drawer and fished out a small stack of envelopes, tied in a ribbon. McGowan immediately spotted one envelope that was smaller than the others, and he knew what it contained. He read the telegram quickly:

133A EDT OCT 10 03 MA022 M
M TLA004 WUB021 CTA009 MM CT WA024
XV GOVT PDB4
EXTRA
FAX WASHINGTON DC 4 1151P EDT
MRS MONIQUE TETRA SR DON'T DLVR
BTWN 10PM AND 6AM. DON'T PHONE
ROSEDALE RD, FREDERICK MD

THE SECRETARY OF THE ARMY HAS
ASKED ME TO EXPRESS HIS DEEPEST
REGRET THAT YOUR SON, VICTOR TET-
RA, DIED IN IRAQ ON OCTOBER 8, 2003
AS A RESULT OF A WOUND RECEIVED
DURING AN ENGAGEMENT WITH A
HOSTILE FORCE. PLEASE ACCEPT MY
DEEPEST SYMPATHY. THIS CONFIRMS
PERSONAL NOTIFICATION MADE BY A
REPRESENTATIVE OF THE SECRETARY
OF THE ARMY.

KENNETH R. RAWLEY MAJOR GENERAL
USA
F63 THE ADJUTANT GENERAL (1263)

McGowan handed the telegram to Darrow. She and Monique were crying steadily now, quietly passing the box of tissues back and forth. Only two letters remained in the stack, and McGowan read them quickly.

The writing was childish, the language unsophisticated, but the letters were thoughtful. They compelled McGowan to read, to finish each sentence, and to read them again, even though he understood everything the first time through. Trained as a soldier to observe and report what he saw, Tetra recorded the facts with simple eloquence, without judgment or opinion. *He could have been a reporter*, thought McGowan, unconcerned with Tetra's marginal literacy. He was disappointed, however, that Tetra mentioned no names or hometowns of his comrades, as if he believed his parents would be more interested in the sights and sounds of guard duty than in the personal aspects of his life or the lives of his friends. Still, the letters spoke of the dreariness of garrison life, the hellish conditions in which the prisoners lived, and disdain for the war and for Iraq. Tetra's letters were the same as those written by every soldier who ever served in combat.

While McGowan and Darrow pored over the letters, copying each one word for word into their notebooks, Monique fetched the coffee she had prepared for their visit. She sensed that Darrow's tears were sincere and she forgave the girl for being pretty and rich. She thought how nice it would be to introduce Darrow to her son, until she remembered that Vic was dead. So Tetra's mother simply watched them work, grateful that a reporter from New York found her son's letters so important.

Finally they finished. McGowan stretched his cramped fingers and drained the last of his coffee. As he rose to leave, Monique touched his arm. "They sent me this just yesterday," she said, handing McGowan an envelope containing

only a photocopy of an official army memo. The name of
the sender had been sanitized—blacked out. But the recipi-
ent was clear:

Date: 15 OCT 03
FROM: XXXXXXXXXX
TO: MG Robert Tannerbeck
             Deputy Commander
             CJTF-7, Baghdad

A REVIEW OF RECENT EVENTS AT
THE BAGHDAD CENTRAL CONFINE-
MENT FACILITY ABU GHRAIB LEAD-
ING TO THE DEATH OF SGT VICTOR
TETRA CONFIRM THAT SGT TETRA
WAS NOT INVOLVED IN EXTREME IN-
TERROGATIONS OF HIGH VALUE PRIS-
ONERS AND WAS NOT INVOLVED IN
PREVIOUSLY REPORTED ABUSES OF
DETAINEES.

"Mrs. Tetra," said McGowan, struggling to control his
excitement by forcibly slowing his speech, "is there any way
you could allow me to take this with me?"

Darrow and Mrs. Tetra both detected the sudden intensity in McGowan's voice. Darrow read it and asked, "What
does it mean, Doug?"

"This absolves Victor Tetra of any involvement with the
abuses at Abu Ghraib, but it also proves that General Tannerbeck, Deputy Dog at HQ in Baghdad, was fully aware of
them long before they were exposed. This implies that the
medal would have been withheld if Tetra had been among
the abusers."

Monique Tetra closed her eyes and nodded her head gently.

"I hate to ask," added McGowan, "but can I also borrow the group photo?"

"Yes," she said. "Take whatever you need."

They found Jacob Tetra back in his chair, staring into space with a beer in his hand. "Mr. Tetra," said McGowan, "I'm very sorry to intrude on you like this."

Jacob Tetra nodded.

To Darrow's surprise, McGowan stepped forward and knelt next to Mr. Tetra's chair. He mumbled quietly as Tetra stared ahead. To Darrow, both men seemed older than their true ages. Suddenly, Tetra's eyes locked onto McGowan's and neither of them spoke. Then the newsman rose and headed for the door. "C'mon, Angie. We've got a long drive ahead of us."

Darrow flopped against the seat of the car. "Thank God that's over. What the hell did you say to him?"

As McGowan started the engine, he refused to look at her. "I told him that it wasn't his fault that his son died. I told him that sons learn to become men by watching their fathers, and that given the way his son died, his old man must have done a good job of raising him. And then I told him it was time to get off his ass and start taking care of his wife."

They drove in silence for many miles. In the darkening car, his profile was powerful, devoid of the lines that betrayed his age in the light. She could see what he had looked like as a young man and wondered why no woman had managed to marry him. Darrow asked, "Doug, what was your father like?"

"A bastard."

"I guess that explains it, then."

He stared ahead for a moment, not getting the joke. Finally, he turned to her and smiled.

They chatted quietly, the conversation polite and boring until the subject turned to politics and religion and current events. Darrow was passionate, determined to change the world, and McGowan was inspired as well as amused by her idealism. For once, he listened more than he talked.

Conversation dwindled as they crossed the George Washington Bridge into Manhattan. McGowan followed Darrow's directions to her apartment building, where he killed the engine and rolled down the windows.

He said, "I'm glad we did this together."

"Me, too, boss."

"I was thinking about a good-night kiss, until you called me 'boss'." As he spoke, he leaned over the center console.

Darrow, alarmed, fumbled with the door release and hopped out of the vehicle. Turning back to the open window, she said, "I learned a lot today, Doug. I'll see you tomorrow, OK?"

Her scent lingered as McGowan watched her jog up the steps to her building. He slumped back in his seat, feeling more foolish than he had ever felt in his life.

CHAPTER 13

June 29, 2004 (Tuesday)
West Point

The United States Military Academy received the Class of 2008 in much the same way it had received Robert Tannerbeck when he was an eighteen-year-old boy in 1969. A shuttle of busses collected the cadet candidates from their parents in the parking lot of the football stadium, whisking them to the barracks complex where one bus-load of young civilians after another would be stripped of their clothes and shucked of their dignity while simultaneously being outfitted with new uniforms, haircuts, eyeglasses, name tags, and room assignments. Upper-class cadets ran the show while officers skulked in the background, Lieutenant General Tannerbeck, the Superintendent, among them.

When Buckner reported to the United States Military Academy at West Point on the sultry day of June 29, he knew better than most of his 1,500 classmates what to expect. He had been through basic training as an enlistee, and the first nine weeks of every cadet's West Point career—called "Beast Barracks" to those who endured it—were simply basic all over again. Buckner was not the only candidate with prior service or combat experience or a Purple Heart. Older, poorer, and tougher than most of their classmates, these candidates arrived without their parents. Buckner spotted a couple of other men in uniform and they hopped the next shuttle together. As the bus arrived at Thayer Hall, the folding doors swung open to accept a female member of the cadet cadre.

"Candidates, you have twenty seconds to exit this bus! Let's go!" The civilian candidates fell all over themselves to line up on the sidewalk, while the uniformed soldiers debarked from the bus like the veterans they were.

"Eyes straight ahead at all times!" barked the cadet, decked out in white gloves, polished brass, and spit-shined shoes that sparkled in the sun. "You may not speak unless spoken to. Stand at attention, hands cupped." She pointed a white-gloved finger at the windowless building directly in front of them. "Keep your eyes on my wall, nothing else." The vets had heard it all before, but Buckner stole a glance at the candidate to his right to see if the civilian found this to be as amusing as he did.

"What are you looking at?" bellowed the cadet. "Eyes on my WALL!"

Buckner complied calmly, but not before noticing that the boy next to him appeared ready to shit his pants. A memory flashed through Buckner's mind: the image of a T-shirted woman at Abu Ghraib shouting at one quivering prisoner among a dozen others.

The cadre herded them into the building, where the male and female candidates were sent to separate classrooms to exchange their civilian clothes for gym shorts and T-shirts. There was no privacy, no time to think as Buckner doffed his Class A uniform and slipped on a jock strap while the cadre barked at them to hurry it up. Every candidate had been instructed to report wearing comfortable black oxfords, and these they retained, rendering them ridiculous in their shorts and shoes, ultimate nerds.

Their tattoos were cataloged, something not necessary in Tannerbeck's day, when any form of body art was a ticket home. The Corps was more colorful now, but still composed mostly of high school hotshots, seasoned with a surprising assortment of born-again Christians, professional truck drivers, inner-city gangsters, and one Hindu monk. In their shorts, it was hard to tell them apart.

Buckner exhibited a tattoo on his bicep, the name "Lydia."

"Girlfriend?" asked the cadet at the register desk.

"No, sir."

The cadet looked up, expecting an explanation, but Buckner offered none. The man shrugged and sent Buckner back to his upper-class cadre, who continued his personal assembly line: haircut, uniform, and paperwork pursuant to his induction into the army and his contract with the United States Military Academy. After lunch, the candidates received rudimentary training on the procedures for saluting and marching and the proper position of attention. Buckner knew it all, and while the cadre raved at his civilian classmates, Buckner began to realize that Beast Barracks would be different from any of his previous army experience. He had completed his basic training at Ft. Benning, Georgia, where his fellow privates, all poor volunteers like himself, seeking adventure or training or simply a path out of the ghetto, had been trained like animals, with brute force and violence, and were somehow molded into soldiers. But Beast Barracks was basic training for white boys, most of them enthusiastic volunteers from good families and good schools and good neighborhoods. They reacted to absurd commands with reason and with questions, and tried to respond logically to illogical orders. And Buckner saw that not one of them knew a damned thing about anything.

As he was herded about by the ranting cadre, Buckner had never been so close to so many white people, and he had never felt more conscious of his color. He spotted a couple of other black men among the cadet candidates and was gratified to observe that they seemed more composed than the white boys, who had blown their cool completely. He could not imagine these kids in Iraq, giving orders under fire.

The day wore on until Bucker was finally delivered to a member of the cadre known as the Cadet in the Red Sash. As he took his place in formation, a boy fell into line behind him. With his head shaved, the boy's ears stuck out and his glasses threatened to slide off the tip of his nose. Buckner listened to the boy's panting until the Cadet in the Red Sash ordered Buckner forward.

Buckner stepped up to a joint line in the concrete, oozing with tar in the heat. With a snappy salute, he recited, "New Cadet Buckner reports to the Cadet in the Red Sash for the first time as ordered."

The man stared Buckner down for a moment, surprised that one of the cadet candidates had reported flawlessly on his first try. Unable to find anything to criticize in Buckner's posture or appearance, he returned Buckner's salute and assigned him a room in the barracks. As Buckner jogged away, the boy behind him stepped forward.

The Cadet in the Red Sash was the most terrifying human being that most of the New Cadets had ever met. When Joseph Boyer toed the tar line, he was as intimidated by the things the man did not do as he was by the things he did.

In heat that turned the tar joints in the concrete into trickles of oil, there were no sweat stains on the man's shirt, no subtle flexing of the knees, no hint of fatigue. He stood like a post, rooted to the concrete in an impossibly rigid position of attention, as surreal as the shimmers of heat that reflected off the pavement and rose around him. Neither the remorseless sun nor the endless parade of New Cadet Candidates caused the slightest waver in his posture or demeanor; the man was as stiff as if he had been in his uniform when it was starched.

When he spoke, no part of him moved except his mouth. Every word was enunciated with mechanical precision. His voice, though not loud, pierced every corner of the parade ground. He did not bellow, but projected his voice with as little distortion as a laser. At a hundred yards, the Cadet in the Red Sash could inject a whisper into a man's ear.

Boyer never saw his eyes, hidden beneath the spit-shined visor of his hat. The man was shorter than Boyer, but he never raised his head, never moved at all when he spoke.

"Step up to my line, Mister."

Boyer shuffled forward an inch, until his nose nearly touched the brim of the man's hat. "Sir! New Cadet Boyer reports to the Cadet in the Red Sash as ordered, sir!" He shouted at the top of his lungs, but his voice warbled.

"How many "sirs" do you think are standing here, Mister?"

"One, sir!"

"Only marines say 'sir' at the beginning and end of a statement. Understand?"

"Yes, sir!"

"Get to the end of the line and do it again."

Boyer returned to the queue, waiting while his classmates struggled with their own mistakes and fell back in line behind him. He worked his way to the Cadet in the Red Sash three times before he got it right. "Sir, New Cadet Boyer reports to the Cadet in the Red Sash for the first time as ordered."

"How old are you?"

"Seventeen, sir!" Boyer was one of the youngest members of his class. Barely a month out of high school, he would not reach voting age until October.

Boyer imagined that he heard a snort of disgust. He stood stock still, mimicking the man's extreme posture. Beads of sweat clung to the stubble of hair on his freshly shaved head, and by his feet, a duffel bag bulged with newly issued equipment.

"New Cadet, you are now a member of Charlie Company, Cadet Basic Training regiment. As a member of Charlie Company, you will be expected to maintain the highest standards of performance and appearance at all times. Is that clear?"

"Yes, sir!"

"Take this equipment to your room and wait there for further instructions." The man's head moved an iota, just enough to facilitate a final once-over. Suddenly the volume of his voice jumped, but he spoke effortlessly, as if someone had simply increased the power behind a stereo speaker. "GET OUT OF MY SIGHT, MISTER!"

The room was austere: ten feet wide, barely larger than a prison cell. Two closets flanked the doorway, and a row of windows on the opposite wall offered a view of the emerald parade ground and the Hudson River. The furniture consisted of two metal cots and two desks, which mirrored each other against the opposite walls. Closer to the door was a sink and a mirrored medicine cabinet. Except for the empty gun rack with slots for two M-14s, the room was not unlike those in a monastery.

The only object of interest to Boyer was his roommate, who sat at one desk staring back at him. The man held a black shoe in his left hand while he rubbed Kiwi polish on the toe with his right index finger. Already, the shoe rivaled those of the Cadet in the Red Sash in brilliance. He seemed disinterested in Boyer's entrance.

"I chose a rack," said Buckner, pointing at a duffel bag identical to Boyer's resting on one of the metal bunks. "But I don't have a preference, so you can take your pick if you want." Without further conversation, the man returned his attention to his shoe.

Boyer tossed his bag on the other bed, conscious that his roommate had called it a "rack." He also noted that his roommate had the fully developed musculature of a man, causing Boyer to be immediately self-conscious of his adolescent shoulders and spindly legs. He struggled to emulate the expressionless mask of the Cadet in the Red Sash, but alarm welled up within him. The future was complex and uncertain; doubts were already entering his mind as to whether he had done the right thing in accepting his appointment to the Academy. The last thing he needed now was a Negro roommate.

Boyer did not consider himself a racist. Indeed, he was offended by the concept of discrimination and he empathized with the civil rights movement. But there were not many black people in Wilbraham, Massachusetts, and Boyer had never met the two black students in his high school. His only exposure to the black population of America was through the media, in a litany of articles about poverty, welfare, gang violence, hip-hop music, and gangster rap. Even on a personal level, his experience with the movement for equal rights had been unpleasant. His appointment to the Academy had been delayed while his congressman sought a qualified black candidate. Fortunately, there had been none.

But someone, however, had obviously had found a qualified black candidate, and it was apparent that he was to be Boyer's roommate. Boyer had hoped for someone like himself: a middle-class Eagle Scout from a suburban community with an A average and a passion for chess. West Point was going to be difficult enough without culture shock.

"Room, ATTEN-SHUN!" Boyer's roommate sprang to his feet and tucked his chin down against his Adam's apple in a brace more severe than even that of the Cadet in the Red Sash.

Boyer spun around to discover the doorway occupied by an upperclassman that radiated foreboding authority. Following Buckner's example, Boyer gathered his lanky body into a vague position of attention. He pushed his glasses back onto the bridge of his nose, awaiting developments.

"You!" bellowed the man. "Goofball!" He stared at Boyer in a way wholly different from the inscrutable Cadet in the Red Sash. Like all members of the upper classes, his uniform was impeccable, and his manner oozed contempt. His eyes zeroed in on Boyer as if he were a target. A sneer pulled back his lips, revealing teeth as straight and square as everything else about him. "Come to attention when an upperclassman enters your room!" He also had The Voice.

Boyer made himself rigid until the man was at last satisfied enough to look away and consult his clipboard.

The upperclassman turned his attention to Buckner for a moment, noticing the perfect posture and the single shining shoe. "Prior service, Mister?"

"Yes, sir!"

The man leveled his eyes on Buckner and faced him so closely that Boyer thought their lips might touch. "You look pretty sharp, Buckner. But your roommate is the biggest bozo I ever saw, and he's your baggage. You help him out, understand?"

"Yes, sir!"

The man walked to the center of the room and lifted Boyer's duffel bag, dumping the contents onto the floor in a shower of shirts, trousers, shoe polish, rain gear, gloves, hats, underwear, and toiletries.

"My name is Matterhorn. I am your squad leader, and I shall control every aspect of your lives for the next two months." He sorted through the items on the floor with his foot, kicking aside the shirt he wanted, followed by a pair of gray trousers, white gloves, a gray wheel cap and belt. "That's the uniform for the rest of the day. Put it on and line up against the wall in the hallway. You have five minutes."

Matterhorn marched to the door. Without looking back, he said, "Don't ever leave your door open again, gentlemen." The door slammed so hard that the mirror on the medicine cabinet swung open on its hinges.

Boyer could not see his classmates because his eyes were fixed on Matterhorn. The squad struggled to keep the backs of their necks and the smalls of their backs against the wall in the hallway outside their rooms while Matterhorn instructed them in the rudiments of saluting and marching. He adjusted their hats and tucked in their shirts and berated them with blistering profanities that Boyer had never heard before. At last presentable, Matterhorn surprised them again by facing the first boy in line and demanding, "What were you famous for?"

There were ten of them, nine men and a woman, every member of the squad a high school standout. West Point scoured the land for the hometown heroes, the natural leaders, packing the ranks of the Corps with more football captains and all-Americans than any college in the country. The squads were assigned by height, and Matterhorn's squad was heavy with basketball players. Donovan, the tallest woman in the class at five feet eleven inches, had been an all-state fencing champion. Two boys were football studs. Boyer was the only member of his squad not to have been a varsity athlete, having achieved his appointment through academic distinction.

As he surveyed his new squad, Matterhorn asked the question of each of them. The question was phrased in the past tense, to remind them that they were now famous for nothing.

"I was my class valedictorian and chess champion of Massachusetts!" Boyer squeaked, as his new glasses slipped down his nose. Matterhorn practically snickered as he pushed the black plastic TEDs-Tactical Eye Devices-back onto Boyer's face with his index finger. The squad leader moved on, not even bothering to put the question to Buckner.

Outside, the ten members of Matterhorn's squad were herded into a company of 150. Nine such companies formed on the concrete apron which fronted the barracks. A full military band played music by Sousa, and flags moved gently in the breeze. From the front rank, Boyer watched the tourists gather along the route to Trophy Point, where his mother had photographed him the day before. She was in the crowd somewhere, and he was eager to march past her. His father was there, too, checking the batteries in his video camera and sporting a new West Point golf shirt and baseball cap.

Around the periphery of the phalanx, upperclassmen in perfect summer white-over-gray uniforms patrolled the lines like border collies. From a distance, the crowd could not hear their corrections and insults.

"Keep your eyes straight ahead, civilians." Everyone was a civilian until sworn in, pathetic by the standards of the cadre. "If I want you to see something, I'll put it in front of you."

The music stopped, the insults ceased, and, for a moment, silence prevailed. Then an upperclassman wearing a red sash commanded, "Forward, march!"

The band struck up a stirring march and the company surged forward. The cadre resumed their final vitupera-tions until they reached the street and wheeled to their left to pass through the gauntlet of spectators. The upperclass-men ceased talking and found their stride, and Boyer found himself gliding in cadence with the music. No one would have guessed that one day earlier these had been teenage civilians, hanging out at the mall.

They took the oath of allegiance on a promontory over-looking the Hudson River, fifty miles upstream from New York City. Here, mountains pinched the river into a narrow channel, and an oceangoing tanker beat a frothy wake as it squeezed through against the current. The foliage on the mountainsides was saturated with chlorophyll, green be-yond belief, and the sky, fluorescent in the late afternoon sun, reflected off the water. Later, Boyer's memories of West Point would be colored gray, like the uniforms, the winter skies, the defoliated hills, and the granite buildings, but as he raised his right hand to swear fealty to the Constitution, he was overwhelmed by the glory of the setting and the ex-quisite solemnity of the moment.

A group of commissioned officers waited for the 1,500 new members of the Corps of Cadets. They stood at somber attention, immaculate in gold braid and full dress uniform, flanked by battle flags and the Stars and Stripes that billowed gently in the breeze. Eagles and oak leaves gleamed from their epaulets, and three men wore stars, glinting in the sun.

Lieutenant General Robert Tannerbeck stepped to the microphone. In his finery, the Superintendent projected the squared-away image of a military man. He was taller than the men around him, straight as the salvaged flagpole from the USS *Maine* that now supported the American flag that fluttered on Trophy Point. His face was unscarred, but strong and sad enough to communicate a familiarity with combat. With drawn-back shoulders that alluded to a profession founded upon raw physical courage, there was no softness to him, not even in his eyes that squinted in the sun. Small and clear and as blue as the sky, they reached out to each of the New Cadets and claimed them.

The general spoke briefly to the families, telling them gently but firmly that their sons and daughters now belonged to the U.S. Army. Without further ado, he led the induction ceremony. Following Tannerbeck's prompts, Boyer recited along with the others:

"I, Joseph Boyer, do solemnly swear that I will support the Constitution of the United States, and bear true allegiance to the National Government; that I will maintain and defend the sovereignty of the United States, paramount to any and all allegiance, sovereignty, or fealty I may owe to any state or country whatsoever; and that I will at all times obey the legal orders of my superior officers, and the Uniform Code of Military Justice."

The wail of a bugle knifed across the plain, followed by a preparatory flourish of drums. The cadet commander issued the order to pass in review, and the band took its cue. Unimpressed by the New Cadets' induction into the army, the cadre sniped at them under their breath, even as the column passed again between the rows of applauding spectators. They entered the shadow of the barracks, and the ferocity of the upper-class invectives increased in inverse proportion to the sound of the fading music. Behind the bleak walls, the earlier humiliations of the day paled as the cadre turned on them with tongues sharper than bayonets. One by one, the New Cadet companies passed under the barracks' sally ports and through the looking glass into a world they had never imagined.

CHAPTER 14

June 29, 2004 (Tuesday)
West Point

The Hellcats stayed on the field long after the last company of cadets disappeared behind the granite walls of the barracks. The band switched from a marching cadence to an entertaining martial swing while the crowd thinned out and the tourists made their way back to their cars.

The reviewing party relaxed and made small talk, while lieutenants and captains stood by awaiting orders. General Tannerbeck chatted with the undersecretary of the army. Mrs. Tannerbeck, escorted by the general's aide, excused herself and rushed to her quarters in order to oversee the last-minute preparations for the cocktail party which was to precede a reception at the Officers' Club. The generals and distinguished guests followed moments later, an impressive parade in their own right.

As they approached the Superintendent's quarters, Tannerbeck sensed something familiar about a civilian who stood on the sidewalk, watching him. It was not unusual for members of Tannerbeck's previous commands to pay their respects, even after leaving the army. Obviously, this man was no longer on active duty; his hair was over his ears and he wore a cheap suit under a rumpled raincoat. The general approached the man directly, with the high-ranking entourage in tow.

"General Tannerbeck," said the man. It was a polite statement, not a question.

"Where do I know you from, soldier?"

"Sorry, General. I took the oath as a marine. Doug McGowan, *Citizen Times*."

Tannerbeck had never met McGowan or seen his face, but he recognized the name immediately. He seemed smaller than the general had expected, though the intensity in his eyes commanded attention. McGowan held his ground while the dignitaries in Tannerbeck's entourage filed by. The general urged them along, adding with a smile, "The press cannot be denied."

"I've been trying to arrange an interview with you for three weeks," said McGowan.

"Not interested," Tannerbeck replied.

"I'm an editor now."

"Congratulations."

"It's my reward for having the shit beat out of me at Abu Ghraib." McGowan read irritation on Tannerbeck's face, but detected no fear or surprise. "We both know what happened there," said McGowan.

"I can't discuss it with you, McGowan. You'll have to take it up with the PIO office at the Pentagon."

"Already did. Those idiots are hanging on to the party line for dear life, all that crap about a few bad apples. You know as well as I do that the abuses at Abu Ghraib were authorized at higher levels."

Tannerbeck turned to leave. "Sorry, McGowan. I have no comment."

McGowan reached into his pocket and withdrew a sheet of paper. "I have proof that you knew that things were not right at Abu Ghraib."

"Most reporters wouldn't know the truth if God whispered it directly in their ear," said Tannerbeck, although he accepted the document and started to read.

McGowan smiled good-naturedly. "Why would someone send you a memo to reassure you that Sgt. Tetra was not involved in the 'extreme interrogations' if you didn't know about them? It sounds to me like you must have inquired about Tetra, because you didn't want to award a Silver Star to a war criminal."

Tannerbeck lowered the document, baffled. "I have guests waiting, McGowan." He knew he had never seen the memo before.

"C'mon," said McGowan, "you know I'm a good reporter. I let the facts speak for themselves. Unless you are guilty of something, why not talk to me?"

"I've seen what your newspaper does with facts, McGowan. One of your staff members reported a cadet parade as an 'armed demonstration.' And an editorial branded the entire West Point class of '03 as 'accomplices' in an illegal war in Iraq," said Tannerbeck. "Well, seven members of that class have already died there while your reporters snicker."

"Those were not my stories, and there won't be any more reporting like that."

"Then report what you saw here today: fine young men and women dedicating their lives to the defense of their country."

"Our readers want to know about Abu Ghraib."

"Submit your requests through channels."

"I have. The army covers its tracks pretty well. They have arrested a few of the alleged 'bad apples,' but I know of at

least two more men out there who have never been identified. I plan to identify them so the army can bring them to
justice. That is what we all want, isn't it?"

"You have a name?"

"Not yet."

Tannerbeck merely nodded and tugged gently on his
earlobe. Never emotional, he could shut down his face
when necessary. It hardened now, no hint of light escaping
his eyes. "I have guests waiting," he repeated. "Excuse me."

McGowan watched as Tannerbeck met his wife on the
porch of his quarters and slipped his arm around her waist.
He had received no help from the general, and had not really expected any, but McGowan had sensed a brief shadow
of worry that had passed through Tannerbeck's mind. Instinct told him that it was not yet time to destroy Tannerbeck by publishing what he had discovered. He had showed
his hand, and he bet the army would now show theirs.

CHAPTER 15

July 4, 2004 (Sunday)
Washington, DC

Although General Piersal made a point of looking like a civilian, he had served in uniform for too long to blend in easily. He dressed for the part in penny loafers and a golf shirt, and his hair was just long enough behind his ears that he could be mistaken for a middle-class business-man. But he waited now in the back corner of a bar too far removed from the beaten path for any white-collar patron. The bartender made him right away: government.

He was halfway through his second beer when a man approached the table and casually sat down.

Piersal said, "I was getting worried."

"You have a talent for clandestine meetings, General. How did you find this place?"

"It's my business. I like dark places."

"I feel as white as an iceberg in here."

Piersal laughed a little harder than the joke merited in an effort to humor the aide to Senator William DuFossey, the Democratic candidate for president. He signaled to the bartender for another beer as he gave Donald Ross a careful once-over. Although they had chatted before at various diplomatic functions, it had taken Piersal some time to warm up to Ross, perhaps because they were so similar. Both men were about power, each of them convinced of the righteousness of their views and determined to implement them any way they could. After months of coy flirtation, they were ready now to commit to a partnership in which two men who trusted no one would have to trust each other.

"Icebergs eventually melt into the all-inclusive sea. Isn't that what our party is all about, equality for all?"

Something about Piersal filled Donald Ross with insecurity, and he affected a Machiavellian air to conceal it. "The party doesn't give a damn about anything except winning the election."

"Of course," said Piersal, with an enigmatic smile.

"Once we're in office, we can save the poor and balance the budget and get the hell out of Iraq. You won't have a problem with peace, will you?"

"I view my profession as a guarantor of peace, not an instrument of war."

"I wish more men in your profession felt that way."

"They will soon enough. Iraq is driving more and more hardliners into retirement. Nothing like losing a war to make a soldier embrace peace."

"Victory would be a disaster for our party, but the voters are ready to kick the bums out as long as casualties keep mounting." The aide checked his watch, as if the war was scheduled to end in the next few minutes.

"The lives of a few good men are a small price to pay to keep this conflict going long enough for us to win the election, eh?"

"Of course not. You know that's not what I meant."

"We're all bastards, Mr. Ross. Your party wants the presidency and I want my next star. And I've put my ass on the line to help you get it. If your man loses, the warriors in the Pentagon will consolidate their hold on the administration and I'll be put out to pasture."

"American politics has become an all-or-nothing game, General. You threw in with us. You'll be destroyed with the rest of us if we lose. You'll be the next chairman of the Joint Chiefs if we win. I haven't forgotten our deal."

"I have no doubts. But you'll need my support after the election even more than you do now," warned Piersal. "Du-Fossey has almost no support among the Pentagon brass."

"I'm sure we will find ways to support each other, General. Like the information you sent over about General Tannerbeck."

"Don't misconstrue my actions. While it is true that there is no love lost between Tannerbeck and myself, my reasons for bringing this incident to your attention are purely professional. Tannerbeck has 'Joint Chiefs' written all over him, but he is a Neanderthal like the rest of them; a threat to the peace process. His disregard for the Geneva Conventions, and his determination to settle conflict with violence, are bad enough, but his future influence throughout the Pentagon will undermine every effort to disengage our troops. It was men like him that got us into the war in Iraq in the first place."

"That's baloney, General. Our civilian politicians got us there. Even I know that, although I certainly have no fondness for men in uniform—present company excepted, of course. But what would you have me do about this?"

"Initiate an investigation. There's more to this story than meets the eye."

"Like what?"

"I have become aware of further details regarding Abu Ghraib. The story is starting to fade, but this is our chance to keep it in the limelight, to further tar the military—and the administration—with the abuses that occurred there. We have a witness to the abuses—an abuser himself—who can confirm that Tannerbeck was aware of the crimes committed there, and in fact cut a deal to keep this man silent. It seems that some people have gone to a lot of trouble to keep him hidden, including reassignment to West Point, where Tannerbeck can keep an eye on him."

The senator's man checked his watch again, for the time spent finding Piersal had made him late for his next appointment back on Capitol Hill, six blocks and a world away from Anacostia. "West Point? The American people worship that school. We can't be perceived as going after an icon like that."

"I don't propose to attack West Pont; I propose to defend it. Accuse the administration of compromising the bastion of Duty, Honor, Country to conceal their own horrific acts. We'll show the voters that nothing is sacred to these people. And after the election, we can reform the values taught there to be more international, more negotiable. We can wean our military of its outmoded warrior spirit and keep a leash on the dogs of war, men like Tannerbeck."

The aide was not sure if Piersal really believed what he was saying or whether he was saying it because he thought that it was what Senator DuFossey would want to hear. He hoped it was the latter, for he preferred cynics to ideologues, regardless of party. "This is fascinating. But it will take more than another congressional investigation to get people's attention. We need to air this in the press where it can be sensationalized, not in some obscure hearing room in front of a bunch of sympathetic Republican senators." Ross swallowed the last of his beer and stood up to leave.

The men shook hands. "Just keep reading *The Citizen Times*, sir. You'll get all the sensation you need." Piersal remained seated while the senator's aide walked quickly to the door. The general dropped a modest tip on the table and followed a few minutes later.

CHAPTER 16

August 2, 2004 (Monday)
West Point

Boyer did suffer culture shock during his first week at West Point, but it had nothing to do with Buckner. Like all New Cadets, he was stripped of his brief history and social standing until all that remained was the raw essence of his character and personality. He was absorbed into a society where his life before Beast Barracks counted for nothing.

Matterhorn was everywhere, correcting their posture, inspecting their rooms, monitoring their hygiene. Unnoticed in the misery was the fact that he was also a teacher. His squad learned the proper way to eat, speak, and march, how to make their beds, shine their shoes, and shoulder their rifles. An enormous amount of time was spent learning to tuck in their shirt tails. There was nothing nurturing about Matterhorn, who dubbed them Dull Squad.

Little time was spent in their rooms, except to sleep, and some members of the squad barely knew the name of their roommate. They took each others' measure in public, where Matterhorn aired their failures with withering humiliation and group punishments. The spirit of cooperation became the formula for success, and persistently inept members of the squad became targets of group resentment.

One member of Dull Squad, a huge boy with a quick mind and extraordinary athletic prowess, was an all-American linebacker. At six foot five, with 240 pounds of muscle that draped his body like armor plating, he barely fit within the Academy's size and weight limits. The football coaches wondered why an athlete with a shot at the pros would consider an education at the United States Military Academy, but Lowry's father was a West Point alumnus, which was explanation enough.

Matterhorn, however, was unimpressed with Lowry's credentials or promise, for, like most cadets, Matterhorn had also been a talented athlete in high school. He spotted in Lowry the smugness of a boy who felt he had the system licked, who tolerated Matterhorn's impositions as a necessary irritant to be endured only until football season started. The fact that Lowry could run faster and march better than his classmates, and could handle rifle manual as if he were twirling a baton, only seemed to infuriate Matterhorn. And when Lowry would stare back during one of Matterhorn's profane tirades with a look that asked *Are you done yet?*, it drove Matterhorn berserk.

But Lowry was only one of Matterhorn's problems. The other was Buckner, whose taciturn manner contrasted sharply with Lowry's. While Lowry at least made an effort to support his classmates, Buckner shepherded only Boyer, and then only enough to keep them both out of trouble. Lowry and Buckner were destined to be enemies, for Lowry's sanctimonious efforts to lead were frustrated by the fact that the squad gravitated toward Buckner, who made no effort at all.

As squad leader, it was Matterhorn's duty to mold his plebes into an interdependent and committed group that acted together, thought together, and watched each other's backs. It was not acceptable to allow two men to go it alone. So while Matterhorn's invective fell on everyone, he reserved special vituperations for the two sharpest plebes in his squad, pitting them against each other, knowing that one would destroy the other.

Prior to meals, the cadets formed on the apron in front of the mess hall, rows of plebes at rigid attention, scrutinized by tired members of the cadre who circled the New Cadets like hungry wolves. To his surprise, Matterhorn found little to complain about as he looked Dull Squad up and down. Their posture was perfect, their BDUs immaculate, all creases and starch. Ten pairs of boots sparkled like diamonds, though none so lustrous as Lowry's or Buckner's.

Nevertheless, Matterhorn refused to be satisfied. "These boots look like crap!" He paced the length of the squad, stopping at Boyer. Without bothering to glance down, he said, "Buckner! Why aren't you teaching your roommate how to shine his boots?"

"No excuse, sir!"

"You don't give a damn, do you Buckner? You and Lowry are a pair of prima donnas, but he at least helps his roommate shine his boots!"

Buckner said nothing while Matterhorn stared him down. Suddenly, Lowry spoke up. "Sir, I'll volunteer to teach everyone how to shine shoes tonight in the latrine!"

Matterhorn sprang at him, his nose an inch from Lowry's, his carotid artery bulging. "Who the fuck do you think you are, Mr. Lowry?" The presence of women at West Point had tempered the level of profanity permitted among the cadre, and Matterhorn reserved his expletives for moments of particular dissatisfaction.

"Cooperate and graduate, sir. I just want to help my classmates!"

Matterhorn inhaled deeply, as if to explode with debasements. Fourth classmen were allowed three answers—yes, sir; no, sir; and no excuse, sir—and such impertinence was an invitation for abuse. Dull Squad waited for the explosion, but instead Matterhorn turned to Buckner and said pleasantly, "What do you think of that idea, Buckner?"

"Sir," said Buckner, "if I wanted my boots to look like Mr. Lowry's, I just wouldn't shine 'em for a week."

Upperclassmen in nearby squads burst into laughter, while their plebes struggled to suppress snickers. Even members of Dull Squad bit their lips as Matterhorn glanced from Buckner to Lowry and back again. Then, he calmly stepped on the glass-like toes of Buckner's boots and twisted his foot, as if putting out a cigarette. Finally, he announced, "Since Mr. Lowry has the shiniest boots in the squad, he will teach the rest of you his superlative techniques. There will be no liberty on Sunday until after Mr. Lowry's class on spit-shining shoes."

The damage to the shine on Buckner's boots became irrelevant a few hours later, when the Third New Cadet Company began its midnight hike to the rifle range. Matterhorn had known from the beginning that a few minutes of tramping through the woods at night would erase the gleam on everyone's boots. The route meandered through the wilderness of the military reservation, and for the first time since reporting to West Point, Boyer felt like a soldier. He was miserable, as men in combat were supposed to be, treading through swamps in the wild darkness. *I am bad news,* he thought, relishing the feel of his M-16 and the company of other dangerous men like himself, invisible and silent in the pitch-black night. But as they waded deeper into the quagmire, Boyer became aware of soldiers around him besides his classmates, the ghosts of West Pointers who had trod this trail before, who sneered at the pretensions of callow boys with blank cartridges in their magazines. Boyer accepted their reproach with a nervous sigh, and a shiver of apprehension that when the time came to fire real ammo at a living target, he might not measure up to their expectations.

The swamp was a slurry of mulch, like wading through oatmeal. Twelve inches of mud sucked at his boots, and rain trickled down the back of Boyer's neck. But worse was the darkness; the only thing Boyer could see was the tiny fluorescent patch stapled to the back of Buckner's Kevlar helmet ahead of him. Each New Cadet wore the patch, turning Dull Squad into a silent row of glowing postage stamps bobbing in the night.

They held their rifles above the water to keep them dry, although the rain mocked the effort. The weapons also blocked the vines and branches, which flipped back into their faces, invisible slaps in the darkness. Boyer brought up the rear, an assignment reserved for the men with the longest legs who could wade through the muck most easily. If a man fell behind at the end of the squad, he could disappear into the night.

Despite his height, Boyer found the going difficult. Depending upon the obstacles in their path, Dull Squad bunched up or surged forward, accordion-like, and Boyer found himself standing still or racing to catch up with the bobbing fluorescent patch on Buckner's helmet.

Suddenly, a root snared Boyer's foot. While struggling to wrench it free, he lost sight of the faint light ahead of him, and as he turned around in the disorienting blackness, he realized with a bolt of forlorn panic that he was alone.

"Buckner!" Boyer whispered in the darkness, so softly that he could barely hear himself over the gentle hiss of the rain falling through the foliage. He called louder.

"Buckner!"

Still louder he called, until he could hear his voice echo through the swamp. Boyer waited, but there was no response. Unsure of any direction, blind in the darkness and unable to hear anything but the rain, he could feel his skin crawl as real fear began to set in.

"Buckner!"

"*Shut up.*"

Boyer felt Buckner grab the shoulder strap of his rucksack and then tug him forward at breakneck speed. The reassuring sight of Buckner's fluorescent patch floated in front of him as they splashed through the water, desperate to catch up with the others before Matterhorn discovered they were missing. Finally, a glow materialized in front of them, wraithlike, and Boyer rejoiced that Buckner had found the rest of Dull Squad, the tail end bunched together again while the men in front struggled on. Buckner released his grip.

"Thanks," whispered Boyer.

"How many times do I have to tell you to shut up, Boyer?"

Gradually, the swamp became shallower. An hour later, the muddy, soaked men struggled onto dry land. Sunrise followed, igniting a plume of fog up and down the Hudson

Valley. Imperceptibly, the darkness gave way to light, but visibility remained limited to the dim figure of the man ahead. The New Cadets were cold and exhausted, but their spirits rose when the trail turned to gravel, crunching solidly under their boots. The firing range could not be far ahead, where a field kitchen waited with a hot breakfast. Boyer hiked happily downhill, relishing the feel of his weapon and the mud in his boots, despite the doubts that continued to grow within him.

The squads worked together at the rifle range, where a line of twenty firing pits faced three hundred yards of grass and weeds and shrubbery. Boyer took his position eagerly, reverently placing his weapon on the sandbag in front of him. He had never fired anything more powerful than a BB gun, and he itched to pull the trigger on a truly deadly weapon. Buckner lounged in his firing hole with professional insouciance, while Matterhorn patrolled behind the firing line helping other squad leaders assign their members to act as spotters, one to each shooter. As the spotters moved into position, Boyer noticed that one man, an African American New Cadet named Richard, shuffled his position in line so as to be the spotter for Buckner. Boyer was certain that the two black men did not know each other, but they greeted each other with a quick dap, like old friends.

The morning was devoted to zeroing their weapons, adjusting their sights to compensate for each rifle's unique variation of trigger tension and previous settings of elevation and windage. In the foxhole next to Buckner, Boyer struggled to place his shots in a tight group on his paper target, but his pounding heart and excited breathing conspired to throw his bullets in a wild pattern. Buckner zeroed his carbine with three wicked shots, and then entertained the enlisted instructors by drawing a face on his target, one bullet hole each for the eyes and nose, followed by a row across the bottom to represent the mouth. Richard cracked jokes and called out impossible targets ("Mosquito at two hundred yards! Hit!"), which everyone found hilarious. On the other side of Buckner, Lowry fired one neat shot group after another, prompting Richard to observe that Lowry's shot groups were tighter than his asshole.

"He shoots that gun even better'n he shines his shoes," quipped Buckner, loud enough for Lowry to hear. Everyone laughed, including Lowry's own spotter, and Lowry's face turned red. Matterhorn observed the scene sternly, but did not step in to enforce Fourth Class decorum. The range belonged to the enlisted instructors, each a combat veteran who regarded upperclassmen and plebes with equal disdain.

They fired for score in the afternoon; serious business, where any man who failed to qualify earned a ticket home. Targets popped up at various intervals, sometimes as close as fifty yards; sometimes at 300. As the exercise progressed, Buckner maintained a perfect score while bantering with Richard and slapping high-fives with each hit. Boyer struggled, unable to control his breathing or his TEDs as they slipped down his sweaty nose.

Aware of the scores, Matterhorn had migrated to Boyer's firing position.

"You have two targets remaining, Boyer. You gotta score with both shots, or you're out of here." Matterhorn had already concluded that Boyer was not West Point material, but he was nevertheless responsible for the overall performance of his squad. "Calm down," he cautioned. "You're holding that weapon like it's going to attack you."

Buckner turned his head to look at Boyer and saw the panic on his roommate's face. He tapped Richard on the knee and nodded in Boyer's direction, eliciting a smug snort.

The next targets popped up at fifty yards, all quickly dispatched in each lane except Boyer's. After an eternity, Boyer fired and the target dropped.

The final target appeared. Spotters pointed and called out the range.

"Three hundred!"

Slowly this time, the New Cadets aimed and fired, the brittle crack of the high-powered .223 rounds gradually reaching an irregular crescendo like microwaved popcorn. Many missed, for the drop was considerable and numerous targets were barely discernable in the shadows cast by the trees at the back of the range. Two targets remained: Boyer's and Buckner's. Boyer fired first, Buckner a split second later. Boyer's target fell; Buckner's did not.

Richard jumped up from his stool, dismayed that Buckner had failed to achieve a perfect score with a miss on the final shot. But Buckner nodded toward Boyer, smiling now, high-fiving with his spotter as Matterhorn gave him a pat on the helmet before glancing quickly at Buckner.

"Damn," muttered Richard. "Sylvester don't even know," he said, using the term he had learned from Buckner, who had learned it from his father, the language of black men in Vietnam who considered all white boys to be weak sisters and named them all Sylvester.

As the enlisted instructors converged upon Buckner to tease him for missing the final shot, it went unnoticed that the only perfect score of the day belonged to Lowry.

The final magazine was dedicated to free fire, one of the few occasions when cadets were allowed to blast away at whatever they wanted, with no thought to score or accuracy. More than simple fun time, the twenty rounds served to familiarize the New Cadets with the kick and travel of a high-powered rifle fired in rapid bursts. The newly qualified marksmen peered downrange through the iron sights of their M-16s, picking out targets and anticipating the command to commence firing.

A range monitor held up a green flag. "Clear on the left! Clear on the right! Clear on the firing line!" For three seconds, silence prevailed across the range. "Commence fire!"

The crash of gunfire split the air as twenty New Cadets blasted bushes and trees and pop-up targets, every fifth round a tracer streaking and ricocheting in a low-level fireworks display. Suddenly, at 200 yards, a deer bolted from behind a blasted tree stump, bounding like a rabbit across the range. With thoughtless gusto, every rifleman swung the muzzle of his weapon toward the terrified animal, instinctively determined to put his deadly weapon to the use for which it was designed: to kill.

The instructors responded as quickly as the New Cadets, but their commands to "Cease fire!" were inaudible in the barrage.

Boyer emptied his clip at the moving target, but the deer seemed charmed. It sprinted one step ahead of the tracers which kicked up spurts of soil behind it. Then Buckner fired one shot, lost in the din. The deer somersaulted in mid-leap, continuing through the air in a shallow arc. It landed in a heap as the firing stopped, magazines empty, bolts locked back, the smell of cordite drifting in the air.

"Cease fire!" Their faces mottled with fury, the enlisted instructors and upperclassmen alike finally broke through the noise and enforced fire discipline.

Matterhorn yanked each member of Dull Squad from his foxhole by the back of his collar. They stood at rigid attention for an hour while Matterhorn and the range instructors took turns berating them with language more violent than anything Boyer had yet heard, demanding to know who had killed the deer. Matterhorn focused his attention on Buckner while the instructors spread their venom more equally, but in the end nobody admitted to the fatal shot.

An instructor retrieved the deer and dumped it at their feet. The largest dead animal that Boyer had ever seen was a bird, and the sight of the corpse made him shiver. Barely larger than a dog, the deer seemed smaller than it had through the sights of his rifle. It lay there, stiffening by the moment, eyes glassy, its short fur matted and streaked with blood. Boyer hid his revulsion and stared straight ahead.

An enlisted instructor detected a hint of unease in another member of Dull Squad, the fencer Donovan, and the instructors circled her like sharks.

"If you can't handle this, sweetheart, what the hell you gonna do in Iraq?"

Another instructor approached, rolling a fifty-five-gallon oil drum which had been used to support pumpkins in a demonstration of wound ballistics. They placed the drum in front of Donovan, then picked her up and dumped her in headfirst. The deer was stuffed in after her and the lid slammed shut.

Matterhorn approached the instructors, while the other upperclassmen observed at a distance as they squared away their own squads. The three enlisted marksmen faced him together, sensing that they had overstepped their authority.

But the relationship between cadets and enlisted men was ill-defined, characterized by the enlisted instructors' sense of amusement toward the cadets who, theoretically, outranked them. Even upper-class cadets were intimidated by the technical skills and combat experience of the enlisted instructors, and rarely did a cadet issue a command to any enlisted man.

"You guys can't do that," said Matterhorn quietly. The sound of gagging escaped from the drum.

The instructors shuffled their feet and glanced at each other. Matterhorn was a towering authority to Dull Squad, but without a CIB he was still an unblooded wannabe to the men he would presume to command. "This range is our responsibility," replied one man, a sergeant E4 and a qualified sniper with twelve kills to his credit. "You find out who killed my deer, sir, and we'll let her out."

A silent standoff ensued, while the instructors strengthened their resolve and Matterhorn contemplated his duty. At last Matterhorn returned to Dull Squad, humiliated, where he paced the length of the squad, his hands on his hips, contempt pouring from his eyes. Buckner kept his eyes on the oil drum, surprised that Matterhorn—not the sort of man to back down easily—had not taken a stronger stand. He knew that Donovan would be released as soon as a commissioned officer found out what was going on, and the instructors would have hell to pay for both their abuse of a trainee and their insubordination. Matterhorn understood that as well as anyone, and Buckner wondered what was going on in his squad leader's mind.

"We'll stand here all night, and all day tomorrow, and all day after that, until someone admits to shooting that deer," said Matterhorn, his voice unusually calm. Boyer was sure he meant it, but Buckner glanced at the afternoon sky.

Army schedules were inflexible, especially at West Point. Dinner was in three hours, reckoned Buckner, and even if Matterhorn didn't allow them to eat, he at least had to have his squad present and accounted for. Dull Squad would be on the trucks headed for the barracks in two hours, he concluded.

Matterhorn suddenly stepped in front of the sun, the visor of his cap an inch from Buckner's helmet. He could not ask Buckner directly if he had shot the deer, for using a cadet's honor against himself was a violation of the Code. So he screamed to the squad, "There is only one man in this squad good enough to shoot a running target at 200 yards, and I want that cowardly son of a bitch to step forward! *Who shot the goddamned deer?*" He bellowed the question a dozen times directly into Buckner's face, each time an accusation. Buckner stared straight ahead and watched the sun begin to set, his thoughts drifting with memories of Abu Ghraib even as Matterhorn howled at him. How different was Matterhorn, he wondered, using the torment of Donovan to find out who shot the deer, from himself, kicking a man to death to find out who smuggled a weapon into Camp Vigilant? With each repetition of the question, Matterhorn's intention became clearer: Buckner would confess to save his classmate and thereby commit himself to the team, or he would earn the scorn of his classmates and surrender his leadership to Lowry. Matterhorn placed the brim of his cap against Buckner's helmet, and eye to eye with Buckner, he whispered, "What are you going to do, Buckner? Are you a soldier, or just some punk sent here by mistake?"

Where are the officers, thought Buckner, *and where had they been in Abu Ghraib?* In the silence between Matterhorn's queries, the sound of vomiting escaped through the holes in the oil drum. Buckner felt his resolve waiver, but as he opened his mouth to confess, Lowry suddenly bellowed, "Sir! I shot the deer!"

Dull Squad made it to dinner on time, though Donovan resigned as soon as they pulled her from the drum. Everyone went hungry that night, but as word of the deer spread to other companies, upperclassmen from throughout the Corps came by to join in the vilification of Lowry. He made it through dinner, and suffered well into the night as the cadre visited his room in shifts, an unending nightmare of abuse. At 0200 on Sunday morning, Lowry broke down in tears and admitted that the bullet that had killed the deer was not his.

CHAPTER 17

August 8, 2004 (Sunday)
West Point

Thayer Hall was one of few buildings that might have fit in at a civilian institution, although from the river even Thayer had the appearance of a crusader's fortress; granite walls perched somehow on a cliff above the river, with turrets that concealed an asphalt parking lot on the roof. Because so much of the building was underground, the cadets never saw much of its structure except from the inside, where it would have resembled any other utilitarian warren of classrooms, were it not for the exquisite maintenance of the hallways and perfect alignment of the student desks in every room. Boyer disdained Thayer Hall because it held no relics of war like most of the other buildings at West Point, most of which were museums to one degree or another. Unique among his classmates, Boyer appreciated that the traditions at West Point were born of valor and blood. When other cadets marched obliviously past the statues of Patton, Washington, or Eisenhower, or watched their feet as they passed by the captured cannon at Trophy Point, Boyer felt the sensation of being watched, as if the statues and cannon were all animated by the ghosts of men who died in uniform. The eerie sensation did not bother him. Indeed, he found it comforting.

Thayer Hall had its allure, however. The building contained Robinson Auditorium, named for another forgotten hero, where the New Cadets were subjected to lectures about rules, regulations, rifle manual, or the Honor Code. For many New Cadets, these lectures were a chance to catch up on lost sleep, despite the lurking upperclassmen. Once each week, however, the cadre marched the New Cadet companies to Robinson Auditorium for Chaplain's Time, where they left their frazzled subordinates unsupervised in the hands of the West Point chaplain, himself a commissioned officer, who provided pizza and soda, and a chance to relax, socialize, and get to know each other. Religion was in the air, but never proselytized. The chaplain kept an eye out for distressed cadets who needed help, and there was plenty of counseling for those who needed it, but West Point also saw fit to encourage camaraderie among classmates and this was the other point of Chaplain's Time.

Boyer and Buckner sat in the front row of folding seats, each with two slices of pizza and a can of Coke. During regular meals, the cadre saw to it that New Cadets rarely consumed all the food on their plates, and most men went to bed hungry every night. The auditorium was packed with men eating themselves sick while the chaplain walked among them, making small talk. "How you men holding up?" he asked.

Boyer said nothing, unsure of how forthcoming he should be among his classmates, none of whom seemed inclined to unburden themselves. The chaplain seemed almost disappointed.

"No problem," mumbled Buckner, with his mouth full. He withheld the "sir" and failed to stand up, knowing he could get away with that level of rudeness to the chaplain, and to discourage the man from staying.

"Getting enough to eat?" asked the chaplain.

"Yes, sir," said Boyer, who started to stand, until the chaplain motioned for him to remain seated. The chaplain sensed that Boyer and Buckner needed nothing from him, so he nodded and moved on.

"Enough to eat?" muttered Boyer, who attended church regularly enough that he could snicker good-naturedly about men of the cloth. "The only thing I think about is food."

"I don't think about nothin'," answered Buckner.

"You must think this is pretty chickenshit compared to the real army."

"Bunch of smart-ass white boys and girls runnin' around singin' Airborne Ranger songs as if everybody's got blood drippin' from their teeth. Then we come eat pizza with the chaplain to make sure we ain't nuts. Crazy shit, man." Buckner felt suddenly ridiculous, talking as if he were Sgt. Rock. *I was nothin' but a prison guard*, he thought, until he remembered Tetra, KIA. He felt hubris swell inside him, a combat vet among combat virgins, and Buckner wondered how many had what it took to keep their heads in combat, and how many were fools like his roommate.

Daunted by such straight talk from a veteran with a Purple Heart, Boyer merely nodded humbly. "I owe you, Buckner. If you hadn't found me in the swamp, I'd still be there." Boyer spoke quietly and without looking at his roommate, for expressions of gratitude were difficult among men who measured themselves against each other.

"I didn't do it for you, Boyer."

Buckner's comment was like a slap in the face, and Boyer looked away, chewing slowly on his pizza. He did not notice Richard approaching until he dropped into the folding chair next to Buckner. Boyer recognized him as Buckner's spotter on the firing range.

"Buckner!" said Richard. The two black men shared a dap and Buckner introduced Boyer. Richard said, "I remember you, Sylvester. That was pretty gutsy shooting, to qualify on the range with your last shot. You sure you didn't shoot that deer?"

"That was Lowry," said Boyer, not realizing that Richard was teasing him.

Richard laughed. "All you white dudes look alike." Buckner chuckled, too.

Boyer stopped chewing. Since the day he had met Buckner, he had evaluated everything his roommate had said or done within the context of Buckner's color. Yet not once had either of them mentioned the issue of race. Now, Boyer saw that he was not alone in his constant awareness of the difference in the color of their skins. In the presence of the two black men, he felt conspicuously out of place, despite the fact that the room was packed with 150 other New Cadets, almost all Caucasian.

"Is that true?" asked Boyer, his seriousness spoiling the joke. "Do we all really look the same to you?"

"Hell, yeah!" answered Richard. "Y'all walk the same. Y'all talk the same. I ain't seen you dance yet, Boyer, but I bet you move real tight, like you don't want nobody to notice you."

"I'm pretty self-conscious on the dance floor," acknowledged Boyer.

"Shit, man!" Richard lifted his hands over his head and snapped his fingers, swaying in his chair to unheard music. "Gettin' noticed is the whole reason we black folks invented dancing."

Buckner said quietly, "Boyer's OK." As Richard lowered his arms, Buckner added, "Whites look like everybody else. You just gotta pay attention to what you're lookin' at. There ain't nothin wrong with being white."

Boyer smiled, basking in Buckner's acceptance of him. "Nothing wrong with being black, either."

Richard and Buckner glanced at each other and laughed. Buckner said, "Boyer, I make you nervous as hell. You tiptoe around the room like I'm some sort of gorilla gonna eat you or something. You probably write home to your mama about how *interesting* it is to live with a Negro!"

"Well," said Richard, "we are a fascinating race."

"I thought 'Negro' was a racist word these days," said Boyer. "I tell my mom about living with an African American." He spoke with a half-smile on his face, not sure whether the other men would find his comment amusing.

"Everybody's a racist," said Richard. "Even sweet natured Negroes like me."

"I don't care what color you are!"

"But you think about it all the time."

"I can't help it," conceded Boyer defensively.

"Don't worry about it. We think about it all the time, too."

"I never think about being white."

"You would if you lived in my neighborhood," said Buckner, ending the conversation.

For the first time since the day he arrived at the U.S. Military Academy, Boyer prepared for bed without dreading the coming dawn. He stood at the sink and shaved his adolescent fuzz quickly, not bothering to lather, for Matterhorn would be doing bed checks soon. Buckner sat quietly at his desk, shining his shoes without making conversation. Ordinarily, Buckner's silent moments would fill Boyer with insecurities, but Buckner's casual acceptance of him with Richard had rid Boyer of his doubts. He was a barracks animal now, a soldier. The next day would be another exercise in misery, but nothing he couldn't handle.

The door opened, its sudden movement startling Boyer so that he nicked himself with the razor. New Cadets were not permitted to visit each others' rooms at night, and members of the cadre always knocked before bursting into a room like a gust of wind. Reflexively, Boyer snapped to attention. His surprise was no less than Buckner's when Lowry stepped into the room and closed the door quietly behind him.

"What are you doing here?" whispered Boyer, a hint of panic in his voice. "Matterhorn said you resigned."

Lowry ignored him and strode directly to Buckner, who rose to face him. "I covered for you."

"I don't need no favors from you," replied Buckner.

Their eyes locked, on guard, each man expecting the other to throw the first punch.

"How long were you going to leave Donovan in that drum?" demanded Lowry.

"A dead deer never hurt anyone. Matterhorn was bluffing. He ain't got any more guts than you."

"Is that what you learned in Iraq, Buckner? Fuck your buddy?"

"You don't know nothin' about Iraq."

"I don't need a Purple Heart to know that you don't leave one of your classmates stewing in a can for something she didn't do."

Boyer interrupted. "What are you talking about, Lowry?"

Lowry turned to Boyer, his manner condescending. "Are you the only moron in Dull Squad who really believes I shot that deer? Boyer, I resigned because I committed an honor violation when I admitted to killing the deer. I'm living down in Boarders' Ward for the next forty-eight hours until they can process my paperwork and muster me out."

Like everyone else, Boyer had suspected his roommate of shooting the deer, but his suspicions had turned to relief when Lowry confessed. Now, the mere realization that Buckner had dared to stare down Matterhorn while Lowry took the rap sent a shiver through Boyer. There would be hell to pay, and the real losers in any contest between Matterhorn and Buckner would be the other members of Dull Squad.

Turning away from Boyer, Lowry continued, "I did what any classmate would have done. I did what you should have done." Lowry pointed his finger into Buckner's chest, and Buckner slapped it away. "What kind of man leaves a classmate in a fifty-five-gallon drum with a dead animal?"

"You never gave a shit about Donovan," said Buckner. "You just wanted to be a hero. You're no better than me."

Outside their window, a bugle sounded. "Taps!" exclaimed Boyer. "Lowry, you gotta get out of here! Matterhorn will be doing bed checks!"

"What's he going to do? Send me home?"

As if on cue, Matterhorn's fist hit the door. He stuck his head into the room, expecting to see Boyer and Buckner in bed, the lights out. Everyone sprang to attention, even Lowry, despite his resignation.

"What the hell are you doing here, Lowry?" Matterhorn's voice boomed, and Boyer felt his heart leap into his throat.

"Just came to say good-bye, *sir.*"

Matterhorn stepped into the room and jerked his thumb toward the door. "Get out of here, Mister. If you got anything to say to these men, you can write 'em a letter when you get to Harvard."

Lowry relaxed his position of attention and strolled away. He did not look back, but said, "Watch your back, Boyer."

Matterhorn focused on Buckner. "You got anything to tell me, Mister?"

Buckner stood silently, until the sounds of taps echoed down the Hudson Valley and died away. "No, sir," he said at last.

Matterhorn paused for a moment, then followed Lowry from the room and slammed the door. In the hallway he yelled, "Everybody in bed! Lights out!" When Matterhorn reopened the door thirty seconds later, the room was dark and Boyer and Buckner were under the sheets. Outside, the bugler marched away, the taps on his heels clicking on the pavement, the only sound.

CHAPTER 18

August 27, 2004 (Friday)
Washington, DC

In three months, Darrow filed a few routine stories, specific assignments from McGowan. She met her deadlines and her articles required little editing, as much to her surprise as McGowan's. When her male colleagues offered to show her the ropes every night at the local bars, Darrow begged off, preferring to spend her time on the Internet rummaging for references to names of members of the 229th MP Company in newspaper articles written by hometown newspapers in the aftermath of the Abu Ghraib scandal. She was concerned, too, about the water cooler gossip that had a way of infiltrating her cubicle, speculation about her relationship with McGowan and her qualifications for the job. She distrusted her coworkers and they distrusted her, and she was convinced that any male friendships would lead to even more gossip. Since none of the women made an effort to get to know her, Darrow isolated herself with work.

The army continued to strangle the request for the Abu Ghraib duty rosters in red tape. Darrow knew her way around the Internet, however, impressing McGowan with discoveries that ranged from hometown news releases about individual soldiers to declassified sworn statements by persons interviewed in conjunction with one Abu Ghraib investigation or another. All names were blacked out in the official documents, but a simple Google search of "229th MP Company" yielded contact information at the Virginia National Guard. So, Darrow made calls every day from her cubicle in the *Times'* newsroom in Washington, leaving messages at the HQs of every unit that served at Abu Ghraib. Rarely did the recipients of Darrow's messages respond to her, and when they did they did not stay long on the phone when they learned who she was. She was surprised, therefore, when her phone rang in between outgoing calls.

"This is Darrow," she answered.

"*Citizen Times?*"

"Yes. Who's calling?"

"Captain Harp, Public Information Office of the Virginia National Guard. I have a message that you called."

Darrow racked her brain, finally remembering. "Yes," she said. "That was about three weeks ago."

"The Guard only works one weekend per month."

She sensed curtness in his manner, but hoped it was simply military efficiency. "Thank you for returning my call."

"What do you want?" asked Harp, almost hostile.

"I'm trying to locate a particular soldier who served in the 229th MP Company at Abu Ghraib last year. I don't have his name, only a photo. I was hoping you might be able to identify him."

"Why?"

"I have reason to believe that he was involved in the abuse of detainees."

"I can't help you," said Harp. "I am not at liberty to cooperate with your investigation. The 229th has not been implicated in any alleged abuses."

"Then why not talk to me? Off the record." She gave him the number of her cellular phone. "Call me twenty-four seven."

"I'm sorry. I cannot comment." The phone went dead.

Darrow crawled into bed that night exhausted, without knowing why. She looked forward to the weekend, to sleeping late and browsing the malls, although the challenge of locating Buckner occupied her mind more constantly now than did the sales at Macy's. The rumors about her sex life and the weeks of fruitless phone calls in search of Buckner had taken an emotional toll. She doffed her sleep shirt and lay between the sheets nude, wishing she had someone in bed with her, to make love to her and to hold her while she fell asleep afterward. She was still awake at midnight when her mobile phone started to chirp.

"I understand you need someone to identify a photograph," said a male voice.

"Who is this?" She was wide awake.

"I might be able to help you."

"How do I meet you?" she said, fumbling in the dark for a pen.

"Can you be at the Korean War Memorial in Washington at 1600 hours tomorrow?"

"I think so."

"I'll see you there."

Like most women her age, Darrow vaguely understood that there had once been a war in Korea, a country that today produced Hyundais, a car she would never consider driving. She could not find Korea on a map, and she required a tourist guidebook to find the Korean War Memorial on the Mall. Twice per day on weekends, Amtrak made the trip from New York to Union Station in Washington, DC, arriving at one p.m. Indifferent to the latest wave of tropical heat that suffocated the Eastern seaboard, Darrow set off for the memorial on foot. After crossing Constitution Avenue, she followed the trail through the Capitol Mall past the Vietnam Memorial, where old men like McGowan stood reverently in front of the black granite slabs while their families and grown children stood respectfully behind them. The Wall was a popular monument, always crowded, but the Korean War monument on the opposite side of the reflecting pool was deserted, its veterans dying off and the war itself now little more than a hot footnote in the history of the cold war. She wondered how long it would take for the Vietnam War to recede into memory like Korea, and for the MIA kooks at the Lincoln Memorial to pack up and finally go home.

She saw the memorial without at first realizing what it was, a squad of bronze soldiers slogging through the Mall on another pointless patrol. Slightly larger than life-size, their faces portrayed not heroism or hope or despair or fear or anger, but the essential emotion of soldiers: misery. Dressed in ponchos, the men appeared resigned to the rain that was forecast for Washington later that night. The afternoon was dark, for the clouds had already arrived.

The soldiers were alone except for a man who stood on a granite viewing patio at the head of the column of statues, placed there for people too timid to trudge alongside them. He wore baggy cargo pants and a knit polo shirt with the Nike swoosh on the chest. Darrow could feel his eyes on her, despite his sunglasses. He seemed sinister, even when he withdrew his hands from his pockets to show that they were empty.

"Darrow?"

"How did you find me?" she asked, keeping her distance. The voice was new, not one she recognized.

"You've been leaving messages all over the area, haven't you?"

Darrow had left plenty of messages, but only to Harp had she given her cellular phone number. She wondered if Captain Harp had posted her contact info on the bulletin board so that someone else might come forward to help her, or to warn others to beware of her. "Can you tell me your name?"

"No. I can't be caught talking to a reporter. The press has portrayed us all as a bunch of savages because a few idiots put panties on some prisoners' heads. Most of us had nothing to do with it."

"I get the impression that you really don't think those guards did anything wrong."

"Shit happens in a war. Those guys dishonored the army, but in some ways I don't think they did anything to those bastards that fraternity brothers don't do to each other in college."

"So why do you want to help me identify them?"

The man struggled to respond. She could almost watch his mind in conflict, loyalties snapping back and forth between his comrades versus the honor of the army they had damaged. Finally he said, "Show me the photo."

She pulled the photograph of the 229th MP Company from her portfolio and handed it to him. He turned to the fading sunlight. "This man," Darrow said, pointing at Victor Tetra. "Do you know him?"

He glanced at her hard. "That's not the man you're looking for. He's dead."

"I know," she said, satisfied that her new source knew what he was talking about. She pointed at a black face in the back row. "I'm looking for the man standing next to Sgt. Tetra."

He lifted his sunglasses and studied the photo quietly, while Darrow waited, conscious of the heat again as a bead of sweat trickled between her breasts.

"Buckner," he blurted suddenly, so crisp that the word startled her. "Morgan Buckner." He handed the photo back and flipped his glasses over his eyes.

"Are you sure?" she asked, stunned to have a name so easily.

"I don't know what you think he did, but Buckner was an attitude case, a tough guy. Good soldier, though, a PFC I think. Not many friends, except Tetra. They were an odd pair."

"Do you know where he is now?"

The man sighed. "He left the unit early, but not because of any problems that I was aware of. Nobody really missed him, you know."

Darrow recorded Buckner's name on the back of the photo and slipped it back into her portfolio. A breeze kicked up a few fallen leaves that swirled around the feet of the miserable sculptures, and she felt as if they were suddenly watching her, wondering what she was going to do with the name of a fellow soldier who might or might not have betrayed their legacy. The sun set behind the Watergate apartments, and the sudden chill and deepening darkness made her shiver.

The stranger seemed eager to be on his way. "I hope you know what you're doing," he said.

"Are you Captain Harp?" she asked.

"Harp is a professional. A lot of us are. We love our country. Those guards did not live up to the soldier's code. They may not be bad men, but they were bad soldiers. Harp wants them out of the army, but he's an officer. He can never talk to you."

"Are you in this photo?"

"Could be." He turned and hurried away then, mingling with the statues, almost a ghost himself.

She notified McGowan immediately, calling on her cellular phone as she hiked northward along Constitution Avenue. Clearly annoyed that she had not informed him of her plan to go to Washington alone, he was nevertheless excited by her progress. "Now that I'm here," she asked, "what do you want me to do?"

"Do you remember how to get to the Pentagon?"

"Not really."

"Well, I'm sure you can figure it out. I want you to go back to the Personnel Office and find out where this fellow is."

"How do I get through security?"

"You have your credentials with you?"

Self-consciously proud of her first professional license, she carried her press pass everywhere, as McGowan had instructed. She told him so.

"Use the day tomorrow to get to know Washington. Forget the monuments and museums; ride the Metro and learn the neighborhoods. If you want to be a reporter, you're going to need to know your way around that town. On Monday, go to the Pentagon and find Buckner. Call me if you need anything."

"You paying for the hotel?" she asked.

"Find a cheap one."

Access to the Pentagon was easier now that Darrow was certified by the *Times*. Her application for a security clearance was still being processed, but the Pentagon had issued a press pass after her initial background check.

She could not yet attend classified briefings, but she could at least get through the door. Nevertheless, the security checks were as thorough as ever. Darrow fumbled to put her watch back on her wrist while the security guards x-rayed the contents of her briefcase in search of dangerous materials. Finally, she was free to wander the halls in accordance with the rules of access defined by the color of her badge.

At first, the building terrified her: four million square feet of office space; six thousand offices on five floors. Like most rookie reporters, however, she quickly learned that the Pentagon was laid out in a series of rings connected by intervening corridors that broke the building into pie-shaped sections. Each section was labeled and color coded, and soon she was striding the halls as confidently as she had previously negotiated the New York subway. The only difference was the artwork, which continued to amaze her. *If the army wanted to create its own art museum,* she thought, *it would put the crap at MoMA to shame.*

Darrow remembered the way to the Media Relations Division and stepped inside after passing her badge across the security scanner. Martha Rose greeted her without the warm smile she had given Buster Lambeau during Darrow's previous visit to her office.

"Hello, Martha," said Darrow, careful to display her access badge.

"Good morning." Rose seemed chillier than she had the first time they met. Darrow wondered if Rose was one of those women who responded to any man who flirted with them, but gave the cold shoulder to any woman more attractive than they were. Old men like Lambeau and McGowan could be charmers when they wanted to be. "What can I do for you, ma'am?"

Darrow was getting a feel for the military, but she still had to fight the urge to turn around and see who was behind her whenever anyone addressed her as "ma'am."

"I'm Angie Darrow," she said. "I was here with Buster Lambeau a few weeks ago."

"I remember," said Rose. "I gave you some Next of Kin information that I shouldn't have. You can tell your boss that *The Citizen Times* has run out of favors from this office." Rose's tone was sullen and hurt.

"I don't understand," said Darrow. "Is something the matter?"

"Well," said Rose, "One hour after you left this office, my boss got a call from some higher-higher who wanted to know what you were doing here. Let's just say that I'm lucky to still have my pension."

"I'm sorry," said Darrow.

"And here you are again. Whatever you want this time, it had better be routine, because I expect my boss will call me the minute you walk out that door." Rose's complaint was clear, but Darrow picked up a second message as well, a warning. *People are watching you.*

"We never meant to cause you any problems."

Suddenly, Rose softened. "Only bad reporters mean to cause the problems they do. Good reporters just let the chips fall. I'm a big girl. I can take care of myself. Now, what can I do to take care of you?"

"I'm trying to locate a soldier this time. A live soldier."

Such requests were routine. Servicemen were constantly being sought for any number of reasons: deaths in the family, indebtedness, paternity suits, people seeking to return personal effects left at previous domiciles. The army itself sought out the current assignments of certain personnel with unique skills; lately, Arabic speakers were in high demand. Rose didn't know why Darrow needed the information, but she had an access pass and that was enough. "Fine. No need to bend the rules for that. I'll need the name and Social Security number."

"All I have is a name and a photo."

Rose rolled her eyes. "My, you are difficult. What's the name?"

"Morgan Buckner," said Darrow. "Previously assigned to the 229th MP Company in Iraq." She handed the company photo to the woman and pointed him out.

Rose accessed the army personnel database and went to work. "Do you know how many men named Buckner are in the U.S. Army?" In less than two minutes, however, the records of three men named Morgan Buckner were available to download. The only African American among them was assigned to the Third New Cadet Company, U.S. Military Academy, West Point, New York.

CHAPTER 19

August 28, 2004 (Saturday)
West Point

Boyer began to believe that West Point was the only place on earth where it was possible to hike uphill to a destination, then return uphill. Earlier in the day, Third Company had climbed the academy ski slope, no small accomplishment with a full pack and a rifle on a sweltering day. Eighteen miles later, the New Cadets approached their goal, and Boyer could not remember a level step throughout the entire hike.

They crested a ridge and were rewarded by the glint of sunlight dancing off the serene surface of a mountain lake. Company by company, the New Cadets paused to catch their breath and savor their arrival. Not only did Lake Frederick mark the physical end of the day's march, but it signified the psychological end of Beast Barracks. The entire class would spend the last week of their summer training encamped on its shores. Upon their return to West Point, they would be officially initiated into the Corps of Cadets.

Officers were on hand to witness Third Company's debouchment from the forest onto the meadow that surrounded the lake. Matterhorn whipped his troops into a tight formation, and they marched the final 200 yards in step, cheering lustily while Matterhorn sang cadence under a cloudless August sky.

The members of Dull Squad pitched their tents in precise rows while the cadre scurried about, ensuring that the tent poles were straight and the canvas was tight and waterproof. When the rows were unerring enough to satisfy even the most meticulous upperclassman, a warm meal was served from the portable kitchen that would make the trip every day from West Point.

The men lounged near their tents as the final hour of twilight lingered. Richard came to visit from Second Squad, and regaled everyone with tales and rumors of other companies and classmates. They felt like veterans.

They all sprang to attention as Matterhorn strolled into their midst.

"At ease. Everyone sit down," said Matterhorn. "Not you, Buckner."

The young men sat in the grass and eyed each other, suspicious of Matterhorn's friendliness.

"Buckner, you have been selected to volunteer to represent Third Company in the pugil stick championship."

Pugil sticks were nasty objects, wooden staffs five feet long used in bayonet training because they were slightly less lethal than a real blade. Padded at each end, they looked like giant Q-tips, but they were brutally effective in demonstrating the proper execution of a vertical butt stroke series. In competition, however, the bayonet techniques of thrust and parry were quickly forgotten. A pugil stick battle was primitive combat at its most fundamental: no rules, no quarter; only two men beating each other to death with clubs.

Buckner glanced at his classmates, who carefully controlled their proud grins.

"You'll fight tomorrow night at 1900 hours. Find yourself a corner man to assist you with your protective gear." Matterhorn tossed a package of chocolate chip cookies to the squad. To all of them, he said, "Good job, men." He turned and walked away.

"Huah," said Boyer, uttering the all-purpose expletive to communicate gung-ho enthusiasm: *Yes, sir! Damn right, sir! Bet your ass, sir! Airborne Ranger, sir! Grrr!* Buckner thought the term was ridiculous. "Huah!" repeated Dull Squad. *We eat this shit up, sir!*

An awkward guest among the satisfied members of another squad, Richard rose to return to his own tribe. He held his fist behind him and Buckner casually dapped it. "Later, warriors."

Buckner was half asleep when Boyer crawled into the sleeping bag on his side of their two-man tent. "I found out who you'll have to fight tomorrow in the pugil stick quarterfinals," he whispered.

Buckner seemed uninterested.

"Did you choose your second yet?"

"Richard."

They stick together, thought Boyer, mortified that his own roommate had honored another man to assist him in combat. He stared blind into the darkness inside the tent, where not a photon of light penetrated, pushing his disappointment into the emotional lockbox that all New Cadets eventually found within themselves. After a while he stopped thinking about it. His rifle, which the New Cadets kept inside their sleeping bags to ward off the rust-forming dew, lay hard and uncomfortable against him, but it made Boyer feel soldierly. He imagined the coming day's maneuvers and wished he were going into real combat, like other men his age who were in Iraq at that very moment.

Buckner tossed in his sleeping bag and moaned quietly. *Another nightmare*, thought Boyer. He envied Buckner, as he envied anyone with combat experience, bad dreams, and bullet wounds. Outside, the cadet guard strolled by, and Boyer imagined he heard the footfalls of cadets long dead who had bivouacked on that very spot. Suddenly, Buckner sat upright in the tent as if punched in the stomach by a ghost. Even in the dark, Boyer saw the flaming whites of Buckner's eyes. With a scream that terrified Boyer, he flung himself from the shelter, taking the tent pole with him and collapsing the canvas. Buckner landed on his hands and knees, where he roared again in an indistinguishable flow of words and fear.

Flashlights popped on throughout the rows of tents, and upperclassmen yelled above the confused hubbub of voices. "Turn off those lights! Get back in your tents!"

Boyer scrambled from the crumpled tent as Matterhorn arrived and placed his hand firmly on Buckner's shoulder.

"Buckner! Wake up! Pull yourself together!" He shook Buckner's shoulder, being careful to maintain a safe distance from a man experiencing something dangerous in some distant place. Though he spoke sternly, Boyer detected paternalism in Matterhorn's voice—an exasperated big brother.

As suddenly as the dream had begun, Buckner stopped screaming and sagged slowly to the ground. Boyer saw cognizance return to his eyes, though they glanced around in confusion. Matterhorn, too, saw that the dream was over. "OK," he said, announcing the end of the drama. "Everybody back to sleep. You, too, Buckner." To Boyer, he added, "Fix the tent in the morning. Don't let this happen again."

As Buckner crawled sheepishly into the ruins of their tent, Boyer wondered how Matterhorn expected him to control his roommate's dreams.

CHAPTER 20

August 29, 2004 (Sunday)
West Point

On Sunday morning, the New Cadets formed up in combat gear for a hot breakfast in a dense fog, followed by a battlefield sermon by the chaplain. Boyer remembered seeing photographs of soldiers in Vietnam and World War II taking communion in the rain, muddy and wounded men staggering toward a priest wearing vestments over BDUs who would place the wafer in each man's mouth. Unlike his warrior classmates, Boyer felt his own mortality as he listened to the sermon in the fog alongside the ghosts of the men in the photographs. He suggested that Buckner join him for the chapel service, and was disappointed by Buckner's snort of contempt.

Training commenced after the sermon, drills designed to simulate combat more realistically than any others the New Cadets had experienced thus far. Dressed in pads and gas masks and armed with pugil sticks, Boyer and his classmates charged up steep, wooded hills through clouds of smoke and tear gas. Every twenty yards, an upperclassman burst through the fog and assaulted them, battering them mercilessly before ordering them, exhausted and wretched, forward to their next combat further up the slope. Sickened by the tear gas ingested every time his mask was dislodged by the proficient pugil stick thrusts of the upperclassmen, Boyer did not feel heroic or exhilarated. Upperclassmen came from everywhere, like evil spirits in the smoke, to vociferously point out that his classmates were passing him by. Boyer imagined how ridiculous he was, his nose running with gas-induced mucus, too tired to wield his padded club in make-believe war. As a female New Cadet stumbled by him, he heard the phrase "High school hero, West Point zero," but wasn't sure if a member of the cadre had yelled it at him, or if he had thought it himself. For a moment he considered resignation, but somehow Boyer pushed himself to his feet and staggered on up the hill, blind in the fog and smoke and gas, his mask sliding all over his face made slippery by slobber and tears.

Dinner that night was quiet as the New Cadets took stock of their class, like veterans after a battle checking on survivors. Someone had seen a dozen resignees leave camp in the back of a deuce 'n a half. Cadet memories could be cruelly short, however, and the departed men were forgotten as thoughts turned to the night's entertainment: the pugil stick championships. Even Boyer, rejuvenated by the hot meal, felt his excitement grow as the hour of combat approached. He joined a group of his classmates as they wandered toward the field where the matches would be fought. They swaggered, and Boyer felt accepted despite his performance on the hill; he was still there, and twelve others were civilians now. But he wondered how many of his remaining classmates had come as close as he had to throwing in the towel.

"Buckner!" Matterhorn approached. "Chaplain wants to talk to you about your nightmare last night." Matterhorn pointed to the east end of Lake Frederick where a man stood, his hands clasped behind his back, and the white collar of his uniform clearly visible.

"What about the pugil stick fights?" asked Buckner.

"That's not your problem. I'll find someone else."

"Sir, I don't need a chaplain."

"You need what the army says you need. That's an order, Buckner."

A ring twenty-five feet in diameter was defined by the circle of men which crowded around it. One thousand blood-thirsty spectators sat shoulder to shoulder, yelling for their champions and lunging vicariously with each blow. A powerful stroke to the head sent one combatant reeling into the crowd, which set him on his feet and sent him back into the ring. Like gladiators, the two powerful men pummeled each other until only one remained standing. The cadet from Second Company raised his stick in triumph as his classmates roared, "Huah!"

A hundred yards away, Chaplain Yates sat on a boulder, absentmindedly tossing pebbles into Lake Frederick. When Buckner approached, the chaplain rose and extended his hand. He was long and linear, pensive, with a sorry glow about him.

"New Cadet Buckner reporting as ordered, sir."

"Have a seat." Yates motioned for Buckner to sit opposite him. "And forget the 'yes, sir, no, sir' bullshit."

"Yes, sir."

Yates grinned. The brass joked that the chaplain could size up a plebe in five minutes and predict whether he would still be around on graduation day. He still exchanged Christmas cards with men he had counseled as plebes who were now full colonels.

"You created quite a disturbance last night. Do you have nightmares often?"

"No, sir."

"The army can't afford to have officers who wake up screaming with nightmares. You could expose the position of your entire command and jeopardize the security of your men."

Buckner did not respond.

"You know," began Yates, "most cadets don't give a damn about me; they don't need a chaplain. But they do believe in God, so somebody has to do the sermon every Sunday." The chaplain had the expression of an old angel, tolerant of the indifference that most people felt toward his ministry. "Do you believe in God, Buckner?"

"Never gave Him much thought, sir."

"It doesn't matter. My job isn't to convert anyone; I'm here to help soldiers deal with the trauma of combat."

"This isn't combat," observed Buckner.

"I guess you'd know."

Silence prevailed for a moment. Behind them, the roar of the crowd carried across the field. Two men wielding sticks tilted at each other, and Buckner heard the sound of wood on muscle in the distance.

"But," resumed Yates, "you don't need to experience combat to be traumatized. I just spoke with three good men who are on their way home tonight because they couldn't handle the pugil stick drill up on the hill today. Each of them would rather die than face his family."

"What does this have to do with me?"

"Nothing, Buckner. I'm just talking. But I wanted to talk to you about your experiences in Iraq. You went through a lot of shit over there."

"So what?" said Buckner. "Lot of people went through stuff worse than mine."

"But they don't have nightmares."

Buckner again kept his mouth shut, wondering how the army expected him to control his subconscious.

"Don't worry," said the chaplain, reading his mind. "Nightmares are a sign of a conscience, an occupational hazard for anyone in uniform. If the army gave the boot to every soldier who had nightmares, we'd all be civilians. Sometimes, my wife is more afraid to go back to sleep than I am. My job is just to make sure you're not nuts."

"Isn't that a job for a psychiatrist?"

"Probably. But the brass seems to think that a priest is as good as a shrink when it comes to stuff like feelings and regrets. So here we are."

Buckner nodded as if in agreement, for it was true that cadets in general had little regard for any sort of doctor whose specialty was something other than fixing bullet wounds.

The chaplain continued. "I've reviewed your record so far and I've determined that you're a superior soldier and leader of men, but you seem to have little concern for the men you would lead."

"As long as they follow, what difference does it make?"

"A good soldier will sacrifice his life for his men. Would you do that?"

Buckner felt as if this quiet priest had suddenly stood up and punched him. He thought of Boyer, and Buckner knew that he would not trade his life to save his roommate. He suspected, however, that Boyer would forfeit his, or at least claim that he would until the final moment of truth. All of the New Cadets would scream bloody murder and charge into an ambush until someone replaced the blanks with real bullets. Then you'd see who punked out. That was the reason for the training, thought Buckner: to let men practice sacrificing so that some of them might actually do it when the time came. Buckner said, "You wouldn't understand what it's like to get shot at unless you've been there, sir."

"I've been there," said Yates. "I've been an army chaplain for thirty-five years, starting in Vietnam in 1970, where I earned my first Purple Heart. I've seen a fair share of battlefields and hospitals. And graveyards. I even have a Top Secret clearance. Why don't you tell me what happened in Iraq?"

Buckner measured the chaplain carefully, wanting to tell him about the source of his nightmares, but knowing that no good would come of it. He felt no need for forgiveness, and the chaplain was ultimately just another officer. Nevertheless, there were things to say, things that had been eating at him since the day he had started at Prep School and that could not be told to Boyer or Richard. With a deep breath, Buckner began his story about Tetra and Tannerbeck and Levi, and the man he kicked to death in a cell in Abu Ghraib.

Boyer found Buckner sitting on a rock ledge above the lake. While the rest of the class relived the pugil stick combat and enjoyed the last vestiges of twilight, Boyer sat alongside his roommate, tossing rocks into the water, forcing himself to wait for Buckner to open the conversation.

"Who won?" asked Buckner quietly.

"Some guy from Seventh Company. You could have beaten him."

"Nah. Not with Richard in my corner. He doesn't know shit about fighting."

"He's your friend."

"So are you."

Boyer glanced sideways at Buckner, who stared into the water. He said, "I thought I was the wrong color to be your friend."

"You take some getting used to, is all."

"I suppose that's why you tell your war stories to Richard."

Buckner stared at Boyer quizzically. "Richard's just another jive-ass brother. I never told him shit."

Careful to keep an offhand tone, Boyer asked, "What did the chaplain want?" He waited in silence for an answer.

At last Buckner answered quietly, "You want to be a soldier, Boyer? Then you should'a known Tetra." Boyer listened while Buckner told him how Tetra lost his life.

CHAPTER 21

August 30, 2004 (Monday)
New York

Washington, DC, was exhilarating for Darrow, who reconnoitered the city with the efficiency of a military field manual, riding the Metro from one stop to the next. At each stop, she exited the train and went to street level, where she took notes about the nearest hotels and restaurants and jotted down comments about the people she saw, learning more about the nation's capitol for twelve dollars' worth of Metro passes than most congressmen learned during an entire term of office.

Darrow liked big cities, although New York was the only one she had known with any intimacy. Washington excited her in ways that New York did not. Washington was about power; New York about money. Both were cynical with respect to their purpose, but the citizens of Washington waded around in a percolating stew of political deceitfulness mixed with fragments of honor that occasionally bubbled to the top. One of those fragments had popped to the surface at the Korean Memorial, and though she now found herself wondering if it was as noble as it seemed to be, she had nevertheless been titillated by it.

On the train back to New York, Darrow decided that three months was a sufficient apprenticeship for an ambitious woman with legs like hers. Increasingly irritated by the office scuttlebutt, she was ready to leave New York behind. Lambeau needed a reporter, and based on her evaluation of her more experienced coworkers, she didn't see why she wasn't as capable of filling the slot in the Pentagon as anyone else. Having decided what she wanted, Darrow also decided what she was willing to do to get it.

McGowan reclined at his desk, his feet propped on an open drawer, reading glasses perched on the end of his nose. Darrow sat across from him, legs crossed, showing plenty of thigh. The search for Morgan Buckner had brought them together professionally and personally, and their behavior had become simultaneously familiar and edgy. He admired her moxie and disdained her naiveté, while she respected his savvy, though not his condescension. The hint of sex was heavy between them, even though they had never kissed, a fact that others in the office would never believe if either of them had bothered to address the rumors. What social life they had was masochistic: she teased him with her body and he teased her with hints of what he could do for her career in exchange for it. She never came across and neither did he, but they both wondered if the day would come. Given that whatever integrity she had was already compromised by rumor and innuendo, Darrow had begun to seriously consider the advantages of a sexual liaison with McGowan.

"Remind me why we aren't publishing the story on Tannerbeck?" she said, with an interrogative inflection.

"Because that is exactly what someone wants us to do," spat McGowan. "We're being played for idiots. The only thing we have on Tannerbeck is the memo about Sergeant

Tetra. It's not sufficient evidence to take this story to print; plus, it's suspicious evidence anyway. Who sent it? And why was a copy sent to the Tetras? It seems a little too convenient that the memo would arrive at the Tetras' house the day before we did."

Darrow voiced her own suspicions. "And what about Captain Harp of the National Guard? I left my office phone number with all my messages, except for him. He had my cell phone number. He gave it to someone so he could contact me and provide the ID on Buckner. What's his motive?"

McGowan looked over the top of his reading glasses at her, wondering how such a smart woman could have been such an indifferent student at Bard. "Motive is the key to everything, Angie. You're asking the right questions."

"Do you think Harp is the same person who sent the Tannerbeck memo to the Tetras?"

"I don't think so. More to the point, why would *anyone* send that memo to the Tetras? There is nothing in it that the Tetras need to know. Could it be just a bureaucratic fuck-up? No, too coincidental. That memo was meant for us. We're being manipulated."

"Let's print the story and see what happens. So what if we are being manipulated?"

"Angie, every reporter gets manipulated once—and only once-in his or her career. I learned my lesson in Panama when I was a hotshot war correspondent. It taught me two things: first, verify your damned facts; and second, the manipulators are usually hiding a bigger, more interesting story than the one you're already working on."

He caught her watching him with an amused look on her face. "What's the matter?" he asked.

"Nothing. You're pontificating again."

Like many men his age, McGowan believed that his life's lessons and memories were important, for he had nothing else to justify the life he had led: no roots, no ties of affection, no children, no ex-wives. There had been women over the years, even some that he loved, but none that he cared about now. He had been alone all of his life, but never lonesome until recently. Abu Ghraib had taught him that he was old and mortal, and whether he died in a cell in Iraq or in his apartment in New York, his death would be a matter of indifference to the world. He caught himself rambling sometimes, and he would stop, feeling foolish. Not because his lessons were unimportant, but because he knew it was his way of flirting—of ameliorating his loneliness—and he was too old and ridiculous to be chasing women like Darrow.

Darrow was not ungrateful for what he had taught her about reporting and about the newspaper business. "The business end of it is a bunch of crap," he told her. "But the reporting, now there's the opportunity to do something noble." She almost believed him, for somewhere under his cynicism was a layer of righteousness. He had betrayed himself at the Tetras' home and she had teased him on the trip back about being a softy, which he pretended to find irritating. But things had been awkward ever since he had tried to kiss her good night.

"Doug," she said, "I want to go to Washington."

"What are you talking about?"

"I can cover the Pentagon. I did a good job this weekend. You know I did."

He simply stared at her, incredulous. "You don't have the contacts or the experience for that beat. And I need you right here."

"You don't need me; you just like having a pretty girl around. But you taught me a lot and now I'm ready for bigger things."

"Ready? Most reporters work ten years before they get assigned to anything important, or even get a byline."

"Most reporters don't have to endure the humiliation of having everyone think they're fucking the boss."

"Don't kid yourself. Most women in this business actually do fuck their bosses."

"Doug, you've got a vacancy. Let me try." Then she added, "I'll sleep with you." She had known it would come to this and she had bided her time carefully. Doug McGowan might never again be in a position to catapult her career like he could at this moment.

McGowan sat up and stared at her expressionless face and into her eyes, which looked back at him frankly. With a sigh, he acknowledged that she could probably get the job done. And Darrow worked for almost nothing. He would miss her, but McGowan understood that if he did not let her go, he could lose her anyway. And she might even be useful in Washington.

"If you go, I'll expect you to keep working on the Abu Ghraib contacts."

"Absolutely." She felt her heart beating higher in her chest.

"And I want you to start looking into the Tannerbeck memo."

"You mean I can go?"

"I want you to start running down the members of the Senate Investigating Committee. Whoever fed us that memo has probably been feeding it to other people as well.

Schmooze the legislative aides. You'll never get to the senators, and they never do any of the real work anyway."

"So I can go?" she repeated.

"Lambeau will know how you got the job, Angie."

Fine, she thought. *I'll fuck him, too, if I have to.*

CHAPTER 22

September 1, 2004 (Wednesday)
West Point

Boyer and his classmates broke camp at 0500 hours. By 0600, they were on the trail, moving quickly and in high spirits. Lake Frederick had been a blast, but it also marked the end of their basic training. Soon, their M-16s would be turned in one last time to the armory, replaced by the M-14s they kept in their rooms, weapons more suited for Saturday drill and rifle manual than the stubby M-16. The march back to the barracks was marked by motivational signs along the way: Duty, Courage, Country, Heart. Inspired, Boyer sang lustily and self-consciously led a few marching songs himself. For once, the hike seemed downhill, a breeze. West Point was drawing them back to close out the summer, where, in thirty-six hours, the Class of '08 would be ceremoniously inducted into the Corps of Cadets.

Matterhorn, who had relaxed discipline slightly at Lake Frederick, regressed with each step nearer to West Point.

"Dull Squad, get your eyes off the ground! There is plenty of time for me to send one more of you losers to Harvard! Understand?"

"YES, SIR!"

Matterhorn laughed. "Gentlemen, I'm your fairy god-mother compared to what's waiting for you at West Point! At this moment, three thousand upperclassmen are return-ing to the barracks after advanced training in regular army units. And each one of them is waiting to take a bite out of your ass." Matterhorn stopped and stood with his hands on his hips as his squad hiked past. "I've spent all summer try-ing to get you people ready for tomorrow. What a waste of time! My classmates are going to eat you alive." Disgusted, he kicked the dirt and resumed the march. Up and down the line, all of the upper-class training cadre nagged and ranted at their squads, each with his own version of Matter-horn's warning.

The next day, Dull Squad was broken up, its members scattered among the thirty-six companies which made up the complete Corps of Cadets. The plebes lay low while up-per-class strangers gradually filled the barracks. Unfamiliar voices floated through the hallways as the older cadets greet-ed each other, or bitched, or roared at a passing plebe.

Buckner and Boyer were assigned to F Company, 2nd Regiment, a band of men known for their athletic prowess more than their academic accomplishments; a company of 110 men and women known throughout the Corps as the "Zoo." The company commander, Mark LaForge, was a raw-boned and taciturn oak of a man, a "Firstie" with large arms befitting the numerous stripes he wore. A combat veteran of Afghanistan, he sported a row of ribbons and an Airborne badge on his chest. Somehow, the Academy had found thirty-six cadets like LaForge, natural soldiers packed so tight that even their molecules moved in formation, and made them company commanders. But in spite of their intimidating command presence, company commanders had mundane responsibilities that kept them involved in the daily lives of every soldier under their command. Among the voices in the hallway, LaForge's was the most ubiquitous, greeting his soldiers, squaring them away, hustling them up, answering questions, and kicking ass when necessary.

LaForge had lost half of his original classmates through three years of academic attrition, simple resignations, and disciplinary expulsions. The survivors were veterans of the system who had prevailed over calculus, thermodynamics, nuclear physics, and the Office of Physical Education. Graduation, the light at the end of the tunnel, was at last visible, and the Firsties were too war-weary to concentrate on much else. For a plebe, an encounter with an angry Firstie was a terrible experience, but few first classmen actually went to the trouble to hunt them down.

Matterhorn was a member of the second class, juniors, or "Cows" in Academy slang. They were angry men and women, burdened by an overwhelming academic load and the responsibility for the continuing discipline and training of the plebes. For Cows, the light at the end of the tunnel was but a pinpoint. Harassment of the plebes was their sworn duty and only diversion. It did not take long for the fourth classmen to learn the first rule of survival in an environment where upperclassmen were suddenly everywhere: Firsties were dangerous only when disturbed; Cows were to be avoided at all costs.

The third class, sophomores called "Yuks," were allies. Only weeks removed from their own plebe year, they had few obligations other than academic survival. They were friends in an environment where not screaming at someone in the hallway was considered a friendly act.

Buckner and Boyer were assigned to the squad of a Cow named Ajax. He was a short and slightly built cadet with standard issue TEDs that constantly slid down his nose. After weeks of trying to emulate Matterhorn's recruiting-poster image, Boyer found Ajax's owlishness reassuring. Unlike the other upperclassmen whose voices boomed up and down the corridors of the barracks, Ajax's nasal whine was more befitting a civilian teenager with a skateboard than an aspiring officer in the U.S. Army.

When Ajax burst into their room, Buckner and Boyer sprang reflexively to attention. Their new squad leader examined every thread of their uniforms, paying special attention to Buckner. "I've heard about you," he said. "I eat prima donnas for breakfast."

Buckner nearly snorted with contempt. Rumors were a two-way street, and friendly Yuks had already spread the word about Ajax. Every class had its share of martinets, men like Ajax who struggled as plebes and metamorphosed into fire-breathing "regulations Nazis" as soon as they had subordinates of their own. Buckner could have gripped him by the throat and lifted him off the floor, but he maintained his position of attention until Ajax finished blustering and left them alone.

On Saturday, the plebes of Company F-2, along with their classmates from other companies, were ceremoniously accepted into the Corps of Cadets. The sky was overcast; the river and the granite buildings blended into a monochromatic landscape, highlighted only by the verdant brilliance of the Plain, so green it tinted the air. The cadets themselves wore starched summer whites. A rainbow of flags snapped in the breeze, which brought with it a hint of fall. The parade ground was surrounded by spectators, there to see the new class of plebes march for the first time with the full Corps.

Thirty-six phalanxes of New Cadets in white gloves and polished brass marched onto the parade ground. Minutes later, their individual companies took to the field and swallowed them up. Out of earshot of the spectators, the upperclassmen muttered insults and the plebes dug in their chins. But when the command was given to pass in review, the Hellcats struck up a tune that silenced everyone. The class of '08 prepared to strut for the first time to the stirring sounds of the official West Point march.

Mark LaForge turned to face the company. "For-WARD!" he commanded, judging the tempo of the music. The guidon bearer raised his staff and the men of F-2 tensed. "MARCH!"

Boyer was flying, carried along as if surfing by the surge of bugles and drums that echoed off the face of the barracks and down the Hudson Valley. The squeak of polished leather and the rattling of bayonets conjured in his mind's eye the glory and horror of war, and the sacrifices being made by other Academy men at that very moment. He thought of his father, who had fought in Vietnam. As they passed the reviewing stand, LaForge commanded, "Eyes right!" Boyer snapped his chin over his shoulder and saw Tannerbeck and the other generals salute them. He imagined the ghosts of MacArthur and Patton and Lee, and a thousand others, standing beside them.

The glory of the moment faded as soon as the company passed through the sally port into the inner compound behind the barracks, away from public scrutiny.

"Company, HALT!" commanded LaForge.

The F-2 Zoo took two steps forward and stopped dead in its tracks.

"Order ARMS!"

Hands slapped against rifle stocks and butt plates slammed onto concrete as M-14s were lowered from shoulders to the ground. On command, bayonets were returned to their scabbards.

"Dismissed!" yelled LaForge.

"Buckner!" screeched Ajax. "Start the 'Days.'"

The 'Days' was a compendium of upcoming mess hall menus, augmented by a summary of news articles in *The Citizen Times*. A piece of cake for Boyer, the 'Days' were a daily debacle for Buckner, who never read the newspaper and had no idea what a bing cherry was or what potatoes au gratin consisted of. Each failure to recite the 'Days' elicited demands from Ajax for more and more plebe knowledge, and each hour spent cramming his brain with useless trivia was an hour less for studying calculus, Portuguese, military history, and English. The 'Days' were just another way to force cadets to master priorities and deal with distractions, but within a week, Buckner was failing in all four subjects.

Boyer was one of few freshmen who managed to memorize all fourth-class trivia and still keep up with the academic workload. No longer did he crawl into the rack each night wondering if he would still be there twenty-four hours later. Now, it was his classmates who were hanging on by the skin of their teeth, and who came to him for help.

Calculus ate them up and spit them out. Three hours per day, five days a week, each day commencing with a graded exam in which each cadet wrote the solutions to his assigned problem on the blackboard for everyone else to evaluate. Determined to repay his roommate for carrying him through Beast Barracks, Boyer spent an hour each night with Buckner, explaining the mathematics of each problem. But Buckner lacked the academic background to do little more than memorize formulas. His muddled jottings on the board were nothing like Boyer's sublime solutions of the night before.

Buckner tossed his books onto his desk and threw himself into his chair, consumed with frustration. "What do any of us need with calculus in combat? None of us in Iraq would know a fuckin' *theorem* if it shit in our helmet."

"Only officers can see them," said Boyer, deadpan.

Buckner stared at him. "That's the funniest thing you've ever said, Boyer."

There was no time to talk as they buffed their shoes and brass in preparation for lunch formation. In the hall, Ajax could be heard berating the minute caller, who announced the final two-minute warning before formation.

Mark LaForge knocked twice and stepped into the room. Normally, a visit from the cadet company commander could only mean trouble, but before Buckner could spring fully to attention, LaForge opened the cabinet below the sink and snatched up a can of Brasso. "Polish your belt buckle," he directed, tossing the solvent to Buckner. He next reached into the closet for Buckner's other shoes, a second pair issued to all cadets, but rarely worn except for parades and Saturday morning inspections. "Put these on and come with me."

Lunch was a mandatory formation for members of the Corps, all of whom crowded into the gothic mess hall and found their assigned seats among the 400 tables that seated ten cadets each. Divided into four wings, each cavernous enough to hangar a dirigible, the mess hall seemed to have been transported from the Middle Ages. The walls were covered with medieval weapons, coats of arms, and the fifty state flags. The oak-beamed ceiling was as solid as the slate floor forty feet below. In the center, where the four great wings met, was the granite tower of the original Academy mess hall. It jutted from the flagstone floor and rose almost to the ceiling, a shaft of stone that commanded attention and drew every cadet's gaze upward, like a cathedral. There, among the turrets above the ancient gate, was the poop deck, a Gothic reminder of the Academy's heritage and a practical place from which to call the Corps to order.

The Brigade Adjutant, his sleeves bedecked with even more stripes than LaForge's, stood on the poop deck and surveyed the Corps below him. "Battalions, attention!" His voice rumbled among the rafters and penetrated the babble of a thousand conversations. The Corps fell silent, four thousand cadets standing behind their chairs anticipating the command to be seated. But the Adjutant surprised them.

"Attention to orders!"

The Corps froze, Firsties glancing uneasily at each other. Cadets attended more funerals than most college students, and they usually found out about the deaths of their friends when the Adjutant announced from the poop deck that another graduate had been killed in action in Iraq or Afghanistan. Upperclassmen braced themselves, praying that the deceased was a member of another company, another regiment, someone they had not known. Today, however, the Adjutant had better news: "Presentation of award!"

Curious upper-class eyes drifted upward toward the poop deck while the plebes kept their eyes straight ahead.

"Presentation of the Bronze Star with Valor to Cadet Fourth Classman Morgan Buckner! Citation to accompany the award." He then read the following:

> On October 8, 2003, while assigned to 229th MP Company, in the Baghdad Central Confinement Facility (BCCF), FOB Abu Ghraib, Iraq, Private First Class Morgan Buckner

distinguished himself while responding to a disturbance by Iraqi detainees within the compound. As a member of the internal reaction force, PFC Buckner, armed with non-lethal weapons only, entered the wired enclosure to subdue the disruptive elements that had commenced to throw stones and tent poles at American personnel. One detainee brandished a smuggled handgun and fired several shots into the American reaction force. Wounded and under fire, and at great peril to himself, PFC Buckner pursued the individual and disarmed him. The prisoner was subsequently restrained and delivered by PFC Buckner to a secure cell for interrogation. Upon removal of his restraints, the prisoner attacked the interrogators. PFC Buckner again subdued the prisoner before the prisoner was able to inflict any wounds on the interrogators. The actions of PFC Buckner reflect great credit upon himself and upon the United States Army.

There was a moment of reverent silence. The flash of silver stars twinkled on the poop deck as General Tannerbeck pinned the medal on Buckner's chest. The general and Buckner exchanged salutes.

A Firstie from Company F-2 yelled, "Go, Zoo!" Two or three others picked up the cue and bedlam broke out. Buckner marched to his table amid a chorus of cheers while Tannerbeck smiled down from above. Not even Ajax could spoil the mood, offering his grudging congratulations as

Buckner reached his seat. But as Boyer stared across the table at his roommate, he was startled to see the confusion in Buckner's eyes. Boyer furrowed his brow to communicate his concern, to ask Buckner what was wrong, but Buckner looked away.

The Adjutant ordered, "Take seats!"

CHAPTER 24

September 1, 2004 (Wednesday)
West Point

That night, as he had done every night since the beginning of the academic year, Boyer explained the principles behind the day's calculus lesson. Each day, Buckner failed as badly as he had failed the day before. Boyer had begun to notice that Buckner paid less attention each night to the explanations, and more attention to simply memorizing Boyer's solutions to the homework problems. Finally, Buckner gave up every pretense of trying to understand anything; he memorized it all, top to bottom, page after page, night after night.

Boyer cooperated grudgingly, as Buckner's contempt for understanding ran counter to everything Boyer believed about higher education. Why would a prestigious institution impose such a rigorous academic regimen upon men as ill-equipped as Buckner, he wondered, only to allow them to beat the system with brute force and mindless memorization? The reason, concluded Boyer, was that the army did not need theorists in combat; they needed men of action who got the job done, one way or another. The curriculum at West Point was not there to teach anyone anything about the subjects studied, but was simply part of the overall obstacle course that taught a man to function under pressure. The concept made Boyer uncomfortable, for he realized that his academic skills were no longer an end in themselves. There was a new yardstick now, with only one grade: a man graduated or he didn't.

Boyer tossed two pages of equations on his roommate's desk. "Buckner, how come you never told me about your Bronze Star?"

Buckner shrugged. "I didn't even know I'd been put in for it."

"You don't seem too happy about it."

"They give 'em out like candy. Every officer comes back with one."

"You weren't an officer."

Buckner turned to the calculus, his face as inscrutable as the equations on the paper. He read the same equation a dozen times before tossing the homework aside and reaching into his desk drawer for the jewelry box that contained his Bronze Star. He reread the citation carefully, knowing that no matter how many times he read it, it would not accurately portray the events as they had happened.

"Boyer," he said, "I didn't do what the citation says I did."

At last Boyer started to understand his roommate's subdued behavior. Some men collected medals gratuitously while others pretended not to care, but an award accepted under false pretenses violated the conscience of any man who called himself a soldier. Boyer turned to Buckner and asked, "What's inaccurate about it?"

"All of it."

"No. They always exaggerate those things, don't they?"

"Not in my unit. We never gave out cheap medals."

"Who wrote you up for the award?"

"Could'a been anybody, I guess, maybe some fobbit company clerk at Division."

"Well, maybe the facts are wrong, but you apprehended the prisoner, didn't you? I'd say you earned the award, whether or not they got all the details right."

"I didn't apprehend anyone. He dropped his gun and lay down in the dirt with his hands behind his head. Another member of the Quick Reaction Force just walked up and cuffed him. I didn't do shit except to escort the prisoner to the hard site." Buckner could not bring himself to explain that he had witnessed the capture while lying prone on the ground.

Boyer pointed at the tiny scar next to Buckner's eye and said, "He shot you, Buckner. That's combat in anybody's book." Boyer was thrilled to be the roommate of a man who had faced death, and had made horrible decisions and carried the ghosts of those decisions with him. He refused to allow Buckner to diminish his romantic notions of war.

"I beat the shit out of that prisoner." Buckner withdrew the Bronze Star from its box and hefted it in his hand. "The guy was just lying on the floor."

"What are you talking about?"

"He didn't attack anyone after we got him into his cell. He was lying on the floor with his pants around his ankles, smiling at me like some asshole, and I just kicked the everlovin' shit out of him. Like I was kicking a fuckin' football."

"Why would the citation say he attacked the interrogators?"

"That's what I'm telling you, Boyer. He didn't do it."

"Oh, for Christ's sake, Buckner. The errors in the commendation do not constitute any sort of honor violation," said Boyer with finality, returning to his books. Case closed.

Buckner glanced at Boyer, who refused to look back. He wondered if it was a Caucasian thing, this constant emotionless analysis of the world in which every event is merely another asset or debit in each man's personal portfolio. What would Boyer do, wondered Buckner, if he was to someday receive the Nobel Prize by accident? "I'm gonna tell Tannerbeck," said Buckner.

"The Supe? You think you can just knock on his door?"

"The chaplain will help me."

Boyer shrugged and shook his head with disappointment. He imagined that technically a case could be made within the honor code that would permit Buckner to keep the truth to himself. Mistakes were not lies, and Boyer saw no reason to risk having to return something as precious as a Bronze Star. Yet, even with all the rules and regulations that governed military lives, he was slowly beginning to understand what Buckner had always understood intuitively: technicalities were for civilians. The realization frightened Boyer, for it meant that he had not internalized the values of the profession of arms. In Boyer's view, honor did not require martyrdom. To Buckner, it did.

Boyer tossed four more sheets of equations onto Buckner's desk.

CHAPTER 25

September 7, 2004 (Tuesday)
Washington, DC

The amazing thing about Washington, DC, was not that there were so many scandals, but so few. In a town where ambitious young women were eager to trade sex for influence, and where ridiculously young men were players in the halls of Congress, sex and information were traded like currency. The bed-hopping was limited to the aides and assistants, however; the sycophants and briefcase carriers who worked behind the scenes to hammer out deals and operate the bureaucracy. The powerful men themselves usually had the good sense to keep above the dirty business of governance, just as the talking heads on the evening news never actually wrote the stories they reported.

At the crowded Luna Restaurant just off DuPont Circle, Darrow waited impatiently for Brian Joad, administrative aide to Senator Collingsworth, minority leader of the Senate Investigating Committee on Abu Ghraib. Joad was not late, but Darrow checked her watch minute by minute until a man slightly older than she approached her table. "Angie?"

She rose nervously and shook his hand. Joad was a handsome fellow and the flirtatious waitress was upon them instantly, disappointed when they ordered only coffee. He opened the conversation with flattery, his slow Carolina accent giving the illusion that he had all the time in the world. "Print journalists are seldom so attractive," he said with a disarming smile. "Shouldn't you be in television?"

She found him repulsive, although his smooth self-confidence flummoxed her nevertheless. As with everyone she met in Washington who knew more than she did, Darrow sensed that he thought he knew how she had obtained her assignment there, as if she had a scarlet letter emblazoned on her chest—maybe a "W," for "whore." She wondered if Joad was setting her up for further sexual favors in exchange for information. Ignoring his compliment, Darrow said, "I have some information that implicates some very high-ranking military officers in the abuses and cover-up at Abu Ghraib."

"That's what you intimated on the phone, Angie." He repeated her name as if they were old friends. "What have you got?"

She handed him a copy of the Tetra memo. "I assume you have a copy of this?"

He examined it perfunctorily enough to convince Darrow that he had read it before. "I can't comment," he said. "I'd like to know where you got it, however."

"I work for Doug McGowan. Does his name mean anything to you?"

"I'm aware that he carries some weight among the members of the press."

"Doug—Mr. McGowan—was captured in Iraq while embedded with Iraqi insurgents and was imprisoned in Abu Ghraib for six months. During that time, he was tortured by men who have never been identified in any of the abuse allegations. Doug and I are going to find them and expose them. We believe that this memo leads not only to the men who abused him, but to General Tannerbeck, and possibly even other high-ranking officers who knew about the abuses but did not stop them."

He studied her with new respect. "That could be a blockbuster. Why haven't you gone to print yet?"

"Someone wanted us to see this memo. We believe it is someone in the government. Before we allow ourselves to be manipulated, we want to know who leaked this memo and why."

"Me, too."

"If you knew, would you tell me?"

"On the record, the proceedings of the investigating committee are confidential."

"Off the record?"

"Depends on the quid pro quo." He touched her hand with his index finger as if to make a point. She jumped at his touch, not sure if she had been propositioned or not.

"What are you suggesting?" she asked, withdrawing her hand.

He harrumphed, reading her mind. "I'd certainly be interested in getting to know you better, but I wouldn't let you off so easy. No, I'd want something more valuable, like the name of the guards who allegedly abused Doug McGowan."

"You'll be able to read the names in the paper soon enough."

"How much of a heads-up can you give me? The committee will want to get to them before their lawyers do."

"I'll do what I can."

"Fair enough. Off the record, I can tell you that we've had our eye on Tannerbeck for a while. I've seen this memo before, but we need more than an ambiguous memo to destroy a man's career, especially a hero like Tannerbeck. Even being called to testify on such thin evidence would be devastating to anyone with a reputation to protect."

"Do you plan to depose him?"

"Probably not."

"Why not? This doesn't seem like such thin evidence to me."

"First of all, the Republicans control the committee. This scandal isn't about Tannerbeck, it's about the White House. They're not going to undermine their own president on innuendo and anonymous memos."

"But the Democrats would."

"Of course. We want a full criminal investigation. Whoever leaked this memo was probably a Democrat, who should also now be subject to a criminal investigation for leaking confidential documents, God bless him."

"You think this is about the election?"

He looked at her as if she were an idiot. "Everything is about the election."

"Who first brought the memo to the attention of the committee?"

"One of the members on the committee came up with it and initiated a request to the Pentagon to supply the names that were redacted and all other communications to Tannerbeck involving Abu Ghraib."

"There were other memos?"

"I can't tell you."

"Can you tell me the name of the committee member who came up with it?"

He smiled and shook his head, and signaled for the check. Opening his wallet, he withdrew a credit card, which he placed atop the bill, and his business card, which he handed to her. "Any chance we can meet again?"

She fumbled for her own card. "Depends on the quid pro quo," she said, learning fast. The man was an unctuous ass, aware that his proximity to power carried an allure that many women found irresistible. Darrow imagined that he had bedded half the women in Washington. Still, Joad had what she wanted, so she said, "Just tell me which one of your members got that memo."

"I've always been a sucker for women with New York accents. You sound so hard-boiled, like my mother, except she's a Southern woman who hides her steel under big hair and sugar. You're very hard to resist."

"How many of us Yankees have you seduced with that line?"

"Are you feeling seduced?"

"Yes," she confessed. "But you were going to tell me the name of the senator who obtained the documents."

"Was I?"

"Off the record, of course."

"Of course," he repeated silkily, his smiling lips as fixed as a ventriloquist's. "Senator Joanne Sarafin."

The first breath of autumn arrived in the Hudson Valley that afternoon, with the rumor of precipitation spreading through the barracks. Rain developed during the afternoon parade, but by nightfall it had abated to a drizzle, and then tapered off into a chilly mist that lingered across the ridges of Storm King Mountain. The ground was barely dampened, but it caused enough rust to the cadets' rifles and ruined enough spit shines that second regiment was up an extra hour that night fixing the damage.

The cool air sluiced down the river and washed across Manhattan, flushing the smog from the urban canyons and reminding McGowan than another winter was coming. He worked late every night because that was the nature of the job, and because he had nothing to interest him in his mid-town apartment. The phone on his desk rang at all hours of the day or night because his staff knew they could reach him there. So when the phone rang, he answered it routinely. "This is McGowan."

"It's midnight," said Darrow. "Don't you have anything better to do?"

"Like what?"

"Go on a date, maybe, like me."

"I'm too old for that."

"Too grumpy, too. I had coffee with the aide to Senator Collingsworth."

"Coffee's not a date."

"It was for him."

"Don't start sleeping with your sources, Angie. Besides, Democrats are lousy in bed, you know."

"I'll do a statistically valid sample and verify that. Do you want to know what he told me?"

"I'd rather talk about sex. What are you wearing?"

"The Senate Investigating Committee has seen the memo before," she said. "Someone leaked it to Senator Sarafin, but the committee thinks they're being played."

"Of course they're being played. That's why God created leaks."

Darrow relayed the rest of her information to McGowan, who listened intently. Finally, she asked, "How do we flush out the source?"

After a few moments of thought, McGowan said, "We create a leak of our own. We embellish our story a little and watch where they run."

"You think Sarafin will lead us to the leak?"

"No. Senators never get their hands dirty with that sort of thing. The aides handle it all."

"That's what Brian said."

"Who?"

"Brian Joad. Assistant to Collingsworth."

McGowan cringed. The boy sounded like a Southern twit, a typical full-of-himself congressional aide. He wondered if she had already slept with him. "Contact Sarafin's office and find the aide supporting the senator's work on the committee. Then tell the aide that we have proof that Tannerbeck was just the tip of the iceberg. Tell him we've got the goods on the president, and if he wants to see our evidence, then we want to know his source for the memo that he delivered to the committee."

She was quiet for several moments while she took notes. Finally, she said, "Doug?"

"Yeah?"

"I'm not wearing anything at all."

Senator Joanne Sarafin (D) of Wisconsin had won two election campaigns by wide margins. A savvy politician with no illusions about the nobility of her profession, she represented her constituents with Machiavellian ruthlessness. Her professional staff, however, was composed of the sons and daughters of wealthy campaign donors—a useful arrangement for raising money, but a liability when it came to performing the behind-the-scenes functions for which congressional aides earned their pay. But Sarafin was more interested in staying in office than she was in passing good legislation, so the lack of a professional staff was of little consequence to her.

Sally Boskin was a young woman nearly as pretty as Darrow, the wholesome daughter of a dairy farmer with five thousand acres just outside of the metropolis of Wausau, and a legislative aide who was way out of her depth in Washington, DC. She sat now with Darrow, nervously sipping her latte while the reporter laid it on the line for her. For once, Darrow did not feel her imaginary letter, for it was clear that the woman sitting across from her was better prepared for milking cows than negotiating legislation for a United States senator.

"Pretty exciting stuff, isn't it?" asked Darrow. "All this cloak and dagger."

"I'll say. You were pretty mysterious on the phone."

"Some conversations are better held in person." Darrow felt wise and worldly talking to this girl. Recalling a lesson learned from Martha Rose at the Pentagon PIO, she added, "People think that reporters are in the business of betrayal, but we are really in the business of trust. You and I need to trust each other, and you cannot establish that sort of personal relationship over the telephone."

"Absolutely," said the girl, clueless.

"I know that Senator Sarafin delivered this classified memo to the Abu Ghraib investigating committee." Darrow placed the Tetra memo on the table.

Boskin's eyes betrayed her surprise, but she had enough sense to keep her mouth shut.

"It's a felony to traffic in classified documents," said Darrow, "but I'm not interested in sending you or the senator to jail."

"Jail? You must be kidding. The senator asked me to go pick up an envelope. I do that sort of thing all the time. I never know what's inside the envelopes. I just deliver them." She spoke with enough confidence that the reference to illegalities clearly had not intimidated her in the way Darrow had hoped it would.

"Who gave you the envelope?"

The girl shook her head.

"I'm on your side," said Darrow. "It's my job to expose the bad guys, and the higher up the chain of command, the better. I want your help, not your hide. And I'm prepared to offer you something in exchange."

"Like what?"

"That memo about Tannerbeck is just the tip of the iceberg. I've got the goods on the secretary of defense and the president, himself. They knew about Abu Ghraib and they knew it was a violation of the Geneva Conventions. I can prove it. And when I do, the Democrats can take back the White House." Darrow listened to herself talk, fast and nervous, and wondered if this girl was savvy enough to detect the bluff in her voice.

"I'm nobody," protested the girl. "I fetch coffee and deliver envelopes. You need to talk to Senator Sarafin."

"The senator does NOT want to talk to me. It would be unseemly for a U.S. senator to go after a war hero like Tannerbeck. As soon as I printed her name in the newspaper, the right wing would crucify her and every redneck in Wisconsin would be mobilized to defeat her in her next election. That's what we're for, you and me. We can expose corruption without getting your boss implicated. And once the Democrats are back in the White House, your senator rises to committee chairmanships, or even a job in the administration. All you have to do is give me the name of the person who gave you that envelope."

"Really, I could lose my job," protested Boskin. "I can't give you what you want."

Darrow shook her head sadly. "In the absence of this information, I will have to print that the senator acquired the document and passed it along to the committee. Instead of me quietly asking questions of her aide, she'll have the entire DC press corps camped out on her doorstep."

"You would do that?"

"I have deadlines."

"I'll call her right now," said Boskin, reaching for her cellular phone. "You can talk to her."

"Don't be silly. As soon as she talks to me, she's on the record. You'll compromise her, and you'll be on the next plane home to Milwaukee. The best thing you can do is to simply pass me on to the person who gave you that envelope, without involving anyone else."

"The man you're looking for has reasons to remain anonymous."

Darrow felt the girl's resolve weakening, and intuitively changed her approach to be more supportive, a girlfriend rather than a reporter. "Everyone has reasons. You're not sleeping with him, are you?"

"Gracious, no!"

"Good. I made that mistake once," said Darrow, trying now to express sisterly concern, although she secretly wondered if it had really been a mistake. McGowan had upheld his part of the bargain and the sex hadn't been all that bad. Returning to the subject, she continued, "He'll never know where I got his name."

"If you already have evidence of a cover-up, why do you need my source?"

"On a story of this importance, we need dual verification of everything we print. If your guy can confirm what I've got, I can deliver the president's head to you, personally, on a platter. You'll be able to write your own ticket with the Democratic Party. Otherwise, I'll have to get my verification elsewhere, from a source that might not care if I take your senator down for trafficking in classified material." Shamelessly, Darrow added, "Let me help you."

Boskin chewed her lower lip for a moment, and then surrendered as meekly as a fawn. Snatching a pen from her purse, she wrote a name and phone number on the back of a napkin. "Do you recognize the name?"

Darrow shrugged her shoulders to indicate that she had never heard of Donald Ross.

"He works for DuFossey."

"DuFossey?" repeated McGowan. "You've confirmed that?"

"Yes. He's on DuFossey's staff as a legislative aide, but DuFossey is now so busy with the presidential campaign that Ross pretty much runs the office in the senator's absence."

"Well done, Angie. Do you know what to do next?"

The compliment pleased her, as she sensed that for once McGowan was not thinking about her breasts. He was teaching now, leading her with his questions and making her think like a professional.

"Set up a meeting?" she ventured.

"No. We are about to touch a hot nerve. Someone is leaking classified information to the DuFossey campaign and DuFossey is passing it on through Senator Sarafin. This is incredibly risky for DuFossey. If he gets caught, he'll be tap dancing all the way to Election Day. But if the information can undermine the president, it could get him into the White House. Unfortunately for DuFossey, Senator Sarafin has her own reasons for not going public with whatever DuFossey sent her. Meanwhile, the investigation is going nowhere until after the election." McGowan laughed. "Ross must be pulling his hair out."

"So maybe he'll talk to us. He can use us to make the case against the administration."

"No. If Ross has a brain in his head, the last thing he wants to do is to talk to the press. As soon as we ask him where he's getting his information, he's screwed. Abu Ghraib will cease to become a Republican scandal and will become a Democratic one."

"We can threaten to expose him."

"Now you're talking."

"But not a meeting? Do we blackmail him anonymously?"

"Blackmail is a crime, Angie, although it can be useful. But we really don't have any evidence with which to perpetrate blackmail. Just the word of some bimbo in Sarafin's office. Ross could deny everything and Sarafin would surely back him up."

"So what do you want me to do?"

"Give Ross the same bullshit you gave Sarafin's little milkmaid. Let him know we've got the goods on the president and we want his source so we can verify."

"You think that'll work?"

"No. He can't give up a primary source without acknowledging the illegality of his contacts. And he won't talk to his source on the phone, either, certainly not from the office, where all calls are logged, or even his cell phone."

"A stakeout?" she asked.

"Good girl," he said, praise for his best student.

Darrow did not know how to conduct a stakeout, but she was glad that he hadn't told her. She had wanted the junior assignment in Washington, and McGowan had given her the job and the responsibility to produce. Strange, she thought, that after making her sleep with him to get the job, he had enough respect for her afterward to allow her to do it.

Like most Americans, Darrow had heard plenty about William DuFossey. A ten-year veteran of the Senate, he had come to national prominence within the last two years for his careful opposition to the war in Iraq. His refusal to support the president had made enemies within his own party, but hordes of college students had rallied to his rhetoric, urging him to run for president himself. Many of those students were from DuFossey's tiny home state of Rhode Island, where the likes of Brown and the University of Rhode Island produced college students in a disproportionate number. Thus, free to attack the war without concern for the Silent Majority that lurked among the constituency of his colleagues, DuFossey had secured the presidential nomination on a wave of antiwar sentiment from the left wing of the Democratic Party.

With an eye on the polls, he had been swimming back toward the mainstream ever since. Despite the continuing bloody headlines from Iraq, however, the public had stayed the course with the president. Only the breaking scandal in Abu Ghraib had nudged the numbers his way, with the press reporting the race dead even. But internal polls, less imaginative than those used by the media to guarantee an exciting horserace, showed that the voting in a couple of swing states would make the difference. Without Ohio and Florida, the Democrats would lose the election, and the voters there still had faith in the president and did not support surrender. Their faith in the military needed to be undermined.

Campaign business was not permitted from federal offices, so DuFossey's campaign was run from an office of the Democratic Campaign Committee in Rhode Island. Nevertheless, the business of the Senate did not stop, and senatorial functions continued from DuFossey's office in the Hart Senate Office Building, one city block of white marble. The structure was impressive for its size, if not its architecture. The interior was utilitarian, except for the massive slab of steel that soared eighty feet in the atrium, topped by a pair of crude steel wings that seemed as aerodynamic as a battleship. Darrow found herself baffled by the sculpture, for unlike the evocative artwork in the Pentagon, it had no relevance to the work done there and was evocative of nothing. The building and its artwork seemed related only by their mutual size.

Darrow had no trouble gaining access, for the press was always welcome. The guards paid more attention to her miniskirt than they did to her credentials as she passed through the metal detector. The hallways were actually balconies that overlooked the atrium, with senatorial offices on the opposite side. The entrance to DuFossey's consisted of dual glass doors flanked by an American flag on one side and the flag of Rhode Island on the other. After the Democratic Convention, the state flag had been joined by the black POW/MIA flag. A plaque on the wall identified the distinguished occupant.

She found DuFossey's office and paused briefly as she passed, since her real destination was a bench installed at the end of the corridor for those visitors who arrived early for appointments or who simply wanted to stare at the grotesque artwork as it soared past them. The bench also made a comfortable spot to chat with some degree of privacy on a mobile phone.

Darrow had never spoken to a member of Congress as she now dialed DuFossey's office, but she had learned that the words "*Citizen Times*" opened doors in Washington. A woman answered the phone and Darrow identified herself. "This is Angie Darrow of *The Citizen Times*. I recently received some confidential information regarding Senator DuFossey that I need to confirm with him prior to printing it. When might I be able to speak with him?"

"I'll refer you to the press secretary."

"No," responded Darrow quickly. "This information is very sensitive, and I do not believe that the senator would like us discussing this with anyone but him. I must speak with him directly. I have a three p.m. deadline tomorrow afternoon. Can you have him call me?"

"One moment."

A silent minute passed while Darrow waited, and then a man's voice said, "This is Donald Ross. Who is this, please?"

Darrow managed to stammer out her name. Quickly, she added, "I'm a reporter with *The Citizen Times*."

"Yes, we got that part already. What can I do for you, Miss Darrow?"

"Thank you for taking this call," she began.

"We always take calls," said Ross, "especially from a reporter for a powerful newspaper who hints darkly that she has some sort of information that is too sensitive for regular channels. Now, I've never heard of you, miss, but I hope you know better than to throw your credentials around for routine matters. You start doing that, and nobody will ever take your calls. This is a small town that way. Now, what is it you want? You have sixty seconds."

Darrow wondered if he was bluffing, even as she began her own Big Lie. "I'm sure you are aware that we have been following the reports of torture and abuse at Abu Ghraib."

"Yes, we've been reading your articles with great interest."

"Sir, I have recently received information documenting a conspiracy at the highest levels of the U.S. government, directing the torture and abuse of prisoners at Abu Ghraib. According to my sources, General Tannerbeck, currently the Superintendent at the U.S. Military Academy at West Point, was directed to carry out those orders by higher authorities."

"That's very interesting," he said calmly. "We've suspected it all along."

"My sources tell me that you have been privy to several documents that support these allegations, and that you have submitted this proof to the Senate Investigating Committee."

"You seem to be the one with the proof, not me."

"I have a couple of sources that provide information to me, Mr. Ross. I know that one of them is also supplying you with classified documents pertaining to the cover-up of the Abu Ghraib scandal. I am also aware of physical torture committed at Abu Ghraib by a guard named Buckner, who has yet to be indicted for his acts."

"I have no idea what you are talking about."

"Frankly, Mr. Ross, that is the answer I expected, at least on the phone. If you need some time to consider your response, I can meet face-to-face with you tomorrow. But we plan to go to press in the next day's edition, and at this time we do intend to include the involvement of the DuFossey campaign in the acquisition and distribution of classified memos related to Tannerbeck's knowledge of the abuses and subsequent cover-up." With a final flourish, she tacked on her lie: "And I can prove that the president himself approved the abuses and ordered them covered up."

"Now, wait a minute," said Ross, genuinely perplexed.
"Are you accusing Senator DuFossey of anything? What is it
that you want from me?"

"Confirmation of your source and verification of our
information."

"Well, I have no comment." Ross's breathing grew shallow as he focused his mind and thought fast. The response
to a political ambush was the same as an ambush in combat:
attack. Ross knew a thing or two about bluff and innuendo, about anonymous accusations, and about the politics
of personal destruction. Only truth defied political attack
or counterattack, but it was because of the truth that Ross
now hesitated. The girl knew something, and he needed
to know if that one kernel of truth had enough power behind it to take out the DuFossey campaign like a sniper's
bullet.

How had she made the connection to the DuFossey campaign? General Piersal, he knew, was one of her
sources—the two men had plotted the leak together—but
the leak was supposed to be anonymous. Ross wondered
if she had tracked down Piersal, or worse, was Piersal
playing both sides? Or was someone else talking to her
about the investigation? Piersal had never provided him
with any documents linking the president directly to the
scandal at Abu Ghraib. So who was her source and what
could she prove? Her story was almost believable. Hell,
he *wanted* to believe it; such revelations would undermine
the entire government and open the door to DuFossey's
candidacy, as long as DuFossey himself remained untaint-
ed by Ross's partnership with Piersal. Darrow had given
him twenty-four hours, and he needed every minute of it.
"Give me your number and I'll get back to you before your
deadline."

Darrow provided her number and snapped her cellular phone shut. She did not know how long she might have to wait, but the miniskirt, she knew, was a mistake. The bench was uncomfortable, so she turned sideways and held the phone to her ear, as if listening, while keeping an eye on DuFossey's office door. She tried not to glance at the clock at the end of the hall, but minutes passed slowly and even the second hand seemed to slow down.

A suspicious guard asked her business, but Darrow smiled and pointed at her phone as if she were on a call. The guard glanced at her legs and moved on. The wait seemed to go on forever, but after an hour, DuFossey's office door finally opened and Donald Ross marched out, sporting his trademark bow tie. He made a beeline to the elevators, not bothering to glance up and down the hallway. Though Ross had never seen her and did not look in her direction, Darrow turned away. She dared not leave the bench to follow, so she watched from the balcony as the elevator descended and Ross strode into the atrium. Immediately, she dashed down the three flights of spiral stairs that wrapped around the elevator and landed in the lobby just as Ross strode purposefully through the exit to the street.

Darrow immediately gave chase, struggling through the crowd as Ross jogged quickly down the granite stairs to a line of cabs at the curb. Only by shoving aside another woman was Darrow able to secure the taxi behind his.

"Follow that cab," she ordered.

"Lady," replied the man, humorless, "I've been driving a taxi for fifteen years and you're the first person ever said that to me. I'll follow him, but I ain't runnin' any red lights."

"Just don't lose him."

"I suppose there's an extra twenty in it for me."

"Of course," she said, not sure whether she had any cash on her at all.

The taxis headed south through rush-hour traffic, then east across the John Philip Sousa Bridge into Anacostia. There were parts of Washington, DC, where the business of government had little impact, where the residents took only a cynical interest in any of the great issues that were debated so emotionally a few blocks away. Anacostia was such a neighborhood, and it was only with reluctance that Darrow's cab driver followed her emphatic instructions to veer down the empty off-ramp in pursuit of Ross into a sullen cityscape. Traffic roared overhead on the elevated highway, thronged with drivers grateful to bypass this part of town, but Darrow's taxi plowed through a pair of potholes and pulled up behind Ross's cab at an intersection.

"What now, lady?" said the cabby, clearly unhappy. As if to punctuate the dreariness of their location, he switched on the windshield wipers, for it had begun to rain.

"Stay with him," said Darrow, fascinated that Ross should take a taxi here. "Give him some room."

They drove on through the shadow of the highway's underbelly into a warped dimension, where prowling poverty had long ago sucked the idealism from the Great Society, where concrete and chain-link fences and shuttered storefronts defined a crumbling civilization. They passed liquor stores and bar fronts among gutted entrances in adjoining buildings. Black men huddled on corners or in abandoned doorways, stuporous with booze or crack, soaking up the rain.

Darrow retreated further into her seat. She felt naked in her whiteness, helpless in a grotesque world of hollow black buildings and hollow black people. Tightly packed row houses loomed over them; one house burned, empty, vacant, like a missing tooth. The sidewalks were empty, too, except for trash scooting before the wind and spiraling in urban dust devils. But there were businesses here—a catfish restaurant, an auto parts store, a bar on each corner—and a steady flow of traffic on the street. When Ross's cab suddenly pulled to the curb and the brake lights illuminated, Darrow directed her driver to continue on past. "Let me out around the corner," she added.

As her taxi cruised by, she watched through the rear window as Ross flipped a bill to his cabby and stepped into a bar named Ileen's, a brick and windowless joint with a malfunctioning neon sign that sputtered and flashed. She found some money in her purse and tipped the driver twenty dollars. "You want me to wait?" he asked. "This ain't no place for a girl like you."

"What kind of girl is that?" she said, as the breeze blew up her short skirt. The streets were in shadow and chilly with the early fall weather.

"White kind."

"Can I afford you? My purse isn't full of twenties, you know."

"I'll wait as long as the other guy waits, no charge on the meter until you get back. You ain't planning on leaving with the man you're chasing, are you?"

"Not a chance," said Darrow, realizing that her driver didn't miss much; the other cab was parked, too, waiting.

She skipped across the street, hugging herself against the cold precipitation. *I've done everything wrong*, she thought, *and I'm freezing my ass off in this outfit.*

Ross spotted Piersal immediately, the only white patron in the nearly empty bar, sitting as always against the back wall at the last table next to the restrooms. As DuFossey's aide sat across from him, Piersal said, "You've got to be more punctual, sir."

"You picked this place," growled Ross. "We are not exactly inconspicuous here." He glanced about like a wary little dog.

"The president himself could have a beer here," snorted Piersal, taking command of the meeting with a barely concealed sense of authority. "We're just two honkies in this part of town. Somebody might mug us, but they sure as hell won't recognize us."

"You'd better be right."

Piersal exuded an aura of gloominess and wisdom that implied knowledge of things best not discussed. "Why are we here? What couldn't you talk about on the phone?"

"I think someone's followed me here."

Piersal did not move, but his eyes glanced at the door. "Don't get paranoid on me, Ross. What's going on?"

"I received a phone call from that woman, Darrow, at the *Times*. She knows a lot more than what you were supposed to tell her."

"Like what?" Piersal leaned forward, intent, one eye on Ross, the other still on the door.

"She knew I had access to that memo. How would she know that?"

"I don't know. You obviously left a trail."

"Perhaps you've talked to her." The aide stared across the table at the stoop-shouldered general and trembled slightly.

"Don't annoy me, Ross."

"She also has proof that the abuses were ordered by the president or the SecDef. How is it that she has this information and I don't?"

"Because she made it up. It's bullshit."

"I don't think so. She wouldn't have called me if she didn't have something to back it up. We've always suspected the president was in on it."

"It's a bluff," reiterated Piersal, impatient with the amateur before him. "I know positively that nobody in our government ordered any heavy-handed bullshit at Abu Ghraib."

"How can you be sure?"

"The president didn't order it, because I ordered the goddamned abuse myself."

"You?" gasped Ross, stunned.

"Damn right. We'd still be electrocuting those raggedy-ass bastards if some idiot hadn't taken those damn photographs." Piersal watched with disdain as Ross's jaw dropped.

"What were you thinking?"

Piersal laughed. "Believe it or not, Ross, I value the lives of our soldiers more than the lives of the enemy. In a guerilla war, military intelligence is critical to mission success. If we can gain enough intel to save an American life by putting a woman's panties on some Iraqi's head, don't you think we should do it?"

"That was your idea?"

"Local commanders were screaming for better intel. I knew how to obtain it. Nobody asked if it was legal. We were saving American lives, after all."

"But I thought Tannerbeck was following orders from the Pentagon, or higher. That's why we're fingering him— to compromise the current administration."

"And that's what the investigation will show, Mr. Ross. The Joint Chiefs knew we were pushing the envelope. My techniques developed at Gitmo were close to the line, but still legal. When we got to Abu Ghraib, however, we lacked the time and trained personnel to reproduce our success in Guantanamo. So, like musicians who make up in volume what they lack in talent, we increased the intensity of our interrogations. Fortunately, we got excellent results. When I realized that nobody was going to tell me to stop, I saw an opportunity to compromise the entire chain of command by documenting my concerns about the legality of the very measures I had implemented. The chain of command was dysfunctional. I ran the OGAs behind the scenes while encouraging the FOB commander to send outraged memos to Tannerbeck about the abuses. But Tannerbeck couldn't pass anything up-channel without giving up the intel he wanted, and without creating an embarrassing situation for his commanders that might make them reconsider his appointment to West Point."

"My God. This could completely backfire."

"Not if you keep your mouth shut. The Darrow woman doesn't know anything except what we want her to know." He spoke reassuringly, despite his desire to grab Ross by the shoulders and give him a good shake.

Unmollified, Ross continued, "She asked about someone named Morgan Buckner, another guard at Abu Ghraib, not yet named or arrested for torturing prisoners. Is that true?"

"Yes, Mr. Ross. Buckner is our ace in the hole. He will bring down the Superintendent at West Point, and humiliate the entire U.S. Army and Defense Department."

"Who is he?"

"Exactly who she said. I'm surprised it has taken her this long to find him." For once, Ross had contributed some useful information, confirming that McGowan and Darrow had successfully followed the Tetra memo. He still wasn't sure how much they knew, and it concerned him that they had not yet named Tannerbeck or Buckner in the newspaper.

"I'm becoming dubious of the value of discrediting Tannerbeck," said Ross. "Is it worth all this risk? We could end up humiliating ourselves if this ever got out."

"Remember, Ross, the goal is to demoralize the voters. As the war destroys our military heroes and reveals them to be criminal or incompetent, a new wave of voters flocks to your banner. We're going to lose this war, and the truly patriotic thing to do is to ensure that some good comes of it. Once we get your man elected to the presidency, the warriors will run for cover and thinking men like us will ascend to power."

"Save the pillow talk, General. You're a real bastard, aren't you?"

"What's the matter, Ross? Shocked to be conspiring with a war criminal?"

Ross stared at Piersal, struggling not to look away, but finally unable to match Piersal's intense gaze. "I can live with it," stated the aide. "Sometimes, the ends must justify the means."

"Indeed they must," agreed Piersal. "And I'll tell you something else about Darrow."

"What?"

"She just walked in the door."

Ross jerked his head around and spotted Darrow as she seated herself at the bar. The few other patrons turned their heads as well, wondering what business a pretty white woman might have there. "Christ!" cursed the senator's man. "What an idiot I am!"

"No, sir. You're merely an amateur, just like she is."

"What do we do now?"

"We get the hell out of here. Now listen up: she already knows who you are, so I want you to walk right past her, keeping yourself between her and me. Look her in the eye;

keep her attention, but do not engage her. I'll slip out the back."

"How do you know there is a rear entrance?"

"Ross, do you think I just pick these places out of a phone book?"

Darrow held her hands against her cheeks to warm them. The bartender slapped a paper napkin in front of her and waited expectantly.

"Something warm," said Darrow. "Tea?"

"Coffee's all I got." The bartender's tone was as chilly as the outside air. He had nothing against white women, especially girls as pretty as Darrow, but they were bad for business. His was a bar where black men could meet black women, but when a white woman came in looking for a black man, nothing followed but trouble. The brothers made fools of themselves and the sisters went home mad. Nothing but trouble.

"Fine," said Darrow. "Cream and sugar." She was conscious of the stares from the few other patrons, but it took only a moment to spot the two white men seated in the rear of the bar. The man with his back to the wall glanced up and studied her carefully for a moment before returning to his conversation with Ross. The room was dark, but bright enough to make out the man's features: high forehead, short hair, and a mustache. She chided herself again for not bringing a camera, for not being prepared.

The black woman next to Darrow laid a bill on the counter and stood up to leave. "Honey," she said, "this ain't no place for you. Good people come here." Before Darrow could respond, the woman walked away.

The bartender scooped up the money and wiped down the bar. Noticing the perplexed look on Darrow's face, he said, "She thinks you're a hooker."

Darrow glanced at her hemline, thinking that the woman's assumption was not unreasonable. "And what do you think?" she asked the bartender.

"Hookers that look like you don't waste their time in neighborhoods like this."

"I'm a reporter," she said.

"Even worse."

Suddenly, Ross stood up and began striding toward her, his eyes furious and locked on hers. Darrow turned to confront him. She had no questions prepared. *Was he going to speak first?* When he was within an arm's reach, Ross spun on his heel with almost military precision and headed for the door. Darrow's eyes followed him briefly, but a flash of movement in the rear of the bar caught her attention. She turned her head toward the table where Ross had been seated, but the man was gone.

Darrow hurried to the rear of the establishment and realized that the hallway that led to the restrooms also led outside. The exit door opened into an alley, empty except for the trash swirling in the drizzle. She skipped across a rain-filled pothole to the main street in time to see Ross enter his cab and drive away. The other man had disappeared like a ghost. She stood for a moment, cognizant that her hair was getting wet, wondering what to do.

A V-8 engine roared to life and a pair of headlights suddenly blinded her as they approached. Her first thought was to run, but the car splashed up alongside the curb and the rear door opened. "Hurry up," said her cab driver. "Do you want to keep following him?"

Darrow jumped into the cab. "No. Just take me home." She gave him the address and her last twenty-dollar bill.

CHAPTER 26

September 8, 2004 (Wednesday)
Pentagon, Washington, DC

Lt. Colonel Makin spun the dial on his office safe, securing classified documents before heading home, when Piersal stormed through the door. The general threw his wet raincoat on the coat rack and barked, "Elliott, I need your help."

Makin grabbed a notebook and followed his boss into his office, where he took a seat in a leather side chair, poised to start recording his instructions. He was both alarmed and excited when Piersal sputtered, "What do we know about Angie Darrow, the reporter from *The Citizen Times?*"

Makin had noted her name while tracking Lambeau's movement through the Pentagon during the quest for Tetra's NOK, but he had dismissed her as McGowan's girl Friday. "Not much," admitted Makin. "We assume she's around for McGowan's entertainment."

"She seems to be growing out of the cub reporter role. She trailed DuFossey's aide and spotted us together."

"Can she identify you?"

"I don't think so. The bar was dark, and I doubt that she would have any idea who I am even if she got a good look at me. Still, Ross tells me that she asked him about Buckner."

"If she knows Buckner's name, then it is only a matter of time before she contacts him."

"We must assume that she already has, which is good. Buckner actually committed abuses at Abu Ghraib. He can demolish Tannerbeck, but he has no link to us at all. Buckner has never heard of us, has he?"

"No, sir. I never met him at Abu Ghraib. He was Levi's project from beginning to end."

"Buckner and Tannerbeck are linked. They met in Baghdad. Not only is it reasonable to assume that they discussed Buckner's actions at Abu Ghraib, but Tannerbeck just awarded him a Bronze Star."

"I know," said Makin, "I wrote the commendation myself."

Army recommendations for award were often submitted in conjunction with a soldier's departure from any unit. When Piersal arranged for Buckner's departure from Iraq, he had directed Makin to submit Buckner for the Bronze Star. Makin had written the informal summary of events and submitted it to Levi, with instructions to forward it to the new JDIC commander, who in turn passed the recommendation to Buckner's company commander. With no access to the MI wing to verify the events that had happened there, and having received the recommendation from a ranking field grade officer, the company commander simply copied Makin's summary onto the formal documentation and forwarded the award up-channel for routine approval by the commander of the 800th MI Brigade.

Piersal allowed himself a smirk. "Now we just have to make sure that Buckner is revealed as a fraud, and that his appointment is related to Tannerbeck's efforts to hide his own cover-up of events at Abu Ghraib."

"How do we leak it?" pondered Makin. "Anonymous call?"

"Leaks are of dubious value to the press, unless they come accompanied by some sort of proof, such as the memo we forwarded to the Tetras. Even that could be faked, which I suspect is why McGowan and this Darrow woman have not published anything yet. They need a source they can trust, put a face to."

"Should we have Ross feed it to them?"

"Yes. We've already succeeded in compromising him, but he's getting cold feet. I want to lock in our relationship so tight that he won't even consider double-crossing us once DuFossey is in office. He's a weasel and I don't trust him."

"If Darrow exposes Ross, he won't take the fall alone," observed Makin. "He'll roll over on us."

"No doubt. But if that happens, we've lost the election anyway. And reporters never reveal where they get their information. It's like a badge of honor for them to spend time in jail for protecting a source."

CHAPTER 27

September 9, 2004 (Thursday)
Washington, DC

William DuFossey spent the day in a boat on Lake Erie, fishing in the rain for an audience of miserable journalists who dutifully snapped photos of a few PCB-laden steelhead before the senator threw them back. To the DuFossey spin machine, the day was hailed as a two-for-one publicity coup: not only did the candidate demonstrate his "real man" appeal by catching fish, but he appeased the environmental community by tossing the diseased animals back into the water and commenting on the need to clean up streams and lakes so that fishermen could eat their catch without fear of tumors and heavy metals in their food.

The Republicans pointed out with a snicker that this was the first day of his life that DuFossey had not worn a necktie, let alone wielded a fishing rod. They added that "real men" had enough sense to come in out of the rain.

While the Republicans laughed and the Democrats strutted and the voters paid no attention whatsoever, Donald Ross met Angie Darrow at Café Renee in Union Station. The coffee shop was perched above a row of retail stores in the vaulted departure area, close to the ornate ceiling.

Accessible via its own staircase, Café Renee was an upscale version of the bar where Darrow had spotted Ross and Piersal—a good spot to watch others without being watched. Ross was relieved to have reached her before the train departed for New York, and he noticed that she glanced at her watch as she sat down at his table. "I'll make this quick," he promised.

She had a few minutes. Crossing her legs, Darrow congratulated herself on finally learning how to dress for the job. She wore blue jeans and a Burberry jacket, which despite its stylishness and expense was nevertheless warm and comfortable. In her Bandolino boots, she presented a glamorous image, and Ross found himself undone by her attractiveness.

"Funny," he said, "if I'd realized how pretty you were, I might not have run so fast when I last saw you."

She allowed him a moment to look at her. "It was dark," she said, not bothering with any false humility. "I'd love to listen to your compliments, but I have a train to catch."

He nodded and got down to business. "I have some information about Morgan Buckner." As she withdrew a pad and pen from her purse, he added, "Off the record."

"Writing it down doesn't mean it's on the record."

"Of course not. Just remember, I must remain an 'unnamed source.' You may never mention my name. I'll deny everything. I can be of great assistance to you in the future, especially if we win the election. Not many reporters at your stage in their career have access to the Oval Office. You understand what I'm offering you?"

"I certainly do, Mr. Ross. I understand my obligations and my rights when it comes to protecting my sources. You don't need to offer me any sort of bribe."

Her choice of words frightened him. "I'm not violating any laws, Angie. I'm just providing information to help you find those who have. If either one of us were to start revealing our sources, the whole foundation of the fourth estate would crumble."

Whatever, she thought. "What's your information?"

"This boy Buckner is a murderer." Ross was pleased to see that Darrow was too surprised to respond. "He killed a prisoner at Abu Ghraib about a week before McGowan arrived. Apparently, he kicked the man to death during an interrogation. The prisoner was identified as C-237, and was never heard from again. His death was never reported."

Recovered from her initial shock, Darrow scribbled notes furiously. "Who told you this?" she asked.

"That I cannot tell you. But there's more."

She checked her watch, desperate now to see McGowan, but knowing that she would skip the train if she had to, if Ross dragged this out. Recalling one of McGowan's infernal lessons, she knew that she could not prompt Ross to hurry. "Sources are filled with ego," McGowan had explained to her. "You have to coddle them, let them talk and be the center of attention. As soon as you act as if they are wasting your time—as most of them are—they'll clam up and find someone else to talk to. The trouble is, you never know which ones are wasting your time and which ones are handing you a Pulitzer Prize." Conspicuously, she removed her watch and tossed it into her purse. "You have my full attention, Mr. Ross."

"You already know that Buckner is now a plebe at West Point, right?"

She nodded.

"Do you know how he got his appointment?"

She raised an eyebrow and leaned forward.

"Buckner is a black kid from Baltimore with a useless public school education who never took the SAT exams. He joined the Guard because it was the only job he could get. Prison guards are not exactly the best and brightest members of their generation, you know."

"You're saying he does not meet the minimum qualifications to be an officer?"

"He barely meets the requirements to be a private. The army makes exceptions for certain men who exhibit extraordinary leadership skills, and even provides them with special education in an Academy Prep School, but there was nothing special about Buckner. All members of Congress appoint kids to the academies every year, and even Senator DuFossey's appointments are rarely the white-bread Boy Scouts that the Academy wants, but not even we would appoint someone as unqualified as Buckner."

"So how did he get the appointment?"

Ross shrugged knowingly. "You tell me. Personally, I think General Tannerbeck knew about Buckner's abusiveness at Abu Ghraib and got him the hell out of there. The army couldn't prosecute him without calling attention to its procedures for conducting interrogations, so he was sent to West Point and given a medal to shut him up."

"What medal?"

"A Bronze Star. Tannerbeck pinned it on Buckner's chest personally just a few days ago."

Darrow recalled McGowan's comments about medals during their visit to the Tetras, and she wondered if the Bronze Star meant anything or not.

"This is explosive stuff, Mr. Ross. You know I will have to verify it."

"I expect you to. I want the truth verified as much as you do." Ross smiled unctuously. "The press and the Congress may not appreciate each other, but that isn't to say we can't be of service to each other. There are already half a dozen investigations ongoing regarding the events at Abu Ghraib. I am confident that the proper authorities represented in these investigative bodies will follow the evidence and root out the guilty parties. I simply want to ensure that they have the evidence. For that, I must rely on the press to expose the facts."

"Why not just present your facts to the committees directly?"

Ross scoffed at her naiveté. "The committees are not interested in the facts. They are interested in protecting the army, and in protecting the commander in chief. The committees are all run by the party in power, as you know."

"Are you manipulating the press in order to expose the truth for the benefit of Senator DuFossey?

"If the truth facilitates my candidate's election, is that so bad?"

Darrow knew she was in over her head, just as she had been in McGowan's office the first day she met him. Then, with nothing to lose, she had bluffed her way through with vivacity and gall. But Ross had called her here for a reason and he clearly expected professionalism from her. So, she returned to McGowan's advice: If someone wants to talk, just listen.

"But the biggest scandal of all, the greatest insult to our servicemen who have sacrificed everything, is that the Bronze Star awarded to Buckner is a fake. He never earned it."

"How do you fake a medal?"

He reached into his pocket and passed a sheet of paper across the table. She read the bold letters at the top of the page: *Citation to accompany the award of the Bronze Star to Morgan Buckner.* Ross waited while she read the entire text. "Every award is accompanied by a citation," he explained. "This citation makes reference to events that did not happen."

"How do you know?"

"I can't prove it. All I know from my source is that, contrary to this citation, Buckner did not apprehend any prisoner and was not attacked by the prisoner after he was taken in for interrogation. On the contrary, he kicked an unarmed and fully restrained prisoner to death. It's up to you to verify it."

The public address system announced the departure of the 4:10 train to Grand Central Station. "That's my train," said Darrow.

"Then I guess you'd better hurry."

She stood to leave, but remembered another of McGowan's lessons: Get everyone's contact info, because you never get the full story the first time around. "I need your cellular phone number," she said.

CHAPTER 28

September 10, 2004 (Friday)
West Point

The Highland Falls gatehouse was a cute granite castle the size of a toolshed occupied by an immaculate MP with polished brass and leather. The crenellated sentry post provided merely a hint of the awesome fortress beyond it, but the expressionless MP was more informative, advising McGowan that cadet visitors usually found Grant Hall a convenient place to rendezvous. Another Gothic structure, Grant Hall was as hollow and shadowy as a church, with dozens of couches distributed throughout and huge oil paintings of famous generals hung on the walls. A bored first classman sat alone at the guard desk, playing with the tassels on his red cummerbund as upper-class cadets and their guests came and went.

McGowan wore a tweed sport jacket on which he had pinned his Purple Heart and Silver Star, old medals from an old war. Unlike many Vietnam veterans who tossed their awards into the garbage, McGowan had kept his medals in his jewelry box for thirty years, remembering them occasionally whenever he went searching for a pair of cufflinks. He kept his medals initially as a tribute to his own bravery, but as he grew older and saw men die in other wars, the awards became reminders of the level of sacrifice that men would make for trinkets. He told Darrow, however, that he had purchased the medals at a pawn shop. She had never known a soldier; she would not understand why an old man would still have his fruit salad.

He stopped at the guard's desk and leaned heavily on it. Behind McGowan stood Darrow, wide-eyed and excited by the dramatic architecture and the stunning landscape of the Hudson Valley. She had driven past West Point a hundred times during her years at Bard, barely thirty miles upstream, but it had never occurred to her to cross the river for a closer look. She had no concept of a military post, but West Point was the kind of army base she could appreciate, a fortress on the scenic Hudson River, surrounded by wooded hills and populated with intelligent men. It was reassuring to know that not every military facility was a godforsaken hellhole in some incredibly hot southern state. She gazed at the ceiling thirty feet above her and let McGowan do the talking.

"Excuse me, Cadet."

The guard stood. He noted the decorations on McGowan's chest, another old grad coming back to West Point like a salmon. McGowan saw the cadet's eyes dart to the medals on his jacket, then back again.

"I'm looking for a freshman cadet named Buckner, Company F-2."

"Fourth classmen are not permitted to entertain guests on weeknights, sir."

McGowan had not considered that Buckner was a plebe, or that his freedom to come and go might be restricted. He realized how sequestered Buckner was, what a cozy place this was for keeping a man out of sight. Unfazed, he said, "I

have to get a message to Morgan Buckner. A buddy of his in
Iraq died. I'm here to tell him."

The guard nodded with understanding, for such things
were not unusual at West Point. "Hang on, sir. Let me make
a couple of phone calls."

Although members of different regiments did not normally have much association with each other, Firsties often
had inter-regimental friends. Even if not, there existed a
special rapport among classmates who could ask favors of
each other, sight unseen.

The guard hung up the phone after a brief conversation. "Sir, I was able to get through to the commander of
Company F-2. Mr. Buckner is in class right now and can't
be reached. However, the company commander assured me
that Buckner will be permitted to call you tonight."

McGowan provided his name and room number at the
Thayer Hotel. Then, with a few hours of daylight remaining,
he snatched a tourist guide from the guard's desk and took
Darrow by the arm. The interior of Grant Hall was of interest to historians and architects, but the real glory of West
Point could only be measured outdoors. As they walked toward the Plain, the cadet chapel seemed to float above them
in a cloudless sky while the breeze-whipped river glided by
at the base of the cliff upon which the United States Military
Academy was perched. The whole place was simultaneously
brooding and exalted, fitting sentiments for a place dedicated to the pursuit of war. As Darrow watched the hardy
and purposeful cadets returning from classes, she recalled
what she first had felt when McGowan had taken her to the
Pentagon—a sense of surprise that warriors understood the
seriousness of their profession far better than did the politicians who shrugged away their lives. Even McGowan seemed
cowed by the majesty of the place, and by the time they re-

turned to the Thayer Hotel to await Buckner's call both were in a reflective mood. Darrow joined McGowan in his room, where they watched TV to pass the time, comfortably quiet with each other, neither of them compelled to make suggestive comments regarding Darrow's presence alone in McGowan's hotel room.

After an uneventful dinner, Buckner returned to his room quickly, curious about the message instructing him to call an old friend from Iraq at the Thayer Hotel. McGowan's name meant nothing to him. Telephones were now items of standard equipment issued with each room in the barracks; an awkward convenience, considering the lack of privacy and the number of sad, whispered calls with high school sweethearts who had moved on. Buckner dialed quickly, hoping to resolve the mystery before Boyer got back from the mess hall and started asking a million questions.

"This is McGowan."

"This is Morgan Buckner."

McGowan felt the hair on his neck rise as he recognized the sound of Buckner's voice on the phone. A year had passed, but goose bumps pimpled McGowan's forearms as if he were back in Abu Ghraib and Buckner was telling him, "*We kill people here.*" The reporter swallowed hard, and Darrow noticed the involuntary shiver.

"Morgan, my name is Doug McGowan. You broke my nose and threatened to kill me at Abu Ghraib. Do you remember?"

Buckner remembered McGowan clearly, though not his name or voice or face. McGowan was not a human memory, but the memory of a feeling. Buckner recalled, as if he were still in Cell Block 1A, the hatred and the shame he felt for

McGowan, for Levi, and for the others who had watched him reduce another man to groveling. "Abu Ghraib was a long time ago," answered Buckner carefully.

McGowan heard the wariness in Buckner's response, as he had expected it. "I've been looking for you for a long time."

Silence. "What do you want?"

"Is it possible for us to meet tomorrow?" McGowan asked.

"Why?"

"Remember the dead man in the shower room wrapped in plastic? I wake up at night dreaming about him."

Darrow had been listening intently, her eyes staring at her feet, but they snapped into focus now on McGowan's face. He seemed to have left the room, unaware of her presence, and she knew that he was lost in his memories. Listening to him as he parried with Buckner, she noticed the quiver in McGowan's voice and she trembled herself.

Buckner recalled his nightmare at Lake Frederick and the others that not even Boyer knew about, when the man in the plastic wrap opened his eyes and yelled at him. He found it frightening that he and the man he had tortured shared the same dreams. "Meet me at the chapel steps tomorrow at 1300 hours," he instructed McGowan. The chapel was a convenient meeting spot, away from upper-class eyes, where two men could talk in private.

Boyer entered the room as Buckner gently returned the receiver to the cradle. "What up, Buckner? Who was on the phone?"

"Nobody." Buckner sealed off Boyer, his emotions encapsulated in some hardened corner of his personality, where all plebes retreated when the odium became unbearable. Cadets knew immediately when their roommates dropped into that cocoon, so Boyer headed quietly to his desk to crack the books. Buckner ignored Boyer, lost in his calculus, and stood at the window staring at the early stars above the darkening river. He thought of his mother, who sobered up enough each Sunday to write him a clumsy letter.

"Boyer, did your mother ever tell you that every time someone dies their soul becomes a star in sky?"

Boyer looked up from his books, puzzled. "No, my mom's not much of a romantic."

Buckner had never thought of his mother as anything but a drunk, when he thought of her at all, but she was with him now, as if the ghost of a dead man at Abu Ghraib had kicked down the wall around Buckner's heart and let in everyone he had ever abandoned. He thought of Tetra, but his memory was already fading, lost in the constellations, and the grief which descended upon Buckner was all the more debilitating because of the enigma: who was this man who he had tortured at Abu Ghraib and who now shared his nightmares? Buckner's eyes misted, but he refused to release the tears with Boyer in the room. So he stared through the window as his heart was sucked out into the universe.

Only the next day, when they had returned from the noontime parade, did Buckner mention to Boyer that he planned to meet someone at the chapel. Boyer understood from the tone of his roommate's voice that he was not invited, but he could see that Buckner was uneasy about the upcoming meeting.

"I don't trust fast-talking white dudes," explained Buckner.

"You trust me," observed Boyer.

Buckner eyed his roommate with a smirk. "You're different, Boyer. Nothing ever comes out of your mouth except arithmetic."

"Math is Truth."

"Truth is Horseshit."

The exchange had become their personal rap, spoken every time Boyer handed over the calculus homework. Boyer had come to relish his relationship with Buckner, and sought every opportunity to deepen it. "Why don't I come with you? I can vouch for you in case God doesn't like the idea of someone like you setting foot in His house."

"God's gonna listen to you?"

"He loves me."

Buckner tossed his roommate's hat to him. "Come on, then. But when we get there, my business is personal."

Like so many other buildings at West Pont, the Cadet Chapel was perched on a knob of rock overlooking the Hudson Valley. Fittingly, the chapel's aerie was above all of the others, offering a breathtaking view not only of the river and the surrounding mountains, but of the Academy complex and the Plain itself, where cadets paraded like tiny squares of uniformed figurines. Boyer attended church services each Sunday in the Catholic Chapel closer to sea level, and so was eager to see what he had been missing. Two hundred and thirty-six stairs of worn granite climbed from the back alley of Washington Hall through a wooded glade to the heavy oak doors at the entrance of the Cadet Chapel, and both men were breathing hard when they emerged into the chapel parking lot.

McGowan had planned to come alone, for he knew that the things he and Buckner had to say to each other were best said man-to-man. But after watching McGowan replace the receiver in its cradle with trembling hands, Darrow refused to wait at the Thayer Hotel. She was baffled and excited by the emotions that McGowan struggled to contain, and she realized that she had underestimated the human drama behind her search for Buckner. Reporting was not merely the pursuit of facts; it was the pursuit of the human spirit, and she resolved not to miss the lesson that lay in the meeting between these two men.

Watching from the sheltered doorway of the chapel, McGowan spotted Buckner and Boyer as they approached the last few stairs that led to the flagstone terrace at the chapel entrance.

"That's him!" exclaimed McGowan in a whisper. "I was afraid I wouldn't recognize him."

"He has someone with him," Darrow observed.

"Keep the other kid company while I talk to Buckner."

She turned to McGowan and saw that his eyes were riveted on Buckner, his breath detectable only by the barest flare of his nostrils. Darrow had never spent a moment with McGowan when his attention wasn't trained at least partially on her, but his concentration on Buckner sobered her with its single-minded focus. She found his fixation exciting, for there was passion and pain at work behind his eyes. Darrow felt that she had worked as hard as anyone to find Buckner and deserved to meet him, but she had enough sense not to argue now, and instead zeroed in on Boyer as the two cadets began their ascent up the final flight of granite steps to the chapel doors.

As Buckner crested the top stair, McGowan stepped forward to greet him. "Buckner. I'm Doug McGowan." He extended his hand.

They tested each others' grip. McGowan was unprepared for Buckner's poise, wary but self-assured. He chided himself for being intimidated by a boy young enough to be his son.

Buckner ran his eyes over McGowan quickly and without comment. He did not recognize the man who accused him now of inhumane treatment so many months ago and so many continents away. He remembered what he had done; not much else. What most surprised Buckner, however, was McGowan's age, for he looked far older than he had during their first brief meeting in Abu Ghraib. Soldiers were young, and the only man as old as McGowan that Buckner had ever seen on a battlefield was the company first sergeant. He wondered why he had not noticed how old McGowan was when he had threatened to kill him.

McGowan suggested they talk on the wide balcony that ran across the chapel entrance, high above the Plain and away from the crowds of tourists who piled in and out of busses in the chapel parking lot. The newsman almost regretted his suggestion when Buckner picked a spot close to the low stone railing. A gentle push could send a man into thin air, one hundred feet above the rocks and woods below, and McGowan had no idea what a West Pointer might do when accused of war crimes.

"Hell of a view," said McGowan, though he kept his eyes on Buckner rather than the river or the distant hills. "Shame your friend Tetra never got to see this." The newsman was gratified to see the surprise in Buckner's eyes at the mention of Tetra's name.

"What do you know about Tetra?" demanded Buckner, a hint of anger in his voice.

Pleased that there would be no small talk, McGowan answered, "He died well. I met his mother; we had a good cry together. She showed me his Silver Star."

Buckner resented that McGowan had met Tetra's parents; he had never even sent them a note of condolence. He

was unaware that Tetra had received any award for his valor, and it surprised and irritated him that McGowan would know this—would know Tetra at all. Jealous of his memories, Buckner said, "You don't know anything about Tetra. Did you know he was funny? He was hilarious."

McGowan could only stare.

"He was the funniest guy in the world. Funny and innocent. Everybody liked him. Innocent people don't deserve to die like that."

"He was a soldier. He was no more innocent than anyone else, Buckner, just like you."

Buckner shot a fierce glance at him, and then looked off into the distance. "What do you want with me?"

McGowan steeled himself and got down to business. "You beat me up pretty good. And then the bastards from MI worked me over. No sleep, no treatment for my injuries, cold, naked. It was four days before I got any medical treatment. The infection almost killed me. I've been in and out of hospitals for the last ten months. I've invested a lot of sweat and blood trying to find you. And now that I've found you, I want an apology."

Buckner did not flinch, but turned to look McGowan square in the eye, like a gunslinger at high noon. The newsman glanced quickly over the side of the balcony as if the sheer power of Buckner's presence was enough to shove him over.

Buckner turned suddenly and leaned on the railing, bent at the waist, supporting himself on his elbows. "I'm sorry." Buckner stared up the Hudson Valley, darkening as the shadows of the western mountains began to stretch across it. His mind was blank, the almost hypnotic spell he had felt just prior to kicking the bastard who had shot Tetra. "You should go now," said Buckner.

I'm sorry. There it was, an apology, as if McGowan were serious. As if a simple heartfelt apology was all that was required to make things right between them. And yet, to McGowan's surprise, the months of anger suddenly evaporated—gone, absorbed in two anticlimactic words.

"I can help you," said McGowan. "I can keep you out of this."

Buckner stared ahead. "Out of what?"

"Out of the shit that's going to hit the fan when I print my story in the newspaper. I'm a newspaper reporter, remember?" McGowan realized that Buckner had no idea that there was anything more than a personal connection between them.

"I never paid much attention," said Buckner, turning to the newsman as a shadow of worry crossed his face.

Some men seem older than their years, especially combat veterans, and McGowan had seen plenty of thousand-yard stares in the eyes of teenagers who could pass for forty. But Buckner now seemed suddenly younger, despite his composure, childishly naïve enough to imagine that his acts would not someday be the focus of intense media or political scrutiny. "Did you think you would just go on with your life, Buckner, like nothing ever happened in that cell in Abu Ghraib prison?"

Buckner said nothing.

All reporters find silence exasperating, but McGowan did not sense that Buckner was keeping his mouth shut in order to hide anything. On the contrary, men with secrets often talk too much, telling others what they should believe. Quiet men often had the courage to allow the facts to speak for themselves, and McGowan wondered if Buckner had already resigned himself to whatever fate had in store.

"You don't have to take the rap for what you did, Buckner."

Buckner remained mute, but McGowan could see him hardening, his mind starting to work.

"You're small fry, Buckner, just like the other lowlife grunts who've been court-martialed so far for the abuses at Abu Ghraib. I want the big fish. I want the secretary of defense, the president himself. I need for you to confirm that the chain of command knew what was going on at Abu Ghraib."

Buckner shook his head, but he recalled the visit with Tannerbeck in CJTF-7 HQ in Baghdad.

"You were awarded a Bronze Star recently." A shadow of worry crossed Buckner's face. "I've read the citation and I know it contains factual errors."

"You don't know shit."

"I know more than you think. You're a murderer, Buckner, but the army decided to let you get away with it rather than expose the abuses at Abu Ghraib. That's why the army sent you here. You think you have any qualifications to be an officer? Wise up, Buckner. Tannerbeck sent you here for a reason."

Buckner's head slumped to his chest.

"Talk to me, Buckner. You killed a man. They'll put you in prison for that. Give me Tannerbeck and I can keep your name out of it." McGowan almost felt compassion for Buckner, until he reminded himself that he was talking to the man who had tortured him and had murdered at least one defenseless human being, maybe more. Buckner was now a source to be manipulated, just another fool with more information than he knew what to do with. He waited to see if Buckner would reconsider his position, but Buckner stared out across the Hudson as if he were somewhere else. Mc-

Gowan slipped his business card under the palm of Buckner's hand. "Call me if things get rough."

Darrow stepped briskly up to Boyer, grabbing his hand before Boyer understood that this woman was intent upon meeting him. With the grace of a politician, she held his elbow and steered him gently away from the terrace, back down the stairs. Over his shoulder, Boyer saw that Buckner was already engaged with McGowan, with no apparent thought to his roommate.

"They need to talk alone," said Darrow, "and so should we."

"Who are you?" he asked, flustered. Her hand still grasped his as she pulled him away, and Boyer spotted the disapproving glance of an upper-class cadet who was showing the chapel to his own date. A fleeting sense of smugness passed through him at the idea that someone would mistake this pretty stranger for his girlfriend, and he risked an extra moment of contact.

"Angie Darrow," she replied, refusing to release his hand. "I'm a reporter and research assistant for Doug McGowan of *The Citizen Times.*"

"I can't talk to you," said Boyer, realizing with a start that two reporters from *The Citizen Times* could only want to talk to Buckner about Abu Ghraib.

Darrow looked at him sharply, with new respect. She found the shaved head and black plastic TEDs repugnant, but Boyer was the first person she had met since leaving Bard who seemed to have ever read a newspaper. Even her colleagues at the *Times* were morons, more interested in speculating about Darrow's relationship with McGowan than about the news they wrote.

"Why not?" she asked. "Has the army abridged your freedom of speech? Have you been ordered to keep you mouth shut about something?"

"No, nothing like that," said Boyer.

"How well do you know Morgan Buckner?"

"My roommate," said Boyer, with a self-important shrug and a fast glance at her breasts. He knew that he should head back to the barracks, but energized by her beauty and her challenging questions, he resisted the impulse to leave.

"Can we take a walk?" she asked suddenly, exercising leadership before he had a chance to retreat. She had noticed his once-over; a little flirtation would encourage him to try to impress her with his intelligence. She remembered again what McGowan had taught her: smart people talk too much.

Flustered, Boyer withdrew his hand from hers, explaining that holding a woman's hand was serious business at West Point. Any Public Display of Affction, innocent or not, could result in hours of punishment tours in Central Area, marching back and forth with a rifle on one's shoulder. The Central Area was filled on weekends with lonely cadets whose indiscretions were gleefully announced from the poop deck at lunch, and whose mortified girlfriends often refused to come back. The restraint which cadets eventually internalized would perplex West Pointers' women for the rest of their lives, just as it perplexed Darrow as Boyer avoided her hand.

He explained PDA, which Darrow found bizarre, but his agitation confirmed her suspicion that he had enjoyed her touch. For an hour, she flirted viciously, concealed her boredom as Boyer described how plebes ate, shined their shoes, and memorized the "Days."

Twilight came early at West Point, tucked as it was against the eastern flank of Storm King Mountain, a massive bulge of granite that shouldered up to the river and blocked off the Academy from civilization. Cadets knew that there was a moment, just before sunset, when the bright and pale sky would contrast starkly with the penumbral darkness in the Hudson Valley, slashed by a reflected ribbon of silvery blue as the last photons of sunlight caromed off the river. On Saturday evenings, upperclassmen and plebes alike gathered with their dates at Trophy Point, an arrow of land above the granite cliffs with a view upriver, to watch the display flash down the valley. Boyer led Darrow to Trophy Point self-consciously, nervous that she might ridicule such a romantic gesture, but she took his arm in a manner approved by cadet regulations and gleefully pointed out poorly concealed examples of PDA among many of the upperclassmen and their dates. She watched the colors shoot across the sky with appropriate awe, and as the darkness settled about the dispersing crowd, she knew it was time to get down to business.

"It's been a fabulous afternoon, Boyer, but I have to ask you some questions before I go."

He knew her inquiries would be about Buckner, and he was leery, but was also anxious to prolong the day.

"Has Buckner ever talked about any of his duties in Iraq?" she asked.

Boyer shrugged. "No. Not much."

"Never? No war stories between roommates?"

"It's not cool to ask too many questions," said Boyer.

"I know that Buckner was recently awarded a Bronze Star."

"Yes." He wondered how she had done her research. Were awards posted on the Internet?

"And that the citation was a lie. I read it, and I know it didn't happen that way."

Boyer stopped walking, chilled by a sense of panic. How could she know? "Combat is confusing," he said. "The people who write the awards don't always get their facts straight."

Boyer's careful sidestepping of her question alerted Darrow that he had something to hide. "What are you telling me?" she asked. People love to talk, McGowan had told her. They want to be the center of attention. Keep your mouth shut, and they'll dig their own grave. Darrow touched Boyer on the arm to encourage him. "Do you know the facts?"

"I can't talk to you."

"You have to talk to me. Otherwise, the truth will be printed in *The Citizen Times* and your roommate will have a lot of explaining to do."

"It's not his fault," protested Boyer, with growing unease. "He didn't know anything about the award until it was pinned on his chest. Someone just screwed up when they wrote it."

"So he really doesn't deserve the medal?

"He earned it. Just because the citation got the facts mixed up doesn't mean he didn't earn it."

"Well," she said, with an air of helplessness, "you need to tell me what happened, or I have no choice but to print the facts as I know them. If you don't set me straight, what else can I do?" She pleaded with syrupy eyes.

Boyer needed to talk to Buckner, but as they returned to the chapel steps, he spotted McGowan sitting on the top step alone. McGowan rose when he saw them, but Darrow signaled for him to wait while she turned to face Boyer in the parking lot. She stood close and Boyer caught another whiff of her perfume. "I need to know what happened," she said, "or McGowan is going to destroy your roommate."

Boyer glanced at McGowan, who stood scowling at them, wondering what Darrow was up to. "A detainee killed one of Buckner's friends," blurted Boyer.

"Tetra."

In a flash, Boyer realized that Darrow knew more than he did, and that he had given her the confirmation she needed that the citation for Buckner's Bronze Star was falsified. He knew that he'd been had. "It's getting late," he mumbled, as he spun abruptly on his heel and headed for the barracks.

CHAPTER 29

September 15, 2004 (Wednesday)
West Point

By mid September, sunrises turned chilly in the Hudson Valley. Boyer stood shivering in the sally port with his hands in his pockets, an unmilitary posture unacceptable to an upperclassman who might have been motivated enough to get out of bed at that pre-dawn hour. Two other plebes, one from each company in the battalion, waited with him. Nobody spoke. They slept on their feet, their ears tuned only to the sound of the delivery van.

The truck appeared suddenly. Panel doors opened and three bundles of *The Citizen Times* were tossed out as the driver drove away without a word. Boyer lifted a bale of newspapers by the string that bound them and climbed three sets of stairs to Company F-2's barracks area.

He popped the string with his bayonet and proceeded to deliver one copy of the newspaper to each cadet room. In upper-class rooms, he closed the windows so the slumbering occupants would awake to a warm environment. In twenty minutes, he was back in his room.

The reveille cannon would roar in five minutes, though only those plebes with newspaper duty ever heard it anymore. Boyer was tempted to crawl back into bed, but the exercise had roused him to consciousness.

Buckner tossed slightly when Boyer turned on the desk lamp and opened the paper. As he settled down to scan the front page, his recently energized heart stopped.

WEST POINTER COMMITS WAR CRIME
by Douglas McGowan and Angie Darrow

In later years, West Point graduates would be plagued by a dead spot in their memory regarding world events during their years at the Military Academy. One of few surviving total institutions in the United States, only in prisons and monasteries could life go on as indifferent to the universe as it could within the granite fortress perched on the bluffs above the Hudson River. To ameliorate the effects of the Corps' isolation, the brass mandated that *The Citizen Times* would be required reading for all cadets. But the events of the world were irrelevant to men whose primary concerns centered around sleep and food, and even among those cadets who did have the leisure and interest to keep abreast of world affairs, the *Times* was not considered a newspaper worth reading. Most of the issues which Boyer delivered went directly into the trash.

Still, there were enough readers so that by noon word of the article had spread to every company. Newspapers were retrieved from trash cans and read aloud while cadets quick-shined their shoes and spruced up their uniforms in preparation for the lunch formation.

Buckner never read the newspaper, and Boyer's nerve had failed him during the ten minutes he shared with his roommate prior to breakfast and morning classes. Throughout the morning, nobody had said a word about the article.

Now, before lunch formation, there were things to do: shoes to shine, menus and news articles to memorize. As the minute caller announced five minutes, Boyer fell in behind Buckner and prepared to march out the door.

A dozen upperclassmen waited in ambush in the hallway, reviewing the article and discussing what to do about it. The company's Yuks, sensing blood in the water, had scurried for cover. A rumbling, ominous intensity filled the hall. When Buckner opened the door, a dozen voices snarled his name.

"Buckner!"

The two plebes threw themselves against the wall in a rigid position of attention.

"Boyer!" yelled Ajax. "Get out of here!" Boyer stepped forward, initiated an abrupt left face, and double-timed to the stairwell. Behind him, hell broke over Buckner like a tsunami.

Cornered against the wall, Buckner could only stare straight ahead as the circle of upperclassmen closed around him, leaning forward like hyenas, their mouths and teeth and tongues working an inch from Buckner's face, spewing vitriol. The hurricane of abusive voices combined into a nonsensical blast of noise, rendering Buckner helpless to distinguish one voice from another. This was not professional hazing, designed to instill discipline, but the condemnation of men obviously struggling to control themselves. The crescendo washed over him and down the hallway, until one Firstie took command, speaking not to Buckner but to his screaming classmates.

"Shut up!" The hallway fell silent.

Frank Gastogne was a Cadet Lieutenant, a platoon leader in F-2 known for his prowess in the boxing ring, but otherwise a Firstie who kept to himself. Ferocious in combat but laconic in manner, he felt no need to prove his masculinity, but he had an unending obligation to study. This combination rendered him relatively benign to most plebes, and he would often ask them personal questions and tell jokes while they stood at attention in ranks, waiting for the rest of the company to form up. He was unguarded and cocky in a way appropriate for the brigade boxing champ, which he was. Plebes liked him—or at least they didn't hate him—and his frequent ridicule of Ajax filled all of them with glee. It was a surprise to everyone that Gastogne would take part in the attack on Buckner, though it was understood that if Gastogne had something to say, everyone else would listen.

"Tell me about that Bronze Star of yours, Buckner."

Buckner's eyes unglazed, as the veil of mental distance that most plebes managed to put between themselves and irate upperclassmen dissolved. No soldier could tolerate an accusation that his awards for valor were unearned, and Buckner knew immediately that the word was out about the inaccuracies in the citation for his Bronze Star. In a steady but angry voice, he said, "Sir, there were errors in the citation."

Gastogne understood immediately that *The Citizen Times* had gotten it right. He leaped into the air with a scream, throwing his fist into the wall an inch from Buckner's ear. Spittle flew from his mouth, followed by an unintelligible torrent of words that baffled even his own classmates. The others stepped back, sharing glances, shocked by the insane vehemence of Gastogne's attack on Buckner. It was not common knowledge, however, that Gastogne's brother was an invalid, his legs blown off by an IED Samara. For his sacrifice, the army had awarded him a Purple Heart and a Bronze Star—the same as Buckner.

"Knock it off!" LaForge elbowed his way through the crowd, which now filled the hallway. Buckner still stood against the wall, Gastogne heaving with anger an inch from his nose. "Everyone get out to ranks," ordered the company commander. "You too, Frank. We're all late for formation." He put his hand on Gastogne's shoulder, but his classmate shook it off and stormed away.

The mess hall was turbulent. Throughout the building, the entire plebe class said the "Days" in atonement for Buckner's notoriety. Buckner and Boyer added their voices to their classmates' chorus until the command to take seats was announced. Buckner poured the iced tea, while Boyer carefully sliced the pumpkin pie into ten equal portions.

"Sir," announced Buckner, "the fourth classmen at this table have properly completed their duties and are prepared to eat!" Every plebe in the Corps could recite the words in his sleep.

Gastogne looked up. Boyer and Buckner sat at attention, eyes downcast, food untouched. The fourth class lifestyle, which had begun to relax as the academic year progressed, had been instantly reimposed upon the entire plebe class— Beast Barracks all over again.

Gastogne stood up. He held a copy of *The Citizen Times*, which he hurled at Buckner. The paper struck Buckner in the face and fell into the food on his plate.

"Boyer," he said, "take your roommate's food. He won't be needing it."

Ashamed, Boyer scraped the meal from Buckner's plate onto his own. At Gastogne's command, he ate.

"Start reading, Buckner!" Gastogne stood at the opposite end of the table, leaning on his fists, his eyes zeroed on Buckner. All others waited, glancing from Buckner to Gastogne, their heads turning as if they were watching a tennis match. Only Boyer obediently addressed his lunch.

Slowly, Buckner took the paper and began to read.

West Pointer Commits War Crime, by
Doug McGowan and Angie Darrow.

"Louder!" ordered Gatogne. "I want everyone in the regiment to hear you!" Indeed, a thousand men strained to listen as Buckner raised his voice.

It was learned today that the U.S. Army has gone to extreme lengths to conceal the events at Abu Ghraib prison, where Iraqi prisoners of war were tortured and humiliated by members of the 372nd MP Company. Not only has the Army reassigned General Robert Tannerbeck, Deputy Commander of Combined Joint Task Force 7 who authorized the abuses, to West Point, but they have also sent at least one enlisted guard, Morgan Buckner, there as well. Buckner not only abused this reporter, but was awarded a Bronze Star for his performance. Sources at the Pentagon, confirmed by sources close to Buckner, have indicated that the citation to accompany the award of the Bronze Star was falsified. Contrary to events chronicled in the citation, Buckner did not apprehend a dangerous detainee who attacked his fellow guards. Nor did he protect an interrogator from attack by the same detainee, but instead kicked the prisoner to death while the prisoner lay on the floor in restraints.

293 OF HONOR   293

Boyer realized immediately that he was the "source close to Buckner." He nearly vomited his food when Buckner ceased reading and glanced his way.

"Keep reading!" yelled Gastogne.

All around Buckner, cadets cocked their heads to listen. With each sentence, Buckner's voice grew huskier.

> *Major General Tannerbeck established a reputation for combat brilliance while commanding the 4th Infantry Division during the assault on Baghdad. Following the conclusion of official combat operations, Tannerbeck was selected to serve as Deputy Commander of CJTF-7, the operational command responsible for operations within Iraq. Tannerbeck's duties included oversight of operations related to the detention and interrogation of POWs. Previous investigations of the abuses at Abu Ghraib have identified a dysfunctional command structure that resulted in the relief of officers up to and including the commander of the 800th MP Brigade. Until today, no evidence existed of malfeasance or incompetence at higher levels of command. Recently, however, classified documents obtained by this reporter confirm communications from unnamed officers at Abu Ghraib directly to Tannerbeck, referencing "extreme interrogation methods" and "previously reported abuses."*
>
> *In November 2003, Tannerbeck was reassigned to West Point, New York, where he now serves as the Superintendent of the U.S. Military Academy.*

Cadets listened, rapt, the only sound in the normally riotous mess hall the husky voice of Morgan Buckner. Even the nearby plebes cocked their ears to hear while keeping their eyes on their plates. Buckner paused, but Gastogne, following along in his own copy of the article, growled, "Keep reading."

> *During the month of September 2003, this reporter was in Iraq, embedded with insurgent forces. On the night of October 20, 2003, while traveling in a convoy of three insurgent vehicles, we were ambushed by American snipers. I was the sole survivor of the attack and was subsequently delivered to Abu Ghraib prison, where, on the night of my arrival, I was interrogated and tortured by two men who have not been identified or arrested by American authorities. Subsequent investigation has revealed that one of those soldiers was Pvt. Morgan Buckner of the 229th MP Company. It has also been learned that soon after my incarceration at Abu Ghraib, Buckner was unexpectedly reassigned from Abu Ghraib to West Point, where he is now a plebe in the U.S. Corps of Cadets. Prior to Buckner's encounter with me, he had been involved in another incident of prisoner abuse in which he kicked a restrained detainee to death. According to sources close to the investigation, Buckner was never disciplined for his actions, but was in fact awarded a Bronze Star for his efforts. The citation to accompany the award of the medal was falsified. General Tannerbeck pinned the award on Buckner's chest during a ceremony at West Point.*

Buckner reached the last paragraph and his voice broke.

"He's going to cry," someone said.

A dozen cadets leaned forward. Boyer hated whatever it was in men that made them turn as vicious at the sight of a tear as they did over a drop of blood in the boxing ring. Weakness was the ultimate offense.

Ajax jeered, "You lied about your medal, Buckner. It's a little late to whimper about it now, don't you think?"

Buckner reached out with his left hand and grabbed Ajax by the necktie of his class uniform, then slammed his right fist into Ajax's mouth, sending the wreckage of his squad leader's teeth clattering across the table. Gastogne threw his chair into the aisle as he bolted to Buckner's end of the table. As he reached for Buckner's throat, he was stunned by the suddenness of Buckner's hands closing around his own neck. The two men stood face-to-face, choking the breath from each other, trembling against their perfectly matched strengths, while the other cadets scrambled out of the way.

LaForge appeared from nowhere and pried them apart. He commanded sternly, "Sit down, Frank." To Buckner, he ordered, "Report to your room. Wait there until someone comes to get you."

Buckner said nothing, but as he turned to retrieve his hat from under his chair, his eyes locked on Boyer, who still sat at attention, his eyes fixed properly on his plate, obediently chewing his lunch.

When Boyer returned to his room, he found Buckner lying on his bunk, staring at the ceiling, his flat nostrils flaring gently with each breath, as motionless as a deer just before an earthquake. But Buckner's quiet demeanor belied the bleak thoughts of dismissal that floated through his mind.

There was no doubt that he would be expelled from the Academy. He tried to remind himself that it was a miracle that he was there at all, but rationalization failed to assuage the pain of failure. He had coped with calculus; he was well-liked by his peers, and—until today—respected by his superiors. He deserved to leave on his own terms, not in shame.

Buckner thought of his mother. She wrote a letter every week, full of praise and pride and encouragement. He knew how she would handle his expulsion; already he could feel her consoling arms around him, but he could also smell her breath and hear her crying herself to sleep at night. *I'm sorry, Mama. I tried my best.*

Buckner heard his mother as clearly as if she had been standing next to him. *They don't let you out of the ghetto for trying your best, boy.*

As Boyer gathered his books for afternoon classes, he stole glances at Buckner, who refused to acknowledge his presence. The expression on his roommate's face reminded Boyer of Patton's statue: hard, cold, disdainful. "Those reporters already knew about the medal," said Boyer, looking away. "I didn't tell her anything she didn't already know." Buckner stared ahead, silent. As Boyer left the room, he noticed the handkerchief wrapped around the knuckles of his roommate's right hand. A splotch of blood had seeped through the cotton, and Boyer automatically worried that Buckner might get a drop on his uniform.

Buckner allowed himself to blink only after Boyer shut the door. He wondered how middle-class white boys ever survived in the world, even a world designed especially for them. Boyer was like the rest of the Corps, a little smarter and a little weaker than his classmates, but generally in the mold. Idealistic, motivated, patriotic; boys that the country could be proud of.

But Buckner could not figure where the yellow streak came from. He'd seen it in other members of his class, not only in Boyer. They were physically courageous; even Boyer had stood toe-to-toe in the boxing ring with the guy who had broken his nose. But Boyer craved the well-defined path; he was bred to be a cadet, hobbled like a trotter since birth until the exuberant urge to gallop was associated with vague feelings of dread. *That must be what it's like to be middle class,* thought Buckner. *Too much to lose to take risks, but not rich enough to lose and laugh it off.*

Two thunderous knocks preceded LaForge's entry. The door flew open and bounced against the stop. Buckner lay on his bunk and stared at him.

"Get up!" LaForge reached down and grabbed Buckner by his shirt, lifting him to his feet and slamming him against the wall. Buckner grabbed his commander's wrist with one hand and made a closed fist of the other.

"Don't try it, Mister. I won't come apart like Ajax."

Buckner felt no fear or intimidation, but his respect for a fellow veteran who had always treated him fairly made him relax his grip.

"Until I say otherwise, Buckner, you are still a plebe in my company. Now stand at fucking attention!"

Buckner obeyed sullenly. He watched curiously as La-Forge reached into his closet and pulled out his dress gray uniform and his gleaming inspection shoes.

"Get dressed," LaForge ordered. "You have an appointment to see the Supe, immediately."

While Buckner dressed, LaForge talked.

"Aside from the honor implications, do you have any idea what you've done? By accepting an award under false pretenses, you cheapen the medals of all those men who earned them. I earned my Bronze Star, and it makes me want to stuff yours up your ass!"

Both men eyed each other. Buckner volunteered nothing, and LaForge's eyes simply poured out their reservoir of disgust.

"Fuck you," said Buckner. "I resign."

"Resign? If the facts in *The Citizen Times* are true, you'll be able to resign after twenty-five years in Ft. Leavenworth."

They walked together to the administration building. Buckner had never crossed the barracks area when the sidewalks were not jammed with cadets who, like himself, were en route to or from classes. Under LaForge's wing, he took the liberty to look around, a privilege denied to plebes within the barracks compound. The Gothic buildings surrounded him like a medieval fortress. They reminded Buckner of the tenements where he had lived as a boy, but more sterile. In Baltimore, there was constant noise—music, fighting couples, crying babies. Here, masculine silence prevailed. He could hear his footsteps echo across the concrete, and almost imagined that he could feel the ghosts of old soldiers that Boyer swore were there.

Tannerbeck's office was on the sixth floor of the headquarters building. LaForge led Buckner to the elevator, a luxury not available in the barracks, and they quickly found themselves in the foyer for the administrative offices of the U.S. Military Academy.

"End of the line, Buckner," said LaForge. He stepped back into the elevator and disappeared.

Buckner stood in a short hallway with three doors, one with a pane of frosted glass. On the glass was stenciled

Administrative Offices

U.S. Military Academy
Enter

The room was large and comfortable, carpeted with thick pile. In one corner, a pair of vinyl easy chairs flanked a coffee table where a copy of the *Army Times* lay. Two doors led from the room. One bore a small brass name-plaque which read "General Robert Tannerbeck."

In the center of the room, a silver-haired woman sat primly at a desk, working on a group of forms: travel vouchers or Officer Evaluation Reports.

"Can I help you, Cadet?"

"Yes, ma'am," Buckner answered. "I was ordered to report to General Tannerbeck. My name is Morgan Buckner."

"Oh, yes." Her manner was suddenly cool, efficient. "Have a seat. I'll inform the general that you are here."

Buckner sank glumly into a chair while the woman announced his arrival on the intercom. After several minutes, the intercom buzzed and Buckner heard Tannerbeck's voice. "Send him in, Gladys."

Like a man en route to the electric chair, Buckner marched slowly into Tannerbeck's office, coming to rigid attention two steps from the general's desk.

"Cadet Buckner reporting as ordered, sir." He saluted smartly.

Tannerbeck remained seated and returned the salute. He did not order Buckner to stand at ease, but studied him coolly while Buckner remained frozen in place. The leather desk chair groaned slightly as the Supe leaned back and stared out the window at the Hudson River. "You must have a hell of a punch, Mister Buckner. Cadet Ajax will be in the hospital for a couple of days. The army will have to provide him with a complete set of front dentures; he lost four teeth altogether."

Buckner said nothing, so Tannerbeck continued. "As a cadet, you are subject to army standards of conduct, including the Uniform Code of Military Justice. Do you have any idea what can happen to you for striking someone of superior rank?"

"A court-martial, sir."

Tannerbeck nodded as if preoccupied, not really interested in the answer. "Yes, well, cadets fight all the time, and we don't court-martial them. There are better ways to handle things like fighting, such as punishment tours on the Area and restrictions to quarters. Sometimes, we simply allow the two men to settle their differences in the boxing ring. Trial by combat, you might say. But you present unique problems, Mr. Buckner."

Tannerbeck continued to stare out the window, as if his comments were merely a mindless prelude to the real issue. Buckner stole glances about the office, which was wood-paneled and carpeted in the same thick pile as the outer office. A row of photographs on one wall caught his eye. Buckner would have expected the general to display a collection of celebrities, but the photographs were of young men in uniform, mostly smiling. There was not an officer among them. On the desk was a photo of a woman, mature, but still handsome. An American flag stood in one corner, and a display case housed a score of tacky plaques and memorabilia of the type traditionally awarded to members of military units upon their reassignment to other duty stations. Among the plaques was only a single *objet de guerre*, a standard-issue army Baretta 9 mm sidearm with a damaged chamber. Buckner was surprised that he saw no enemy flags or patches or weapons.

"We made the front page of *The Citizen Times*," continued Tannerbeck. He turned abruptly to face Buckner, ready to get down to business. Buckner immediately cast his gaze at a spot directly above the general's head. "That puts us in pretty exclusive company."

"Yes, sir."

"This article will ruin my career. It accuses me of authorizing war crimes, including murder. Worse, it implies that I awarded a Bronze Star to the man who did the killing, and falsified the citation to conceal the truth. If all this were true, I could face a court-martial myself, Buckner."

Buckner lowered his eyes and dared a brazen look at the superintendent. It occurred to him that Tannerbeck might have no memory of their previous meeting in Baghdad.

An awkward silence settled upon them.

Tannerbeck's shoulders suddenly sagged. He rose from his chair and walked to the wall bearing the photographs. "See these men? All of them were under my command when they died. I wrote to their parents and asked for pictures of them so I would never forget them."

Buckner remained at rigid attention.

"At ease," ordered Tannerbeck.

Buckner clasped his hands behind his back and spread his feet apart, exactly shoulder width. Otherwise, he remained as rigid as a Beefeater, eyes straight ahead.

Tannerbeck continued, "This article is going to make life very difficult for both of us. There are already official inquires underway, and I expect that McGowan will keep fanning this fire until Congress demands someone's head. He will try to contact you, but under no circumstances should you talk to him."

"I met with him Saturday, sir. I didn't know who he was."

Tannerbeck sank back into his chair with a sad, pneumatic sigh. "What did you tell him?"

"Nothing, sir."

Tannerbeck leaned back again, impressed by Buckner's self-possession. There were times when a commander drew inspiration from his men, certain men whose composure exceeded his own. Despite his culpability, the general considered himself an honorable man, and he saw in Buckner the same qualities of dignity and absolutism that had characterized his own career.

"And what about the Bronze Star?" asked Tannerbeck.

"Sir, I spoke to the chaplain about that shortly after it was awarded," said Buckner. "I said nothing to McGowan about it."

"The chaplain reported to me this morning," said Tannerbeck quietly. "You did the right thing."

Silence returned while Tannerbeck continued to stare out the window. Each day he spent moments studying the geography of the river and the low hills along the eastern bank. The view never changed, except for the barge traffic on the water or the sunlight or shadow on the hills, yet the general could not resist the urge to look outside whenever the window crossed his line of sight.

Buckner shifted his weight. He scanned the office again and took a more studied look at the photos on the wall. The general had shared something private with him, and Buckner was beguiled and flattered. A cynic would have felt manipulated, but West Pointers were not cynics, and even Buckner had begun to believe in chivalry and romance and vainglorious tradition.

Tannerbeck continued. "That isn't to say that I don't intend to shut you up. Until further notice, you will remain confined to your quarters. You will make no statement regarding the article in the *Times*, or to any members of the press, or to any other cadets. There will be no official or unofficial response to the article. Understand?"

"Yes, sir. What about the other cadets, sir? The upper classes are demanding an explanation."

"You will not discuss this with anyone: cadets, officers, civilians, or otherwise."

"Yes, sir."

"Mr. LaForge and your tactical officer will determine your punishment with regard to the fight in the mess hall. I expect that the next several months will be very difficult for you, Buckner."

"Yes, sir."

"You are dismissed, Cadet. Go back to class."

Buckner saluted and executed a precise about-face.

CHAPTER 30

September 17, 2004 (Friday)
West Point

Fall colors erupted across the hills as if on command. Rain commenced that afternoon, a cold drizzle that floated down among the turrets and made the stones glisten in what pale light there was. The opaque sky muted the blush in the trees and lent its pallor to the river, now sullen like the barracks that huddled below the granite spire of the chapel, rocketing into the clouds. Only the Plain retained a hint of color.

That night, after the fourth class was ensconced in their rooms for study, the upper classes gathered in their companies across the Corps. The cadets of F-2 congregated in front of Mark LaForge's room, curious because of the order to wear a proper uniform. Suddenly, the door opened and General Tannerbeck entered the hallway, LaForge behind him. The men in the hallway snapped to attention. For many of them, this would be the closest they would ever get to the Supe, and all eyes focused on the stars and the ribbons and the combat stripes on the sleeves of Tannerbeck's uniform. Throughout the Corps, company officers met with their cadets to present the same message that Tannerbeck had chosen to deliver to Company F-2 in person.

"At ease," ordered the general. "Fall out. Sit down, if you want." A few men exchanged glances, and one or two took the Supe at his word, seating themselves on the floor, their backs against the wall. "I'm here," began Tannerbeck, "to discuss with you the recent article in *The Citizen Times*. Is anyone not familiar with the article on the front page of the paper this morning?" He held the *Times* aloft. All had read it, or declined to admit that they had not.

"Before I get to Cadet Buckner, let me tell you something that each of you will probably learn sooner or later: war is chaos. I have been in dozens of battles, big and small, and I never knew what the hell was going on in any of them. The closer the bullets, the more narrow your focus, and two men in the same foxhole might have completely different versions of the same firefight. Thus, it is not unusual for confusion to exist regarding who did what when the time comes to prepare citations to accompany awards for heroism.

"Regarding the Bronze Star awarded to Cadet Buckner, I am proud to inform you that Mr. Buckner himself brought the discrepancies to the attention of the chaplain long before he was aware of any interest in the award by the press. I have decided to rewrite the award rather than rescind it."

Several eyes turned toward Frank Gastogne as Tannerbeck verbalized their thoughts. "Although Buckner is a plebe, some of you may owe him an apology.

"Second, much of what you read in *The Citizen Times* is classified and cannot be acknowledged or denied. Most of us will never know the truth. As professional officers, however, it shall be your responsibility to live by the West Point motto of Duty, Honor, Country. Sometimes, these concepts will come into conflict, and you will have to choose one over the other. While I cannot reveal specific facts in this case, I want you to know that I performed my duty as honorably as I could under the circumstances, and my conscience is clear."

"What about Buckner's attack on Mr. Ajax this afternoon, sir?" asked a particularly courageous Yuk. "Will he be disciplined?"

"His behavior was unacceptable," answered Tannerbeck, "regardless of provocation. But I feel there are mitigating circumstances. I have been discussing some options with Mr. LaForge."

The group fell silent.

"There is one more thing, gentlemen. Apparently, an antiwar demonstration has been scheduled to be held here at the Academy tomorrow, in response to the article in the newspaper. You are ordered to have absolutely no contact with the demonstrators, regardless of provocation. No matter what those flag-burning bastards do, you will not confront them, talk to them, or acknowledge their existence."

Heads nodded and a few mumbled "Huahs" filtered down the hall.

"That is all, gentlemen. Good night." The Zoo sprang to attention as Tannerbeck turned abruptly and departed the company area.

While Tannerbeck talked to the upper classes, Boyer and Buckner sat wordlessly at their desks, struggling vainly to keep their minds on the open textbooks before them. Boyer knew that Buckner could not possibly understand the assignment, and he wondered whether Buckner would accept the solutions to the nightly homework assignments as usual, or if he would throw the pages back in disdain.

An hour later, Boyer tossed the completed homework onto Buckner's desk. Buckner had not moved, not even to turn the page.

"I don't know what happened," said Boyer, trying to explain again how Darrow had confirmed the facts in the article regarding the award of the Bronze Star. "She knew already that something was fishy about the commendation. She started asking me about it and I tried to explain that it wasn't your fault."

Buckner shifted his eyes to the sheaf of papers covered with the gibberish of Boyer's calculus solutions. He ignored them and said nothing.

"You going to use the homework solutions?" Boyer asked.

Buckner shrugged.

"You know you're not smart enough to do it on your own," said Boyer, trying to lighten the mood with some of their previously typical banter.

"Smart enough? Me? What the fuck were you thinking about, Boyer, talking to that bitch? You gotta lotta brains, but skinny white boys like you wouldn't last ten minutes in my neighborhood. Sometimes you gotta know when to keep your fuckin' mouth shut!"

"Buckner, she knew what she was doing."

Buckner turned slowly with a sneer on his face.

Except in boxing class, Boyer had never been in a fight in his life, but he jumped to his feet now. He knew he could not win any physical confrontation with Buckner, but he lusted for the release and punishment and redemption.

Bucker stared at him with amusement as he rose slowly from his chair. "Show me what you got, Sylvester."

Boyer lunged forward. He wrapped both arms around Buckner's chest, pinning his arms, and allowed his momentum to propel them both to the floor. The back of Buckner's head slammed against the sink, and star points of light flashed onto his retina. But he was on his feet before the pain set in, and one powerful punch sent Boyer crashing against the closed door of their quarters.

Before Boyer could recover, the door flew suddenly inward, propelling him forward as LaForge stepped into the room. Both plebes snapped to attention, though Boyer kept his hand to his face, fearful that his nose was broken again. LaForge stared at Buckner's torn undershirt and the blood under Boyer's nose, and nodded. Relationships between roommates were too important to allow them to be poisoned by unresolved conflicts, and nothing resolved conflict faster than a brawl.

"You like to fight, Buckner?"

"No, sir!"

"Too bad. You seem to be pretty good at it." LaForge wandered around the room as if inspecting it while the plebes remained at attention. "Unfortunately for you, Buckner, you should have told someone that you had already reported the problems with that Bronze Star, rather than punching your squad leader. Normally, you'd spend the rest of your life walking punishment tours for something likc that, but given the circumstances I have decided to let you and Ajax settle your differences one-on-one, which is something I wish I could do with him myself. But since he is in no condition to take you on in the boxing ring, Frank Gastogne has volunteered to stand in for him. So you have a choice, Buckner. You can get in the ring with Gastogne, or you can spend the next six months in your room and on the

Area for knocking out Ajax's teeth at lunch today. Which will it be?"

Few men survived longer than one round in the ring with Gastogne, but even if Buckner could go the distance, three rounds were nothing compared to months of confinement and weekends spent walking punishment tours. The challenge to box was as close as Gastogne could come to offering Buckner an apology, and as close as the Academy could come to ignoring the attack on Ajax.

"Sir," said Buckner, "I want Mr. Boyer in my corner."

LaForge glanced back and forth at the two men and shrugged. Loyalty between roommates had always amazed him. In four years, he had witnessed numerous fights between roommates, swinging with fists one minute and best friends the next. He himself had squared off more than once against his own roommate, but could not imagine living with anyone else. "I don't give a shit who's in your corner, Buckner." he said. "The date and time will be decided later, when the whole company will be available to witness it. Be ready."

"Yes, sir."

"In the meantime, you are confined to your room, except for classes and meals. Now get this room cleaned up." LaForge walked out and slammed the door behind him.

Boyer and Buckner stood rooted to the floor for a moment after the door closed. Finally, Boyer turned to Buckner. "Gastogne will clobber you."

"Not if you tell me how to fight him."

"The smart way to fight him," said Boyer, "would be to go down with the first punch and take the ten-count."

Buckner snatched Boyer's pages of calculus from his rack and settled into his chair to memorize them. "Well, you know I'm not very smart."

CHAPTER 31

September 17, 2004 (Friday)
West Point

Charlotte Tannerbeck had been an army wife for more than twenty years. She had never held a paying job, for she had married Bob Tannerbeck while still in graduate school at the College of William and Mary, where she had studied psychology. The moment she met him, she knew she would be a soldier's wife, but the strain of a military marriage had tested her emotional and psychological fortitude more than she had anticipated. The first few years were difficult, but she had expected that, and had prepared herself for the frequent separations and the assignments at godforsaken army posts where Tannerbeck tried to mend the devastated army in the aftermath of Vietnam. She told herself that things would get better as her husband achieved higher rank and was promoted into more stable, administrative jobs. But she had underestimated Bob Tannerbeck. Just as Charlotte began to hope that their life would become less nomadic, the Pentagon began grooming her husband for his stars. One command assignment followed another, each lasting just long enough for Tannerbeck to get the feel of it before moving on. Charlotte did enjoy the prestige of being the wife of the battalion commander, then regimental commander and on to post commander. And the assignments at the Pentagon were fun, hobnobbing with powerful people in the government. But Charlotte was not born to wander, and she resented the army's control over her life. She had never had children, and although she knew it was irrational, she blamed the army for that, too. *You can't raise a baby out of a suitcase*, she told herself.

But Tannerbeck's appointment as the Superintendent of the U.S. Military Academy made up for their previous itinerant life. When her husband returned from Iraq, she had demanded that he guarantee her at least three years at West Point. She was surprised by how readily he had agreed, and was pleased to note that some of the old military fervor had gone from him. He had changed, and Charlotte liked her new husband. For the first time in their marriage, she was living with a man who did not bring his troubles home with him or brood about his career. Tannerbeck was home every day by five thirty and he watched the six o'clock news while she prepared dinner. Sometimes, he even helped in the kitchen, or he would read to her while she cooked. And she could hardly believe her ears when he suggested one night that they make love on the living room floor in front of the fireplace. She felt like a newlywed again.

Charlotte moved into the gracious old mansion which was reserved for the Superintendent, and filled it with the kind of warmth and hominess that a woman lavishes on her first real home, before too many moves destroy the furniture and the fine china and the nesting instinct. From time to time, cadets were invited to dinner. Charlotte loved to cook for them because they were so grateful and polite and she would wave to the ones she recognized on Saturdays when the Corps passed in review on the Plain.

The cadets appreciated Charlotte, too, and for more than her food. Despite her forty-five years, she was still extraordinarily sexy, with twinkling green eyes, auburn hair, and high, square cheekbones. She was getting a little thick through the middle, or so she thought, but she was still the center of attention when cadets visited, a situation she enjoyed because her husband noticed it, and became possessive and romantic as soon as the last cadet went back to the barracks.

Charlotte did not impress the women of the Officers' Wives Club as much as she did the cadets. The women were dismayed that the Supe's wife would refuse to assume the duties normally reserved for the wife of the highest-ranking officer on the post. Politely, but with the subtle firmness typical of genteel Southern women, she advised them that she did not want to be drafted to chair committees or host tea parties. She was not a member of the army, Charlotte explained, and she preferred to devote her time to her husband and to their marriage. To everyone's astonishment, Tannerbeck supported her.

That night, however, dinner was subdued, conversation strained as they both contemplated the article in *The Citizen Times* and both refrained from mentioning it. Only later, when Charlotte brought tea and Tannerbeck stoked the first fire of the season, did she finally broach the subject that had frightened her all day.

"Bob," she asked, "how long are you going to pretend that *The Citizen Times* forgot to publish a newspaper today?"

With a sad chuckle, he placed a condescending kiss on her forehead as if to say, *Don't worry. Everything will be OK.* He knew she wouldn't buy it.

"How much of the article is true?" she asked, refusing to be coddled.

He retreated from the fire and joined her on the couch, where Charlotte snuggled against his side sipping her tea. "None of it," he lied. She held him silently but with rising anger, for she knew her husband to be a decent man and she could not fathom why men like Doug McGowan would seek to destroy him. "I'm sorry," he said, "after all these years, you deserve better than to go to bed at night with an accused war criminal."

Charlotte put her cup on the coffee table and took his hand. "Bob, you've never said anything so stupid. I'll always be proud of you. This last year has been the happiest year of my life. Your tab is paid up, General."

He kissed her again, then got up and poured a brandy for himself and another for his wife. Tannerbeck kicked off his shoes and allowed the fire to warm the soles of his feet as he lay down on the couch with his head in her lap. *Amazing*, thought Charlotte, *how a man fifty years old still needs mothering.* It was amazing, too, that she still wanted to nurture him. "Now, General," she said, "when, exactly, did you first begin to imagine you were Napoleon?"

He laughed aloud. "You mean I'm not?"

The phone jangled. Tannerbeck bolted to a sitting position, but his wife, with unladylike strength, forced him back into her lap. Calmly, she lifted the receiver. "Tannerbeck residence."

"Hello? Charlotte Tannerbeck?"

"Yes, it is." She recognized the voice of the army deputy chief of staff. "General Paxton?"

"Hi, Charlotte. I'm sorry to trouble you at home, but I need to speak to your husband."

"Of course." She lowered the receiver to her lap, where Tannerbeck held it to his ear. She was astonished by how meekly he remained where he was, and how nonchalantly he took the phone. In the past, she'd seen him snap to attention whenever the Pentagon called. Tannerbeck reported directly to the chief of staff of the army, but the chief's deputy often handled political issues the chief preferred to avoid, just as Tannerbeck had handled Abu Ghraib in Iraq when the CINC wouldn't touch it.

"Hello, Jeff."

"Bob, I'm sorry to bother you so late."

"Don't worry about it."

Lieutenant General Jeffery Paxton had departed Iraq within a month of Tannerbeck to assume his duties as deputy to the chief of staff of the army. The war had benefited both their careers, although there were rumors that Paxton had received his promotion as a graceful way to ease him out of Iraq for his failure to build the new Iraqi army into any kind of fighting force. The men were more than acquaintances, though not close friends. The fraternity of army generals was sufficiently small so that they all knew each other, yet competitive enough that genuine friendships were an exception. Still, they were bound by their profession.

The two men did not communicate often, for the position of Superintendent was extremely autonomous and commanders at that level required little guidance. Their relationship was cordial, but Tannerbeck was certain the call was not social, and he found himself reverting to the protective skills he had learned as a plebe, a career ago: *Yes, sir. No, sir. No excuse, sir.*

"Are we going to beat Navy this year?" asked Paxton, reluctant to get down to business.

"Absolutely," lied Tannerbeck, in the only occasion at West Point where falsehoods were not only acceptable, but required. The war had started to erode army recruiting efforts not only for front-line soldiers, but for Army football players as well. Big men made big targets. Ships made for safer duty than infantry, and Navy was going to kick Army's ass again this year. "But you didn't call me at home to ask me that, Jeff. How come the chief's got you doing his dirty work?"

Hesitantly serious, Paxton said, "You know why I'm calling. *The Citizen Times* has really stirred up a hornet's nest here."

"I'll bet."

"The Chiefs have received inquiries from every committee investigating Abu Ghraib, not to mention the press."

"I see," said Tannerbeck.

"We are feeling pressure, unbelievable pressure, directly from individual members of Congress as well as the Armed Forces Subcommittee. I'm calling to advise you that you will be called upon to respond under oath to the matters described in McGowan's article. The testimony will be confidential, at least until the investigating committee publishes its findings."

"Are you talking about an Article 31 hearing?"

"Yes."

Charlotte watched in amazement as her husband's face turned to stone, like a plebe in suspended animation before an irate upperclassman. Under the Uniform Code of Military Justice, an Article 31 investigation was convened to examine the facts behind allegations of a crime. The army didn't respond to every peace-minded crackpot who complained about war crimes whenever an army recruiter showed up on a college campus, but McGowan's article had enough facts behind it to attract the attention of powerful people.

"Jeff, I appreciate your notifying me personally." Tannerbeck's voice was filled with irony, as if to ask why the chief couldn't pick up the phone himself to notify his own subordinate that his career was over. "When will the investigation begin?"

"Very soon. The Judge Advocate General's office will be selecting the investigating officer within the next couple of days." An awkward silence ensued until Paxton added, "I know that none of us got out of Iraq perfectly clean. We might be able to provide some cover about the abuses in general, since even the SecDef will have some explaining to do on that one. But this business with Buckner is a problem. Is there any truth to McGowan's article?"

"No."

"No dead prisoner? No deal to send him to West Point?"

"No."

"Good," said Paxton, adding for good measure, "Fucking reporters." The DCS reclined in his chair and gazed out his top-floor window onto the darkened center courtyard of the Pentagon, the largest exterior "no cover, no salute" area in the world. He recalled the fury among the Pentagon brass when the Abu Ghraib scandal broke. There were rumors among the Chiefs that the chairman had almost come to blows with the secretary of defense during a screaming match in the SecDef's office, in which the chairman had stripped off his uniform tunic, laden with ribbons and badges and four stars, and hurled it at his boss's feet in a spectacular act of insubordination and resignation. The resignation was not accepted, but the relationship between the Pentagon brass and the civilian leadership had remained strained ever since.

The investigations had come fast and furious after that, the army in an angry and self-flagellating mood, almost hoping that the trail of evidence would lead to the secretary's office, where the politicians were already doing their Kabuki dance of denial. But the evidence disappeared into a morass of confusion at the brigade level, where poor leadership and an untenable chain of command conspired to facilitate the abuses and diffuse responsibility. It had always seemed odd to Paxton that nothing had filtered to CJTF-7, and now he suspected why. Tannerbeck had sealed them off, plugged the up-channel leak to protect them all. And now he was lying about it, protecting them still.

"McGowan was imprisoned at Abu Ghraib for six months after being captured while embedded with the enemy," said Tannerbeck. "He suffered a bit and he's determined to make the army pay."

"I know. Don't talk to him, don't cooperate with him, and keep your boy Buckner away from him."

"It's been done. We expect some antiwar demonstrations here tomorrow. Buckner will be restricted to his quarters. The rest of the Corps, and all other Academy personnel, have been ordered not to make any statements whatsoever to anybody."

"Good," said Paxton. "Bob, I hope this blows over quickly. It's embarrassing to the army to have the Superintendent of the Academy implicated in stories about war crimes and cover-ups. People tend to believe the bullshit they read in the papers." Paxton had noticed, however, that *The Citizen Times* had started to get its facts straight in other articles regarding the GWOT, the Global War on Terror, and he wasn't sure if that was a good thing or not.

"Don't worry," answered Tannerbeck, irritated by Paxton's lecturing tone.

Paxton paused for a moment and added, "Bob, if the investigation finds that you were derelict in the performance of your duty, I won't be able to help you."

"I know. I understand." He also understood that Paxton wasn't buying his story.

"You sure you want the chief's job?" asked Paxton, trying to end the conversation on a jocular note, making a joke of the speculation within the army that Tannerbeck was headed for the Joint Chiefs someday.

"I may never get the chance."

"We eat our young too often."

"I don't feel so young anymore."

"Me neither." After an awkward pause, Paxton signed off. "Good night, then."

Tannerbeck hung up the phone with trembling hands. His conscience, clear this afternoon, was clouded now with the reality that he had lied to his superior officer. The Code was absolute: a West Point graduate does not lie, cheat, or steal, or tolerate those who do. But the Supe did not waste his time justifying his actions or dissembling. Tannerbeck understood what he had done and resolved to live with it.

Charlotte replaced the receiver on its cradle. She waited for her husband to speak, but he lay there silently, eyes closed. She stroked his forehead for a long time until finally she whispered, "Tell me."

His eyes were fiery and dry when he opened them, clear as the day she had first felt them on her, the day she fell in love with him. He sighed, a man resigned. "There will be an official inquiry. It looks like McGowan might get his pound of flesh after all."

"Oh, for God's sake," she said. "You couldn't help it! The Joint Chiefs must know that."

"They know. It's politics." Even as he spoke, however, he heard the rationalization in his voice. It was politics to the politicians, for whom everything was a game, but Abu Ghraib was a blemish to the army that no soldier could tolerate, and Tannerbeck knew he was finished.

"Damn politics!" Her voice wavered. "What will they do to us?" Despite her refusal to join the Officers' Wives Club, Charlotte was an army wife and she used the word "us" automatically.

"Nothing will change," Tannerbeck promised. "The investigation is only for show, something to placate Congress."

Charlotte appreciated the lie, but there was a toughness to her that her loveliness belied. Mentally, she calculated the outcome, who would testify for her husband and who would testify against him.

"What will you tell them?"

"That I was unaware of any abuses and I didn't make any deals to cover them up," he said.

"As long as that's the way it happened, what is there to worry about?"

"It's a lie, Charlotte."

She had suspected it from the beginning, so his confession caused no visible reaction. "Is this the end, then?"

"Probably," he said. "It depends on what the others have to say. I'm worried about Buckner. He's young, and he'll be scared. He's as compromised as I am—he killed a prisoner, for Christ's sake. But there is something about him, something fearless. Courageous men are honest men. He's got something to hide, but he's the kind of man who might throw the truth in our face and challenge us to do something about it."

Charlotte nodded, though she did not understand.

"And I'll insist they question General Piersal."

"Will he tell the truth?"

"That bastard has never told the truth in his life. Who knows what he'll say? He's as guilty as I am, but those MI boys always have some other game going. I have enemies there."

"What about Volpe?" she asked.

"Rick is an ascetic, completely incorruptible. He'd blow his own brains out if I asked him to, but he won't lie."

"What will happen if the board of inquiry determines that the article in the newspaper is true?"

He reached for her hand and held it in his own. "A court-martial," he said quietly. "Dishonorable discharge, maybe even prison if they listen to the press and declare it a war crime. You would be left with nothing—no pension, nothing."

"No matter what, darling, I'll always adore you."

His eyes glistened.

CHAPTER 32

The word on Darrow among the *Times'* staffers in the Washington office was that she was McGowan's girl—don't touch. She was too young and too pretty to have earned the job anywhere but in the bedroom, and the contempt she felt from her Washington coworkers was even more palpable than that in New York. She visited the staff offices as little as possible, writing from her cubicle in the Pentagon and filing her stories via modem. The other reporters resented her absences from the office, and griped that the bureau chief let her get away with it. But the chief was watching Darrow as closely as he watched them all, and he did not concur with the feelings of his subordinates. Buster Lambeau had seen his share of doe-eyed cub reporters and sexy girls with more ambition than brains, but Darrow was not one of them. She used her face and her body to her advantage, but what woman didn't? Lambeau saw in Darrow the makings of a reporter, for however luscious were her lips, they did not babble with mall-rat repartee. The woman could put words on paper and tell a good story, even if she didn't always fathom the importance of one lead over another. She took his editing without offense. And if she spent more time chasing a story than she did writing it in her cubicle, good for her. Still, Lambeau kept his distance. The others were wrong about Darrow's talent, but they were right about how she'd gotten the job, and if there was any coaching to be done he'd let McGowan do it.

Lambeau stared at her now, perfect as always, leaning against his office doorjamb.

"Buster," she said, "Do we have a sketch artist? Somebody who draws witnesses and defendants at trials we cover?"

"Go see Latour," he growled, more irritated than usual. Nobody except Martha Rose called him "Buster."

Janet Latour was a freelancer, on retainer with the *Times*, but free to sell her services to anyone. She had started her career as a sketch artist for the police, but as computer technology began to replace her skills, she worked now mostly in courtrooms where cameras were prohibited, drawing in charcoal various faces of interest. Like Darrow, she rarely visited the *Times'* office except to drop off her work. At fifty years of age, she was as old as the parents of the reporters she worked with, and not privy to their gossip. When Darrow explained her mission, Latour was eager to help. "I would be delighted," she said, "to help you identify this man." They agreed to meet for lunch at the Tortilla Coast restaurant, a popular hangout for Congressional staffers just east of the Library of Congress.

As the waitress delivered chips and salsa, Latour withdrew her sketch pad from a huge all-purpose leather purse. "We'll start with his overall shape," she said. "Big guy, little guy? Fat or skinny?"

"I just need his face."

"Fat guys have round faces." She drew a circle on her pad. "Skinny guys have rectangular faces." Latour smiled reassuringly. "Trust me."

"He was chunky, I think."

Latour drew an oval, marking it here and there for future additions of ears, eyes, nose, chin, mouth. "Hairline?"

"Receding."

"You're very observant."

"No," said Darrow sadly, "I'm terrible with faces. I couldn't describe you if I had to, even sitting here looking at you."

Latour waved her pencil, as if to dismiss Darrow's worries. "Was he wearing glasses?"

"No." Both women smiled, and Darrow was grateful to be in the hands of a pro.

"Mouth. Big or little?"

"I don't remember." Darrow's smile faded. "I can see him in my mind's eye, but I just can't describe him. I don't see how witnesses ever provide enough information for sketch artists to render anyone with accuracy."

"Too bad he didn't have an eye patch and a beard. But don't worry. It'll come to you."

Darrow brightened. "He had a mustache."

"See what I mean? Simple." Latour drew a quick handlebar mustache on the oval where she imagined it might be. "Too big?"

"Yes."

Latour shortened it, adding a mouth for reference.

"That's about right," said Darrow.

"A military man."

"Military? A round face with a mustache and you know he's in the military?"

"Of course," said Latour. "The only cosmetic reason for any man to grow a mustache is to make his mouth appear wider. Wide mouths are considered sexy in our society, as I'm sure you know. I certainly wish I had *your* lips. Anyway, men accomplish this act of vanity by growing the ends of the mustache out onto the cheek past the end of the lips. But the military restricts mustaches. They may not extend beyond the edge of the mouth like a handlebar, or grow over the lip like a walrus. The end result is that military mustaches all end up looking like Hitler's." Latour drew in a small mouth and gave the mustache more detail. "It's always the guys with small mouths that grow mustaches," she explained. "Wide-mouthed guys don't need them."

"Amazing," said Darrow. The drawing was coming to life even without the eyes.

Latour drew a pair of generic eyes, and then aged them with wrinkles. "Men get crows feet, too," she said. "About my age, eh? You know, I could really go for this guy, if his mouth wasn't so damned small."

Darrow laughed heartily for the first time since she had arrived in Washington. She decided that Janet Latour was going to be her first friend. Slowly, a face emerged on Latour's pad, a face that Darrow had seen before. She stared at it, humbled and grateful for the unusual talents of others. "How do you do it?" she asked. "Even if I had your talent as an artist, I could never have drawn this from memory."

Latour gave Darrow a frank once-over that would have been offensive if Latour had been a man. "In our society, most people never really look at each other. We glance, and then look away. Art training helps force you to understand the basic human shapes, but it takes a certain level of brazenness to really stare someone down. I was always a little rude that way. You should be, too."

Darrow held up the drawing. "It's wonderful. What do I owe you, Janet?"

"Lunch. The chichimangas are great."

The doors to the Pentagon briefing room opened at 1445; the daily briefings commenced punctually at 1500. Many reporters arrived as soon as the doors opened, for it was a chance to socialize and spread gossip. The young guns among them were more cutthroat, sharing information with no one, but most of the correspondents on the Pentagon beat were old salts and combat veterans who were content to finish out their careers where they were respected for their experience and where their contacts had value. Their relationship with the Pentagon Public Information Office was cordial, but antagonistic. The reporters wanted information and the PIO provided it when it suited the military. More often than not, members of the press already had the answers to their questions and simply wanted the briefing officers to admit to what everyone knew. It was a daily game of "Gotcha!" called the "Three O'clock Follies," in which the briefers lied, the press knew they lied, and the briefers knew that the press knew that they lied.

Darrow attended the Follies religiously, but wisely kept her mouth shut during the sparring matches, smiling at the old guys when they managed to really stick it to the PIO officer behind the podium. Condescending they were, but the Pentagon correspondents began to tolerate Darrow, even providing her with juicy tidbits of information from time to time. They were surprised by how frequently she was able to reciprocate with tips of her own.

She approached one group now, three senior correspondents from Reuters, UPI and *Time* magazine, who chatted amiably among themselves.

"Hey, Hargrove," she said, calling one man by his last name, the way they always addressed each other.

"Darrow." He nodded his head as they all eyed her with amusement.

"You guys got a minute?"

"Have you ever met a man who didn't have a minute for a pretty girl?"

She gave them her most luscious smile as she took Janet Latour's sketch from her shoulder bag. She handed it to them without comment.

"You taking up the police beat, Darrow?" Hargrove held the drawing at arm's length rather than don his bifocals. "Looks like an accountant."

"Do you recognize him? I think he's in the military."

"Well, that narrows it down to a couple million souls." Hargrove handed the sheet to the man from UPI.

"What'd he do?" asked the man, tilting it back and forth as he studied it.

"I don't know," she said. "Depends on who he is."

The three studied it in silence for a minute and then returned it, shaking their heads. "Ask Sonderstrom," said Hargrove at last. "He knows everyone who wears a uniform in this town. Been on this beat for twenty years."

"I've never heard of him," said Darrow.

"He writes for the *Army Times.*"

She nodded her head, as if to express familiarity with a newspaper she knew she should be reading but which she found too dull to tolerate. Darrow had no interest in the army budget or weapons development programs.

The three men glanced at each other knowingly. "Come, child." Hargrove took her elbow and guided her through the other correspondents. The doors to the conference room had opened and the crowd now funneled slowly into the room.

Suddenly, Hargrove cupped his hands to his mouth and uttered a loud stage whisper. "Hey, Sonderstrom! Get over here!" Then he stepped aside and allowed the other reporters to pass. Some members of the press hung back, curious, but Hargrove shooed them through the door.

Against the tide, a small man with glasses emerged from the room, a puzzled expression on his seasoned face. "Hargrove, what the hell is the matter with you?"

"Sonderstrom," said Hargrove, "you've met Darrow from *The Citizen Times*?"

Darrow offered her hand and Sonderstrom shook it brusquely. "No, I have not," he said, speaking to Hargrove. "If I have business with the *Times*, I go directly to Buster Lambeau."

"I know you're a busy man," interjected Darrow, "but I only need a minute or two of your time."

"Well, dear, you seem to have gotten me out here, I've lost my seat at the Follies, and if I don't get back in there they will close the door and we'll all be locked out. Now that I'm here, what is it that you want?"

The other reporters smirked as Darrow handed him the sketch.

Sonderstrom had begun his stint at the *Army Times* after a lackluster career as a journeyman reporter for various city rags around the country. A man of limited ambition and few social skills, Sonderstrom somehow found his niche at the *Army Times*, a civilian newspaper dedicated to covering issues related to the U.S. Army. He had never progressed beyond the rank of beat reporter, but his beat for the last twenty years had been the Pentagon, where he knew every office and every officer assigned there. The old man studied it for five seconds and handed it back.

"General John Piersal. Deputy chief of staff for Military Intelligence, U.S. Army, here in the Pentagon."

"Thank you," said Darrow, impressed. Even Hargrove raised an eyebrow.

"That's it? You drag me out here to perform this favor for you, and all I get is 'Thank you'?" Sonderstrom stared at her intently. Darrow was not certain if the twinkle in his eye was from malevolence or mirth.

"Do I have to sleep *everyone?*" she asked, dead serious.

Sonderstrom stood dumbly, his mouth half open while the other reporters burst into laughter. The man from Reuters spun the old man around and led him back into the briefing chamber which the PIO Major had just entered.

Hargrove put his arm on Darrow's shoulder and said, "You know who Piersal is, don't you?"

Her blank expression was all the answer he needed.

"He's the army's chief spy. I don't know what you've gotten yourself into, sweetheart, but he is going to be furious that you've identified him."

CHAPTER 33

September 18, 2004 (Saturday)
West Point

While the Tannerbecks slept, the vanguard of an army of antiwar activists began to invade the town of Highland Falls. They came from college campuses throughout New York, Connecticut, and Rhode Island, where *The Citizen Times* was well read and where college zealots were well organized. Most of the contingent knew each other from previous rallies to save whales, spotted owls, trees, the ozone layer, and the civil rights of convicts. The caravans gathered in the parking lot of the local branch of the Marine Midland Bank. Marijuana smoke and the mellow sounds of Elliott Smith wafted into the night.

Highland Falls was a military town sustained by its proximity to West Point. Main Street fed directly into the South Gate of the Academy, but unlike most army towns, the approach to the gate was not a gauntlet of bars, used-car dealerships, and fast-food joints. Highland Falls was a tiny, picturesque community, with a pair of white-steepled churches lending it an aura of respectability. The major industry was tourism, which supported a dozen motels and a couple of gas stations, a drugstore, a Safeway, and a few souvenir shops. The townsfolk were proud of their association with West Point, and they found the odd assortment of protestors in their midst extremely irritating.

The Highland Falls police chief rousted the campers from the bank parking lot at dawn. They were young men and women filled with mindless contempt for anyone in uniform, but the more experienced members of the antiwar movement among them successfully discouraged a premature confrontation. Instead, they joined a caravan of motley vehicles inching its way toward the South Gate, where expressionless MPs directed them to a makeshift parking lot on muddy Soldier Field, a mile away from the Plain and the cadet barracks. As they waited for other protestors to arrive, some of the more ardent activists led antiwar chants and waved banners at passing traffic, but the predominant scene was one of confusion. The demonstration had been convoked too quickly, and leaders of the various contingents spent more time exercising their authority and yelling at each other than in organizing the carnival of masked anti-WTO anarchists, militant lesbians, pacifists with tambourines and pierced noses, NOW grandmas, tattooed college students, and professors with gray ponytails. Ninety people milled about in the mud and none knew what to do.

"Looks like our article started something," observed Darrow from the entrance to the Thayer Hotel, a convenient vantage point from which to view the action.

"It doesn't take much to mobilize the Chronically Outraged," agreed McGowan. "But bizarros make the news. Without these fruitcakes, half the reporters in the country would be out of a job."

A military officer approached a smoldering knot of zealots, his starched uniform a transfixing contrast to the unkempt protestors. "You will be permitted to express your opinions within the confines of the field," stated the liaison officer, a rangy, rawboned Midwesterner with huge wrists and hands. His name tag and collar insignia identified him as Major Ruskin. The civilians regarded him contemptuously, ignorant of the sacrifices behind the Ranger tab on his shoulder or the Combat Infantry Badge on his chest.

"You'll *permit* us?" snarled one young man wearing cool wire-rimmed spectacles and an adolescent beard. He lisped slightly due to the stud in his tongue. "It's your job to protect our *right* to express our opinions," he reminded the soldier.

"If you attempt to disrupt the parade," continued Ruskin, "you will be deterred." His voice was as even as a drum roll, his face utterly blank, as if the species before him was not worthy of an emotion of any kind.

"What parade?" said another boy, staring at the muddy field. They had performed no reconnaissance of the Academy grounds, or had any understanding of the world they had barged into. A few yards away, a gaggle of coeds suddenly squealed over a butterfly that fluttered into their midst, as though beautiful things were not supposed to exist on a military institution.

"Get everyone together," suggested one of the young men to his comrades. "We'll conduct a peoples' march onto the parade ground. We'll march right alongside the cadets."

The others nodded in agreement and signaled for their lieutenants to round up their contingents. Whether they demonstrated peacefully by intermingling with the Corps in front of the reviewing stand, or whether they created a melee, it would be a victory for the peace movement. The press was on hand; it would undoubtedly make the papers.

"Any attempt to interfere with the parade will be deterred," repeated Ruskin, as imperturbable as a howitzer. The officer's composure began to rattle the demonstrators, accustomed to the indulgent personalities of deans and bureaucrats who smiled when challenged and always backed down.

"How you gonna deter us?" demanded the boy with the beard. He pointed to the row of armed MPs that surrounded the field. "Blow us away?"

At last, the major showed his teeth, but it was not the acquiescent kind of smile these students understood. The major turned and marched back to his troops.

Despite their misgivings, the young men mustered their followers into groups. Like platoons of the soldiers they so despised, their eyes blazing, the rabble began a disorderly route step to the Plain.

Throughout the morning, while the ardent protestors greeted each new busload of reinforcements at Soldier Field, a festive mood permeated the area of the barracks and the Plain. The sky turned blue, with clouds scudding before a crisp breeze. Spectators already encircled the parade ground, energized by the fall weather and thoughts of football.

Saturday mornings were reserved for inspections, white-glove affairs in which company Tactical Officers went through every room checking for dust, unauthorized items, and the proper placement of toothpaste tubes in the medicine cabinet. The "Tacs" were commissioned officers of superior achievement assigned to oversee the development of the cadets throughout their years at West Point. They were gung-ho role models, every one a combat vet with a stunning array of ribbons and badges, and every one a hard-core son of a bitch. During the room inspections, cadets stood at attention by their desks and were themselves inspected while the Tac called out violations to LaFarge, who recorded them for the future award of demerits. A stickler for regulations, Boyer always had the room shipshape and escaped with only three demerits, for excessive dust on the bristles of the push broom stowed under his bunk.

Word came down: room inspections were complete; prepare for personal inspections in ranks.

Boyer stripped off his class uniform and reached into his closet for the full dress jacket, the traditional cadet uniform with tails and a dozen brass buttons, while Buckner closed up the closets, cabinets, and desk drawers to put the room back into its normal configuration. Restriction to quarters did not normally include an excuse from parades, but in light of Buckner's public notoriety, the Academy PIO had included parades as a public appearance from which Buckner was restricted. So Buckner helped Boyer struggle into his shoulder belts.

Buckner unwrapped Boyer's uncomfortable shako from its felt sack. He inserted the pompon and adjusted it, leaving the hat balanced precariously on Boyer's head, which itself seemed barely balanced on his skinny neck. The chin strap hung uselessly between his chin and lower lip, per regulations. On windy days, cadets held their straps in their teeth to prevent the ridiculous "tar buckets" from blowing away. The minute caller announced five minutes to inspection as Buckner handed Boyer's M-14 to him. Boyer snatched it in his gloved hands and held it at port arms as Buckner opened the door. "Go get'em, killer."

At 1130, the demonstrators began to arrive at the Plain. They gawked like ordinary tourists at the barracks, the Cadet Chapel, the panorama of the granite mountains, the river, and the emerald Plain. They found it incongruous that a place of such beauty produced men of violence who had ranged with insouciance across the killing fields of Dak To, Normandy, and Gettysburg. Through the sally ports, they caught glimpses of the cadets at attention as officers walked the ranks, inspecting each cadet's rifle, shoulder belts, spit shine, shave, haircut, and brass. For Firsties and plebes alike, inspections in ranks were an ordeal of standing at attention. By the time the bugle blew to start the parade, everyone was anxious to march, to put on a show, just desperate to *move*.

The sidewalks were crowded with spectators, camera-toting tourists with children riding on their fathers' shoulders waving little American flags. Despite the exhortations of a few hotheads, the brave plan of the demonstrators to march onto the Plain dissolved during the march from Soldier Field as a lack of discipline undermined their resolve. So, they stood meekly behind the barriers with the other tourists and waved "WAR IS TERRORISM" banners while yelling obscenities calculated to inflame not only the cadets, but everyone else as well.

The Hellcats began to play, and even the demonstrators fell into awestruck silence.

Company F-2 marched onto the Plain to the strains of John Philip Sousa. The guidon flapped in the breeze and everyone bit down on his chin strap while the upperclassmen grumbled and cursed the demonstrators, inaudible to the throngs surrounding the Plain. Boyer sailed with the music, marching proudly with the ghosts of the Long Gray Line who inhabited the supernaturally green parade ground.

From the stands, the companies appeared to move across the field as solid phalanxes of a hundred men. En masse, individual cadets blended together into a ribbon of motion; only the cadet commanders at the head of their troops were distinct entities. One by one, each company found its spot on the field and halted. The cadets lowered their arms and awaited commands. Unlike many companies, F-2 had never had a strong military tradition, and the cadets chatted and told jokes while they waited at attention for the final order to pass in review. When the entire Corps stood assembled on the field, the Hellcats played the National Anthem. The demonstrators stood among the reverent spectators and yelled vituperations with studied disrespect, relishing the disapproving stares of those around them. The Corps presented arms; orders were read and commands issued, military folderol that not even the cadets understood.

Finally, the first captain issued the command, "Pass in Review!" The words echoed across the plain and bounced against the window where Buckner stood watching. To the cadets, the distorted echo was inchoate, but they knew the routine. With an indiscernible twitching of their wrists, the four thousand men of the Corps rattled their mounted bayonets in mock enthusiasm over the imminent opportunity to perform. The spectators speculated about the faint clatter that floated from the Plain.

The band struck up. The companies began to move. One by one, they fell in fifty paces behind the company ahead of them, four thousand men in thirty-six squares marching to the beat of Wagner. One company after another, the Corps marched initially toward the crowd, and then turned left, marching parallel to the rope line for fifty yards before executing another left turn, away from the spectators and toward the reviewing stand where they passed in review.

As Company F-2 approached the crowd, the taunting of the protestors swelled. Some tossed flowers and called for peace, while others bellowed, "Criminals!" and "Murderers!" A murmur of outrage arose from the legitimate tourists, joined by the cadets' own revilements muttered through clenched teeth. Inspired by the fact that Buckner was one of their own, and determined to put on a show for the people who would presume to judge them, the cadets of Company F-2 marched with newfound enthusiasm. They were surprised, however, when LaForge led them past the normal turn point and directly toward the crowd. The protesters were initially perplexed by F-2's failure to turn away like all the others, but then recoiled as the company advanced, marching to the driving rhythm of the Hellcats' drums with the implacable precision of a harvester. At the last moment, LaForge gave the command, "Left Turn, March!" and the cadets of F-2 veered away with a perfect pivot, ranks as straight as rifle shots. Inches away from the spectator fence, the men found their professionalism, marching silently, eyes ahead, rifle butts in perfect alignment, every foot placed in the footprint in front of it.

Suddenly, LaForge issued the preparatory command, "Eyes…!"

Excited now, F-2 realized that their company commander was about to salute the crowd, an act of irony that would be lost on the civilian demonstrators. The cadets grading the parade and the reviewing officers on the stand, already appalled by F-2's intentional deviation from the proscribed route of march, could only watch while LaForge committed professional suicide. His saber snapped through the air in a quick flash of chrome as he completed the command: "Right!"

One hundred men snapped their heads to the right, in perfect unison, crisp as robots. Instantly face-to-face with so many grim faces, several spectators stepped back. Boyer's chest swelled as he realized that F-2 had projected power directly into the crowd and had cowed the demonstrators with their precision and professionalism. LaForge belted out the next command, "Ready...Front!" The men and women of F-2 snapped their heads forward again, as if disinterested in what they had seen.

The company proceeded to return to its place in the parade. As they passed in review, General Tannerbeck returned their salute sternly, and every member of the company understood that LaForge's intimidation of the crowd would not go unpunished. Nevertheless, F-2 was in high spirits as they left the Plain and passed through the sally port to the assembly area, where LaForge dismissed them on the march without even bringing the company to a halt. As the perfect formation dissolved around him, LaForge marched directly to his room to await the inevitable arrival of the company Tactical Officer.

CHAPTER 34

September 20, 2004 (Monday)
West Point

Due either to a unique collection of personalities or to fortuitous timing, some graduating classes from West Point made a greater mark upon the army than others. The Class of '73 was such a class. Its graduates received their combat baptism in Panama and Serbia. They were seasoned in Desert Storm and became generals in Iraq. By 2004, thirty-nine members of that class wore at least one star. They held positions of power around the world, and twelve of them worked in the Pentagon. Although every Academy class forms a fraternity, the generals of '73 were a special clique among their classmates. They were sons of the army who had persevered during peacetime when promotions were slow and glory hard to come by. In war, they fought each other as hard as they fought the enemy; combat commands were fewer and fewer at higher ranks and each successive rung up the military ladder required more politicking than the last. Still, they had loyalty and honor, and a member in trouble could count on his classmates. It was true when they were plebes, and it was true in 2004.

General Tannerbeck had known Tom Roby only casually when they were classmates at West Point. During the early years of their careers, the two men heard of each other occasionally, and once served briefly together in Panama. Only later, when both men had advanced to the top of the personnel stew and began their parallel and meteoric promotions through the ranks, did they become competitors and friends. By the time Lieutenant General Roby arrived at West Point to lead the investigating committee appointed by the chief of staff of the army, his wife had already received Charlotte's birthday card.

When Gladys announced Roby's arrival, Tannerbeck came out of his office to greet him. The Supe noted that his classmate had lost more hair and gained some weight since he had last seen him in Iraq. Even as a cadet, behind thick glasses with eyes too sensitive to be a soldier, Roby had more the aspect of a math teacher than a leader of fighting men. But Roby's star had risen in the Republican Defense Department because he supported the SecDef's vision of a smaller, more lethal military, and because he had the management skills to cut personnel without cutting operational readiness. Still, nobody made it to the top through management talent alone, and Roby had compiled a respectable combat record with a reputation for efficiency, if not glory.

Tannerbeck greeted his classmate cordially. "Good to see you, Tom. How long has it been since you were back at the Point?"

"A long time," Roby answered, smiling, "but not long enough. I'd forgotten how chilly the wind can be here."

Both men nodded grimly.

Roby sank into one of the Superintendent's leather chairs and formally announced, "Bob, I've been appointed by the chief of staff of the army to conduct an Article 31 pretrial investigation of the events of September 2, last year, in which troops under your command allegedly committed abuses against prisoners of war in violation of the Geneva Conventions. Are you familiar with Article 31?"

"I've been studying the UCMJ all week," said the Superintendent, pointing at two thick binders on his desk: *The Uniform Code of Military Justice* and *The Manual for Courts Martial.*

"Me, too," confessed Roby. "This will be an informal investigation, but the consequences can be equally serious. I wish we could take this lightly, but a lot of people have their eyes on us. I can't whitewash this."

The Superintendent said, "Why are you leading this investigation, Tom? You're not JAG."

Roby shrugged. "I received this assignment because I outrank you by a few weeks, Bob, and there just aren't many three-star lawyers in the Judge Advocate General's Office. Can't have junior officers investigating senior officers."

"Of course," said Tannerbeck. "But are you qualified?"

"Hell no. But I've been assigned legal counsel, Colonel Harkins from JAG. He's never seen combat, but he's a whiz with procedures."

"Fine. When do you want to begin?"

"We'll start tomorrow, but I probably should not discuss any aspect of the investigation with you, other than aspects that involve you directly. You're entitled to legal representation. I assume you have a lawyer?"

"I can answer my own questions."

Roby nodded his head ruefully; he had suspected that Tannerbeck would testify without legal advice. West Pointers never quibbled or manipulated the truth, so what purpose was served by a lawyer? Still, Roby warned his classmate,

"Bob, this guy Harkins is a shark. He lives for the courtroom razzle-dazzle."

"However," added Tannerbeck, as if had not heard Roby, "I would appreciate it if you would see to it that Mr. Buckner gets the best JAG officer available."

CHAPTER 35

September 20, 2004 (Monday)
West Point

To civilians, Colonel Richard Volpe was a specter. The jagged scar down the middle of his face suggested that he was a man who had survived something he wasn't supposed to. Stoop-shouldered and laconic, he spoke with the peculiar precision of a military poet. His remaining eye ricocheted around the room until it focused like tracer rounds on one thing after another, recording details invisible to others.

When he arrived at Tannerbeck's office, he presented himself to Gladys as if he were reporting to a superior officer. It made no difference that Gladys was a civilian or a woman old enough to be his mother. Volpe treated everyone in a brutally respectful manner until he or she gave him reason to do otherwise.

"Good morning, ma'am. Colonel Volpe to see General Tannerbeck."

Few men impressed Gladys, who had served West Pointers for thirty years and had become accustomed to routine gallantry. But Volpe embodied a sense of tragedy, the dark side of West Point, and even Gladys found his presence disconcerting. With one eye fixed on Volpe, she reached for the intercom, but the door to Tannerbeck's office suddenly opened, as if the Supe had sensed Volpe's eerie presence.

"Hello, Rick."

"General."

The two officers stood silently for a moment, awkward, until Tannerbeck stepped forward and threw his arm around Volpe's shoulder. To Gladys' surprise, Volpe responded with a hug of his own. They slapped each other on the back like brothers, then disappeared into the general's office while Gladys watched, embarrassed. She had never seen Tannerbeck shed his courtly demeanor, and in a society where expressions of affection between men and women were taboo, an embrace between two men was shocking.

Volpe took a seat in the leather side chair occupied earlier by General Roby. His darting eye settled for a moment on the wall of photos and he knew immediately who the men were. "I'm sorry it came to this, sir."

"We both knew it was inevitable. I'm surprised it took McGowan as long as it has to pin this on us."

"We knew what we were doing, sir."

"Yes, we did."

Volpe caught Tannerbeck glancing at the wall of faces. The Old Man acted as if the photographs were alive, weighing him down with guilt. *Sentimental men should never be allowed to wear stars*, he thought. "Don't be so hard on yourself, sir. Whatever we did was necessary."

"It doesn't matter. We'll be judged by people who don't know the difference between right and wrong, or don't care. Congress and the press, sanctimonious idiots who would presume to tell us about honor."

"How high do you think the purge will go?"

"It depends on our testimony, I suppose."

Volpe dropped his eyes to the floor, and then looked back at Tannerbeck, miserable.

"Don't worry about me," said Tannerbeck. "I'm washed up no matter what happens. But I refuse to accept the judgment of people who have never seen combat, who can't understand the burden of command, and who have never had another human being die for them." Tannerbeck glanced at the photographs on the wall and continued, "I'll be damned if some little bitch from Bard is going to pass judgment on me." His stare lingered for a moment on the faces of his men before his eyes drifted irresistibly to the window, where the gray river ran and the hills beckoned beyond.

Volpe sat uncomfortably in the leather chair. Leaning forward, his elbows on his knees, he stared at the floor and said, "I'm going to testify truthfully, sir."

"I know, Rick. You are incapable of doing anything else."

"I'm sorry."

"Don't be," said Tannerbeck. "Honor demands different things from each of us."

Fifteen minutes passed while they sat in silence, old friends unable to say good-bye. The intercom buzzed.

"Sir," said Gladys, "I just received word that a boxing match involving Mr. Buckner is about to get underway at the gymnasium."

Volpe recognized his cue and stood up, refastening the buttons of his uniform jacket. "Good luck, sir."

Tannerbeck opened his desk drawer, rummaging among the pens and paperclips until he found what he wanted: a pair of silver stars, an extra set he kept in case of emergencies. He tossed them to Volpe.

"You'll be wearing these soon enough, Rick. Think of me when you pin them on."

Volpe twisted his face into a dreadful smile and walked out the door.

CHAPTER 36

September 20, 2004 (Monday)
West Point

The cloud cover lowered throughout the Hudson Valley all morning. By noon, the ceiling hovered just above the chapel, and drizzle floated in the wind. Tendrils of mist scraped across the turrets of the barracks while Second Regiment stood at attention below.

Weekday parades without crowds were a miserable waste of time, especially in the rain, when two hours of marching could mean two days of cleaning rust from an M-14. Even the men and women of F-2, mysteriously gung-ho since their triumphant brush with the demonstrators, longed to retreat from the elements. Cancelled parades meant rack time, and nothing, not even the wrath of the Tactical Officer, could motivate a cadet to sacrifice an extra hour of sleep.

Like Eskimos with a multitude of words for snow, cadets could differentiate a thousand forms of rain. All eyes were on the Regimental Staff, who would decide if the form of precipitation warranted cancellation of the parade. These high-ranking cadets conferred with each other like umpires, one eye on the clouds and an ear to the telephone.

Authority to cancel would come from the Tactical Department.

G Company started the chant.

"Odin!"

Other companies joined in. Slowly, with deep, resonant supplication, a thousand men called upon the god of thunder to wield his hammer and strike rain, heavy rain, from the clouds. It did not occur to anyone that the god of thunder was not Odin, but Thor.

"Ohh...din, Ohhhhhhh...din."

The call rolled between the buildings like the marching cadence of ogres in the pagans' forest. Civilian pedestrians stopped to listen, unsure of the meaning or the source of the haunting cry that emanated from behind the barracks and rose into the gray sky.

"Ohhhhh...din, Ohhhhh...din."

The cadets, too, listened, their own chants causing them goose bumps. There was spirituality in those sounds, echoing among the barracks in the dreary air. For a moment, it was easy to believe that Odin was real, especially when the clouds finally released their burden and the rain fell in earnest. When parade practice was cancelled, few men believed that it had been a mere coincidence that the frontal zone had closed in.

Cheers erupted as company commanders dismissed their companies, but the delight in F-2 turned to keen anticipation when LaForge announced, "F Company, reform in fifteen minutes! Buckner and Gastogne, your uniform is gym alpha; it's time to fight!"

The company formed below the windows of other companies. Gastogne, in sweat pants and parka, waved to well-wishers who called to him from their rooms. He stood aside from the rest of the company and bounced on his toes and threw shadow punches. In similar athletic gear, Buckner waited with the rest of his classmates, rooted to the pavement at rigid attention while upperclassmen strolled among them, muttering corrections. They ignored Buckner, for each of them had done his time in the ring, and none had the malice to harass a condemned man with the courage to take on Frank Gastogne.

Word spread so quickly that men from other companies loitered at the gym even as F Company arrived. LaForge ordered them away, then assigned a guard to the boxing room door and the arena was sealed.

The room was huge but the ceiling was low, the air heavy with the peculiar musk of human fear and the pungent sweat of men at the limit of their endurance. The concrete floor was spotted here and there with old drops of blood, brown reminders of past agonies. A dozen heavy bags hung at one end of the room; speed bags lined the other. Along one wall, dozens of boxing gloves hung on hooks, each with protective leather headgear. The gloves weighed sixteen ounces, heavy as bricks. The instructors called them "pillows," but years of punching had compacted the padding to the consistency of gravel. The greasy headgear was stiff from the sweat of a thousand foreheads and still reeked of the day's earlier combat.

In the center stood the floodlit ring, taut and spotless, a shrine. Plebes tended it after each fight, reverently toweling away blood and tightening ropes like pugilistic altar boys.

LaForge assigned the fighters to their corners. He directed the upperclassmen to one side of the ring, the plebes to the other. Gastogne slipped into the ring and doffed his parka and T-shirt. A murmur rose from the crowd, like breeders judging horseflesh, as Gastogne strutted his stuff. He was a young man in prime physical condition, broad-chested, hard-bellied, and with a jaw like an anvil. His shoulders, a boxer's source of power, were massive epaulets of muscle, every striation defined and engorged with blood and adrenalin. Gastogne was quick; he could dance and jab when he wanted to, but he usually won his fights through sheer brute power.

The lessons taught in the boxing ring, however, were not about fighting, but about controlling fear. Few cadets anticipated upcoming bouts without knots in their guts, but Gastogne was one of those few who had long since outgrown the butterflies. His supreme confidence was yet another weapon in his arsenal; his hungry smile terrorized his opponents, the bravest of whom responded with mere shit-eating grins.

Buckner was an efficient boxer, but his style lacked the classic elegance taught at West Point. He was a brawler, one of few cadets who had at some time during his life actually thrown a punch with the malicious intent of taking someone out. He tended to push and butt and strike below the belt. Buckner had learned early in his life what it was like to square off in bare-fisted combat, where only the winner walked away. It took more than a smile to intimidate him.

"How long can you punch without stopping?" asked Boyer. He jammed the leather helmet tight against Buckner's forehead and tied it under his chin.

"I don't know. Never had to fight longer than a minute."

Boyer fed him his mouthpiece. "Charge him as soon as the bell rings."

"He'll throw a jab to keep me away."

"Yeah. Wait for it, then throw your head in his face and go after his midsection. Don't stop punching. Keep him on the defense."

Buckner nodded.

"Can you punch for two minutes, nonstop?" asked Boyer.

"No, but neither can he," said Buckner.

"Yes, he can. But if you keep him running for the first round, he'll lose his confidence. He'll fight more cautiously after that. He won't be so eager to attack."

Buckner tossed his head back and forth and pounded his gloves together. "What do you know about boxing, Boyer? You can't punch your way out of a paper sack."

"War, boxing, chess; they're all the same."

They were ready. LaForge called the fighters to the center of the ring. "Three rounds, two minutes each. You know the rules. Any questions?"

Buckner and Gastogne touched gloves and retreated to their corners.

"Chess?" said Buckner. "I'm fucked now."

The bell rang.

Only the sentry guarding the door snapped to attention as General Tannerbeck slipped into the room, for every eye was on Buckner. He shot across the ring, covering the distance before Gastogne was barely out of his corner. The champ jabbed to slow him down, but Buckner followed Boyer's orders and stopped in his tracks. The punch found air, then Buckner threw his head into Gastogne's face, an intentional butt, and the upper-class audience cried foul. The protests were drowned by the furious exhortations of the plebes. Buckner began to pummel Gastogne's midsection and the fourth classmen rolled their shoulders vicariously with each punch.

Buckner pushed and shoved and stepped on Gastogne's feet. Confused and frustrated, unable to see past Buckner's headgear that was jammed in his face, Gastogne was too busy fending off Buckner's attack to wreak any damage of his own. Although Buckner failed to inflict any physical harm, he took away the upperclassman's psychological advantage.

Gastogne finally clenched. He grabbed Buckner in a bear hug and, exasperated, flung him to the canvas. He turned his back and walked to his corner, expecting the mandatory eight-count, but there was no count. Buckner charged into Gastogne's back and drove him into the corner post. Gastogne turned, and Buckner hit him in the face.

The plebes screamed for more.

"He's trapped!" yelled Boyer. "Crowd him! Don't let him move! Stop swinging for his head, Buckner! Stay in his stomach!"

Gastogne ducked into the center of the ring in ignominious retreat, Buckner in pursuit. Both men threw wild, headhunting punches, and both men missed. They stood, exhausted, nostrils flared and bloody, eyes narrowed, chests heaving. Every muscle was contracted with exhaustion or rage. Aroused by the sight of blood, both camps screamed support for their champions. After an eternity, the round ended.

Boyer swabbed Buckner's face with a towel. "Good job," he praised. "How do your arms feel?"

"These gloves feel like bowling balls." Buckner opened his mouth and accepted a stream of water squeezed from a plastic bottle with a nozzle.

"You didn't hurt him, but he's worried. Can you keep this up for two more rounds?"

"No."

Boyer noticed that his fighter's eyes were brimming with tears. "Are you hurt, Buckner?"

"No."

Boyer put his mouth to the ear hole in the leather head-gear and whispered, "Why are you crying?"

"I don't know."

Boyer's first thought was to exhort Buckner to get control of his emotions, to fight with a clear mind. During boxing classes, Boyer had seen more than one of his classmates, overcome by emotion, go to pieces in the ring. Terrified and angry, bloody and hurting, intoxicated on adrenalin and goaded by a screaming mob, it was a wonder that everyone didn't burst into tears. But they threw punches and took punches, sustained only by the same emotions that undermined their composure. Tears and blood flew in equal measure, and in the end, pure willpower counted for more than good technique.

The bell rang. Buckner stood up and Boyer whisked away the stool. "Crowd him, Morgan. Hold onto him when you get tired. Stay on him and shove him around." *And stay only a little bit out of control.*

Gastogne fired a looping left that swept away Buckner's guard. The following right exploded in Buckner's face. A blow to the chest drove him against the ropes and a crushing uppercut put him down.

"Get up!" screamed the F-2 plebes. "Fight, Buckner!"

Boyer yelled for LaForge to stop the fight, but Buckner struggled to his feet. Gastogne moved in.

"Back off," LaForge cautioned. He looked into Buckner's eyes, which looked back, focused. "Want me to stop it, Buckner?"

"No, sir."

LaForge squeezed Buckner's nose, now slippery with blood, to confirm that it was not broken. "Fight!" he ordered, and backed away.

Buckner charged. Again he planted his headgear in Gastogne's face. He chopped at his abdomen, but his punches were weaker now. Gastogne broke loose more easily than before, and peppered Buckner with punches, but Buckner always came back and tied him up. A one-two combination staggered Buckner and he went down on one knee. But he was up immediately and bulled forward, absorbing more punishment before tying up Gastogne again. He fought not to win, but only to survive. The upperclassmen booed and the plebes held their breath, but when the second round ended, Buckner was still on his feet.

As Tannerbeck watched unnoticed in the shadows, he could think of no sport which could leave a man more chemically disoriented than boxing. The fighters' hearts, he was sure, pumped more adrenalin than blood. Fear and pain spawned other biological compounds, and lactic acid oozed from exhausted muscles. He had seen men so disoriented in the ring, so saturated with natural chemicals, that they became unfocused in midswing—tears streaming down their faces, lost in time and space, fighting from instinct without a shred of understanding. Sometimes, they simply passed out, not from any punch, but from the passion that could suddenly make their circuits go haywire.

The general recalled his own days in the ring, when a scheduled three-round fight, six minutes, had filled him with dread for the entire day. The queasiness always disappeared at the first bell, replaced by the rush of masculine élan. He was smooth, then; he could glide like a shadow across the canvas and his punches had snap. But the fear was always hovering in his chest. Before the bell, he had feared the inevitable pain, but once hurt, and realizing that it could be endured, he recognized the more dangerous fear that lurked within him: fear of failure; fear of quitting; fear of dishonor.

"He's dead on his feet," said Ajax through his wired teeth as he placed the stool in Gastogne's corner. "Pound him steady, and keep away from him. One good punch will put him down."

"I don't have enough strength to put him down," Gastogne panted.

"You have to take his heart."

"He's not going to give up," said Gastogne. "This one's going to the end."

"I'm going to stop the fight," said Boyer. "If you stand up for the bell, I'm throwing the towel. You're through. He's using you for a punching bag."

"No, I'll finish it."

"Bullshit. You'll only get hurt. You're already hurt."

"I'm OK."

Boyer squeezed water into his roommate's mouth and pointed toward the center of the ring. "You're not OK. Whose blood do you think that is all over the ring?"

"If you can't handle this," said Buckner, "I'll get a corner man that can." He pointed a glove at their classmates. They chanted, "Buckner! Buckner! Huah!"

"You can't make it through this round. He's going to drop you."

Buckner's eyes turned watery again and he sniffed, a mixture of tears and blood. "Then he drops me."

Boyer would never understand any situation where there were no options, where retreat or advance were not alternatives of equal weight to be selected according to the most judicious evaluation of the circumstances. In his view, the most sensible course of action now was to surrender. The fight, though valiant, was lost. Buckner had endured his trial by combat and had earned the respect of his classmates and the upperclassmen alike. Boyer saw little to gain by prolonging the fight, and a lot to lose.

But Boyer understood, too, that he could never explain these things to his roommate, or to his classmates who now yelled more vociferously than ever for Buckner to fight on. It was this absolute aspect of Buckner—of West Point itself—that frightened Boyer, and filled him with envy. Buckner understood the ruthlessness of implacable commitment, where there was no turning back, and Boyer had no option but to accept it.

Boyer advised, "Don't throw any punches. Hang on and weigh him down, tire him out. With fifteen seconds left in the round, start swinging with whatever strength you have left and hope for a lucky punch."

The final round began. The crowd noise became ear-splitting. In the shadows, Tannerbeck looked on, still unnoticed.

But Buckner lacked the strength to charge or retreat. His legs were mushy, no spring left. If Buckner confused Gastogne, it was in the way he plodded to the center of the ring and waited dully for the punch that flattened him. Buckner's head seemed to fly from his shoulders as blood flew into the crowd, which recoiled in disgust. The entire room fell silent.

Boyer scurried along the ropes to where his roommate lay. "Buckner! Buckner!" He threw Buckner's bloody towel into the ring, surrender. LaForge caught it and flung it back into Boyer's face as he knelt to begin the count.

"Stay down," Boyer pleaded. Behind him, his classmates screamed, "Get up! Get up!"

Buckner sat up. He stared at the ring and noticed for the first time the drops and pools of blood on the canvas. *It can't all be mine*, he thought. With some satisfaction, he noticed a red trickle still flowing from Gastogne's nostril. He lurched to his feet.

Gastogne released a widow maker. Buckner ducked and rammed his head into Gastogne's stomach. Both men collapsed, Gastogne winded, Buckner exhausted. The fighters struggled to their feet and exchanged blows as both cheering sections screamed for blood. Buckner connected with a left hook and Gastogne began to bleed profusely. He retaliated with a straight right that put Buckner down again. The crowd roared. Buckner got up. The two men clenched and staggered drunkenly around the ring. "Thirty seconds," announced LaForge.

Gastogne stepped away and began to flail with his remaining strength. Like Buckner, he planned to finish with broadsides, and he had the stamina to begin firing sooner. The blows fell heavily upon Buckner, who no longer had the strength to move away.

The fighters stood toe-to-toe and threw punches, left then right, as if they were working on the heavy bags in the back of the room. Every blow landed. Blood flew.

The company was on its feet, screaming and jumping and throwing punches in the air.

Suddenly, Buckner's knees buckled, though he continued to swing until he hit the canvas. Above him, Gastogne clawed at the air until he realized that his target had collapsed. LaForge signaled for the bell and the round ended.

The upperclassmen mobbed the ring, and Gastogne fell into their arms, too spent to raise his own in triumph. Boyer ran to Buckner, still on his hands and knees.

"Quiet!" yelled LaForge, and the room fell silent. He looked at his watch. "Everybody out! Dinner formation in twenty-five minutes. Fourth class, double-time. Everybody out!" He turned to Boyer. "Get him on his feet. I want you both standing tall in formation." He paused and added, "Good fight, Buckner."

The room emptied in a flash. Buckner's classmates dashed pass Tannerbeck with barely a hint of recognition; the upperclassmen paused momentarily, unsure how to proceed past the Superintendent, before simply moving out smartly. LaForge stopped as he passed Tannerbeck. "Good afternoon, General."

"Good afternoon, Mr. LaForge."

"I think Mr. Buckner has paid a fair price for his attack on Mr. Ajax. I recommend that his restriction be lifted, sir."

Tannerbeck nodded. "And what about your own restrictions," asked Tannerbeck, "for your stunt at the parade last week? How many more weekends of confinement do you have ahead of you?"

"Twenty-five or thirty, sir. Every weekend until graduation."

"You're lucky you weren't relieved of command."

"Yes, sir."

Tannerbeck suddenly handed a package to LaForge. "This is an Iraqi flag left on the Plain after those antiwar demonstrators went home. Make sure it remains in Company F-2 forever, passed down from commander to commander as a reminder of the company's performance. Mementos remind us of things we shouldn't forget, Mr. LaForge, however ill-advised they might be. Come by my office sometime, when the walls of your room get a little too close, and I'll show you my collection."

LaForge stared at the bundled flag and mumbled, "Thank you, sir." Tannerbeck touched him on the shoulder and walked away.

CHAPTER 37

September 21, 2004 (Tuesday)
West Point

Like all officers at West Point, the six lawyers that staffed the Judge Advocate General's Office were the cream of the crop. Assignments were normally handed out according to workload and legal specialties, although any one of them would have been well qualified to represent a cadet in an Article 31 investigation. Nevertheless, when General Roby instructed the JAG commander to assign his best lawyer to represent Cadet Morgan Buckner, he pondered the selection for less than sixty seconds.

Captain Mauree McKaen was a barrel of laughs among friends, but in the courtroom she epitomized the reasons that lawyers and sharks are often mentioned in the same sentence. Her appearance was as severe as her attitude: muscular and tall, with prematurely silver hair shorter than required by regulations. The public school system in Detroit was glad to be rid of her in 1980, and her high school classmates—those who remembered her—would have been surprised to discover that McKaen had pulled herself together in community college and gone on to a no-name law school on her way to becoming one of the toughest JAG officers in the U.S. Army. People speculated about her sexual orientation, but nobody asked and nobody told, for she was a good lawyer and nothing else mattered.

Following orders, Buckner presented himself to McKaen's office immediately after his last class of the day. She returned his salute, but withheld the command to stand at ease while she took a close look at him, with a stare frank enough to unnerve him. At last she asked, "What the hell happened to you?"

"Boxing, ma'am."

She shook her head. "I thought you'd be tougher."

Buckner said nothing, and she finally directed him to take a seat on a wooden chair next to her desk. Her office was small and unadorned, purely efficient, with no other furniture except a file cabinet and a bookshelf loaded with leather-bound law books and loose-leaf binders filled with the Uniform Code of Military Justice.

"Do you know why you're here, Mr. Buckner?"

"No, ma'am."

"Do you know what an Article 31 investigation is?"

"No, ma'am."

"The army has initiated an investigation under Article 31 of the Uniform Code of Military Justice of your part in acts of alleged prisoner abuse at Abu Ghraib prison, as were reported in the newspaper recently. You are going to be interviewed by General Roby in an effort to determine if sufficient cause exists to proceed with a court-martial or other judicial or non-judicial punishment. I have been assigned as counsel to protect your rights. Do you understand?"

"Yes, ma'am." Buckner felt his heart beat faster under his sternum and his rib cage seemed to tighten. *So this is it*, he thought. He understood that an Article 31 was investigative only, but he didn't believe that it was anything other than a formality prior to court-martial.

"You have the right to remain silent, which means you do not have to respond to any questions regarding this allegation. And you have the right to a lawyer. Do you have a problem with my being your defense attorney?"

"No, ma'am."

"Good," she said with a nod. "Now, the investigating officer will read your rights to you and all that stuff when he questions you. Unlike the civilian penal codes, in which subjects are Mirandized only when they are arrested, military personnel are advised of their rights as soon as they become a suspect in any investigation. So just because he reads your rights to you, it doesn't mean you are under arrest. Got it?"

"Yes, ma'am."

"The investigating officer will also advise you of the possible charges that might arise from this investigation."

"You mean if I'm guilty?"

"Don't get ahead of yourself. An Article 31 investigation does not determine guilt or innocence. This is a preliminary and informal inquiry only. If the investigating officer determines that insufficient evidence exists to back up the accusations in the newspaper, we all go home and forget the whole thing, cased closed. But if he determines that there is enough smoke here to warrant further action, the army will draw up formal charges and initiate a formal Article 32 investigation. If that happens, the potential charges that you will likely face include dereliction of duty, assault, and murder."

"Murder?" His voice turned husky as his heart suddenly beat faster, filling his chest and forcing the air out of his lungs. For a year he had refused to believe that the prisoner wrapped in plastic had died from the kick he had administered, but the word "murder" pinned him to the reality of his situation like a thumbtack. "I didn't kill anyone."

"That's good, Buckner." She opened a file folder and Buckner was surprised by how thick it was. "But let me explain something to you. First of all, I don't care if you cut the man's balls off and stuffed one up each nostril. Second of all, everything you say to me is privileged information that cannot be used against you. My job is to help you beat the rap, guilty or not. If I'm going to do that, I need the facts. OK?"

Buckner nodded slightly and looked at his lap, trying to regain his composure.

"OK, then. Don't try to defend yourself. Just tell me what happened. Start at the beginning. When did you first encounter the man you are alleged to have killed?"

Buckner met her stare for a moment, then looked down again, intimidated by her intensity yet somehow comforted by it. He had no doubt that she was in his corner, and her brusque manner reassured him that he would not go down without a fight.

"The man was involved in a prison disturbance. I was part of the reaction team called to help put it down. As we entered the compound, the man pulled out a handgun and started shooting. He killed my best friend."

"OK," she said, "we have motive." She peppered him with questions: How many prisoners? How many guards? What were the procedures? Weapons? What was the nature of the disturbance? With McKaen's prompting, the story came out as Buckner led her to the events in the interrogation wing. "What did you see when you entered the cell block?"

"Crazy shit," he said, adding quickly, "crazy stuff," to correct his use of profanity in the presence of an officer.

"I know what shit is. Keep talking."

"Prisoners were standing around naked with the guards yelling at them. They had panties on their heads. Some were in stress positions. All the stuff in the pictures."

"Naked pig piles? Dogs? Electroshocks?"

"No, not that I saw."

"Then it wasn't all the stuff in the pictures, was it?"

"No, ma'am."

"Don't assume anything. I want to know only what you saw personally. No more, no less." She looked at him sternly. Somehow, her businesslike manner bucked him up.

"One guy had a hood on his head, and some had panties on their heads. But mostly the guards were just yelling and screaming at them. The guards slapped 'em around a little bit, too."

"What about your prisoner?"

"We took him to a cell where Levi told me to hold him down while he pulled his pants off."

"Levi?"

"He was a civilian who seemed to be running the show. He had a foreign accent." At McKaen's prompting, Buckner described how Levi had initiated the questioning of the prisoner. He further described Levi's appearance, but could not place the accent. McKaen recorded the information greedily, as if sensing that Levi would be a key witness. "This is good," she said, talking to herself as much as to Buckner. "I suspect that the army will not or cannot produce this guy. None of these civilian OGA contractors have turned up at any of the courts-martial so far." She assumed Levi was a real person, but the thought crossed her mind that Buckner could have invented him out of thin air. "Keep going," she ordered.

"Levi put panties on the prisoner's head to keep him from spitting on us. He was telling me about how Muslim men hate being naked and how they break down in the face of humiliation. I was listening to the screaming going on outside the cell and I thought it was all bullshit. The guy was laughing at us. So I took the panties off his head and stuffed 'em down his throat and threatened to kill him. The guy started puking, and then gave it all up: told us the name of the guard who gave him the gun and contacts outside the prison. Then Levi told me to go back to my unit and keep my mouth shut."

"And that was the last you saw of this prisoner?"

"Yes, ma'am. Except I kicked him on the way out."

"Kicked him?"

"In the stomach. He was lying on the floor crying his eyes out, and I started thinking that a few tears wasn't much of a price to pay for killing Tetra. So I kicked him as hard as I could."

"Wait." McKaen looked up at him sharply, and then began thumbing rapidly through the pages in Buckner's file. She stopped at a document and read it carefully while Buckner sat, wordless, wondering what had caught her attention. She held it up. "This is the report filed by your company commander that documents your self-reported version of events that day, including your actions inside the hard site. Let me ask you something, Buckner: why did you report your actions in the first place?"

"We were briefed on the Geneva Conventions, and what I saw seemed out of line to me."

"Your own actions included?"

"Yes, ma'am. But they told us that if we violated the Conventions, there were times that it was excusable. If American lives were in jeopardy, for example. If that happened, we were supposed to report our actions. I felt that we needed to find out who was helping the detainees get weapons, or other guards could get killed."

"What did you expect to happen to you when you reported your actions?"

"I didn't know."

"What did happen to you? Were there any consequences?"

"No, ma'am. Nothing happened."

"No reprimand?"

"No, ma'am. I never heard anything more about it until I read it in the newspaper."

She tossed the report back into the file folder and slammed it onto her desk. "Buckner," she growled, "why the hell didn't you mention in your report that you kicked the prisoner after you had elicited the information needed to save American lives?"

"It didn't seem relevant."

"Irrelevant? Or did you realize that, at that point, your actions were no longer protected by any hint of exigent circumstances? Your parting assault on that helpless prisoner was gratuitous violence, Buckner; pure and simple revenge, a clear example of prisoner abuse and a violation of the Geneva Conventions. Am I right?"

Buckner squirmed as if she had bayoneted him. He stared at his hands and mumbled, "I don't know."

She rolled her eyes. "At last, a West Point cadet who admits he doesn't know what the hell he's talking about. Did you enjoy it? Kicking the crap out of the man who killed your only friend?"

"No."

"No? Well, I would have enjoyed the hell out of it."

He glanced up and met her eyes.

"Listen carefully," she said. "I already told you this once: I don't care what you did. I just need to know the truth. You got that?"

"Yes, ma'am."

"Shall we continue?"

"Yes, ma'am."

"Was the prisoner alive when you left him?"

"Yes, ma'am."

McKaen fired her questions almost faster than Buckner could answer them. He explained how Levi had summoned him a week later to assist in the in-processing of a civilian, a man who claimed to be a reporter for *The Citizen Times*.

"Was Levi recruiting you?" she asked.

"Maybe. I guess he thought I had what it took."

"It would seem that you do."

Buckner described the interrogation of McGowan, his smug attitude and his scorn for Levi's threats. "He dared us to hurt him. He said Americans never abuse prisoners."

"I guess you fooled him, eh?"

"I showed him the corpse wrapped in plastic and then I broke his nose. He gave it up."

"Don't be so proud of yourself."

"He gave up a lot of information, really good stuff. Contacts and phone numbers in France and in Syria. This was actionable intel that could be used to close down terrorist networks all over the world. Levi was really excited."

"But do you regret torturing McGowan?"

"No."

She wrote furiously. "Tell me about the corpse."

"He was just lying there in the latrine, wrapped in Saran Wrap or something."

She stared at him, demanding more, until Buckner looked down at his lap. She said nothing, and waited for Buckner to resume his account.

"I think the body was the same guy I kicked in the stomach. He had a tattoo on his hand."

She wrote it down. "I'm glad I didn't have to break your nose to get that out of you, Buckner." She added, "You look like someone already beat me to it, anyway."

Buckner wasn't sure if she was joking. McKaen plowed ahead. "All right, then. What about General Tannerbeck?"

"I received orders to the Prep School a couple of days later. General Tannerbeck sent orders for me to report to his office before I left Iraq."

"What did you talk about?"

"Not much. Honor, devotion, duty. That kind of stuff."

"Nothing about Abu Ghraib?"

"He told me to keep my mouth shut about it."

"No deal to send you to West Point in exchange for your silence?"

"Not in so many words."

"In any kind of words?"

"Maybe. I don't know. He said I wasn't really qualified, but I might make it if I worked hard enough. And then he told me not to talk to anyone about Abu Ghraib."

McKaen was writing again, page after page this time. Buckner sat quietly, listening to the scratching of her pen on paper, wondering what the hell she was writing and when she would ask her next question. Finally, she tossed her pen on the tablet and leaned back in her chair with a deep sigh.

"OK, Buckner, this is what I want you to do: from now on, you must not discuss any aspect of this case with anyone. Not your mother, not your girlfriend, not your roommate, and most definitely not anyone on the investigation committee. Our deposition is scheduled for the day after tomorrow. I will be with you, sitting right next to you. I will advise General Roby that you have elected to exercise your right to remain silent. You with me?"

"If I refuse to testify, won't they think I'm guilty?"

"You are guilty."

"I didn't kill that guy."

"Maybe you did, maybe you didn't. I'm not too worried about the murder rap. We can use the SODDI defense for that one."

"Saudi?"

"S-O-D-D-I. Some Other Dude Did It. Like the missing Mr. Levi. I'll know better after they formally charge you with something. At that time I'll be permitted discovery—they are required to show me their hand, show me their evidence. At any rate, I think we can beat the murder rap as long as you keep your mouth shut."

"Everyone tells me that: keep your mouth shut."

"It's usually good advice. You're looking at ten to twenty years in prison, even without the murder charge. But it's one thing for the army to suspect you are guilty; it's another thing for them to prove it. I'm going to make them put up or shut up. If they can't—or won't—produce Levi, all they've got is the word of some traitor newspaper reporter and some unsubstantiated hogwash."

"McGowan got some memo that shows that General Tannerbeck knew about the abuses."

"That's Tannerbeck's problem, not yours. Hopefully, the general's lawyer is as good as I am and he will keep his mouth shut, just like you. You understand?"

"Yes, ma'am."

"You can call me twenty-four seven. I am aware of your nightmares, but you don't seem to be the kind of guy who needs hand-holding at 0200 hours. Nevertheless, I'm here if you need me." She produced her business card and placed it on the desk in front of Buckner. "You're dismissed, Cadet."

CHAPTER 38

September 21, 2004 (Tuesday)
West Point

Volpe looked carefully at Colonel Steve Harkins as General Roby introduced him, recording every aspect of the lawyer's face. The surveillance unnerved Harkins, a career JAG officer with no combat experience. He could not bring himself to stare back at Volpe's scar, so Harkins focused on the oak leaf clusters on the colonel's Silver Star as he swore him in. The men took their seats.

The dean of the Academy had made available a space in Eisenhower Hall for Roby's interrogations, a standard classroom lined with blackboards and filled with twenty-five student desks plus one steel gray desk for the instructor. An American flag had been planted in a stand behind the instructor's desk where Roby now sat. Harkins occupied a student desk to the left of Roby, where he observed the proceedings, took notes, and operated a small tape recorder. Volpe took a seat directly across from him.

"Colonel Volpe," Roby began, "Are you familiar with an Article 31 investigation?"

"Yes, sir."

"Your testimony is required as part of the investigation into the alleged prisoner abuse at Abu Ghraib during the time that you were the FOB commander. You are not the individual under investigation in this case. Nevertheless, you are not immune to prosecution if evidence uncovered by this investigation should implicate you." Almost rhetorically, Roby added, "Do you understand, Colonel?"

"Yes, sir."

Roby glanced at Harkins to confirm he'd gotten it right, then continued. "Any statement you make here can be used against you in any potential prosecution. Therefore, you have the right to refuse to answer any question."

"I understand, General. I also understand that I am entitled to a lawyer. I have declined legal representation and I am prepared to respond to questions."

"Very well," said Roby, with another glance at Harkins. "Let's begin with your appointment as commander of FOB Abu Ghraib."

"Excuse me, General Roby," interjected Harkins. "We should ask Colonel Volpe to state his name and Social Security number for the record."

Volpe responded without prompting, spitting out the requested information as if he were a POW: name, rank, and serial number. He then launched into his testimony without further prompting.

"Upon the recommendation of General Piersal, who had come to CJTF-7 at the behest of the Joint Chiefs of Staff for the purpose of reviewing our handling of POWs, I was assigned to OPCON over all aspects of security at FOB Abu Ghraib, which at that time was composed of a hodgepodge of unrelated MI and MP units, plus OGA civilians. My authority clearly extended to administrative issues and force protection. Personnel issues were handled in part at

Abu Ghraib and in part by the 800th MP Brigade in Baghdad. Actual operations and interrogations were delegated to the JDIC commander, who reported to me."

Flustered that Volpe had begun his testimony without being asked a question, Colonel Harkins fumbled with his papers. General Roby realized immediately that Volpe was not like most MI gasbags, who carefully qualified everything they said with a dozen caveats, so he simply said, "Continue, Colonel. Did you personally witness any severe treatment of prisoners?"

"No, sir."

"Were you aware of abuses?"

"I received a number of reports. In many cases, the abuses were verified and the responsible soldier was reprimanded. These reports generally originated from the reserve army units operating at the soft sites within the various compounds—the tent facilities where detainees were warehoused. These were good units; the fact that these reports rose through the chain of command indicated that they were self-policing. I received few reports from the hard site, the cell blocks where high-value prisoners were interrogated." Volpe spoke in an efficient monotone of cold facts, so dispassionate that even Harkins found himself believing every word that came out of Volpe's mouth.

"How did you become aware of abuses within the cell blocks?"

"I inspected the place regularly and dressed down the commander on more than one occasion. I forwarded my complaints up-channel, but not much came of them. I also expressed my concerns to General Tannerbeck."

"And what was General Tannerbeck's reaction?"

Without a pause, Volpe laid it on the line. "He advised me to stop sending my complaints to him."

Roby and Harkins exchanged glances, a hint of a smirk on Harkins' face. "Why would he not want your reports, Colonel Volpe?"

"I don't know, sir."

"Why do you imagine? If you were to take a guess, why do you think he told you not to forward your complaints to him?"

"I'm not a very good guesser, sir."

Harkins put down his pen and forced himself to look directly into Volpe's one good eye. "Your loyalty is commendable, Colonel, but under oath, it seems evasive. We're asking for your opinion."

The scar on Volpe's face turned a furious purple as he returned Harkins' glare. Had the two men been confronting each other with knives, Harkins would have thrown down his weapon and fled, but in a combat between intellects the lawyer relished Volpe's scorn. But Volpe's color returned as quickly as it had flushed, and he testified slowly and clearly, "The JDIC was producing battlefield intelligence that was saving American lives. I believe that General Tannerbeck wanted to save as many of his soldiers as he could."

Sensing the rising tension in the room, Roby retook control of the questioning. "Colonel Volpe, are you familiar with the allegations made by *The Citizen Times* regarding a guard in the 229th MP Company named Morgan Buckner?"

"Yes, sir. I received a report from the 229th company commander that one of his soldiers, Private First Class Buckner, had reported bizarre and illegal treatment of prisoners while he was transporting a prisoner to the interrogation wing. The abuse was described in detail, including Buckner's own self-reported participation. I forwarded the report up-channel and cc'd General Tannerbeck."

"Did General Tannerbeck take any action?

"You'll have to ask him, sir."

"Are you aware of any action on his part?"

"No, sir."

"Nothing?" interjected Harkins. "You never discussed it with him? Were your reports simply an effort to cover your ass, or did you have some valid purpose for forwarding them to General Tannerbeck?"

Volpe refused to allow Harkins under his skin again, but he knew that the lawyer was getting the best of him. "We discussed my reports, sir. General Tannerbeck ordered me to stop sending them. I refused."

Roby stared sadly at Volpe, as though he found the colonel's testimony physically painful to hear. After a few moments, he glanced over to Harkins, who practically smacked his lips as he scribbled notes, already planning Tannerbeck's court-martial.

Roby moved on. "Did Buckner's self-reported abuses include the fact that the prisoner died as a result of Buckner's treatment of him?"

"No, sir. When I received the report, twenty-four hours after the incident, I checked on the prisoner. He was alive at that time."

"So who killed him?"

"He could have died of natural causes, although I believe he probably died from internal bleeding as a result of Buckner's assault. I was not informed of his death until the body had been disposed of."

"What did you do about it?"

"I reported it to my commander, and to General Tannerbeck."

"Colonel Volpe," said Roby, "you've already been deposed about these matters during previous investigations of the abuses at Abu Ghraib, have you not?"

"Yes, sir."

"Why are your reports to General Tannerbeck only coming to light now?"

"My official chain of command did not include General Tannerbeck, sir. All of the investigations so far have focused on breakdowns within the chain of command. To be perfectly honest, General, nobody asked me."

"Your reports to him were a courtesy?"

"Not exactly. I felt that I was not getting the support I needed from my own chain of command. I had a personal relationship with General Tannerbeck—we've served together in several combat situations. I wasn't intentionally going around my own commander, but there was an element of frustration. As you know, sir, back-door communications are pretty common and not always a bad thing. I kept General Piersal informed as well."

"Piersal? Why were you communicating to him, Colonel?"

"I had my differences with Major Makin, the general's assistant from Guantanamo who set up the JDIC. Apparently, Makin, in turn, expressed his own concerns about me to General Piersal, who gave me a call. He was very supportive, and he asked that I keep him copied on all correspondence regarding my complaints about prisoner abuse. He encouraged me to continue sending my reports to General Tannerbeck."

Roby frowned and shot a glance at Harkins, who also looked puzzled. The JDIC was Piersal's creation, and Pentagon scuttlebutt had already speculated that Piersal's head might be the next to roll. Had Piersal been working behind the scenes to quietly clean up his own mess? Roby resolved to call Piersal to testify.

Volpe sat quietly for a few moments while Roby and Harkins conferred. Roby finally sat back with a sigh while Harkins scribble more notes. With nothing further to ask, Roby turned the questioning over to Harkins.

"Colonel Volpe, when exactly did you first bring to General Tannerbecks's attention that the interrogations at Abu Ghraib were illegal?"

"I expressed my doubts to General Tannerbeck immediately after a meeting with General Piersal, wherein he described the manner in which the prisoners were to be prepared for interrogation. This was during General Piersal's initial visit to Baghdad, before the JDIC was created."

"And what was General Tannerbeck's reaction?" asked Harkins.

"He said I should not jump to conclusions."

"Is it your impression that the general supported the abuses that eventually occurred at Abu Ghraib?"

"I believe you've already asked that question," growled Volpe.

"I asked you to take a guess as to why General Tannerbeck directed you to stop sending your reports up-channel. Now I'm asking you to guess as to whether or not he supported the abuses at Abu Ghraib."

Volpe sat quietly for several moments, staring at Colonel Harkins with his one eye until the JAG lawyer turned to General Roby.

"Colonel," said Roby, "do you understand the question?"

"Yes, sir."

"Do you have a response?"

"I believe that General Tannerbeck supported whatever it took to get those prisoners to talk," said Volpe.

Harkins sensed an effort by Volpe to avoid a yes or no answer, and he knew from experience that witnesses quibbled only when the questions started hitting too close for comfort. Volpe was Tannerbeck's man, but the lawyer could see that he was the kind of soldier who was uncomfortable with any testimony that was less than bluntly truthful. Harkins needed only to ask the right questions, and Volpe would bury Tannerbeck. "Did that include torture?" he asked. "Yes or no, Colonel."

"Yes, if that is what you consider the interrogations at Abu Ghraib to be."

"Why do you believe that General Tannerbeck supported the abuses at Abu Ghraib, Colonel?"

"He told me that he didn't care if he had to stuff a cattle prod up every ass in Iraq, if that is what it took to bring his men home in one piece." For once, Volpe's eye did not engage Harkins', but looked instead at his hands, folded on the desk in front of him.

A palpable silence prevailed for several moments, until Harkins glanced at General Roby, returning the proceedings to him. Slumped in his chair, Roby quietly asked Volpe, "Do you have anything to add, Colonel?"

"No, sir."

"You have the right to make a statement. That includes a statement in support of General Tannerbeck if you wish."

"He knows how I feel."

"Very well," said Roby. "You are dismissed, Colonel. We're adjourned."

CHAPTER 39

September 22, 2004 (Wednesday)
Pentagon, Washington, DC

Darrow had concluded that the men who developed the system for numbering the six thousand offices within the Pentagon must have been civilians, for the army could never have come up with such a sensible scheme. Despite her short tenure in Washington, DC, she knew her way around the thirteen miles of corridors of the "Puzzle Palace" as well as anyone. Piersal was listed in the Pentagon directory, and it required less than three minutes for Darrow to find her way from the daily briefing to room 3D460, accessible like all the others via a sturdy wooden door with a name plaque on the wall, this one stenciled with the words "Deputy Chief of Staff of Army Intelligence." Like many of the doors in the hallway reserved for the Joint Chiefs and their deputies, the door to Piersal's office was open. Darrow took a breath to steel herself, and stepped inside.

The ante-office was surprisingly large, with two massive mahogany desks. One was occupied by a civilian, a motherly woman who typed a blistering tattoo on her computer keyboard. At the other sat an enlisted aide, a crisp female NCO in a starched uniform, her blonde hair pulled back in a bun so tightly that the skin on her face seemed stretched into perpetual narrow-eyed smile. A pair of leather chairs and a leather couch occupied one corner of the room, surrounding a coffee table with copies of the *Army Times* and a few popular magazines stacked neatly on it. The space could have been the waiting room of any doctor's office, were it not for the American flag in the corner and the ever-present military artwork on the walls. The woman looked up sternly as Darrow stepped into her domain, and the reporter sensed immediately that there would be no small talk.

"Can I help you?" asked the woman politely, but without a hint of friendliness. Even with a press badge, reporters could not simply walk into the offices of the Chiefs of Staff without an appointment, and Darrow imagined for a second that the woman had an Uzi in her lap.

"I'm Angie Darrow of *The Citizen Times*. I have an urgent matter to discuss with General Piersal."

The woman gave Darrow's access badge a sharp-eyed glance, then struck a key on her keyboard to display Piersal's calendar for the day to confirm what she already knew. "You don't have an appointment." The female NCO sensed danger and glanced toward them.

"No," confessed Darrow. "I happened to be in the building and I came by to discuss some very important information. Would you inform the general that *The Citizen Times* would like to clarify his relationship with Donald Ross before we go to press?"

The woman stared hard at Darrow over the top of her reading glasses and Darrow felt the temperature in the room drop a degree. "You can't just walk in here, young lady, and ask to meet with the deputy chief for Army Intelligence. I don't care what newspaper you represent."

"I believe he'll want to talk to me."

"General Piersal is a very busy man. Not even the secretary of defense drops in unannounced. You'll have to make an appointment."

"The secretary of defense doesn't have the information I have about General Piersal's links to Abu Ghraib prison. Now, unless you want to see your boss's picture all over the front page of the newspaper, I would suggest that you let him know I am here." Darrow took a seat in one of the leather chairs, with her back to the woman, and picked up a copy of the *Army Times* and pretended to read. She hoped that the woman would not detect the trembling in her hands.

Darrow listened while the woman pressed a key on the intercom unit on her desk. "Colonel, there is a Miss Darrow from *The Citizen Times* here to see General Piersal."

A silence ensued, long enough that the secretary felt compelled to speak again. "Colonel?"

"Send her in."

Darrow stood up and forced herself to kill the triumphant smile that she wanted to flash at the woman. She wondered who she was about to meet, sensing by the delay in his response, followed by his quick decision to meet with her, that the man knew who she was.

The secretary led Darrow to a door to the right of her desk. She knocked perfunctorily and opened the door for Darrow, her face grim. "Here you go, honey." Darrow stepped through and the door closed behind her.

Colonel Makin's windowless office was similar to that of the reception area, except that his waiting area was more functional: a round work table surrounded by desk chairs. As he stood to greet her, Darrow spotted the standard black name plate with white letters on his desk. The name did not mean anything to her when he introduced himself.

"I am General Piersal's aide. We work very closely together. Anything you have to say to the general, you can say to me." Beguilingly polite, he pointed to a heavy wooden chair. "I noticed that you have been certified for access to the Pentagon. That is a very responsible position for such a rookie reporter. You must have really impressed Doug McGowan."

She examined his face fearlessly, rude, the way Latour had advised. But Makin was a pugnacious man and Darrow could not stare him down. Looking away, she said, "Working with Doug has been a great experience, Colonel. He has an amazing number of sources within the Pentagon."

"I'm sure he does," said Makin, admiring her legs but refusing to be taken in by them. He was more concerned with why she was there. Had she discovered that he was responsible for sending Volpe's memo to the Tetras? "You seem to be developing a network of your own," he added.

"Shall I add you to my list?"

"It depends. It is not generally good policy for anyone in MI to be listed in too many little black books."

"Then why did you agree to see me?"

"Curiosity."

"You want to know what I know about General Tannerbeck and Abu Ghraib."

"Of course. I read the article in the newspaper. I'd love to know where you got your information."

"Colonel, do you mind if I just cut to the chase?"

"Please."

"I would like to ask General Piersal why he was meeting with Donald Ross in a bar in Anacostia."

"Miss Darrow," said Makin, sitting up stiffly and considering his words with care. "There are certain things that are better left unreported. I'm not sure what you think the relationship between General Piersal and Donald Ross is, but we can be of more help to you if you keep that information confidential. The press and the army may not appreciate each other, but that isn't to say we can't be of service to one another."

"Are you offering me information in exchange for keeping General Piersal out of the headlines?"

Makin's smile was as humorless as his secretary's. "Perhaps. What information are you looking for?"

"Proof that General Tannerbeck knew about the abuses at Abu Ghraib. Proof that people higher than Tannerbeck knew. The secretary of defense, perhaps? Or the president?"

"Even if I had such information, any release of classified material of this nature would border on treason. Information you have received so far has been low-level hints and scuttlebutt, something to point you in the right direction so you can turn up your own evidence. We want to ensure that the guilty are brought to justice, Miss Darrow, but we are not traitors."

"How do you know what information I have received, scuttlebutt or not?"

Makin's jaw muscles flexed. "Just speculating," he said.

Darrow smiled, but eschewed the urge to corner him the way the old heads would have at the Three O'clock Follies. She needed Makin's help, and for that Makin needed to save face. "What sort of low-level scuttlebutt can you provide that might point me toward such proof?" she asked.

"Off the record, I can tell you that General Tannerbeck is now the subject of an Article 31 investigation regarding his part in the Abu Ghraib scandal. Pending the results of that investigation, he could face a court-martial."

Her eyes widened. "That's pretty important scuttle-butt."

"You didn't hear it from me."

"You can't tell me anything about anyone higher than Tannerbeck?"

"If you break the case, the whole house of cards will come down. You won't need me." He checked his watch to signal that the interview was over.

"What about General Piersal?" she asked. "When can I talk to him?"

"That won't be possible, Miss Darrow. The general is at West Point, testifying at the Article 31 hearing I just mentioned."

CHAPTER 40

September 22, 2005 (Wednesday)
West Point

After the initial formalities, Lt. General John Piersal, DCSINT, took his seat calmly. The proceedings were familiar, for he had already testified during a number of previous investigations into the abuses at Abu Ghraib. He had survived them all due to his meticulous records as well as his physical distance from the scene of the crime. Few officers were as skilled in the art of covering their tracks as were the gnomes of Military Intel, and Piersal's career path had been a calculated climb though a shadowy labyrinth of army bureaucracy and field assignments. Previous investigations had found him blameless in the disaster at Abu Ghraib, and he was confident that this one would be no different.

Giving the sleeve of his jacket a tug, Piersal awaited General Roby's first question. Piersal's uniform reflected an unusually meticulous attention to detail: his shoes polished, his brass sparkling, every ribbon properly worn and aligned, and his three stars twinkling with authority. He sat as stiff as a plebe, not because he was intimidated, but to project himself in a military manner—to let Roby know that he was dealing with an equal.

The two men were not strangers, having encountered each other routinely at the Pentagon. There was no camaraderie between them, however, and Roby immediately got down to business.

"General Piersal," he said formally, "you have testified in regard to the alleged abuses at Abu Ghraib on multiple occasions. Rather than rehash your previous testimony, we will today focus solely on facts related to the investigation of General Robert Tannerbeck and Private First Class Buckner with respect to allegations made against them recently in *The Citizen Times*. Are you familiar with the article and the allegations?"

"Yes."

"What was your relationship with General Tannerbeck at the time of the alleged abuses?"

"We had no chain of command relationship. I was requested by the SecDef and the Joint Chiefs of Staff to go to Iraq and lend my expertise in the interrogations of Muslim terrorists. Responsibility for the implementation of my recommendations was delegated by the CJTF-7 CINC to his deputy, General Tannerbeck. General Tannerbeck facilitated the creation of the JDIC at Abu Ghraib, although the Abu Ghraib chain of command officially ran through the 800th MP Brigade." Piersal spoke slowly and carefully, as if to be able to reach out and grab any misspoken word out of the air before it reached the listener.

"The commander at Abu Ghraib was Colonel Richard Volpe. What was your relationship with him?"

"As with Tannerbeck, I had no official relationship. Colonel Volpe had some issues with my subordinate, Major Makin, who was temporarily assigned at Abu Ghraib to establish the JDIC. I came to know Colonel Volpe in an effort to resolve the conflicts."

"What sort of issues?"

"He was concerned that our interrogation techniques were too extreme. I reassured him that although we were treading into some gray areas, everything we did was approved by legal counsel."

"How did things get so out of hand?"

"I believe that our carefully controlled procedures began to decay after Major Makin returned to Guantanamo. His replacement was unqualified for the position and untrained in the techniques we pioneered. The commander surrendered day-to-day operations of the interrogation units to the OGAs, civilian contractors, who exerted undue authority in the leadership vacuum."

"Were you aware of the situation?"

"Indirectly. I maintained contact with Colonel Volpe, and he kept me apprised of his misgivings. I urged him to report the situation up his chain of command, which he had already done. When it became clear that no relief was forthcoming, I became concerned that Colonel Volpe could be hung out to dry if any abuses came to light. Thus, I urged him to inform General Tannerbeck of his concerns and to copy me on all correspondence."

"What did you do with that correspondence?"

"I followed up with my own admonishments to General Tannerbeck."

"General Tannerbeck must have found your concerns ironic, given that the techniques employed at Abu Ghraib were your own."

"On the contrary," hissed Piersal, taking umbrage. He leaned forward and jabbed the desk with his index finger as he made his points. "The abuses at Abu Ghraib are a perversion of the techniques we pioneered at Guantanamo. We never employed, authorized, or encouraged the use of electric shocks, the use of dogs, naked piles of prisoners, masturbation, or simulated sex acts. I believe that the atrocities at Abu Ghraib are a direct result of enthusiasm by undisciplined and unprofessional soldiers and a lack of command supervision. These problems were exacerbated by actual command complicity. Specifically, I refer to General Tannerbeck himself." Piersal resisted the temptation to fold his arms across his chest, satisfied that his performance conveyed his indignation.

The vehemence of Piersal's response surprised Roby, as did his bold censure of Tannerbeck. "In what way was General Tannerbeck complicit?"

"He specifically directed me and Colonel Volpe to stop sending our 'damn memos.'"

Roby reflexively glanced at the tape recorder on Harkins' desk. He felt overcome by a sense of disappointment, exacerbated when he noticed Harkins slowly shaking his head as he scribbled notes on a legal pad. Only Piersal seemed unmoved by his testimony, staring ahead like a smug student, eager to answer the next question. Reluctantly, Roby obliged him.

"General Piersal, what was your relationship with Private First Class Buckner?"

"Officially or personally, none. I first became aware of Buckner when Colonel Volpe informed me of Buckner's self-reported prisoner abuse in Cell Block 1A. As usual, the chain of command failed to respond to Volpe's concerns, and I am aware that Volpe subsequently reported the problem to General Tannerbeck."

"What was your reaction when you received Colonel Volpe's report?"

"I was alarmed, but I left it in the hands of Volpe and Tannerbeck. I assumed there would be disciplinary action, as there had been for a number of other minor incidents. Granted, this one wasn't so minor."

"So, you were unaware of any effort to transfer Buckner out of the country?"

"Correct. I first learned that Buckner had been transferred when I read it in *The Citizen Times.*" Piersal spoke with an expressionless face. *It'll be Tannerbeck's word against mine,* he thought, *if Tannerbeck admits to it at all.*

CHAPTER 41

September 22, 2004 (Wednesday)
West Point

The first plebe calculus exam consisted of six problems, straightforward exercises in differential calculus designed to measure each cadet's level of drowning in the subject upon which every succeeding course at West Point was founded. Boyer already lay on his bunk, enjoying the luxury of relaxation afforded to academically inclined cadets who could rip through an exam in an hour, when Buckner returned to the room, spent. "How'd it go?"

"I'll send you a postcard from Iraq," said Buckner, flinging his books onto his desk. "Calculus is bullshit!"

"Calculus is the foundation for all physics in the real world," explained Boyer, always the tutor.

"Real world? Can't see it. Can't touch it. Can't smell it or hear it or understand it. There's nothin' real about it."

"You can't see God or patriotism or the Honor Code," observed Boyer.

"There's nothing real about them, either."

Boyer laughed and pointed to a message on Buckner's desk. "Some Firstie from the Central Guard Room came by. You've got to report immediately."

"Why?"

Boyer shrugged.

Buckner checked himself in the mirror, now a habit. "Tell Ajax where I am if I miss lunch formation."

The Central Guard Room occupied a large space in the central barracks complex, close to the mess hall. Two first classmen passed the time by maintaining daily status reports and answering the phones at desks behind a counter. Plebes rarely had business there. The guardroom served primarily as an administrative nerve center for the Officer of the Day and the Commandant of Cadets. It was boring duty for the Firsties unfortunate enough to pull guard detail there.

Unsure of procedures, Buckner approached the counter in the proper fourth class manner. "Sir," he said, saluting, "Cadet Buckner reports to the Central Guard Room as ordered!"

One guard returned a brisk salute. "Where the hell have you been, Buckner?"

"Calculus exam, sir!"

The guard nodded, recalling his own academic frustrations. The Firstie had just finished an exam in Quantum Physics and was as unsure of his future as Buckner was of his. The specter of failure haunted cadets until the very day they graduated.

Buckner followed the guard into the hallway. They passed Boarders' Ward, rooms reserved for failed cadets, those who were being mustered out of the Corps due to military incompetence, academic failure, or lack of motivation. Isolated from their classmates, the ashamed future civilians huddled in their corner of the barracks. The rooms were as quiet as a morgue, and to the rest of the Corps, the inhabitants there might as well have been dead. Buckner vaguely recalled Lowry, who had spent his last days here after the brouhaha over the deer on the firing range.

The guard approached the final door. Suddenly, in a moment of panic, Buckner wondered if this was the way cadets were notified of their dismissal. Had the calculus exam been graded already?

The guard knocked on the door before leading Buckner into the room. "Ma'am," he announced, "I have Mr. Buckner to see you."

Charlotte Tannerbeck stood in the center of the room, as composed as a falcon. "Thank you," she said quietly, as the guard backed out and shut the door. Buckner stood at attention, while Charlotte circled him slowly. "Do you know who I am, Mr. Buckner?"

"Yes, ma'am. I've seen your picture on General Tannerbeck's desk."

Her sternness wilted slightly. "Then I'll get right to the point. I'm here to discuss your testimony before the investigating committee tomorrow." Buckner kept his mouth shut, and Charlotte lifted her head to look him in the eye, disconcerting him with her intensity. "Mr. Buckner, do you know what my husband is doing at this very moment?"

"No, ma'am."

"He is testifying before General Roby concerning the Iraqi prisoner you killed in Abu Ghraib and the abuses you witnessed there. This is the same committee that will hear your testimony tomorrow."

Captain McKaen had informed Buckner of the date and time of his own testimony, but he had no need to know about the schedules of others and was not aware of who else would be testifying, or when.

Charlotte's voice dropped suddenly to a whisper, her firm demeanor wavering. "He's lying to them."

The room fell oppressively silent. From outside, the sounds of cadet companies lining up for lunch formation penetrated the window panes with surprising clarity.

"Does it shock you that I'm telling you this, Mr. Buckner?"

"Yes, ma'am."

"Welcome to the real world, Morgan. The Honor Code is a wonderful thing, but there are times when duty and honor conflict with each other. I'm sure you know that, don't you?"

"I don't know," he stammered.

"You'll discover that sooner or later. I'm here to ask you what you plan to tell the committee."

"I can't discuss it," said Buckner. "My lawyer said—"

"Lawyers are for cowards," interrupted Charlotte. "My husband doesn't need a lawyer and neither do you. It's very simple: You can tell the truth, and definitely go to prison. You can lie, and maybe avoid prison. Or you can get a lawyer and try to accomplish the same thing as lying without actually saying anything. Lawyers are for quibblers who want to define the meaning of 'is.'"

"Mrs. Tannerbeck, did General Tannerbeck send you here?"

She nearly laughed. "My husband would divorce me if he knew what I was doing."

"Then I don't understand what you want me to do."

"I want you to lie, Mr. Buckner. My husband is lying to keep you from going to jail and to protect me from disgrace, as if that mattered to me. I want you to stand by his side and back up his testimony."

Buckner refused to speak.

"Look," said Charlotte, "this investigation is a white-wash. They don't want the truth; they want this whole thing to go away! And your testimony can make that happen. Only two things link my husband to abuses at Abu Ghraib: One of them is you. The other is Colonel Volpe. There are no photographs of you, no evidence, no nothing; just the word of some vengeful newspaper reporter. All you have to do is confirm my husband's story—that you never committed any abuses and never witnessed any. It's your word against McGowan's, and my husband's word against Volpe's."

Through the window, Buckner saw cadets marching to lunch, and wished he was with them, or any place other than that claustrophobic room. He wondered who was Colonel Volpe.

Charlotte continued, "Why would you even consider anything else? You are accused of abuses as serious as anyone else in this miserable affair. You can go to prison. Is that what you want?"

"My lawyer says I can beat it."

"Good for you." Charlotte opened the door to leave, but then turned back. "Morgan, let me tell you something else: powerful people at the Pentagon wanted to kick you out of here, send you back to the ghetto where you came from because you were not qualified to be a West Point cadet. You represented a potential embarrassment to the army, and their fears have been realized. My husband was initially opposed to sending you here at all because he could not stomach compromising the integrity of West Point in a deal to admit a man guilty of murdering a prisoner. But now that you are here, he's been fighting to keep you here, despite your potential to embarrass him. He sees something in you that nobody else does. You tell me: are you worth it?"

Buckner remained at attention even after she closed the door behind her. The last members of the Corps marched past the window on their way to the mess hall for lunch.

CHAPTER 42

September 22, 2004 (Wednesday)
West Point

The bar at the West Point Officers' Club was quiet. The Academy was a family post, and the presence of so many high-ranking officers enforced a decorum atypical of most officers' clubs, where horny, unmarried lieutenants often ruled happy hour at the bar. General Roby and Colonel Harkins reviewed the testimony they had heard earlier in the day as the waitress delivered their martinis. She was less impressed by Roby's stars than she was by the class ring on his finger, a weighty knob of gold and stone that even waitresses recognized. Harkins kept his hands under the table.

"Well," said Roby, "Tannerbeck is quite a character, isn't he?"

"Yes, sir. He was very impressive."

Roby detected a note of crispness in Harkins' response, the method employed by lower-ranking officers to express their desire to *cut the crap.*

"Speak freely, Colonel. We're not jurors and this is not a trial. I'm interested in your opinion of his testimony—good or bad."

"With all due respect to General Tannerbeck," began Harkins carefully, "his testimony was not credible. His account of the incident flew in the face of Colonel Volpe's and General Piersal's."

"I agree." Roby stared pensively at his beer.

"General Tannerbeck simply denied everything, even when we pointed out the inconsistencies with previous testimony from Colonel Volpe and General Piersal."

"Everyone has a different story," said Roby, reminding Harkins that there were also inconsistencies between Piersal's testimony and Volpe's.

"Yes," acknowledged Harkins, "but they agreed that Tannerbeck knew about the abuses."

"Piersal gives me the creeps."

"Piersal was very impressive, as if he testifies all the time. He had every memo he needed at his fingertips. Those MI guys cover themselves well." Harkins spoke with a lawyer's admiration.

Roby could have said exactly the same sentence with contempt. "Piersal is the wizard behind this curtain."

"Piersal did everything right. Tannerbeck authorized everything, even when Piersal warned him of the consequences. Tannerbeck was just stupid."

"He was blind, Colonel. Tannerbeck loved his men too much. He went too far to protect them." Roby stared at his beer again and added, "I wouldn't trust Piersal as far as I could throw him, but I do believe Volpe. Men like Volpe are incapable of falsehood."

Harkins nodded. "He is an odd character, isn't he?" Refocusing on Tannerbeck, he said, "At minimum, Tannerbeck is guilty of dereliction. Either he ordered the abuse or went along with it. But the thing that bothered me the most was his demeanor. He was too haughty, too sure of himself, as if to say 'OK, we all know I'm lying. What are you going to do about it?'"

"He's cornered," said Roby. "What option does he have, except to charge blindly ahead? He's already reported to the Pentagon that he was unaware of the abuses, and that's what the Pentagon reported to the press."

"He must know he's finished."

Roby agreed. "Once he decides what is right, he will fight you to the end."

"He never lies, cheats, or steals except when he's right. Is that it?"

Roby felt the hair along the back of his neck rise. Even after twenty-six years in the army, he had never found a graceful way to deal with non-graduates who expressed their envy of West Pointers with ridicule. He took it personally, because he was certain that the Academy had made him a superior man. It was an understanding which could be shared only with other grads, a conviction interpreted by others as mere conceit.

Unaware of Roby's irritation, Harkins continued, "Tannerbeck must have known what Volpe's testimony would be, and Buckner's story is already public information. To absolutely dispute them was sheer arrogance."

"Maybe," said Roby, spoiling for an argument. "But Tannerbeck commands a bizarre loyalty among his troops, as if they're under some kind of spell. I wonder if he didn't expect Volpe to cover for him."

"He expects a lot."

"He usually gets it."

"Well, I'll be glad to wrap this up and go home. After Buckner tomorrow, we'll still have to depose the reporter."

"Assuming McGowan will talk to us. We have no authority over him."

"In any event, we already know his story, since he printed it in the newspaper. I can't see any way to avoid a court-martial in this case."

"Let's wait to hear what Buckner has to say," said Roby, without conviction.

"He'll invoke his right to remain silent," predicted Harkins. "There isn't a lawyer in the country that would let him testify."

CHAPTER 43

September 22, 2004 (Wednesday)
New York

The whisper of rain against the windows of the *Times'* offices grew infinitesimally louder, just enough to jar McGowan from his thoughts. The rain and the darkness surprised him. Rush hour was winding down. The sounds of horns, a siren somewhere, and tires on wet pavement rose muted through his window, eight floors above the street. The press room was deserted, except for a couple of swing-shift copy editors who sat quietly, hardly moving, checking stories for misspelled words and faulty punctuation. The overhead lighting was off. The night crew eschewed fluorescence in favor of the incandescent oases of light emitted by the desk lamps. That suited McGowan. He preferred the gloom.

He approved of the rain, too, for he knew it rode in on a cold front. McGowan was tired of summer, with people so athletic and full of life, going about their business, making him feel old and grumpy. Despite the anchor of work, McGowan had felt increasingly depressed, less satisfied by the revelations about Abu Ghraib than he had expected. He could feel depression settling in on him, and he told himself to snap out of it and take a night off. He tried to imagine what would constitute a good time, but could think of nothing.

The reporters came and went at all hours, just as he did, so McGowan barely looked up when the door to his office opened. A scent of lilac invaded the office as he turned away from the window.

"Cheer up, McGowan."

McGowan's eyelids snapped up.

"Have you missed me?" she asked.

"Yes." He was too tired to pretend otherwise.

Darrow came around his desk and sat on it. "You like this perfume?"

"You were wearing it the night I made an idiot of myself, when I dropped you off at your apartment after our visit to the Tetras."

She was pleased that he would admit to his foolishness. Younger men wouldn't do that. "French women bathe in this shit."

"Don't tease me, Angie. I'm an old man."

"I'm not here to tease you, Daddy-o. I got a tip that the Pentagon has initiated an Article 31 inquiry into the Tannerbeck story."

"What's an Article 31?" he asked.

"A preliminary investigation to determine if there is evidence to warrant a court-martial. A committee is at West Point right now to interview Tannerbeck and Buckner."

"Who told you this?"

"A reliable source," she said, just like a pro. "But that's the least of it. I tracked down the man in the bar with Donald Ross."

"Who was he?"

"General Piersal, deputy chief of staff for Army Intelligence.

"DuFossey and Piersal?" said McGowan. He was speechless for a moment while he tried to understand the meaning of what Darrow had told him. "What the hell would those two want with each other?"

She puckered her lips and shrugged. "I don't know, but Piersal is at West Point right now to testify against Tannerbeck."

McGowan rubbed his chin, wanting to know more. Eyes closed, his brain bubbled with thoughts as he struggled to divine the meaning of the facts that Darrow had presented. But he could make no sense of it, so he reached for the phone. "Have you got a phone number for Ross?"

He dialed as she rattled it off, and Ross answered on the first ring.

"This is Doug McGowan of *The Citizen Times.* I believe you know my associate, Angie Darrow."

"A charming woman," said Ross carefully.

"She's certainly more charming than I am," agreed McGowan. As if to prove it, the newsman got right to the point. "I want to speak with Senator DuFossey immediately."

"So do a few million other people, Mr. McGowan. Perhaps I can help you?"

"No, I need to ask the senator about his relationship with General Piersal."

"The senator has never met General Piersal. I manage that relationship. I've already discussed this with Miss Darrow. Our conversation was supposed to be confidential, as I expect this conversation to be. What is it that you want to know?"

McGowan continued. "I assume you are aware that General Piersal is at West Point right now, testifying in an Article 31 investigation of General Tannerbeck?"

McGowan was surprised by the silence on the other end.

"No, I didn't know that," stammered Ross. "So what?"

"I will be on my way to West Point momentarily," replied McGowan, "to contribute my information to the committee investigating General Tannerbeck. The senator should call me on my mobile phone. If he calls, I'll keep his name and your name out of my testimony. If I don't hear from him, he and you and General Piersal will be in tomorrow's headlines." McGowan paused briefly and then recited his cellular telephone number. He asked, "You got all that?"

"Got it," said Ross, and hung up the phone.

The Palisades Parkway was an exciting road to drive, especially during the hours before midnight, when the traffic had thinned out. It was smooth but winding, yet not so crooked as to discourage moderate speed. McGowan's Dodge from the corporate fleet held the road well enough for him to travel comfortably at sixty miles per hour. McGowan tried to focus on Tannerbeck, but could think of nothing but Darrow, curled up and dozing in the passenger seat.

At midnight, the reporters entered the lobby of the Thayer Hotel. Erected shortly after the Civil War, the building perched high on a granite bluff overlooking the Hudson River. The lobby boasted Victorian furniture and cascading battle flags around forty-foot columns that supported the beamed ceiling. But the military grandeur of the lobby belied the hotel's antebellum facilities; the tiny rooms lacked air-conditioning and the beds were too soft. The hotel was for civilians—parents and girlfriends—and for Old Grads who came back for class reunions during June Week. Visiting active-duty officers, McGowan learned, stayed in the Bachelor Officers' Quarters.

They took separate rooms, but before heading upstairs, Darrow sat in the lobby with McGowan, admiring the battle flags and combat streamers that hung from the balconies while waiting for his phone to ring. A few months ago, the banners would have seemed ridiculous to her; brash manifestations of battlefield élan and unit pride, silly things that meant so much to men. But as she reflected upon the icons of her own life—rap music and shopping malls—she understood that there was no sacrifice behind her achievements, and without sacrifice there was no meaning. So she stared, realizing with a start that the holes in the old flags were not the work of moths, but of bullets.

McGowan's phone rang.

"I don't like being threatened by *The Citizen Times*," began DuFossey.

"Call it what you want, sir, but I'd like to talk to you about your relationship with General John Piersal, deputy chief of staff for Army Intel at the Pentagon."

"Donald Ross has filled me in on the situation, and as I understand it, your deceitful Miss Darrow spotted him in conversation with General Piersal recently. As a senator, my office has any number of reasons to routinely communicate with our military leadership."

"Cut the crap, Senator. You don't meet the deputy chief of staff for Military Intelligence in a sleazy bar in Anacostia, and you don't leak damaging information about military heroes as part of routine business. Now, I can simply print what Darrow saw, or I can listen to your explanation of why the chief administrative aide for a presidential candidate would be meeting secretly with such a high-ranking member of the U.S. military. I'm sure that such revelations would appall your constituents and would result in demands for an explanation. Basically, you can explain now or explain later."

"And if I explain now?"

"If it's a good explanation, or even just an honest one, I'll keep your name out of print. And I'll do better than that. I sit on the editorial board at the *Times*. We've already endorsed you for president, and I've seen enough of the war in Iraq to believe in your candidacy. But endorsements can be withdrawn or tempered if we conclude that you are dealing in classified information, or are orchestrating a campaign to embarrass the Pentagon and our boys in uniform. You might still carry New York, but not a patriotic American state like Ohio. Yet, despite whatever irritation you may feel with me right now, I'm prepared to keep your name out of this because I don't believe this country can afford four more years of the current administration. Besides, my career is better served if I have intimate access to you as president, than if I simply destroy you as a senator. All I need from you is the truth."

In a voice frosted with disdain, DuFossey said, "You're joking."

"Not in the slightest," said McGowan, sensing DuFossey wavering at the other end of the connection. "I'm at West Point right now, Senator. How do you think it will look to the investigating committee if I tell them that your top aide was meeting secretly with General Piersal? I'm sure you can imagine the speculation. You both will become the focus of investigations. Is that what you want?"

"What do you want to know?" asked DuFossey, beaten.

McGowan sucked in a deep breath and pulled a pen from his shirt pocket. "What is your relationship with Piersal?"

"We're strategic allies. He helps me, I help him. Odd bedfellows, admittedly."

"What does he do for you, precisely?"

"He has proposed to orchestrate the debasement of the current administration by bringing to light war crimes committed by General Tannerbeck in Iraq."

"Why is he working with you instead of going directly through army channels?"

"He has his own agenda," said DuFossey.

"What do you mean?"

"Piersal was invited by the Joint Chiefs to go to Baghdad and create the same sort of intelligence-gathering operations there that had worked so well in Guantanamo Bay. He set up the necessary infrastructure, but the army personnel running the operation made a mess of it, as we all learned when the scandal broke. After he was promoted and had returned to the United States, he contacted my office and proposed to assist in discrediting the current administration in return for his nomination to the Joint Chiefs if I ascend to the presidency."

McGowan scribbled notes as quickly as he could, hardly able to believe the words he wrote. "Senator, did you agree to this?"

"We were horrified, of course."

"But you agreed?"

"We listened. My aide, Donald Ross, was too Machiavellian for his own good. He called just a moment ago and revealed the details of this situation to me. I am furious over his indiscretion and stupidity. I have already directed him to terminate his relationship with Piersal."

McGowan said nothing as he jotted more notes. Unnerved by the silence, the senator felt compelled to keep talking.

"I've told you everything, McGowan. I know you're going to publish this. But we have a deal: if you mention my name, I'll deny everything and I'll have your ass."

"Don't worry," promised McGowan. "You're a confidential source."

"I'm warning you, McGowan. Don't fuck with me."

With a grim smile, McGowan hung up on the senator from Rhode Island.

McGowan escorted Darrow to her room as he related his conversation with DuFossey. He asked her to start putting together a story; they'd finish it together later. She lingered in the doorway and he imagined that she might allow him to kiss her, but as he moved closer she ducked into the room. Her cheap perfume persisted, and McGowan could sense that Darrow was as flustered as he was.

One more phone call remained. Indifferent to the late hour, the enlisted night clerk at the Bachelor Officers' Quarters patched McGowan through to the room of General Piersal.

He picked up the telephone after only a single ring, groggy but lucid. Without his glasses, he squinted to read the clock. "This is General Piersal," he growled.

"Sir, this is Doug McGowan, *Citizen Times*. Sorry to bother you."

Recognizing McGowan's name, Piersal resisted the impulse to slam down the receiver. "Do you know what time it is?"

"One a.m. I would have called earlier, but I just got off the phone with Senator DuFossey."

Piersal jumped out of bed and groped for the light switch. Makin had informed him earlier of Darrow's visit to Piersal's office in the Pentagon, and Piersal concurred with his leaking the fact that Tannerbeck was the subject of an

Article 31 investigation. But Piersal had not expected *The Citizen Times* to show up at his BOQ room door, so to speak, in the middle of the night. "Your girl, Darrow, is a determined little terrier, isn't she? I could use a woman like that in MI."

"I'm not sure there will be anything left of MI by the time she gets done with you."

"What do you want, McGowan?" The two reporters had discovered more than they were supposed to, but Piersal refused to panic. There were always cards to play.

"I want to know about your part in orchestrating the abuses at Abu Ghraib."

"If I were you, I wouldn't bet my life on what you think you know about Abu Ghraib."

"DuFossey and Ross have sold you out, General. But I'm after Tannerbeck, not you. You can talk to me, or you can testify at your court-martial. Take your pick."

Piersal reached for his trousers, hanging across the back of the desk chair in his room. "Meet me in one hour, alone, at the chapel steps."

Piersal stepped from the shadows of the massive chapel doorway as McGowan parked in the chapel lot and killed the lights. The general wore casual civilian clothes, loose-fitting Dockers and a lightweight jacket and gloves. The gloves were an ominous sign, thought the newsman, as the weather was not cold. McGowan recalled his meeting with Buckner at this same spot, except that tonight the view from the chapel porch of the panorama below was hidden in darkness, punctuated by a few streetlights that surrounded the Plain. A sullen moon emerged from behind the granite shoulder of Storm King Mountain; somewhere in the shadow beyond was the Hudson River.

"According to Ralph Waldo Emerson," said Piersal, "Whoso would be a man, must be a nonconformist."

"I'm impressed," said McGowan, baffled by the reference. "Few military men ever read anything other than regulations and manuals."

"We are not all Neanderthals."

McGowan was pleased to sense hubris. All he needed now was a little insecurity. "Do you ever feel like a voice in the wilderness, General? I would think that few of your colleagues would appreciate a literary man among them."

Piersal snorted. "They've never heard of *Beowulf,* but they've heard of Harvard. They listen when I talk."

"Even the West Pointers?"

"Some people never listen to anyone."

"Well, General, I'm ready to listen. I want to know what you told the investigating committee this morning."

"McGowan, I can't help you anymore. You're going to have to get the rest of the story on your own."

"Did you testify that the illegal abuse of prisoners was your idea, executed with your direction via the CIA, despite your official protestations against the abuses?"

"That's ridiculous."

"Senator DuFossey believes it."

Piersal struggled to retain his composure and was flailing about to invent a response when McGowan tossed out the bait. "I know the whole story, General, but that doesn't mean I'm going to print it." To reassure Piersal, he added, "We've known about you and Ross for weeks now, but nothing has appeared in the newspaper, has it?"

"What do you want?" growled the general, increasingly concerned as McGowan played his own hand, each card a trump.

"I want Senator DuFossey to become the next president of the United States. I really don't give a damn about your future, but I want intimate access to the highest levels of government, and this is my opportunity."

Piersal sneered. "Aren't we all a bunch of bastards? If that's what you want, all you have to do is leave me and Du-Fossey out of your articles about Tannerbeck and write positive stories about our campaign."

Our campaign, noted McGowan. *The man thinks he's on the ballot.*

"We could work together," said McGowan, keeping Piersal's hopes alive. "All you have to do is to fill me in on the details."

"You don't need the details."

"But I want them."

"And if I refuse?"

"I'll destroy you."

Piersal was a man who could evaluate risk, who prided himself on his ability to adapt to any situation. He kept his ego under control at all times, and when he was beaten, he made the best deal he could. He was also a man who could spot a liar a mile away, and saw in McGowan a man as slippery as himself. The game was up; *The Citizen Times* would win this one.

Piersal ambled to the edge of the chapel porch, positioning himself next to the low stone wall that protected the cadets from stepping into thin air, one hundred feet above the granite boulders below.

McGowan followed at a safe distance, reading the general's mind as clearly as Piersal had read his.

"I should take you with me," said Piersal, staring into the abyss.

"It wouldn't do you any good. The story is being written as we speak."

"Of course." Piersal's voice was steady, arrogant, full of venom. "I orchestrated Abu Ghraib, alright. But Tannerbeck approved the abuses from the beginning."

"Why?"

"Don't be ridiculous. The ACLU would have us believe that torture is not effective in eliciting accurate and timely information. That's bullshit. Torture saves lives. You yourself gave up information that saved plenty of Americans."

"Why have you been leaking information to us that will compromise Tannerbeck? If his decisions saved American lives, why destroy him?"

"When the scandal broke, DuFossey and I saw an opportunity to change the culture of our military. Men like Tannerbeck are patriots who love their soldiers. But they are warriors, savages who revel in battlefield glory. They lead us into wars that might otherwise be settled by diplomats. They need to be replaced by enlightened men who can settle disputes with less bloodshed."

"Men like you and DuFossey."

"Yes," growled Piersal. "Men like me and DuFossey." The general stepped onto the low stone wall and stared into the void below. "Do me a favor, McGowan."

"Suicide is for cowards, General."

"On the contrary. If Tannerbeck had any moral courage, he'd jump right along with me." Piersal riveted his eyes on the moon and his voice grew husky. "See to it that I'm remembered as a patriot, will you?"

When he stepped off the wall, Piersal seemed to hover in midair for a moment before gravity pulled him into the darkness. Only after he heard the wet pop of impact did McGowan stagger to the wall and look over, but there was nothing to see.

CHAPTER 44

September 23, 2004 (Thursday)
West Point

Buckner snapped to attention and reported, McKaen at his side. Even as Roby returned Buckner's salute, McKaen introduced herself as Buckner's attorney, simultaneously indicating to Buckner where he should sit. Harkins started the tape recorder as Buckner sat uneasily, waiting for the action to begin.

"Mr. Buckner," began General Roby, "I'm glad to see that you have legal representation. I assume that Captain McKaen has advised you of your rights and obligations. You should remember that this is an investigation, not a trial. At this time, you are not formally accused of any crimes. The sole purpose of this investigation is to determine whether sufficient evidence exists to charge you with any violations of the Uniform Code of Military Justice. Do you have any questions at this time?"

Buckner shook his head. "No, sir."

"Excellent," replied Roby. "Before we begin, let's get the formalities out of the way. First, you are entitled to a lawyer. Do you wish to be represented by Captain McKaen?"

"Yes, sir."

"Has Captain McKaen explained your Miranda rights under the Code of Military Justice?"

"Yes, sir."

"Nevertheless, pursuant to the rules of Article 31 of the Uniform Code of Military Justice, I am obligated to read them to you again: you have the right to remain silent in response to any or all of the questions related to this investigation. Anything you say can and will be used as evidence against you in a trial by court-martial. You are entitled to a lawyer. The army will provide one for you, or you may retain civilian representation. Do you understand these rights?"

"Yes, sir."

Roby turned to Harkins. "Anything you care to add, Colonel?"

"No, sir. Your explanation of Mr. Buckner's rights was adequate." Turning to Buckner, the lawyer said, "For the record, Mr. Buckner, state your name and rank, plus your unit and duty assignments in Abu Ghraib."

"Cadet Fourth Class Morgan Bucker. I was a PFC at Abu Ghraib FOB, Iraq, in the 229th MP Company responsible for guarding prisoners and defending the installation from external attack. I was also a member of the Quick Reaction Force."

Harkins nodded and deferred to Roby.

"Captain McKaen," said General Roby, "do you have any preliminary or peremptory remarks at this time?"

"Yes, sir. At this time, Cadet Buckner would like to exercise his right to remain silent regarding any and all questions pertaining to the matter at hand."

Harkins glanced at Roby and nodded smugly.

"Very well," said Roby. "Then I have no choice but to adjourn these proceedings."

"Sir," said Buckner suddenly. "I would like to testify."

Harkins, who had already begun shuffling papers back into his briefcase, snapped his head up in surprise. McKaen, too, responded with a start. "Buckner!" she exclaimed under her breath. "What the hell are you doing?"

Roby stared at Buckner with one raised eyebrow. "Mr. Buckner, it appears that your attorney is advising you to remain silent. I would suggest you listen to her."

"Sir, with all due respect to Captain McKaen, I would like to testify."

"General," said McKaen, "may I have a moment with Mr. Buckner in the hallway?"

"Yes," agreed Roby. Harkins tugged at his shoulder to provide legal advice, but Roby ignored him. One of the advantages of military justice was that common sense prevailed, and Roby did not need a nattering attorney to advise him on such a matter. Harkins returned his pencils, legal pads, documents, and records of previous testimony to his desk, arranging these like his own battle gear while salivating at the prospect of interrogating the man at the center of the legal storm.

McKaen practically dragged Buckner from the room by his ear. "What the hell are you doing?" she hissed again, when they were alone in the hallway. "Your instructions are to stand up when I tell you; sit down when I tell you; salute when I tell you; and otherwise shut the fuck up! Do you not understand English?"

"I want to testify."

"I don't care! I forbid it."

"Then you're respectfully fired, Captain."

"Do you want to go to prison?" she asked, furious.

"No, ma'am."

"Well, if you tell them the same story you told me, you will."

416 Richard H. Dickinson

Buckner simply stood facing her, the muscle in his jaw flexing rhythmically. McKaen was not a woman easily intimidated by criminals, not to mention West Point plebes, and so it was with some surprise that she found herself stepping back, as if a wall had suddenly formed around him. She realized she had underestimated him, that she would not be able to reach him now. She had seen it in West Pointers before—a sense of martyrdom, the willingness to destroy themselves in a blaze of righteousness over some stupid honor violation or other petty crime. Like most lawyers, she found it exasperating. Rarely had she witnessed this phenomenon with so much at stake, however.

"It's your funeral," she said. She opened the door and led the way back into the room.

Back in their seats, McKaen spoke. "General, against my advice, Cadet Buckner is determined to testify."

Roby turned to Harkins. "Any reason not to proceed?"

"Mr. Buckner," said Harkins, "you realize that you have the right to remain silent, and that anything you say here today can and will be used against you?"

"Yes, sir."

"And you choose to testify despite the warnings from your attorney, not to mention the urgings of General Roby and myself?"

"Yes, sir."

"The crimes we are here to investigate are very serious and could result in a prison term in excess of twenty years if you are convicted. Do you understand that?"

"Yes, sir."

Harkins stared long and hard at Buckner, as though processing something before formulating a question. Roby looked quizzically in his direction, but Harkins finally spoke.

"Mr. Buckner, has anyone contacted you with regard to your testimony, other than Captain McKaen?"

Now Buckner sat mute, all eyes upon him, as he waited for the blood to stop rushing in his ears. "No," he whispered, knowing that his delay in answering the question and the tenor of his voice had already given him away. He had not even begun his testimony, and Buckner had already compromised his honor. The colonel betrayed a hint of a smile before he nodded to Roby.

"Very well," said Roby, stern and suspicious. "Let's proceed. Mr. Buckner, I am aware that some of your testimony here today may have already been printed in the newspaper. For the purposes of this investigation, assume that none of us have read the newspapers. Understand?"

"Yes, sir."

"Begin then, with the events of October eighth, last year. It is our understanding that on that date, while assigned to an internal reaction team as a member of the 229th MP Company at Abu Ghraib prison, you apprehended a prisoner during a disturbance and delivered him to the MI facility for interrogation. Is that correct?"

"Yes, sir."

"In your own words, take us through the events of that day."

Buckner stared at his hands, which rested on each knee. Quietly, he began: "During a prison riot, the prisoner fired several shots into the reaction team, killing my best friend. After he was apprehended, my platoon leader instructed me to take him to MI for interrogation. We wanted to know how he got the gun. I escorted the prisoner to MI and turned him over to a civilian named Levi. I then returned to my unit."

Harkins and Roby exchanged glances. McKaen felt her stomach begin to tighten. Harkins asked, "Did you escort the prisoner into the cell block where other prisoners were held?"

"Yes, sir."

"Did you observe any unusual or unprofessional behavior by any guards toward any prisoners?"

"Yes, sir. I observed some prisoners with women's panties on their heads and some of the guards were yelling at them. I reported my observations to my platoon leader, along with a report of my own treatment of the prisoner I escorted to the cell block."

"We have a copy of your report, Mr. Buckner. The newspaper reports that the prisoner died as a result of your abuses, but you make no mention of that allegation in your report."

"He was alive when I left him, sir."

"So you deny the allegations in the newspaper."

"Yes, sir."

McKaen squirmed in her seat. Technically, Buckner was being truthful, if not fully forthcoming. She had seen too many young soldiers try to beat the rap with clever testimony, and all of them had gone to jail.

"Were you ever disciplined for your treatment of the prisoner, Mr. Buckner?"

"No, sir. I assumed the brass figured I was within the rules, given the exigent circumstances."

Harkins and Roby exchanged glances. Harkins then directed a stare at McKaen, who returned a poker face.

"Mr. Buckner," continued Roby, "did you ever kick a restrained prisoner?"

"No, sir."

"Sir!" said McKaen, almost yelling. "May I speak with Mr. Buckner again in the hallway?"

"I believe you'd better, Captain."

Buckner said, "Sir, I do not need to consult with Captain McKaen."

"Buckner, shut the fuck up and come with me," whispered McKaen icily.

"No! I don't need a lawyer."

She put her lips to his ear and said, "Do you want to add ten more years for perjury? I cannot represent you if I know you to be telling lies."

"Then you better leave."

McKaen sat back as if she'd been slapped. "General Roby," she said, "I believe I have just been relieved of my duties as defense counsel."

"Not a chance, Captain. I understand what is going on here." Roby turned his attention to Buckner and said, "Mr. Buckner, is it your testimony that your treatment of the prisoner who shot Sgt. Tetra was justified due to the exigent nature of the situation, and thus was not illegal?"

"Yes, sir."

"And you deny categorically that you ever kicked this prisoner?"

"Yes, sir."

Harkins interjected. "Mr. Buckner, you're familiar with the penalties for perjury? You understand that if you eschew legal counsel you cannot later complain that you didn't get it?"

"He understands perfectly," answered Roby. "Captain McKaen, you will remain as defense attorney for the time being. I understand your predicament. You will do the best you can under the circumstances."

"Yes, sir," she responded. She turned in her chair and gave Buckner a shrug.

"Mr. Buckner," continued Roby, "you've read the article in *The Citizen Times* regarding your alleged crimes?"

"Yes, sir."

"What exactly have you told Mr. Douglas McGowan or Miss Angie Darrow regarding your actions at Abu Ghraib?"

"I've never spoken to Mr. McGowan, except to tell him I had nothing to say to him."

"He claims in his articles that you murdered the Iraqi prisoner by kicking him to death. Do you know where he got his information?" asked Harkins.

"No, sir."

"It so happens, Mr. Buckner, that we have testimony from two sources other than McGowan regarding your alleged murder of the prisoner. Can you think of any reason that both General Piersal and Colonel Volpe would falsify their testimony?"

"No, sir."

Roby moved on. "Mr. Buckner, do you also deny that you interrogated and abused Mr. McGowan while he was in your custody at Abu Ghraib?"

"Yes, sir. I deny it."

"Describe for us your encounter with Mr. McGowan."

"I was called from my rack around midnight to assist in the in-processing of a new prisoner. McGowan was captured while he was embedded with insurgent troops."

"Yes, we know that much. Did you physically abuse him?"

"No, sir."

"Did anyone?"

"Not that I witnessed."

"Why would McGowan accuse you of torturing him?"

"Sir, I do not know."

"If you were never guilty of any abusive treatment of any prisoners or of Mr. McGowan, then I assume there could not have been any secret agreement between you and General Tannerbeck regarding your appointment to West Point, in exchange for your continued silence?" Harkins' question reeked of sarcasm.

"Sir, that is correct."

The questions stopped. The rumble of the HVAC system carried in the sudden silence. Buckner and McKaen stared ahead, refusing to look at each other or at General Roby. Even Harkins and Roby seemed surprised by the quick end of the questioning.

The blood galloped in Buckner's ears; he heard the gunshots at Abu Ghraib and the calls of his teammates: *Tetra. Tetra? Tetra!* Only when General Roby repeated himself did Buckner realize that he was excused.

CHAPTER 45

November 2, 2004 (Tuesday) to
December 18, 2004 (Saturday)
West Point

The first frost of the season sugared the Plain on Election Day, a day like any other to the cadets, who had already voted via absentee ballots. The Corps voted Republican, the anti-intellectual party, for West Point was a unique institute of higher learning where action counted for more than ideas. Few cadets discussed the election, even during dinner while the results still hung in the balance, for none of them believed that either candidate would end the war in Iraq in time to save them from a combat tour. Most members of Company F-2 were asleep when Ohio finally fell to the Republicans.

McGowan watched the returns on the television in his office, increasingly morose as state after state went red. When the networks pronounced the election complete sometime after midnight, he turned off the TV and stood staring out the window for many minutes, idly wondering if the cold weather portended a hard winter. His cell phone vibrated in his pocket and he checked the caller ID: Darrow. He was pleased that she would call, but he guessed she wanted to discuss strategy, how next to pursue the story now that DuFossey had lost. She was too intense that way. McGowan would prefer to forget everything for a while, to spend a day in bed, with or without her. He turned off his phone.

Despite the early frost, an Indian summer settled into the Hudson Valley and the Corps enjoyed several weeks of parades in full dress gray. Classes continued, the academic load taking its toll on all classes as a trickle of cadets resigned voluntarily, not waiting for the inevitable failures at semester's end. Navy beat Army in football, and Boyer—who could swim like a tarpon—nearly drowned in the Olympic swimming pool when learning to survive under water while wearing a pack and boots and a rifle. The air chilled and the hills lost their autumn color, but the Plain remained emerald green. Parades became routine, crisp drills by somnambulant men who, except for Boyer, never heard the music or felt the presence of ghosts among them.

Christmas approached, as did semester exams, a pair of conflicting anticipations that filled the Corps with jubilation on one hand and trepidation on the other. On the day of the calculus exam, Buckner returned to his room, more exhausted than he had been following his bout with Gastogne. He had made no response whatsoever to four of the thirty-six questions and now there was nothing to do but wait. He waited, too, for the army's judgment regarding his Article 31 testimony about Abu Ghraib; six weeks had elapsed without a word.

When Buckner entered his room, he saw his roommate standing with his back to the door, staring out the window at the pewter river. Boyer's bedding was stripped, the sheets and blankets folded neatly under his pillow.

"How'd you get done so fast?" said Buckner, glancing curiously at his roommate's rack.

"We rich people have calculus in our genes, Buckner. We need it for counting our money." Boyer turned, not smiling at his own joke, and it dawned on Buckner that his roommate had changed uniforms.

"What's with the dress gray?" he asked, referring to the traditional Nehru jacket worn at dinner formation and social functions.

"I'm on my way to Boarders' Ward. I wanted to go in style."

"What?" Buckner spun around and peeked into Boyer's closet. Empty, a duffel bag lay before it. "You're leaving?"

An ugly thought crossed his mind: was it possible to master calculus without cheating? Boyer's mathematical aptitude seemed inhuman, as implausible as the idea that Boyer could have violated the Honor Code. There were other options. OPE, the Office of Physical Education, took its toll each semester, and Boyer had not done well in wrestling or survival swimming. He had earned only a few demerits during the semester, but his peer evaluations for military aptitude were mediocre, mostly because his ramshackle body would never fill out a uniform the way it should. Buckner could think of no reason for dismissal that made sense.

"What did they get you for?" he asked.

"Nothing. I'm quitting. Just...resigning. I wanted to finish up the semester."

"I thought you loved this place!"

Boyer dropped into his desk chair, his chin on his chest, his voice barely audible. "I love it, but I'm not cut out to be an officer."

Buckner threw himself onto his bunk. "This is crazy. You'll make a terrific officer." Even as he spoke, however, Buckner knew that Boyer's decision was right.

"I'm smart," said Boyer, grateful for the false vote of confidence, "but I'm no leader. I'm too scared. I'm afraid of the upperclassmen. I'm afraid of making decisions, and of *not* making decisions. I'm afraid of breaking the rules, making mistakes, the Honor Code, everything!"

"We're plebes. We're supposed to be afraid."

"Not you, Morgan. You aren't afraid of anything. That's what it takes to be a leader, not a 4.0 grade point average."

Neither cadet could look at the other. Boyer, his jaw working, struggled with his self-disgust, while Buckner cracked his knuckles. Already, they felt the bond between them weakening.

I'm better than Boyer, thought Buckner. *I'm still here, and he's not.* Ashamed of his self-congratulations, he said only, "I'll miss you, bro."

Boyer hefted his duffel bag. "Don't tell anyone until I'm gone. You know how it is when guys submit their LOR. I just want to disappear."

"Where you gonna go?"

"Harvard. Matterhorn knew from the beginning that I belonged in a second-rate school."

Silence again. Boyer stepped quickly into the hall and closed the door. Buckner was watching from the window as Boyer exited the barracks and trudged across the empty concrete apron to report to the Central Guard Room. The buildings and the pavement and the skies were gray, as was Boyer in his uniform. The river, too, and the granite hills were as gray as everything else. Only the Plain retained its color, emerald, forever green, as if tended by ghosts of past regiments. Nothing moved but Boyer.

Buckner opened the window. "Go, Harvard!" he yelled, and his voice caromed from barracks to barracks and across the Plain. Boyer stopped and turned and saluted, and held the salute long enough to wipe his eyes. It would not be acceptable to allow the Firsties in the Central Guard Room to see tears.

CHAPTER 46

December 24, 2004 (Friday)
West Point

Ice formed on the river; thin scabs of it crashed into the shore, piling up in crystalline ridges like piles of broken glass. By midwinter, the ridges would grow into six-foot walls of beached icebergs. Each new ice flow ground new chunks into the piles, orchestrating a grumbling lullaby lifted to the barracks on the wind. But during Christmas leave, the barracks were silent and deserted, occupied only by the vigilant spirits of dead cadets.

General Tannerbeck felt like the only inhabitant of a granite ghost town as he strode the sidewalk across the Plain and passed by the statue of George Washington on horseback. The huge doors to the mess hall were locked, the windows of the barracks were dark. The general's footsteps echoed softly across the Plain to Trophy Point, where even the reveille cannon stood mute. Tannerbeck reached his office without encountering a soul.

He had promised Charlotte he would be home for lunch, even though he could not provide her with a good reason for going to work at all. Correctly, she had pointed out that there was not much for the Superintendent of the

United States Military Academy to do on Christmas Eve. The Corps had gone home, all four thousand members no doubt sleeping late for the first time in six months. Most of the Academy staff—the instructors and administrative personnel whose sole assignments were to support the Corps—were on leave with their own families or working abbreviated hours, as there was little to do without cadets around.

He had given Gladys the day off because her grandchildren were coming to visit. Tannerbeck stood in the outer office and soaked in the silence. The thought crossed his mind to call Charlotte and ask her to come and sit with him in the office. Just sit, be with him.

The office was so quiet that the telephone seemed to explode when it rang. The receiver practically jumped into the Superintendent's hand.

"Tannerbeck."

"Bob? Are you answering your own phone these days?"

Tannerbeck leaned back in Gladys' little chair and put his feet on her desk. Charlotte would have been pleased to see his nonchalance, with General Paxton on the other end of the line. "I gave everyone the day off. Not much going on around here today."

"Well, I'm glad at least two of us are tending to the national defense." Paxton's voice turned suddenly sober. "I'll get right to the point, Bob. General Roby has completed his report and submitted it to the chief. We've discussed his findings and recommendations."

"I see," said Tannerbeck, his heart suddenly in his throat. After all these weeks, he wondered if the Chiefs were playing some kind of joke, to inform him on Christmas Eve that he was to be court-martialed. "What was his assessment?"

"It's not good, but it could be worse," said Paxton. "In short, Roby concluded that abuses occurred, that you knew about it, and that you intentionally failed to report it. He believes you submitted a false report to this office upon our initial inquiry, and that you offered false testimony during the official investigation."

Tannerbeck said nothing, stunned despite his mental preparations for precisely these findings.

"Is Roby's report accurate?" asked Paxton.

"I'll stand by my story."

"Bob, you know your story is bullshit." Tannerbeck made no reply, so Paxton continued. "OK, be that as it may, there is some good news, at least from your point of view. Of the possible witnesses against you, Buckner tended to corroborate your own testimony. Colonel Volpe, of course, did not do you any favors."

"And Piersal?"

"What a goddamn mess. The investigation of his death was responsible for the delay in concluding the Article 31 investigation, Bob. As you know, we've ruled it a suicide."

"Yes."

"There was some thought that you might have had something to do with his swan dive."

"I know."

"Well, we turned up some very interesting stuff on General Piersal. Lieutenant Colonel Makin was very forthcoming after we offered him immunity from prosecution."

"I never trusted that little bastard."

"For good reason." Paxton debated how much to tell Tannerbeck, since most of the story was now classified. Finally, Paxton said, "Piersal was running the show at Abu Ghraib behind everyone's back. That doesn't absolve you, Bob, because you concealed the abuses there. Piersal then took your malfeasance and tried to deal it to the Democrats to swing the election."

"What are you talking about?" asked Tannerbeck, baffled.

Paxton decided that Tannerbeck deserved to know what had happened to him, and so he related the details learned during investigation.

"You've been sitting on this since October?" said Tannerbeck, stunned by Paxton's revelations.

"If we had released this information to any of the congressional committees, the Republicans would have leaked it immediately. DuFossey would have been disgraced and the election would have been over before it started. We could not allow the military to be part of the political process, so we classified the results of the investigation and let the election play out on its own."

"Piersal should be on trial, not me."

"If you'd done your duty, there would be no need for anyone to be on trial."

"We saved American lives," said Tannerbeck, defiant. "I'd do it again."

Paxton remained silent for several moments, wondering what he would have done if he had been tapped for Deputy CINC in Baghdad instead of Tannerbeck. *But for the grace of God...* "A lot of people support you, Bob, even if they can't say so."

"Do they support me enough to stop a court-martial?" asked Tannerbeck.

"The chief of staff feels that a court-martial of a lieutenant general would create an unbelievable circus in the press and would embarrass the army. A trial would also bring Piersal's machinations to light, as well as our own decision to withhold information about his actions. Furthermore, our legal counsel advises that, given the credibility of the witnesses against you, there is a small but real possibility that your defense attorney, if he's good, could defeat a court-martial, in which case the press would make fools of us all. Therefore, the chief has decided that no further action will be taken. Roby's report has been classified. The official conclusion will be that you were unaware of the abuses at Abu Ghraib, and that there were no deals made to keep Buckner under wraps."

"I see." Tannerbeck took his feet off Gladys' desk as relief, anger, and sadness flooded through him.

"You can thank Cadet Buckner for that interpretation of events," said Paxton. "His testimony backed you up all the way, although his story is as full of holes as yours. I hope to God you did not collaborate with him. Whatever the truth is, I urge you to keep your own counsel."

"I understand."

"And Bob…" Paxton paused for a long moment before continuing. "The chief would like your resignation."

"Very well." If Tannerbeck felt anything at all, it was relief.

"Wait a couple of months. You'll retire with full honors, of course."

"Of course."

Paxton offered his best wishes to Charlotte, and the line went dead. Tannerbeck sat for a moment longer in Gladys' chair, suddenly very tired. After a while, he wandered into his office.

Though more austere than most, the office contained a fair number of mementos proudly collected over the course of a vainglorious career. Some were more treasured than others, like the 9 mm pistol with a bullet hole through the chamber, shot out of his hand during Desert Storm and later recovered by his men and awarded to him as their own tribute to his leadership. But the souvenirs, even the 9mm,

seemed suddenly tarnished, as though they were trinkets offered by a cynical army to feed the egos and sustain the loyalties of idealistic fools like himself. How had it happened,
he wondered, that the fields of glory had turned into waste-
lands?

His eyes drifted to the photographs on the wall, and the
faces rebuked him for losing faith. *You did a good job,* they
told him. *You took care of us.* He studied each photo. He came
to a black-and-white glossy of a private. The boy had died in
Iraq, during the same horrible engagement for which Tannerbeck was awarded the pistol. The photograph showed a
smiling recruit in his dress uniform; it had been a proud gift
to his mother, taken shortly after his graduation from boot
camp. Tannerbeck could not take his eyes from the picture
as he groped for his desk chair. He sat down heavily.

"Oh God," he muttered to the boy. "I'm sorry." He blinked quickly, and then stared across the Hudson River. After a
few minutes, Tannerbeck reached for the phone and dialed
his home number. "I'll be home soon," he said to Charlotte.
"I have to tell you something."

"Is something wrong?"

"No."

"It's only nine o'clock," she observed, wondering why
he was lying.

"I love you." His voice started to break and he covered
the mouthpiece.

"I know, darling. That's the only thing I live for. Hurry
home. I think it's going to snow."

Tannerbeck replaced the receiver and stared again at
the black-and-white photograph on the wall. For the life of
him, he could not remember the boy's name.

CHAPTER 47

December 24, 2004 (Friday)
New York

Darrow lay naked beside him, her head on his shoulder and one arm thrown across his chest. "Not bad, for an old man," she said.

He laughed; it was true that he had never performed with such stamina, even when he was a young man, a couple of decades before.

Darrow sat up beside him and peeked through the venetian blinds to check the weather. The snow had stopped just after sundown and now, barely six hours later, the skies were clear, bathing the white cityscape in violent moonlight. The light through the blinds illuminated her in horizontal bands of shadow and reflection, and McGowan could not take his eyes off her. Moonbeams glanced off her face and breasts and abdomen, while her eyes remained wicked and black, like pools of oil. She dropped the blind and snuggled back down.

She said, "I'm hungry. Is there any place open on Christmas Day?"

"I know a nice little bed and breakfast in Massachusetts. If we leave now, we can make it to the Berkshires by morning. We can sleep on the floor in front of the fire."

"Doug, what are we going to do about Tannerbeck?" She could sense by the lack of tension in his muscles, however, that McGowan was thinking of pleasanter things. "What about Tannerbeck?" she persisted. "And Buckner?"

"Tannerbeck's an old soldier. He'll fade away."

"Buckner's not."

"I stopped hating him after I met him at West Point. He's not evil. Just a poor kid caught up in the bullshit of war."

"Doug, the man tortured you."

He kissed her again and said, "What he did to me, combined with what you just did to me, pretty much evens things out."

She smiled, but refused to be flattered. "We can't just walk away from this story."

"Why not?"

"I want my Pulitzer."

"I'll give you one of mine."

"Can we at least go after DuFossey?"

The image of General Piersal came to him, floating in midair, two seconds before he died. Someday, he would introduce DuFossey to Piersal's ghost, let the candidate know that he had watched the man commit suicide. One more little secret that McGowan could keep until an advantageous moment. "No," he said, "DuFossey can wait."

"You don't care if he gets away with it? He'll be reelected to the Senate unless we expose him."

"I'm counting on it."

"What do you mean?"

"He came damn close to being our next president. In four years, he'll be a stronger candidate. The incumbent will be gone and the voters will be fed up with the war. He belongs to me now, and I'm not going to let him forget it. When he gets to the White House, I'm going to be his press secretary." McGowan hunkered down under the covers with his hands behind his head.

"You're dreaming."

"One dream came true. Why not another?"

"What dream was that?" she asked.

"You."

CHAPTER 48

February 15, 2005 (Tuesday)
West Point

Buckner could see Charlotte Tannerbeck's face clearly. He had never seen a woman cry so many tears without shaking or sobbing. She made no effort to staunch the flow that washed down her face and neck and into her scarf. Her right hand held tightly to her husband, and whenever she spied a familiar face, she forced a smile and waved.

Company F-2 approached the Supe's quarters in perfect formation, ten rows of ten, in step, grim. Five paces in the lead, the company commander judged their cadence and studied the pavement ahead. The Hellcats struck up the *Colonel Bogey March*, the theme song from the movie *The Bridge on the River Kwai,* and LaForge barked the preparatory command.

"Eyes…!"

The cadets counted in their heads: Left, right, music and footsteps, left, right, left.

"RIGHT!"

One hundred heads snapped in the Tannerbecks' direction. All eyes focused on the Supe as F-2 marched by. Tannerbeck saluted; sharp, proud, and regal. His uniform awed them, ribbons to his shoulder. Charlotte broke their hearts.

She spotted Buckner and held his eyes. There seemed to be no anger in her gaze, only sadness and a sense of forgiveness. Buckner saw that General Tannerbeck, too, had found him. Imperceptibly, the Superintendent nodded.

And that was when Buckner felt it.

The tingling presence of invisible spectators hummed in the air like the zip and flutter of bullets. The Hellcats' drumbeat dimmed, replaced by the tramp of soldiers marching, hundreds, thousands of footfalls moving to another rhythm. Against the barracks echoed a faint, mournful song—a ripple among the turrets, a choir, sung by men who had stood bloody and savage and terrified amid the carnage of a thousand battlefields.

Buckner was alone. He saw nothing but Tannerbeck's fiery-eyed face watching him, judging him. But there were others judging him, too—Boyer's ghosts—surrounding him, marching with him and within him. They challenged him and frightened him and accepted him, and Buckner knew they would haunt him forever.

Tannerbeck dropped his salute and the Hellcats broke through the fugue like a burst of daylight. The air thinned and the ghosts returned to their posts. Ahead, LaForge yelled, "Ready...!"

Left, right, left, right.

"FRONT!"

GLOSSARY

Arabush	Israeli term of contempt for Arabs or Muslims
AWACs	Airborne Warning and Control
BCCF	Baghdad Central Confinement Facility
BDU	Battle Dress Uniform
Brigadier General	One star
CIB	Combat Infantry Badge, awarded to U.S. Army infantrymen after their first actual combat
CINC	Commander in Chief
Cow	Second Classman; a junior at West Point
CJTF-7	Combined Joint Task Force 7
Deuce 'n a half	10-wheeled truck with capacity of 2.5 tons
Dustoff	Medical evacuation mission, or the evacuation helicopter
Firstie	First Classman; a senior at West Point
FOB	Forward Operating Base
Frag Order	Fragmentary Order
Gitmo	Guantanamo Bay, Cuba
Hajji	American term of contempt for Iraqi insurgents

HMMV	High Mobility Military Vehicle, a "Humvee"
Humrat	Humanitarian rations
IED	Improvised Explosive Device
IP	Iraqi Police
Lieutenant General	Three stars
LOR	Letter of Resignation
Major General	Two stars
MoMA	Museum of Modern Art in New York
NCO	Noncommissioned officer; a sergeant
NOK	Next of Kin
Non-com	Noncommissioned officer; a sergeant
NVG	Night Vision Goggles
OD	Olive Drab
OGA	Other Government Organizations, such as the CIA
OPCON	Operational Control
SAW	Squad Automatic Weapon
SecDef	Secretary of Defense
Sitrep	Situation Report
Tango	Target
TED	Tactical Eye Device; eyeglasses
Terp	Interpreter
UCMJ	Uniform Code of Military Justice; the army's manual for legal proceedings.
Yuk	Third Classman; a sophomore at West Point

Acknowledgements

This is a work of fiction. Many of the characters in this story are historical figures insofar as their ranks and titles really exist, but any similarity of events, conversations, personality, or physical description is purely coincidental.

I would like to express my appreciation to a number of people who provided invaluable technical advice. Patrick Pierce kept me up-to-date on the many changes at West Point since my graduation. Martha Rudd and Jill Mueller arranged for me to visit the Pentagon and to attend daily briefings in the DOD media briefing room. Julie Forcum and Lynn Fleck advised me on women's fashion. Roger Brokaw was generous in his descriptions of life at Abu Ghraib, where he worked as an interrogator. My extraordinary editor, Emmy Kathryn Eoff, was instrumental in helping me to delude readers into believing that I know anything at all about grammer or punctuation.

As always, numerous writers have provided a foundation of research upon which *Acts of Honor* is based. Following is a partial list of sources deserving credit for some of the ideas that inspired me:

Generation Kill by Evan Wright

Assembly Magazine, March/April 2005 (article by Patrick McNamara, USMA '97)

Absolutely American by David Lipsky

"Five Days in Fallujah" by Robert Kaplan (*Atlantic Magazine,* July/August 2004)

Torture and Truth by Mark Danner

Word of Honor by Nelson DeMille

The Places In Between by Rory Stewart

Matches by Alan Kaufman

Douglas MacArthur's farewell address

Panic on 43rd Street, by Michael Wolff (*Vanity Fair Magazine,* September 2006)

The Road to Haditha, by Bing West (*Atlantic Monthly Magazine,* October 2006)

About the Author

Richard Dickinson graduated from the U.S. Military Academy at West Point in 1973. After accepting a commission in the U.S. Air Force, he served as a Hurricane Hunter and air traffic controller. His duties included flying into the eyes of hurricanes, flying into radioactive debris clouds from Chinese nuclear tests, and observing incoming Russian ICBMs over the North Pacific. He is the author of *The Silent Men*, a critically acclaimed novel of the Vietnam War. His latest novel, *Acts of Honor*, is the first serious literature to emerge from the war in Iraq. He lives in Seattle with his wife and dog.

Other novels by Richard H. Dickinson
Hurricane Alley
The Silent Men
The Warlord

The official website for Richard H. Dickinson can be found at www.richardhdickinson.com

(

1845487

Made in the USA